The story of Josephine Cox is as extraordinary as anything in her novels. Born in a cotton-mill house in Blackburn, Lancashire, she was one of ten children. Her parents, she says, brought out the worst in each other, and life was full of tragedy and hardship – but not without love and laughter. At the age of sixteen, Josephine met and married 'a caring and wonderful man' and had two sons. When the boys started school, she decided to go to college and eventually gained a place at Cambridge University, though was unable to take this up as it would have meant living away from home. However, she did go into teaching, while at the same time helping to renovate the derelict council house that was their home, coping with the problems caused by her mother's unhappy home life – and writing her first full-length novel. Not surprisingly, she then won the 'Superwoman of Great Britain' Award, for which her family had secretly entered her, and this coincided with the acceptance of her novel for publication.

Jo has given up teaching in order to write full time, and her nine previous novels have been immensely popular:

'Tension and drama . . . a book to read at one sitting!' *Prima*

'A classic is born' *Lancashire Evening Telegraph*

Also by Josephine Cox

Don't Cry Alone
Vagabonds
Alley Urchin
Outcast
Whistledown Woman
Take This Woman
Angels Cry Sometimes
Let Loose The Tigers
Her Father's Sins

Jessica's Girl

Josephine Cox

HEADLINE

First published in 1993
by HEADLINE BOOK PUBLISHING PLC

First published in paperback 1993
by HEADLINE BOOK PUBLISHING PLC

10 9 8 7 6 5 4 3 2 1

ISBN 0 7472 4112 0

Phototypeset by Intype, London

Printed and bound in Great Britain by
HarperCollins Manufacturing, Glasgow

HEADLINE BOOK PUBLISHING PLC
Headline House
79 Great Titchfield Street
London W1P 7FN

To Billy and Harry

Life's too short
Don't stay away too long

Uncle John
Thank you for everything

To my readers

Many of you have told me how much you look forward to my dedications and that through them you see a glimpse of my own life. Without betraying too much, I can tell you that these little messages do tell a story all of their own.

Like any family, ours has its ups and downs, its joys and sorrows, but beneath all of that is a great reservoir of love, and we always watch out for each other.

In the dedications, I might ask forgiveness of someone or ask them to come home, or I am fortunate enough to welcome a newborn into the fold. Often I thank a brother or a sister or another member of the family for some kind gesture which has meant a lot to me. Sometimes I say goodbye to a dear one, or I may send a special message to a friend.

In answer to your pleas that I should write my autobiography, I can only apologise and say that I daren't even think about it. Too many loved ones would be hurt and shocked. Maybe one day I will write it, but it would be many years before it could be published.

Meanwhile, all of my novels do reveal the 'truth' in varying degrees, through authentic settings and realistic characters.

I always look forward to your lovely letters and comments.

Thank you so much, and God bless,

Josephine Cox

Contents

Part One

1925

The Newcomer

'Those who have courage to love
Should have courage to suffer'
Anthony Trollope (1815–82)

Chapter One

'I love you more than life itself. You know that, don't you, child?' Jessica's soft brown eyes swam with tears as she gazed at her daughter's face. Then, when the long-guarded secrets returned to haunt her, she turned away, her voice falling to the softest whisper. 'But if you only knew . . . I don't think you could find it in your heart to forgive me.' She closed her eyes but still the images persisted, dark disturbing images of her own brother. With all her heart she prayed he had come to be a better man, for there was nowhere else for Phoebe to go.

Phoebe came forward from the foot of the bed, the ready smile on her face belying her anxiety. 'Oh, Mam! What is it? What's troubling you?' She had heard her mother's murmured words; the same words, always the same. Not for one minute did Phoebe believe her capable of committing even the smallest sin, yet there was no denying that Jessica Mulligan was deeply troubled. When her mother gave no answer, but looked at her with pleading eyes, Phoebe told her gently, 'You don't have to tell me how much you love me, sweetheart. *I know* . . . because don't I love you in the very same way?' Her voice trembled with emotion but she must not be drawn into that long trek down memory lane. There were things

3

there she did not understand. Things that seemed to haunt her mother. Lurking doubts that raised so many questions. Questions that were never answered.

Phoebe had come softly into the room, hoping that at long last her mother might be sleeping. She was both astonished and anxious to see her wide awake. She seated herself on the bed, entwining her long strong fingers around the thin pale hand, willing her own warmth into it. 'Mam, you know what the doctor said,' she gently chided. 'You must rest. How can you expect to get well if you don't do what he tells you?' She shook her head and sighed aloud. 'What will I do with you, eh?' she demanded with a forced smile; her love was plain to see in her brown eyes as they roved that small familiar face and her heart cried out at the injustice. 'Will you rest now, sweetheart,' she implored. 'Please, Mam. For me, eh?'

Sorry that Phoebe had heard her fearful whisper, and choosing not to mind the girl's plea, Jessica told her, 'You've been such a joy to me, child.' She made a small sound that might have been a chuckle but to the watching girl sounded more like a sob.

'Oh, Mam!' Phoebe was remembering the times when she had caused her mother a deal of heartache. 'I'm so sorry.' Her voice broke with emotion as she dipped her head in shame. 'I wish I could have been a better daughter,' she said regretfully.

'No, child.' The woman smiled, a warm loving smile that betrayed her deep love for the girl. Reaching up, she stroked the rich auburn tresses that cascaded over Phoebe's shoulders, 'We might each have our regrets, but thank God we've always had each other.' She rested her loving gaze on the girl. She wished she could have given so much more, but when Phoebe's father had died it was often a struggle just to survive. If she'd had the means she would have dressed this lovely child in the finest clothes. Instead Phoebe's wardrobe consisted of two good dresses – one was a pretty cream thing which Jessica had made for her daughter some time ago, and the other the one she had on now, a brown shapeless shift with a high neck and three-quarter sleeves. It wasn't much but Phoebe never complained. She made the best of what was given her, and her effervescent beauty shone through.

'Look at me, Phoebe,' Jessica said now. When she looked up her mother said, 'I won't deny there have been times when you've driven me to distraction, but I don't blame you, child. And you mustn't blame yourself.'

Jessica fell silent then, looking into those intense brown eyes and remembering how it had been. Her daughter was her reason for living. Oh, it was true that Phoebe had caused her a deal of heartache, that she'd drifted from one place to another since leaving school . . . a sweeper in the mill, assistant to the parish clerk, and now this last position behind the counter at the local paper shop. Only two weeks ago she'd been asked to leave because of a dispute with a customer. There were times when Phoebe was difficult. But the fault wasn't hers because she was a good girl at heart, kind and warm, if headstrong and impossible at times. Jessica laid the blame for Phoebe's restless spirit at the door of her late husband. He had provided for them all those years, it was true, but he couldn't forget how Jessica had come to him. And after his sons died, he could never forgive. It seemed like only yesterday that Jessica had fled from Blackburn, from the man she truly loved. Oh, she had also come to love the man she married, but he had been guilty of one unforgivable thing and that was his resentment of Phoebe.

'It isn't you who should be sorry,' Jessica murmured now as she affectionately pressed the girl's hand to her face, 'Believe me, sweetheart, you've nothing to be sorry for.' Shifting her glance to the windows, she whispered, 'Open the curtains, child. Let the sunlight fill the room.' She tightened her two hands over Phoebe's arm and held it in a vice-like grip, her eyes hardening. 'There's something I must tell you,' she said harshly, glancing furtively towards the door as though afraid she might be overheard. 'Something I should have told you long ago.'

Exhausted by the emotion that surged through her, she relaxed her hold on the girl. Suddenly her face was lit with the most wonderful of smiles; at last she would be rid of her burden, rid of this dreadful thing that had haunted her for too long. The smile faded when she reminded herself that she was only passing the burden on to Phoebe. Suddenly she was torn with doubts. Did she have the right to shift her guilt on to this child who had filled her life with delight? She gazed a moment longer on the girl's lovely face, a face that had always been especially beautiful with its small perfect features and bold fiery eyes that were the golden brown colour of autumn. Whenever Jessica thought of Phoebe, she always thought of those handsome laughing eyes. But they were not laughing now. Not now nor at any time during these past weeks.

'Open the curtains, sweetheart,' Jessica urged again. 'So I can see your eyes brightened by the sunshine.' She smiled, and there was so much love there the girl's heart broke to see it. When Phoebe stayed a moment longer, searching her mother's gaze with anxious eyes and wondering with bitterness why things could not have been different, Jessica knew in her heart that she could never tell her. Suddenly she felt her time was close. 'Hurry,' she said, at the same time drawing her hand from Phoebe's and casting her eyes once more towards the window. 'The daylight will be gone so quickly.'

The girl rose from the bed and walked to the window, her mother following her every move. When suddenly the daylight spilled into the room, Jessica sighed deep within herself. She prayed that Phoebe would find her way on the rough road ahead. Yet she dared not hope for too much because only she and the good Lord knew how evil her brother was. 'I love you,' she murmured, her arms reaching out. She felt wonderfully elated, free at last.

A sensation of glory. An eerie silence. And then only the desperate sound of a girl crying for the one she had loved above all others. Yet all her tears could not bring her mother back.

Chapter Two

'Stop tormenting yourself, Phoebe. It won't do no good to let your imagination run away with you.'

The young woman with the plain face and bobbed fair hair shook her head in frustration. After a moment she stretched her short fat legs and touched the floor with her toes, bringing the wooden rocking-chair to a halt. Widening her eyes until they resembled round blue marbles, she stared at Phoebe, but there was genuine affection in her voice when she attempted to allay her friend's fears.

'There was nothing so mysterious about what were playing on yer mam's mind,' she said reassuringly. 'You only have to read the letter to see what were troubling the poor soul.'

Clambering out of the chair, she reached up to the mantelpiece and picked up the long brown envelope which Phoebe had earlier propped against a metal statuette of a prancing horse. Returning to her chair, she perched herself on the edge, keeping her feet firmly on the ground so as to stop the rockers from tipping backwards.

'We'd best read the letter again,' she said, at the same time withdrawing it from the envelope and carefully unfolding it. Holding the opened document at arm's

9

length, she screwed up her eyes so tightly that they almost disappeared in the fleshy folds of her face.

My dearest daughter,

By the time you read this letter I will have left you. That is my greatest regret for I have no fear of dying, only of leaving you behind. But I want you to know that you are not alone in the world. I pray you will forgive me for depriving you of the truth all these years. So many times I have begun to confide in you, and each time my courage has failed me. Even now, I find it so very hard.

I have an older brother, your Uncle Edward. Unfortunately he is not the most generous of men, nor the most understanding. Edward Dickens is formidable but he has a powerful sense of duty and there are those who say he is a man of conscience. I have no choice but to leave you in his charge and to ask God that you will somehow find contentment.

Enclosed is his recent reply to my letter. In it you will find his address, together with certain instructions. Deliver yourself into his hands as soon as you are able. He will be expecting you.

I hesitate to say this but I must or I will not rest. *Don't let him break you, child.* He will try, I know. But, thank God, you are strong in heart and have a spirit as determined as his.

God go with you, my darling, and have faith. Love is a powerful and wonderful thing, but it can bring its own heartache. No sacrifice is ever too great. Remember that always. And in spite of what you may discover, remember too that my love for you never wavered.

Your devoted mother,
Jessica Mulligan

Lowering the letter to her lap, Dora looked across at her friend. Phoebe's head was bowed, her wild auburn hair tumbling over her forehead and hiding sad brown eyes that gazed downwards, tears spilling over and her heart aching as though it would break. As she stared into the empty firegrate, the iron bars there seemed to Phoebe like the bars of a prison.

'And you think that was all?' she asked in a small broken voice. 'You really think that was what my mother meant to confide in me? She just wanted to tell me about the letters? To explain about this man, this Edward Dickens?' She deliberately kept her gaze averted.

'Your uncle,' Dora corrected. 'Well, o'course that were all! Don't you see, Phoebe? Your mam were feeling guilty because she never told you about your uncle or his family. Happen she thought you might not forgive such a thing. You told me yourself how your mam asked, "Could you ever forgive me?" Like I said, Phoebe, it were playing on her mind. All these years you thought you didn't have another soul in the whole world, and now suddenly you find out you've got an uncle. And who knows? Maybe this uncle of yours has got children too . . . cousins you never knew about. You could have played and grown up with them. When I first came to live in this street, I remember you telling me how lonely you were.'

'But why didn't she tell me?' Phoebe's heart was heavy.

'Not that I ain't forgiven her, Dora, because I have. I know me mam must have had her reasons.' She had tried so hard to understand.

'There might be any number of reasons why she didn't tell you,' Dora said wisely. 'Sometimes a family fall out among themselves and the bitterness stays for years. Sometimes it keeps them apart forever. Whatever happened all them years ago was between your mam and your Uncle Edward. There's no use worrying over it, is there, eh? Your uncle's accepted you back into the fold, and that at least is something to be thankful for. Your mam and this brother made their peace before it was too late, and now you're not alone any more. That's all that matters, isn't it?' Dora was eager to reassure her. Although she was a few years older, she had been Phoebe's one and only friend.

None of the other children in the street had been allowed to play with Phoebe on account of her father being an assistant at the workhouse mortuary. 'He smells of death,' the parents would say, their two great fears in life being first the workhouse and then the mortuary. And so, until Widower Little came to live next-door with his daughter, Dora, Phoebe had never known what it was to have a friend of her own age. Her mother though had always been especially close to Phoebe; she adored the girl. Her father was a private, often morose man who rarely spoke and showed neither emotion nor affection.

Phoebe's mother always defended him: 'Your father never got over the loss of his two sons.' One boy was stillborn and the other was taken by pneumonia when he was only an infant. She never confessed to her daughter how Mr Mulligan would secretly have preferred Phoebe to have died rather than be robbed of his sons. His bitterness was complete when Mrs Mulligan failed to bear him any more children. But he was a good man at heart and had faithfully provided for his family as a man should. His wife understood his sorrow and forgave him. But there was always a distance between them. And an even greater distance between him and Phoebe.

'Oh, Dora, you're such a friend.' Phoebe's brown eyes were bright with tears. Both her parents were gone and but for Dora she had no one. This man who was her uncle was just a stranger. Far from giving her comfort, her mother's letter had only made her uneasy. She had no one to turn to but Dora and thanked God for that kindly creature. Phoebe looked at her friend now, her heart warmed by the sight of that plain homely face and the affection there. 'Whatever would I do without you?' she asked softly, reaching out to hold a plump dimpled hand. She and Dora had grown up together. Through that time they had shared each other's most secret thoughts and Phoebe had come to love her neighbour as she might a sister.

'Away with you!' Dora laughed, slapping her podgy hand over Phoebe's slim fingers before falling backwards in the chair and beginning to rock herself in some agitation. 'You'll do well enough without me, Phoebe Mulligan,' she declared. 'And you'll cope just fine with your new life. What!' She chuckled and winked at Phoebe. 'That uncle of yours won't know what's hit him. "Formidable" or not, he'll bless the day you came into his house. How could he help but love you, eh?'

Dora sincerely hoped that she was proved right and Phoebe *would* win her uncle's affection. Lord only knew how desperately the girl had craved the love of her father. But when that love wasn't given, she had grown bold and defiant, pretending it didn't matter. Only Phoebe's mother and Dora suspected how the girl's proud wilful ways disguised deeper, more heartfelt feelings.

Seven years ago when she was only ten years old, her father had been trampled beneath a carriage and four. Now, at the tender age of eighteen, she was an orphan. Dora looked at her, thinking again how beautiful Phoebe was, a slim vibrant creature full of life and brimming with love. Yet for all that she seemed destined to suffer a turbulent life. Like Jessica Dora hoped that Phoebe would find a place in her uncle's household, but knew only too well that if she was in her friend's place she would be suffering nightmares. All the same, knowing that Phoebe was looking to her for reassurance, she felt obliged to hide her real feelings. There was nothing else she could do; nothing else Phoebe could do, except to follow her mother's instructions. She had no other living relative, no money and soon the men would be here with the cart to empty the house. The landlord would arrive for the house keys and Phoebe would be sent on her way from her familiar and beloved home in Bury to a place that might as well be on the other side of the world. To the faint-hearted Dora, the prospect of living with an unknown relative was daunting and terrifying. She had been secretly frightened by Jessica Mulligan's warning to her daughter: 'Don't let him break you, child . . . for I know he will try.'

Suddenly, and partly to reassure herself as well as Phoebe, Dora blurted out, 'You're not to worry, d'you hear, Phoebe Mulligan? Things will turn out for the best, I'm sure.'

Phoebe raised her face to the ceiling, her white even teeth biting nervously into her bottom lip as she stared trancelike at the dark smoky patches on the wall above the fireplace. After a while she lowered her gaze, her striking brown eyes searching deep into Dora's. She had detected that note of nervousness in her friend's voice and felt compelled to ask, 'Edward Dickens will be expecting to make a lady of me, won't he, Dora? It's no use him trying to make me something I ain't!'

She sighed deep inside herself; there was so much anger in her, so much frustration that often found outlet in wild, wilful behaviour. And judging by Edward Dickens' reply to her mother's letter, he had been told of his niece's lack of self-discipline. Phoebe had been surprised that her mother should have betrayed her in that way but, on reflection, had come to realise that it was done in good faith. It was only right that this man, this stranger, should know what he was letting himself in for. Either he wanted her or he didn't. And if he didn't, then it was best all round if she knew now. However, the fact that he did want her told Phoebe two things . . . firstly, Edward Dickens was indeed 'a man with a powerful sense of duty' who saw his niece as a responsibility he must accept. Secondly, and much worse in Phoebe's thinking, he had a mind to mend her of her rebellious nature, to mould her into the kind of young lady he would permit to reside under his roof. It was this supposition that gave her sleepless nights. More than once in these past two weeks she had thought about running away, but then she realised how futile that would be for she had nowhere to run to, and besides, her uncle sounded like the sort of man who would hunt her down.

'You mustn't talk like that, Phoebe,' Dora reprimanded. 'You're as much a lady as anyone else.' She suddenly laughed, saying, 'All the same, I reckon they won't know what's hit 'em!'

Though Dora believed that Phoebe's good honest character must win her uncle over in time, she reflected again on Edward Dickens' message, a cold unfeeling letter which to her mind, betrayed too much of the man himself. 'I wish it were possible for you to come here and live,' she told her friend. 'There's nothing I'd like better, you know that, don't you? But there's no room, what with Judd having to sleep in the front parlour, and me and our Dad taking the only two bedrooms.' She sighed and suddenly looked old though she was not yet twenty-one. 'I have to be on hand for our Dad in case he calls out in the night,' she explained. 'So I can't have you here, gal, more's the pity.'

Phoebe was stricken with guilt, quick to assure her, 'You're not to worry about me. I ain't your problem, and besides you've got your hands full what with your dad being bedridden an' all. I'll be all right, you'll see.'

'Don't forget I've got our Judd to help me, although more often than not he's all worked out when he gets home from the mines. By the time he's had his meal and a strip wash, I've already seen to our Dad and there's nothing Judd can do anyway . . . apart from spending part of his evening with the old fella, which he allus does,' she said warmly. 'I'm lucky to have such a fine brother.' She eyed Phoebe curiously. 'Our Judd's allus had a soft spot for you, you know that, don't you?'

When Phoebe went a soft shade of pink and seemed uncomfortable beneath her gaze, Dora laughed. 'Oh, tek no notice! What am I thinking of?' Her mood became serious as she added, 'All the same, Phoebe, if there was a way we could take you in with us, you'd be more than welcome.'

'Bless you for that.' Phoebe knew what a heavy burden Dora suffered; her mam had run off some years before when Dora's dad had been struck down with a crippling affliction. He was a short-tempered, demanding fellow who gave her little peace. And, as she had pointed out, although her older brother Judd was a great comfort to her, his main task was providing for the family; a responsibility which he shouldered admirably.

'I'd best be off.' Dora clambered out of the rocking-chair. 'He'll be awake soon and wanting his food.' She hurried across the parlour, pausing just once to tell Phoebe, 'I'll be back soon as ever I can.' When Phoebe nodded she gave a small satisfied grunt and then was gone.

The silence was unbearable. Phoebe leaned back in the chair that had been her father's, her mind filled with memories of her mother: of the way she sang as she went about her work, of the manner in which she would sit opposite Phoebe at the big oak table when they would talk long into the night – women's talk, aimless chatter that was a delight to them both. Never once had Jessica

Mulligan revealed the existence of her brother Edward, and all of Phoebe's questions concerning her mother's family were never really answered.

'Why?' Phoebe murmured. She could see her mother as clearly as if she was here now. 'Why didn't you tell me about him? Was he so awful that you wanted to keep him out of our lives?'

Her gaze strayed to the envelope which Dora had left on the hearth. Her mother's letter was placed on top but there was another letter inside . . . Edward Dickens' letter. For a seemingly endless time Phoebe continued to stare at the envelope. She knew the contents of that letter by heart. She had read it countless times, and each time had grown more apprehensive. Her mother had sent her down a road that would lead into the unknown, setting something into motion over which Phoebe had no control. It was that which frightened her more than anything. And yet, because of her very nature, she could not help but rise to the challenge.

'Happen Dora's right after all,' she murmured, her gaze never leaving that brown envelope. 'Happen my uncle will come to love me.' She hoped so. Oh, how she hoped so!

Stooping to collect the envelope from the hearth, she opened it with trembling fingers. Taking out the letter she unfolded it and laid it on her lap, wanting to read it yet not wanting to. She looked away, searching the room as though to find an escape. There was none. Reluctantly she returned her gaze to the letter then began to read again with deliberation, as though measuring every word.

I was most surprised to receive your letter, especially

in view of our agreement so many years ago. However, being a Christian I will not shirk my duty. I am assuming of course that you have exhausted all other avenues.

I trust you have raised the girl in the strictest discipline, and that she is a responsible and God-fearing creature. She must also be hard-working and mindful of her superiors.

Of course she must be provided with certain items which I am not of a mind to supply: namely a narrow bed, an upright chair, one pair of boots in good repair, and in addition a Sunday best pair.

She will also be required to bring other items which a girl of her years might be in need of, together with a suitable if meagre supply of clothing and personal artefacts although there is neither room nor need for useless paraphernalia.

While I am generously allowing the girl into my household, you must understand that I am under no obligation to provide for her. To this end she will be found a position suitable to her talents. Also, while I accept that you are not a wealthy woman, I will expect that any item of value you do possess will of course accompany the girl. These items will be sold to further her upkeep until she is paired with a responsible suitor who will eventually take the burden from me.

May God in His great mercy cleanse your soul.

Edward Dickens

It was a cruel forbidding letter, one that had filled Phoebe with horror and anger. It was a letter that must have caused her mother a great deal of heartache in those final weeks. Nowhere in those unfeeling words was there a single word of compassion or sympathy for the sister who had written to him in desperation. He had not called her by name, nor had he referred to her as his sister, and he had not signed the letter in the manner which a brother might be expected to use. It was a hard unyielding document which betrayed the measure of the man. In her mind Phoebe had already formed an image of Edward Dickens. It was not a pleasant one. The prospect of living in his house, under his regime, filled her with dread.

Replacing the letters in the envelope Phoebe clutched it in her fist. Heaving a deep sigh, she stood before the mantelpiece thoughtfully peering into the mirror above. 'There's no use fighting it,' she told the face looking back at her. 'These are the cards you've been dealt, Phoebe Mulligan. Play them with the courage your mother gave you. And don't ever shame her.'

The strong classic features stared back, proud and determined. For one fleeting moment the almond brown eyes grew darker, still scarred with grief. All around her the house was unbearably empty, curiously still and bitterly cold. She shivered, hugging her slender arms around her and leaning forward to touch her forehead against the mantelpiece.

'Oh, Mam! Mam!' Her voice broke on a sob. She had tried so hard not to cry but she missed the busy familiar figure who had been the heart and soul of her existence. She craved the sound of that gentle voice, and knowing that she would never hear it again was almost more than she could bear. 'I won't let you down, Mam,' she quavered, 'I promise . . . I'll make you proud of me.'

Opening her fist, she glanced down at the envelope. In her mind's eye she could see the address – Dickens House, Preston New Road, Blackburn – and not for the first time wondered at how near to them her uncle had been. 'Barely an hour's journey away,' she murmured, shaking her head in disbelief. Phoebe had only once been to Blackburn and that was many years ago when her mam had taken her to Corporation Park. Looking back now, she recalled her mother's strange restless mood all the while they walked through that beautiful park and then afterwards on the tram home. She wondered now whether it had been her mother's intention to call on her brother Edward but, for some reason, she had lost her nerve at the last minute . . .

'Anybody there?' The man's voice carried along the outer passageway, jolting Phoebe out of her reverie. 'It's Jolly's wagon . . . come ter collect the furniture.' The shout was accompanied by the sound of heavy footsteps approaching the parlour, followed by a loud insistent knocking on the door and 'Hello. Are yer there, Miss?'

Dabbing the tears from her eyes, she regained her composure just as the door was inching open. 'It's all right, Mr Jolly,' she told the red-faced fellow as he poked his head into the room. 'I've been expecting you.'

'I'll get to it right away then,' he replied dubiously. He knew how the girl had been orphaned and was about to be shipped off to some unknown uncle. Such gossip didn't stay secret long, not in Bury it didn't. Phoebe Mulligan was a strong-minded lass who would likely know how to take care of herself, but she *was* only a lass and it couldn't be easy for her. It wasn't easy for him either. It was never easy emptying a house when the heart was gone from it. Venturing further into the room, he snatched a piece of paper from his waistcoat pocket and held it out for her to take. 'You'd best check the list first, though,' he said gruffly. 'I wouldn't want to tek what weren't mine.'

He thought how exceptionally handsome she was with that long fiery hair and wideawake eyes that suddenly smiled at him. He didn't envy her what she was going through, losing first her da and now her mam. He hoped this uncle of hers would treat her tender.

Phoebe took the list from him and glanced through it. It was all in order. As agreed between herself and Mick Jolly she was to receive the sum of fourteen shillings and sixpence for certain items of furniture and bric-a-brac; things which her mammy had cherished, things which had always been around from the first day she could remember. She was aware that her uncle had insisted that anything of value was to go with her, but there was nothing of any real value. Not in monetary terms anyway, she thought sadly. All of these things were of sentimental value, precious things that were now destined to grace some stranger's house. The rest would be going with her to another stranger's house . . . her own bed and eiderdown; a small cupboard in which she kept her few personal things; the chair which her mammy had sat on when she said Grace before meals, and a small quantity of clothing, together with her one pair of boots which might or might not be considered suitable for walking to Church in. All of these things Judd had kindly gathered together for her, carefully placing them in the tiny front parlour and advising her to, 'Make sure you keep this door closed, and don't let the fella from Jolly's go anywhere near it. Make certain he knows he's to touch nothing in this room.'

Now, as Phoebe remembered Judd's words, her heart gave a curious little leap. She had not realised how much she would miss having him near. 'It's all here,' she told the red-faced man. 'But you're not to go anywhere near the front parlour. There's nothing in there for you . . . only the things that I have to take with me.' She gave the note back, her warm smile belying the ache in her heart.

Taking the note from her, the man nodded. 'Thank you, Miss,' he said kindly, 'we'll be quick as we can. I know how bad you must be feeling.' He had a daughter much the same age and it would break his heart to see such a dreadful thing happen to her.

Phoebe gave no answer except to nod her head and look quickly away. The tears were threatening and she felt ashamed. When the door was quietly closed she raised her head, straightened her long grey cardigan and tidied the folds of the dark calf-length shift which had been her mam's. Then, flicking the stray hairs away from her face, she lifted her chin high in a gesture of defiance. 'Don't fall apart now, Phoebe Mulligan!' she chided herself. 'Remember what your mam told you . . . "Strong of heart", that's what she said you were, and that's what you have to be. Whatever happens to you from now on, Phoebe, you must always remember that.'

It was a moment before she realised that Dora had returned and was standing in the parlour doorway, a smile on her round face as she told her, 'They'll put you away for chattering to yourself, my girl! And it won't be in no Dickens House neither . . . more likely they'll throw you in the Asylum where you'll never be found again.'

'Dora!' Phoebe swung round at the sound of her friend's voice. As always, Dora's presence had a calming effect on her. Yet she was an odd little thing, sturdy and round with thick shapeless legs beneath an equally shapeless dress, and with her fine fair hair bobbed in the latest style she had only succeeded in exaggerating the squareness of her appearance. The thought of cutting her hair into that unattractive basin style was horrifying to Phoebe but Dora loved the trim of her own hair and constantly snipped away at the ends the moment they appeared. She was a darling and Phoebe loved her; something about Dora always seemed to put her at ease.

'Happen the Asylum might be a better fate than where I'm going, anyway,' she said with a rueful grin.

'Don't you make light of the Asylum,' Dora warned. 'There can't be no worse fate than that . . . unless it's the workhouse.' When there was a loud clatter from the upper reaches she glanced nervously towards the stairs. 'Our Judd sent me,' she explained. 'He says is there anything yer need him to do here? He would have come himself only our Dad's commandeered him. But he can be here soon as ever he's washed and changed.'

'No. Thank him all the same but there's nothing for him to do.'

'I'll tell him then . . . if you're sure. But think on, you're to come and say goodbye to us all afore you go.' She waited for Phoebe's reassurance before hurrying away again.

For the next hour Phoebe deliberately busied herself in the small parlour where she and her mother had lived out their lives. She cleaned out the firegrate and black-leaded the iron surround until it looked brand new; she took down the tapestry curtains and folded them neatly in the centre of the table, tying them into a bundle with the green cord tablecloth, then she washed the parlour window and scrubbed the linoleum. She swilled the outer yard with the soiled water and swept it away beneath the door which led to the alley. Drawn into the alley by the screech of excited children, she watched them at play. One snotty-nosed infant with pretty fair curls threw away the jam buttie she'd been eating and out of nowhere a flock of chattering starlings descended on it, their sudden and fierce appearance causing the infant to burst out crying.

'It's all right, lovey.' Phoebe took the child in her arms. 'They won't hurt you.' When the infant was quietened, she returned to the house.

She could hear Jolly's men going up and down the stairs, fetching and carrying the furniture outside to the waiting cart. Soon they would be coming into the back parlour. Her heart sank. Taking her mother's polishing tin out of the scullery cupboard, she turned her energy to the walnut piano that had been Jessica Mulligan's pride and joy. Jessica had been the only one who could play the piano. In spite of many hours of tuition, Phoebe could never master the instrument. 'That's because you'll never be the lady your mam is,' her father had teased. Deep down, though, Phoebe knew it was the truth. She had watched her mother many times, polishing that piano until it shone, warm rich wood grained with swirling patterns, every nook and cranny followed with loving fingers, its pretty tapered feet and the shiny brass hinges, every corner, every surface, until the entire beautiful thing was bathed in the pungent scent of beeswax, and every artefact in the parlour was reflected in its shiny surface. Phoebe now followed the very same pattern, her every movement unconsciously mimicking those of her mother. Of all the things Phoebe would dearly have loved to keep, her mother's piano was the most special. But, like all the other familiar things, it had to go.

Shortly afterwards the man came to pay her for what he had taken. She then carefully placed the fourteen shillings and sixpence in her purse. The money belonged to her Uncle Edward. Like me, Phoebe thought sadly. It belongs to him . . . just like me. Following the man to the door, she watched them take the piano away. She stood on the front step as they loaded it on to the cart, biting her lip when the leg was badly scratched as they roughly hoisted the piano into position. Her quiet brown eyes followed the cart as it went down the street, the horse's iron-clad hooves stamping rhythmically against the cobbles and the man up front indulging in a loud rendering of a bawdy music hall ditty. When the cart turned the corner and was gone from sight, Phoebe waited a moment longer as though willing it all to come back; her mother, the things she loved, and the way they were. But it was gone. All gone. The furniture was on its way to a new home and so was she. A certain thought moved her lovely features in a wistful smile . . . maybe the furniture was going to a better home than she.

Inside the house she went from room to room; upstairs, downstairs, every room save for the front parlour was stripped bare. Nothing looked the same now; nothing could be the same any more. There were faded patches on the wall where the pictures had hung, and where the furniture had stood undisturbed all these years the linoleum was like new. Suddenly it seemed to Phoebe as though the house knew it was empty. It wasn't talking to her any more and the air was heavy with the smell of dampness, as though it had lain in wait only to creep out and engulf the emptiness.

At precisely the same moment as Phoebe's small brass clock in the parlour struck the hour of two p.m. the landlord arrived. Mr Smart was not a bad sort but he was first and foremost a businessman. There were two days still owing on the rent and he needed the keys because the next tenant was eager to inspect the house. 'The agreement was for you to vacate the premises by two-thirty,' he anxiously reminded Phoebe. 'I have prospective tenants coming to view any minute now.'

'You had no right to make such an arrangement!' she retorted, angrily counting the rent arrears into his hand and waiting for him to sign the rent-book which she then quickly recovered to keep safe. 'I still have half-an-hour before I need to turn the keys over. Besides . . . you know I can't go until Jessup collects me.' Phoebe had employed old Jessup to take her and her belongings to Blackburn; the cost for use of horse and cart, and of course Jessup himself, was five shillings. Nobody else had offered to do it as cheaply.

As Mr Smart prepared himself for an argument both

Jessup and the prospective tenants arrived together, Mr Jessup coming into the parlour as though he'd lived there all his life, with the young couple tapping nervously on the door only seconds behind. The interruption did nothing to thaw the frosty silence between Mr Smart and Phoebe.

As he took off his bowler hat and waved it with a flourish, Mr Smart's pointed features were twisted into a rare smile. He instructed the couple, 'We'll start upstairs, I think.' Peering at Phoebe through narrowed eyes he added slyly, 'No doubt this good person and her belongings will be gone by the time we're ready to inspect the lower rooms.' Turning stiffly away, he ushered the couple to the outer passage and the stairs.

'I hope you know what you're doing,' Phoebe called after the couple. 'Don't sign anything until you've examined all the small print!' There was no reply except for a deliberate coughing fit from the enraged Mr Smart.

'Yer little sod!' Old Jessup loved a rumble and it was especially satisfying to see a landlord made uncomfortable. 'Yer did right though, lass. Everybody knows how partic'lar yer mam were about not being in arrears with the rent.' He dipped his workworn fingers beneath the brim of his cap and began frantically scratching, a habit he had when worried. 'Hey! I hope you've paid that fella up to date?' It wouldn't do if Mr Smart had a means of getting his own back on the lass.

Phoebe held out the rent-book for him to see. 'All straight,' she said briskly and with a satisfied little smile: 'So he'll not be able to throw me in the debtors' prison!'

'Hey, lass, it does me heart good to hear it.' He chuckled loudly. 'Oh, but yer a fiery little piece an' that's a fact,' he said. 'I don't think I'd like to get on the wrong side o' you, Phoebe Mulligan.' When she giggled he made a long sound that resembled a sigh then, looking round the empty room, asked in a concerned voice, 'Where's yer belongings, lass?'

'There isn't much,' Phoebe replied in a sober voice. 'A narrow bed and a few odd things. You'll find them in the parlour.'

'Right then, I'd best get to work.' He brushed past her, the smell of stale sweat wafting into her nostrils. 'Soon as ever I've loaded the wagon we'll be on us way. I don't want to be making the return journey in the dark.'

'Judd says I'm to fetch him if you need any help.'

'Naw.' He shook his head. 'I reckon I'm not too far gone that I can't lift a narrer bed on me back. Thank you all the same, lass.' He turned to look at her, saying in a kindly voice, 'If you've got any goodbyes to say . . . friends and such . . . well, happen this is the time, lass. It ain't a pleasant thing to watch yer belongings being loaded on to a wagon.' When she hesitated he winked and smiled, reassuring her: 'Don't worry, lass. I'll look after yer things like they were the crown jewels. Trust me, eh?' He stepped aside for her to pass. 'Go on, lass, keep away 'til it's done.' As she went down the steps, Phoebe knew she would never again set foot in that house. Everything worth taking would go with her on this day.

'Take care o' yourself, Phoebe darling.' Dora's eyes were bright with tears as she hugged her friend. 'Write to me when you're settled. And may the good Lord keep you outta mischief.' Dabbing her brown checked handkerchief against her eyes, she drew away. 'I'll miss you like nothing on earth,' she said in a broken voice. 'And so will our Judd.'

She turned round then, looking at the shadowy figure standing in the scullery doorway – a man of some twenty-four years of age, tall and slim with slightly darker hair than his sister's, thicker in texture and longer too. Coming forward, he ran his fingers through the tumbling locks and flicked them away from his eyes. They were sad at the thought of Phoebe going away. 'You'll miss her too, won't you, our Judd?' Dora insisted.

'Yes, I'll miss her,' he replied in a soft voice. He was standing before Phoebe now, looking down on her, his light brown eyes reflecting his serious mood. 'I'm sorry things have turned out this way,' he said. 'You deserve better.' He didn't say what was in his heart. He didn't beg her not to go; he was so afraid she would refuse him.

'Thank you, Judd. That's a lovely thing to say.' Phoebe felt strangely uncomfortable beneath his gaze. She had only ever seen him as a kind of brother. Now she was pleasantly surprised to realise just how good-looking he was. She wondered how she had never noticed that before. When he impulsively bent to kiss her on the forehead, she realised how much she would miss him too. Anxious now, she glanced at Dora. 'I'd best be going,' she said. 'Old Jessup's likely to charge me an extra shilling if I keep him waiting.' She felt Judd's eyes on her and it made her nervous.

'Wait a minute . . . I've got something for you,' Dora told her. In a minute she was rushing into the kitchen to return with a small bundle. 'This 'ere's some food for the journey,' she said, shoving the bundle into Phoebe's hand. 'And there's a present from me and our Judd inside.' She paused a moment, choking back the tears. 'Whenever you look at it, Phoebe, remember we love you.'

As the wagon pulled away, Phoebe looked back at the two people standing in the doorway. Dora was frantically waving, a reassuring smile on her face as she called out, 'Take care, and don't forget to write to me.' Phoebe waved back, returning Dora's smile, but could not stop the tears from rolling down her face. 'I will . . . I promise,' she cried. Judd said nothing. Nor did he give any sign that he was desperately sorry to see her go. He simply stood beside his sister, a strong quiet man watching Phoebe and her pitiful belongings as the wagon took them out of Albert Street. Then he cast his gaze to the floor, turned away and went into the house.

It was a glorious day, the sun was high in the heavens and the birds sang to them from out of the hedgerows. The cobbled streets had been left far behind. Perched on the seat beside old Jessup, Phoebe had remained silent while he whistled and kept himself amused. It was when she discovered Dora's present of a delicate silver neck-chain which she had cherished above all her possessions that Phoebe's reserve broke. Her emotions burst like a dam; so much pain and grief, so many regrets and so much uncertainty about the future – everything she had suppressed until now poured out of her.

The old fellow watched helplessly when the young girl bowed her shoulders and sobbed as though her heart would break. Shaking his head forlornly, he blinked away his own tears. Still whistling, although on a quieter note, he directed his attention to the road ahead. His old heart went out to her in her awful predicament. But what could he do? What could anyone do?

After a while old Jessup made an effort to draw Phoebe into conversation. He rambled on about things that were close to his own heart, such as the merit of: 'Our new Prime Minister, Stanley Baldwin and this 'ere Unemployment Insurance Act they're all talking about . . . can't see as how it'll make that much difference to the likes of me, though.' He talked with unbridled suspicion about a 'dangerous man' who had only recently been let out of jail on parole. 'Adolf Hitler is a dark horse and needs watching.' He shook his head and chewed his baccy till it trickled down his chin in a brown rivulet. 'You mark my words, Phoebe lass. See if I'm not right!' he warned grimly.

When he saw that she wasn't interested in government or policies, he changed tack. 'What d'yer think o' Charlie Chaplin?' he asked with a laugh. 'I've promised to take my missus to see his film *The Gold Rush*. Folks reckon it's side-splitting. By! He's a funny little thing and no mistake.' He talked about 'new fangled motor-vehicles' and how the ladies would never have dared to show their ankles in his young days. 'Nor fling their legs about, doing this 'ere Charleston dance!' he said, and when she glanced up at him, Phoebe could have sworn he was blushing.

When it was Jessup's turn to sit quiet and concentrate on the road, Phoebe took an interest in the vehicles that passed them by: grand carriages with handsome bay horses up front and proud ladies peering out of the windows; black Ford cars with flat-capped drivers and pretty young things seated beside them, giggling and coy, with short bobbed hair and wide innocent eyes. She wondered what they would say if they knew she was leaving all of her life behind? But then she realised that the course of her life would be of no interest to any of them, and rightly so. Like her, those folk had to make the best of what they had, and she wouldn't be at all surprised if every one of them had some sort of cross to bear, in spite of their brave faces and their bright laughter. The sight of them happily going about their lives only made her feel even more determined to rise above the obstacles which Fate had put in her way.

Chapter Three

'So this is Phoebe Mulligan?'

The young man paused in his labours, straightening his powerful shoulders and passing his bare arm across his forehead to wipe away the sweat. His dark handsome eyes raked the face of the young girl seated high up on the wagon. When he spoke again it was with a curious satisfaction. 'She don't look so wild or bad, does she, eh?' he asked of his brother. There was a certain wicked delight in his voice when he slyly murmured, 'All the same . . . I wouldn't complain if she were to climb into my bed one dark and lonely night.' His soft laughter was unpleasant to hear.

He gazed on her a moment longer, wanting her all the more when she deliberately looked away. In his heart he knew that this beautiful tragic creature was destined to be part of their lives . . . for good or for bad.

'Leave her be, Greg. She's had enough heartache.' His brother also paused in his task of chopping the fallen oak tree into smaller segments of firewood. Stooping to the bucket, he dipped the ladle into it and poured cool water over his head and shoulders. Then grabbing his shirt from the ground where he had earlier thrown it, he rubbed it over his naked chest, soaking up both water and sweat.

That done he flung the shirt down again. He too had heard the familiar clip-clop of the horse's hooves coming down the lane which ran alongside their father's farm and, like Greg, was fascinated by what he saw. The girl was shockingly beautiful. Slim and shapely, she still retained the looks of a child although there was something bold and defiant about her that suggested she was no innocent. In the brilliant sunlight her burnished hair seemed aflame, wild flowing tresses mingling with the harsh greyness of her shabby long cardigan. Her small heart-shaped face was somewhat sad and visibly pale, intermittently hidden by the straying locks which were blown across her features in the teasing summer breeze. The magnificent dark brown eyes glittered and danced as she stared down boldly from her lofty perch.

'She's fair game, I reckon,' Greg retorted, his avaricious gaze willing the girl to look at him. He laughed, a low sinister sound that caused his brother to swing round and stare at him as he went on in a harsh whisper, 'I mean, if we're to believe the rumours . . . Phoebe Mulligan is no lady.'

'Rumours?' Hadley sensed a certain badness in his brother's mood. He had seen it many times before and feared the consequences. 'When do you ever pay attention to rumours?' he demanded in a harsh voice.

'When it suits me.'

'Like I said, Greg . . . her mam's just died. That's enough pain for her to cope with. On top of that, she's got more trouble than she can handle with Edward Dickens for a guardian.' When his brother turned to laugh in his face, he added, 'I'm warning you – don't think I'll stand back *this* time. Stay away from her!' His dark blue eyes blazed and for a moment it seemed as though an argument would ensue. But then the other man abruptly looked away, watching the girl as the cart drew parallel with them, so close that he might have reached out and touched her.

Satisfied that his warning was delivered, Hadley returned to his work, slicing the axe deep into the timber and angrily flinging the chopped logs into the cart which would carry them back to the barn. Occasionally he glanced up at his brother whose whole attention was riveted on the wagon, now preparing to draw into the kerb on the opposite side of the road. Hadley, though, deliberately averted his eyes from the heightened activity. He had seen that same dangerous look too often in his brother's eyes and was suddenly cold with fear. Because of Greg's cruel arrogance some years back, there had been a shocking tragedy. History had a way of repeating itself and, more than anything, he was afraid for the girl.

Hadley and Greg Peters were twins, twenty-six years of age although Greg was the elder by forty minutes. Each was handsome in his own way yet as different as day from night. Greg's was a powerful muscular figure. Six feet tall, he was darkly handsome with thick black hair and dark smiling eyes. Vain and arrogant, he was also deadly charming but possessed of a cruel, sadistic streak. Hadley was fractionally below six feet in height and did not possess the cultivated bulging muscles that were his brother's pride and joy. Instead he had a strong, lithe figure, narrow of hip and broad of chest, whose hardened muscles were naturally honed by long labour and commitment to the land he loved. Where Greg strutted like a peacock or slunk like a creature of the night, Hadley had an easy, confident way of moving, tall and upright, with the long lazy strides of a man at peace with himself. Where Greg's dark secretive gaze sought to probe beneath the surface, Hadley's sapphire blue eyes smiled easily and were incredibly handsome, although they could be delightfully mischievous or intensely brooding as they were now.

'We'd best get this lot up to the barn,' he said, spinning his long-handled axe into the air, his sharp eyes following it until it thudded into the dismantled tree trunk. 'If we try and pile more on, we'll lose the lot. It'll need a second journey to shift it all.' Raising both arms, he ran the flat of his hands through his earth-coloured shoulder-length hair, scraping it back from his face while discreetly eyeing his brother who was still engrossed in what was happening outside the Dickens house. In spite of himself Hadley was curious. He shifted his gaze to the girl. Greg had been right in one thing at least . . . Phoebe Mulligan was very beautiful. A heartbreaker in the making, he mused with some regret.

As she climbed down from the cart, Phoebe knew they were watching her. At first she had been amused and flattered that two very handsome young men had been so taken with her; it was clear they thought she was worth a second look. Certainly the black-haired fellow had not been able to take his sultry eyes off her, and though she had mischievously encouraged him with a coy smile, she was nevertheless disturbed by the intimate manner in which he continued to observe her. She thought him a fine figure of a man, standing there in the field, legs apart, his fists thrust deep into his trouser pockets and his proud arrogant features tilted upwards, compelling her to look on him. In that first tumultuous moment when their eyes met Phoebe had sensed a very real danger. In his secretive smile she recognised a spirit as rebellious as her own; she felt his simmering excitement and knew she must be careful of this one. His dark eyes were beckoning, curiously wicked. Yet, though she was stirred both by his passion and his attraction for her, she was not blinded to her deeper instinct. *This man was dangerous.*

In that moment before the cart passed them by she had glanced at the other young man. This one had not shown the same interest in her arrival and that intrigued her. She had studied him for a while, thinking he made a wonderful picture against the backdrop of that impenetrable spinney with the green rolling fields behind the jewel blue sky above. He was stripped to the waist, his broad back bent to his task, and with that rich earth-coloured hair, unusually long and falling to his shoulders, was unlike any other man she had ever seen. When at last he turned to gaze on her she was wonderfully surprised at the way the sun lit his blue eyes; they were not a quiet blue but a rich, dark and iridescent colour. His eyes reminded her of the dark ocean in a painting that had been her mother's. It was with a sudden shock that she found herself flooded with embarrassment. Quickly she looked away, her heart turning somersaults and a pleasant tinge of pink creeping up from her neck to warm her face.

'That's right, lass.' Old Jessup clambered down from the cart, his tiny bloodshot eyes looking up to where

Phoebe sat, her long fine fingers gripping the reins in the way he'd shown her and a look of apprehension in her serious brown eyes. 'You keep the old horse steady . . . while I fetch the lady of the house.' He shook his head when a certain thought entered into it. 'I ain't unloading one single stick o' furniture . . . not until I know I've delivered yer proper, I ain't!' He took a moment to glance into the field opposite. The two young men were riding away on the flat-cart. He shook his head again, clicking his tongue between his teeth and making a loud tutting noise. He had seen the manner in which that black-haired fella had stared at young Phoebe. He was not so old he didn't know what such a look meant. 'Young 'uns are all the same these days,' he muttered. 'Bloody motor-vehicles, jazz and short skirts!' There was a time, not so long ago, when such things were unheard of. 'Where will it all end?' he asked the sky, quickly answering his own question. 'It'll end in trouble, you mark my words. As sure as my name's Jessup, it'll end in trouble.'

Phoebe stared after his misshapen old figure, her anxious gaze coming to rest on the house. 'It's a grand place,' she muttered. 'Too grand for the likes of me.' She had not known what to expect but somehow had imagined her Uncle Edward might be a wealthy man. Certainly the house bore testimony to that. It was situated in a narrow lane at the end of Preston New Road. A wide thorough-fare snaking out of Blackburn towards Salmesbury, Preston New Road was flanked with houses that were much bigger and finer than the endless rows of back to backs which were built for the cotton mill workers in the town. Phoebe herself had been brought up in such a house in Bury and though they were cold, draughty and depressingly tiny, would have given all she owned to be back there now, with her mother sitting opposite the table or hunched in the rocking chair by the fire, trying to darn in the firelight. So many images invaded her mind: of her mother, of Dora, even the thought of Judd brought a pang to her heart. How she wished it was possible to turn the clock back. Oh, but then she probably would not have been able to change things, because wasn't it Fate? Didn't her own mother tell her, 'When the good Lord calls you . . . there isn't a thing you can do but answer his call.' Fate or not, it didn't stop her from hurting. 'Stop your wishing, Phoebe Mulligan,' she told herself with a wry little smile. 'You can't go home ever again. You're here now and you'd best make the most of it, my gal!'

With sorry eyes, she watched old Jessup go across the pavement and on up the path to the house. Dickens House was situated at the end of a row of large detached Victorian dwellings. With its sturdy timbered gables and tall bay windows, the house was very imposing. There was a garden too with a broad paved path running between two velvet green lawns interspersed with varied trees and shrubs, some of them bursting with blossom and others displaying luscious shiny green foliage. The front entrance was splendid. Three stone steps led to the dark panelled front door, and there was a porch with its own little roof and a collection of flower-pots filled with plants. Every window in the house was dressed with fancy lace curtains, and as Phoebe looked up to the bedroom windows she imagined she saw a figure. When she peered harder, it disappeared into the shadows.

Assailed with an inexplicable sense of guilt, Phoebe concentrated her attention on the open fields, the cattle grazing there, and the seemingly endless miles of pretty meandering stone walls that split one field from the next. 'Why, it's lovely,' she murmured. The realisation that she might be able to wander these fields at will gave her a degree of pleasure.

The woman who answered old Jessup's persistent knocking was a small nondescript creature with pale greying hair and a timid look about her. On seeing Phoebe waiting in the wagon, a look of horror crossed her face. 'Oh, dear!' she exclaimed, her pale eyes staring at Jessup and her teeth digging nervously into her bottom lip. 'Is that Phoebe Mulligan?' she asked in a small voice. She glanced fleetingly towards the wagon but seemed visibly alarmed when Phoebe smiled at her.

'Aye, that's Phoebe,' Jessup replied with a fond look at the girl. 'I've delivered her safe to your door . . . just like her mammy wanted.' He regarded the woman through serious eyes; there was something about her that made him nervous. Frightened, dithering women always did that to him and he wondered in passing why she was so anxious, but then there was no fathoming women, who were a law unto themselves. 'Aye, that's Phoebe, ma'am,' he affirmed. 'So if you'll kindly show me where I'm to deposit the lass's belongings, I'll start unloading. The sooner it's done the better because I've a long trek back home and a missus waiting at the other end.' He smiled to put her at ease, a broad whiskery grin that only served to worry her further.

'Oh, dear me . . . dear me!' She made a small step

sideways, hiding in Jessup's shadow, fearful that Phoebe might overhear. 'I'm not sure what to do.' Her soft whisper caused him to lean forward in order to hear her better. 'You see . . . Mr Dickens isn't here, and I don't know what time to expect him home.' She stared at him, her front teeth biting into her bottom lip again until it was red and sore.

'Not here, yer say?' Jessup leaned back on his heels, prodding his grubby fingers beneath the brim of his cap and scratching at the roots of his hair while he pondered on what was to be done. It was a strange kettle o' fish and that was a fact. 'Look here, Ma'am,' he said at length, 'if yer ask me there's only one thing we can do in Mr Dickens' absence, and that's for you to show me where yer want the lass's belongings put.' He eyed her suspiciously. 'You do know which room she's to sleep in, don't yer?' He didn't like to see her gnawing at her mouth like that. It put him in mind of a mouse nibbling at a crumb of cheese. Aye! That were it. She put him in mind of a mouse. 'I say . . . you *do* know where the lass is supposed to sleep, don't you, missus?' He startled himself when he addressed her as 'missus' instead of the more respectable 'ma'am'. But then it was not surprising, since his respect for her had also been nibbled away.

'Yes, of course I know where she'll be sleeping.' The woman appeared to be offended. 'Mr Dickens has given Phoebe a quiet little room at the top of the house.'

'Yer mean the attic?' he asked, shaking his head in disgust. When she gave no answer he asked impatiently, 'Then don't yer think that's where I should put her belongings?'

43

'Well, yes, I suppose so. Only . . .' She straightened her back and sneaked a look at Phoebe who appeared to be growing restless judging by the way she was tapping her feet and looking towards the house. 'I would rather Mr Dickens was here.'

'But he ain't, is he?' Old Jessup was growing agitated. 'I've already told you that.'

'Well, d'you want me to offload the lass's belongings on to the pavement . . . then yer husband can carry them into Phoebe's room when he gets back?' He had never hit a woman in his life but he felt like doing it now.

'Goodness!' Her eyes almost popped out of her head. 'I'm sure Mr Dickens would have a heart attack if he came home to find the pavement strewn with bits and pieces,' she chided, smartly stepping back as though sensing his growing urge to strike her. 'And you must do no such thing!'

'Good!' At last he'd managed to kindle a spark of life in her. 'Then you'll show me where I'm to put these "bits and pieces"?' When she nodded, he turned about, saying, 'Open the door wide, if yer please, and be ready ter lead the way.' Without looking back, he went at a smart pace down the path and back to the wagon, all the while muttering beneath his breath, 'I'll never complain about my old woman ever agin . . . she ain't no beauty but there's worse things and that's a fact!' He gingerly stroked the back of his head. 'Aye, an' she knows how to swing a bloody rolling-pin, that she does.' He chuckled aloud and began whistling a merry tune.

'What's she like?' Phoebe had seen the woman at the door and assumed it was her aunt although every time she had tried to see the woman's face, it hid itself behind Jessup's bulky figure.

'Oh, she's harmless enough, I reckon.' He stretched up to help Phoebe down. 'It don't look like anybody's rushing to help me,' he said. 'So if yer don't mind carrying the smaller things into the house, lass, I'd be much obliged.' He smiled when he saw that she was already rummaging in the pile of belongings on the wagon. 'That's grand, lass . . . but be careful. We don't want yer precious belongings damaged now, do we, eh?' He cast his eyes over the few meagre possessions and wondered how the girl would fare here in this place. Shaking his head at the pitiful thoughts that flitted through his mind, he went hurriedly to the forefront of the wagon where he began unstrapping the narrow bed.

Cunningly secreted behind her bedroom window, Margaret Dickens followed Phoebe's every move, her blue eyes betraying the dark jealousy in her heart. 'Go back where you came from!' she hissed. 'We don't want your sort here.' A sudden sound made her slew round, her face showing both relief and irritation when she saw that it was her mother. 'For goodness' sake, Mother!' she snapped. 'How many times must I tell you not to creep up on me like that!'

'I wasn't creeping, dear,' her mother apologised meekly. 'I only wanted to know whether you might come down and welcome your cousin.'

'You must be mad! I don't even know the creature. By rights she belongs in an institution.' Her clear blue eyes were hard as washed stones and her full painted lips were drawn into a pout. 'I think Father made a mistake in

45

bringing her here. She's not one of us.' Flicking her fingers at the lace curtain and discreetly drawing it back, she added venomously, 'Just *look* at her . . . she's every bit as wild and unkempt as Father feared.' She peered down to where Phoebe was struggling along the path with a pile of bedding. When she saw Phoebe's lovely face at close quarters, she bristled with envy. 'Common brat! Keep her away from me, that's all,' she ordered in a harsh voice.

Noreen Dickens leaned into the window, her quiet eyes appraising the girl below. She had never seen such a handsome child, so alive and vibrant with her profusion of auburn hair and that delightful figure that was not a child's yet not a woman's. There was something about the girl that touched her heart. And yet she was afraid. It was a strange feeling. Suddenly she was telling herself that it might have been better if Phoebe *had* been put in an institution. She thought of her husband's iron character and of his *real* reason for taking the girl in when he had loathed the very idea. She recalled her daughter's churlish words just now, and her fears for the girl were tenfold.

Turning from the window, she innocently addressed her own daughter. 'She's very lovely, don't you think?' Phoebe's striking appearance was more astonishing to Noreen Dickens, because she remembered the girl's mother well, a good kind soul who had had the misfortune of committing one cardinal sin in her life: a sin that was thrust upon her; a 'sin' which had cast her out from her family and hardened Edward's vindictive heart against her. Phoebe's mother had been very pretty but not possessed of the same vivid beauty as her daughter. In her youth she was not unlike Phoebe although Noreen could now see Jessica had been only a paler version of this girl.

As she watched Phoebe stoop to collect some garments, laughing and chatting to the old fellow when he made fun of her, Noreen found herself smiling. She could not help but be drawn to the girl. Certainly she was very spirited, especially in view of the fact that she must be heartbroken at the recent loss of her mother. She had also been taken from her home and brought here to a strange place, among strange people. With a sinking heart Noreen remembered that her husband would soon be home. Another painful challenge to the girl's spirit. The smile slid from her face. 'I hope we can make her happy,' she said thoughtfully.

'I hope we make her miserable!' Margaret stood close to the window. Her back was straight as a ramrod, her perfectly formed features sternly set.

Noreen was not surprised by her daughter's peevish remark. Margaret was a selfish ungrateful girl who believed the world should revolve around only her. There was a rare anger in her mother's voice as she asked now, 'How can you begrudge Phoebe the little she has? Put yourself in her place, Margaret, and try to show a little compassion.'

'Well, well!' Astonished and irritated at her mother's rebuke, Margaret stared at her for a moment, thinking how dowdy and unattractive the little woman was. Not for the first time she wondered with amusement how her father could have come to marry such a plain placid creature. Thrusting out her chin and eyeing her mother coldly, she retorted, 'So you hope we make her happy, do you, Mother? How very interesting. Who would have thought the brat might have an ally in you?' She laughed softly, leaning back to sit on the window-ledge, her cold blue eyes intent on her mother's face as she said with cunning, 'I wonder what Father would have to say about that?'

'No doubt he would be as disappointed as you are,' Noreen replied cautiously. She was under no illusion where her daughter and husband were concerned. They had each made her suffer in their own particular way. All the same, she would have her say this one time because she had seen something in Phoebe that awoke a dormant feeling in her, a feeling of shame and regret, a feeling that her life was not her own, a feeling which told her how truly empty was her own existence. Facing her daughter she asked in a controlled voice, 'Why is it that you're never satisfied? You have everything a girl could want . . . more clothes than you could ever wear in a lifetime, a freedom which I and many other women could never hope to enjoy. You've travelled Europe at your father's expense, to be taught the ways of a lady, and soon you'll be installed in one of his stores, in a position of some authority. Is there nothing that can satisfy you, Margaret?'

'She really has stirred the tiger in you, hasn't she?' Margaret continued to regard her mother with some curiosity, her eyes growing wider with every word and a curious little smile playing at the corners of her pretty mouth. 'If I hadn't heard you with my own ears, I would never have believed it!' As far back as she could remember her mother had never spoken out with such conviction. It was an intriguing experience and one which she found greatly entertaining. 'You do have a tongue after all, you sly old thing,' she said with some venom, 'although I'm not sure Father would approve. As for me showing "compassion" for *her*,' she glanced towards the window, 'for that creature . . . I don't owe Phoebe Mulligan anything. The plain truth is I never wanted her in this house, and I still don't.'

'Why not?'

'Because she doesn't belong here, that's why not!'

'So where does she belong?'

'Anywhere but here in this house. Father doesn't really want her here and neither do I.' She paused then to stare into her mother's face. 'What is she to you anyway? Anyone would think she was your own kith and kin . . . which she isn't, except in marriage.'

'I'm disappointed in you, Margaret. The girl has no home, no parents, no prospects at all, and still you set yourself against her.' Noreen sighed, shaking her head and saying, 'Somewhere along the way I failed badly as a mother.'

There was a long painful moment before her daughter replied in a cutting tone, 'I can't argue with that.'

Noreen might have said something, but then she might have remained silent as she had done so often before. The shout from below saved the moment. 'Missus!' It was Jessup's voice. 'If you'll kindly show me the way, I'd be very grateful because this 'ere bed's breaking me back!'

'You'd better go, Mother dear,' Margaret said sweetly. 'We wouldn't want to keep the riff-raff waiting now, would we?'

Choosing to ignore the sarcastic remark, Noreen made

no reply. She turned away and hurried towards the door. Without looking back she murmured softly, 'How like your father you are.' Once more she gave thanks that there had been no more children after Margaret.

When her mother had gone, Margaret continued to watch the girl from the window. Phoebe had made many trips to and from the wagon until now it was almost empty and most of the items were piled against the front door. When suddenly Phoebe glanced up Margaret quickly drew out of sight, cursing the girl for having almost caught her in the act. 'Damn and blast you, Phoebe Mulligan!' she whispered into the room. Now, when her mother's words came back to her, she actually laughed aloud. It was true, she was not easily satisfied – but then she saw nothing wrong with that. Her mother's opinion meant little to her, though. If it had been her father who had shown displeasure at her behaviour then she would have been hurt. Her father was as strong as her mother was weak. She had always admired him for that and constantly looked to him for an example. She loved her father dearly yet she had learned from an early age how to manipulate the people around her. Her father was no exception although in the matter of Phoebe he had stood firm. As a rule he could refuse her nothing, but in this case she had been forced to concede. Edward Dickens set great store by his principles, sternly reminding his daughter, 'Your aunt's untimely demise has caused me no end of aggravation. But it is my sorry duty to bring the girl into this house and to teach her the Christian way. So let that be the end to it!' There were other, more sinister reasons for his having brought Phoebe here, but he was not about to reveal those to anyone.

Having her own strong opinions dismissed as though they were of no account was an unpleasant and belittling experience for Margaret who had still not entirely forgiven her father. She had been bitter. She was bitter now. Yet she did not hate him. That emotion was reserved for Phoebe; an emotion that had festered and grown until now it was a cold and dangerous thing.

Crossing the room, she pressed her ear close to the door, listening intently as the unwelcome visitors entered the house. From the landing she could hear her mother calling out, 'Up here . . . mind how you go.' There followed a series of sounds as the procession came slowly up the stairs; amidst all the shuffling and banging, the old man's voice could be heard hurling abuse at all and sundry. 'No! No! Get outta the way . . . I can manage better on me own, dammit.' When old Jessup found it all too much, they paused right outside the door, causing the eavesdropper to draw away, terrified that they might invade her privacy. But then she relaxed. 'A minute,' the old man gasped, puffing and wheezing, 'just give me a minute to get me breath.'

'Don't be stubborn, Jessup!' Phoebe's firm young voice rang out. 'I mean to help you carry that bed, whether you want me to or not.' After a brief exchange of words when she would not be dissuaded, the procession continued with Noreen urging them on, past her daughter's bedroom and up the next flight of stairs.

In the privacy of her room, Margaret Dickens smiled. 'That's right. Take her up to the attic,' she said with a low laugh, 'take her to the hovel where she belongs.' She went to the wardrobe and flung open the door, sensuously running her slim white hands over the many lovely dresses there. 'You're no threat to me, Phoebe Mulligan,' she said in a low voice. 'I was a fool ever to think you might be.' She glanced towards the ceiling, listening to the muffled sounds as they travelled along the upper landing. Her smile was bitter. She remembered what her mother had said just now, 'She's very lovely, don't you think?' Looking deeper into the mirror, she stretched her pretty features into a hideous grimace, cruelly mimicking her mother's words. 'She's very lovely, don't you think?' In a hard voice she answered herself, 'No, Mother! I *don't* think.' Yet in spite of herself she had grudgingly to admit that her cousin *was* beautiful . . . much too beautiful for her own good. But then, she was also very common, so obviously devoid of a proper upbringing, an intruder who had brought nothing with her but the shift on her back and a few worthless articles that should have been left to rot or burned for the rubbish they were.

Phoebe's existence had been a shock to her cousin because Edward Dickens had never spoken of having a sister. Jessica Mulligan's name had been forbidden in this house years before Margaret was born. When his sister's heartfelt letter arrived, begging him to take her daughter, he had called Noreen and Margaret into his study to inform them of his decision.

'Against my better judgment, I shall comply with her wishes,' he said, adding in a formidable voice, 'Of course, in the manner of the girl's upbringing, I shall be answerable to no one.' When Margaret was insistent on knowing more about her aunt and the reason for her 'deserting' the family, her father explained how, 'As a girl, Jessica was always a headstrong, undisciplined creature. She simply ran away one day after an argument with Father. Of course we knew she was in the company of a young man not of Father's choosing. We learned that they were married and soon after that our father died. She and I have not communicated from that day to this.'

His explanation was accepted by Margaret who saw no reason to doubt her father's words. But he had lied. Only Noreen knew the truth. She had liked Edward's sister, and blamed herself for not contacting Jessica when the announcement of her husband's demise was placed in the local paper. But her sympathy for Jessica was over-shadowed by her fear of Edward. And so, over the years, she had remained silent.

Margaret vehemently protested that her father had made the wrong decision. After seeing Phoebe, she believed it more than ever. Her thoughts went fleetingly to a certain young man, a man who had proved to be elusive for too long but whom she hoped was now well and truly under her spell. Lately, and much to her own astonishment, she had found herself to be genuinely in love with him; even entertaining the idea of marriage. Unlike his brother Greg who had proved to be an exciting but selfish lover, Hadley was a quiet, private man whom she had secretly craved. It had taken a long time and a great deal of wily cunning to coax him into her arms. He was a good man, too good for her and she knew it. But she was bored with the same old crowd. Hadley was different, a real man, a challenge, and she was a woman who needed a challenge. She had seen the way both brothers had looked at Phoebe. She knew they had admired her beauty and was beside herself with rage.

Raising her brilliant blue eyes to the ceiling, she murmured in a calm deadly voice, 'Keep away from him, or I swear you'll rue the day you ever came to this house!'

Suddenly her mood changed. Looking into the mirror she quietly appraised the slim shapely figure there. Her smile deepened when with slow provocative movements she slowly discarded her clothes until she stood naked from head to toe. Reaching deeper into the wardrobe she clutched at the emerald green dress. It was a pretty flowing thing, straight at the waist but bound at the hips with a dark velvet band. The voluminous skirt had a scalloped hem that dipped and rose in a profusion of shimmering beads in every colour of the rainbow. Bands of dark velvet trimmed the throat and sleeves, the sleeves being short and scalloped like the hem and the neck shaped into an exquisite sweetheart line. As she drew the precious garment from the wardrobe, the many coloured beads in the lavish folds of the skirt shimmered beneath the light. With a sigh she slipped it over her head, letting it fall on her narrow shoulders. It trickled over her cool body, accentuating every angle, every voluptuous curve. Turning this way and that, she examined herself in the mirror. Satisfied, she reached into the drawer beneath the wardrobe, drawing out a dark feathered head-band which she slipped over her fair bobbed hair, positioning it at just the right angle on her forehead. Teasing out a halo of soft wispy curls to frame her ice blue eyes, she pirouetted in front of the mirror, pouting her ruby red lips and smiling into her own face. 'No, Mother,' she sighed softly. 'Phoebe isn't beautiful . . . not like me.'

She laughed aloud. How could she ever have imagined that the girl might be a threat? Indulging herself, she stroked her long fingers over her hips, touching the dress, smoothing its folds with reverence. This was her favourite outfit, the one she had danced in time and time again with many different beaux, the most memorable occasion being when she had danced in Hadley Peters' arms. In her mind's eye she recalled Phoebe's brown shapeless shift. She need have no fear, she told herself. Hadley was a man of good taste. And he was *her* man. If Phoebe wanted a man of her own, there was always Greg. The idea fired her imagination. Greg and Phoebe. Beauty and the Beast. The more she thought on it, the more the idea appealed to her. She smiled deviously. The smile became a low wicked laugh. Of course! Greg Peters and Phoebe Mulligan. What a wonderful idea!

In the attic room above, Phoebe stood by the window, her dark gaze travelling the room and her heart sinking with every new thing she saw: the bare floorboards covered only by a small peg-rug; the sloping walls that reached up to a high ceiling which was open to the rafters; the room itself, so tiny and filled with shadows, the only light being that which filtered in through the little dormer window. There was no furniture other than what she and Jessup had brought up, and this consisted of her own narrow bed, a chair, a small cupboard, and a bundle of her more personal belongings. Turning her dark eyes to the woman, Phoebe asked in a subdued voice, 'Where will I hang my clothes?' She cast her gaze once more round the room, trying hard not to wrinkle her nose against the damp musty smell that pervaded the atmosphere.

Noreen gave no immediate answer but instead looked

towards the bed. There Phoebe's belongings had been lovingly placed, and the woman could not help but mentally compare the clothes with those of her own daughter in the room below. Margaret's were extravagant and expensive while Phoebe's treasured possessions were meagre and pitiful. 'I'm sure I don't know,' she answered presently, returning Phoebe's smile. 'Your uncle does not appear to have taken that into consideration.'

'My missus allus hangs her things on the picture rail,' Jessup intervened. 'On account of we ain't got no fancy wardrobe neither.' He peered at the clothes on the bed and then at Phoebe, saying in a sorry voice, 'Anyroad, you ain't got but two or three items for hanging, have you, eh? Do like I said, Phoebe . . . hang them on the picture rail. After all, there ain't no weight to pull the rail down, is there?' He made a small chuckle then immediately looked away, sucking his lips in embarrassment. 'Aw, Phoebe . . . I didn't mean that as heartless as it sounded, lass,' he apologised in a small voice. His missus allus did say as how he let his tongue run away with him! 'What I meant to say was . . .'

'It's all right, Jessup,' she interrupted kindly. 'You're right, though. I ain't got enough clothes to worry about. I'll manage somehow.'

Relieved that the matter was resolved, Noreen stepped forward and went at a nervous pace around the entire room; it was soon encompassed. 'You'll quickly get used to everything,' she told Phoebe while averting her gaze. The girl made her feel ashamed somehow. 'There's a small washroom at the end of the corridor.' Her face brightened. 'That will be yours to use. No one else ever comes up here . . . although now, of course, I expect your uncle will instruct Daisy to extend her duties in order that she can attend to your room . . . and, of course, the washroom must be kept clean.' That said, she looked from Phoebe to the old man who was waiting in vain for a small remuneration from the lady of the house. 'You may go now,' she told him. 'Phoebe will be all right.'

'Is that so, ma'am?' he replied, staring into her pale eyes and seeing only shadows. He shifted his gaze to Phoebe's downcast face. He was not entirely convinced. 'You will be all right, won't you, lass?' he asked gently. 'Is there anything else you want me to do before I take my leave?' Suddenly he was eager to be gone. His hopes of a few coppers from the lady of the house had quickly vanished and there was an unwelcoming atmosphere in this place which made him uneasy.

'No, thank you, Jessup,' Phoebe replied. 'You've done all you can and I'm very grateful. It's up to me now.'

'Aye, lass, like you say . . . it's up to you now.' He had been smiling at Phoebe, but now the smile was replaced with a frown as in a bold voice he told the woman, 'She's a good lass, missus. Take care of her, won't you? Her mammy, Jessica Mulligan, was one of the best, and this 'ere lass is made of the same good mettle. See that you and yours treat her right.' Without waiting for a reply, he ambled out of the room, muttering to himself and cursing the Fates for having left the girl at the mercy of strangers. He didn't like the look of things. No, not at all. When he was coming up the stairs just now, he had heard the two women arguing in that room below and didn't like the sound of it. He knew that

Phoebe had heard it too, and his old hackles were up. 'Bloody relatives!' he muttered aloud. 'Better off without 'em, that's what I say!' He paused on the second step when he heard someone call his name. 'What's that you say?' he mumbled, twisting his aching body round and his face lighting up when he saw that it was Phoebe calling him. He almost lost his balance when she threw herself into his arms. 'Now, now, lass . . . what's all this, eh?' he asked with some concern.

'Thank you for everything,' she whispered, hugging him tight. He was the last link with her past. Jessup was a loved and familiar sight in the streets of Bury, and she wondered if she would ever again see him or her two dear friends.

'Aw, lass, bless your heart,' he chuckled. 'It ain't the end of the world, is it, eh?' Though when he glanced into the tiny attic room and saw the woman standing there he thought it might as well be. 'You'll be fine. Just do as you're told and don't go looking for trouble,' he warned. Easy words but all the same he dared not look into Phoebe's dark eyes. Disentangling himself, he went down the stairs as fast as his old legs could take him. Then he went out of the door without a backward look.

Returning to the attic, Phoebe watched the old man from the window. She followed him as he went down the path, she climbed on to the wagon with him, and she was by his side as the ensemble travelled away from the house at a steady pace, her fears soothed by the sound of the horse's hooves as they created a rhythmic clatter against the hard road. At the spot where the road wound away, she and Jessup parted company when the old man turned to wave and she waved back until her arm ached. In a moment the wagon and Jessup were gone, Phoebe's heart went with it, and the tears she had suppressed spilled slowly down her face. 'Goodbye, Jessup,' she murmured. 'God bless.'

'I'll leave you to it then.' Noreen's voice crept into the silence. No one had ever touched her conscience as this girl could. 'I won't stay and help you put things away . . . your uncle has very strong views and I know he would not approve.' She was startled when Phoebe swung round, her face stained with tears. 'You mustn't be afraid, child,' she said lamely.

'What's he like?' Phoebe asked. 'What kind of a man is my mother's brother?' She could not bring herself to call him 'Uncle'. The memory of that awful letter was too fresh in her mind.

Noreen was taken aback by the direct question. She struggled to find an answer. Phoebe wanted to know what kind of man he was. The answer would not have calmed the girl's fears. If Phoebe was to learn in this moment what kind of man Edward Dickens was, she might well be tempted to run from the house and seek sanctuary on the moors or travel the countryside like a gypsy rather than dwell under this roof.

In an attempt to put the girl at ease she answered confidently, 'Your uncle is a quietly spoken man. In all the time I have known him, I've never once heard him raise his voice in anger.' That at least was the truth. She might have gone on to say how he had no need to raise his voice because his hard grey eyes spoke volumes; she could have explained how he had a way of arousing fear without speaking one single word; or she could have warned Phoebe that to cross him was to commit the gravest of all sins.

While this true description of her husband came into Noreen's fearful mind she chose not to convey it because she knew that the girl would learn these things soon enough. Instead, she dwelt on the facets of his character that might redeem him. 'He is a devout and respected man,' she went on. 'Oh, I won't deny that he is a hard taskmaster, but he expects from others only what he himself is prepared to give. I suppose he is a wealthy man . . . although of course it is not my place to know the full extent of his business affairs. What I *do* know is this, as recently as eight years ago your uncle was proprietor of Dickens' general store in Ainsworth Street, Blackburn, the same store which was left to him by his father, your grandfather. Being the shrewd businessman he is, your uncle began to specialise in menswear, not just suits and overcoats but all the accessories such as shoes, ties, shirts and gloves. He now has several shops throughout the north-west, each dedicated to the pampering of gentlemen who can afford the very best.' She tried to give the impression that she was proud of her husband's achievements when in truth she had no regard for either him or his 'gentlemen's shops'. 'So you see, Phoebe, he is much to be admired . . . a man of talent and accomplishment.'

'Do you love him?'

'Goodness!' Noreen was shocked at such bluntness. 'That is not the kind of thing a lady should ask.'

'You think me a lady?'

'Well, I . . . really, Phoebe, I don't know *what* to think.'

'Do you?'

'Do I what, child?'

'Do you love him?'

'Enough!' Phoebe had disturbed her deeply. It seemed Edward had been right when he forecast that his sister's child would not have been brought up in the manner of a lady. 'Please guard your tongue when you address your uncle. He would not take kindly to such boldness. I'll overlook it on this occasion because I believe you to have asked the question in all innocence. But be warned, child, I have little authority in this house so if you're foolish enough to incense your uncle, don't look to me for help.' Afraid that she might be frightening the girl she added in a lighter voice, 'He can't be all that bad though, can he? Not when he's given you a home and taken on the responsibility for your well-being.'

'I think he must be bad.'

'What are you saying, child?' Noreen was horrified.

'My mam wrote to him when she was dying, and instead of travelling to Bury to bring her comfort, he sent her a cruel unforgiving letter. If he was a good man, he would never have done such a heartless thing.'

'Please, Phoebe.' Noreen came closer to the girl, her eyes soft with compassion, and her heart aching. She wanted so much to confirm the things Phoebe had said. It would have given her so much pleasure to discredit her husband in the girl's eyes but it could not be. It could never be. After all these years it was too late. Anyway, she was too much of a coward. 'Listen to me, child. You really must be careful what you say. I can only warn you to think before you speak . . . as we all must.' With the exception of Margaret, she thought cynically. 'Your mother was a wise woman, and I know she loved you dearly. Do you think she would have sent you here if she thought your uncle was a bad man?' She had wondered long and hard as to why Jessica had done such a foolhardy and dangerous thing but she was wise enough to know that the poor woman had little choice. When Phoebe bowed her head she felt a great urge to put her arms round the girl and comfort her, but she could not. She must never get too close. It would be too painful.

'Did you know my mam well?' Phoebe concentrated her gaze on the small flowerbed that skirted the lawn. She could not rid herself of the feeling that her aunt was keeping something from her. She sensed the little woman's fear and it bred a strange anxiety in her.

'Your mother moved away soon after your uncle and I were married. I knew her only for a short while before then, but she was a fine young woman . . . much like yourself, Phoebe, only not quite so lovely. She was a good woman, though, and I liked her.'

Phoebe raised her head and looked at the other woman's eyes. She saw the truth there and her trust was restored. 'I'm sorry I asked such a personal question,' she apologised. There was something else she needed to know. 'Did he tell you how ill my mam was?'

'No. Not until it was too late.' That was the truth.

'Did you see the letter he wrote?'

'No.'

'I've brought it with me. Do you want to read it?'

'No. And I suggest that you get rid of it. From what you tell me, it can only bring you pain.'

'I can't do that. It were my mam's.' Phoebe would keep

it safe and, yes, it would cause her pain were she ever to read it again. But she knew every word. She wouldn't forget. Nor could she forget the pain that letter must have caused her mother. She had never met this man who was her uncle but already she disliked him immensely.

'Your uncle is holding office in the new Blackburn shop . . . interviewing applicants for the vacancies there. He's expected home by teatime.' Noreen had felt the conversation drawing dangerously close to matters that were best forgotten. It would not do to raise the past and all that went with it. Besides which, if she were to breathe one single word of what had happened all those years ago, she would undoubtedly be severely punished. And so in a matter-of-fact voice she went on, 'Meanwhile, you'll find clean bed-linen just outside on the banister so you can make your bed up straight away. I've been given strict instructions that you're to remain up here until he sends for you. I'm sure you can busy yourself, Phoebe . . . you have much to do. When you have everything in order, you'll find a clean towel and soap in the washroom. Your uncle insists that you be presentable when you're summoned.'

There was a brief pause when Phoebe kept her face to the window, her eyes looking at the spot where she had last seen the horse and wagon. Her aunt's voice came to her again, this time a little kinder. 'I know all this must appear harsh to you, Phoebe, but it's best that you do as your uncle asks. You'll learn in time, my dear . . . just as I have. Do you appreciate what I'm saying, Phoebe?'

She nodded but kept her face averted. The other woman made a strange sound then, like a deep-down sigh, and still Phoebe did not turn round. Only when she heard the door being closed did she come away from the window to sit on the bed where she threw herself across the mattress and sobbed as she had never sobbed before.

Halfway down the stairs, Noreen paused at the sound of Phoebe's muffled sobs. For a moment it seemed as though she might return to the attic. Instead she raised her face to the ceiling, listening a while before saying in a furtive whisper, 'Watch over your daughter, Jessica, for I'm not woman enough to keep her from harm.' Squaring her thin shoulders, she lifted her head and continued down the wide carpeted stairway and on to the lower reaches of the house where she would await her husband's return. But she would not plead on Phoebe's behalf. It would be to no avail.

Margaret heard her mother's familiar steps as they went by her door. She heard Phoebe in the room directly above her own. She knew how desperately unhappy the girl was. And the knowledge filled her heart with pleasure.

'Come on, gal,' Phoebe reprimanded herself, sitting up and drying her eyes on the corner of her shift. 'Your mam always told you that tears won't solve anything, and she was right.' Looking round the room she realised it would take a while to get it looking as she wanted it. 'It ain't such a bad room,' she said with a brighter face and her fighting spirit rising. 'Matter of fact . . . all it needs is a set of pretty lace curtains and a bit of elbow grease and you won't know the place at all!' Determined to make the best of what was offered her, she soon set about tidying up.

First there were the clothes to hang, and she had been careful to bring the hangers with her; one by one she shook and straightened the garments which Jessup had laid on the bed and which she had crushed beneath her during her moments of despair . . . the long grey woollen cardigan that had been her mother's together with two straight skirts, one navy, one brown, and a white long-sleeved blouse. Then there was the trim three-quarter-length dark jacket that fitted snugly to her slight figure, accentuating the tiny waist and the small square shoulders. And her cream dress.

This was kept for best, for Sundays and special events, although there had been few of those in her life. Her mother had toiled over that dress for many hours and Phoebe had lost count of the times she had been made to stand there for what seemed ages while Jessica painstakingly turned it in here, dropped the hem there, snipping with her scissors and tucking with her pins until at last the garment was finished.

It was Phoebe's first 'grown-up' dress, and all the more precious because she knew how much her mother had sacrificed in order to purchase the materials with which to make it. The soft cream colour was a perfect complement to her magnificent auburn hair and dark eyes. The sleeves were long, tapering in at the cuffs and fastened with the tiniest pearl buttons; the neck was high, with a pretty lace collar; and the fitted waist was encircled with a narrow belt in a darker shade of cream. The skirt, which reached down to her calves, swirled as she walked. When she wore it with her jacket and best black patent shoes, Phoebe felt like a princess.

Reverently, she hung the dress on the picture rail. It worried her that there was no cupboard in the room. She decided to ask her aunt whether she might have a dust-sheet with which to cover the clothes because, left exposed, they would soon turn grubby and discoloured.

When the clothes were hung, Phoebe shook the mattress and made the bed; it looked pretty enough with the chequered eiderdown and white pillowslip with the primroses at each corner. She pushed the bed against the wall to the right of the window, positioning it so that she could see the sky when lying down, then she plumped both pillow and eiderdown for the umpteenth time. Next, she took up the peg-rug and shook it out the window. Then, coughing and spluttering from the dust which billowed in, she laid it on the floorboards at the side of the bed and surveyed her handiwork.

'That's it!' she said. 'It's beginning to look like home now, Phoebe gal.' The smile slid from her face as she thought about those words. Nothing could ever replace what had been home.

Casting aside the depression that threatened to swamp her, she launched into the pile of paraphernalia that was piled in the corner. In no time at all she had the cupboard in place beside the bed and all her belongings in it, although the whole lot only filled the top drawer. On the small surface she laid out her hairbrush and comb, she hung her mother's small crucifix on the wall behind the bed-head and the picture of a kitten found a home on the opposite wall, out of the shadows, where the sun brought it to life. Lastly she took the framed picture of her mam and herself, kissed her mam's face, and placed the picture on the mantelpiece. Seeing her own things all around her lifted Phoebe's heart and, thinking that maybe things wouldn't be too bad after all, she went out of the room and along the landing to look for the washroom.

The attic was huge, a labyrinth of small dark rooms riddled with cobwebs. Phoebe peeped into every one, then wished she hadn't because now she would lie awake at night wondering what kind of monsters might come creeping out when the house was asleep. 'Don't be daft, Phoebe Mulligan!' she chided herself, forcing a small laugh and going at a faster pace when she imagined she heard a sound behind her.

The washroom was clean and, curiously enough, much larger than her bedroom. In one corner stood a pot sink cracked with age and across the far wall there was a handsome bath which must have been white once but was now faded. The window was small though, and the room alive with shadows. There was no soap and no towel. Phoebe searched everywhere. Her aunt had made a mistake. Exasperated, she made her way back to her own room.

Somewhere in the bowels of the house a clock was chiming. She counted the chimes. One. Two. Three. Four. FIVE! It was five o'clock already. She had lost all sense of time. In the eerie silence that followed the last chime she could hear the rumbling of her own stomach. It had been some time since she had eaten and she was ready for her tea.

Someone was approaching. Running back to her room she closed the door and waited, her back pressed hard to the wooden panelling and her heart in her mouth. At last, she suspected, she was about to meet her uncle. Someone was right outside the door. The sharp knock against it made her heart leap; then her aunt's voice, harder somehow yet noticeably trembling, announced, 'Your uncle wants you downstairs. Right away, Phoebe!'

When she opened the door, her aunt hardly looked at her. 'You're to come with me,' she said. In a moment she was leading the way downstairs to the dining-room where Edward Dickens was waiting. Dutifully Phoebe followed, her head held high and the proud look on her face belying the fact that inside she felt like a lamb going to the slaughter.

'Wait here.' Noreen indicated the place where Phoebe was to sit; as she pointed to the carved wooden settle at the foot of the staircase, her hands were trembling. Realising that Phoebe had sensed her nervousness, she clasped her hands together and hurried towards the dining-room door. 'I'll inform your uncle,' she said. In a moment she had gone into the room and Phoebe was left alone.

The settle was hard and cold to the touch. Phoebe shivered as she sat down but her back was straight, her head held high, her whole confident demeanour belying the nervousness inside her. The sound of voices emanated from the dining-room, low urgent voices, heightening the fluttering in her stomach.

She turned her dark eyes towards the main entrance. Outside it was a brilliant summer's day. The sun filtered in through the fanlight over the door, projecting the colours of the stained glass into the hallway and playing weird patterns on the wall with dancing facets of light, brilliant in their greens, blues and yellows. She watched them shimmer and flicker and was fascinated. She didn't like the house though. It had a hostile feel about it, something that said 'Go away. You're not welcome.' She smiled at her own thoughts. How could a house speak? Yet it could. It was. The old grandfather clock at the end of the hallway loudly ticked the minutes by. It seemed as though she had been waiting a lifetime when suddenly the dining-room door inched open and her aunt appeared.

'Your uncle is ready to see you.'

The door was open wide now and Phoebe could see inside, her eyes picking out a huge darkwood dresser whose shelves were festooned with willow pattern plates and pretty pot jugs. Her inquisitive gaze was drawn to the right of the room, to the magnificent fireplace there; its broad mantelpiece was covered with a red tasselled cloth, which was covered with various ornaments. Directly before it, legs astride, grey eyes intent on her, stood Edward Dickens. A tall, well-built man, surprisingly handsome with his thick greying hair and a small neat beard, his fine features held an odd resemblance to Phoebe's own dear mother. But the resemblance was only fleeting because the next moment he seemed nothing like her at all. His face was wreathed in a welcoming smile.

As she came deeper into the room, Phoebe was aware of her aunt's nearness. Their shoulders brushed and Phoebe was momentarily surprised to hear a whisper in her ear. Something about the furtive action told her to direct her gaze ahead and not to look round. 'Don't be afraid, child,' the murmur said. But she *was* afraid. He was smiling at her, his grey eyes searching her face.

Phoebe told herself that there was nothing to be afraid of but for some inexplicable reason she was deeply disturbed by this man, this handsome stranger who was her reluctant guardian.

She was led to the end of a long oval-shaped table. It was covered with a crimson chenille cloth and its entire centre packed with food: plates of ham and pickle dishes, pork pie and a cheeseboard, daintily sliced bread beside a dish of butter, fresh fruit, and a tiered cake stand decorated with sections of Battenberg. Just a glance at the food set Phoebe's stomach rumbling so loud that it could be heard by one and all. Her embarrassment was complete when the girl with yellow hair giggled aloud.

The table was set with four places . . . one at the very far end, the head of the table, where the tall carver-chair seemed to dominate the whole room. There were two places set opposite each other halfway down the table, one to the left of Phoebe and one to the right. Noreen Dickens and her daughter had dutifully taken up position here.

The girl did not look at her mother but regarded Phoebe with blatant curiosity. Her piercing blue eyes had followed the newcomer's every move. When Phoebe returned her gaze, she quickly looked away, staring down at the table and smiling secretly as though enjoying some private entertaining thought. Phoebe guessed that the girl was not much older than herself and her heart gave a little skip. Perhaps she had a friend and ally after all.

'Would you care to tell us what you find so amusing, Margaret!' The sentence was softly spoken but it charged the atmosphere with a sense of impending doom. The ensuing silence was unnerving. Phoebe's heart turned somersaults and she was uncertain as to whether she should look at her uncle or stare down at the table as the other two were now doing. She could feel his eyes on her. She chose to raise her head and stare back at him.

He appeared to be astonished yet continued to look at her a while longer, his curious grey eyes growing harder as they roved her slim form, noting the plain brown shift and the well-worn shoes, the striking abundance of her russet-coloured hair, and the way she held herself so fearlessly, beautiful and unashamed.

When he took a step closer, Phoebe looked away. She made no move as he rounded the table, his hands clasped behind his back, his face set sternly as he regarded her at greater length. She could not know his thoughts: how he saw his own sister in the child she had sent to him, or how he believed Phoebe to be too handsome, too bold in the way she met his gaze, far too proud for the common creature she was. Above all he was convinced that he was taking on more of a challenge than he had at first anticipated. But he must not be beaten by this slip of a girl. Nor must he forget the sin her mother had committed. The girl must not be allowed to go the same way. He knew where his duty lay. As the girl's guardian and a staunch Christian, he had been given the unique opportunity to exact punishment for his sister's sin. And nothing would deter him.

'You're very lovely,' he murmured, 'much like your mother before you.' He inclined his head in a warmer smile, his eyes appraising her with feigned appreciation.

Taken aback at such an unexpected compliment,

Phoebe made no answer. Instead she found herself stiffening beneath his relentless scrutiny. When it seemed he expected her to comment, she agreed softly, 'My mother was very beautiful.'

'Indeed she was, my dear!' he conceded fervently. 'Indeed she was. But then . . . beauty is not always a blessing.' Raising his hand, he touched his long fingers against the wild auburn curls, flicking them this way then that. His next remark was addressed to his own daughter. 'Your cousin has exquisite hair, don't you think?' he asked sweetly.

Margaret raised her head and locked her gaze with his. They smiled into each other's eyes. When she spoke it was with a certain satisfaction. 'If you say so, Father,' she replied coldly.

'Oh, but I *do*!' he assured her. 'I do.' His gaze shifted towards his wife. His smile fell away at the seriousness of her expression. 'And what about you, my dear?' he asked. 'Don't you think the girl's hair is . . . magnificent?' When she looked away he spoke again, this time in a softer voice. 'I didn't hear what you said, my dear?' he prompted, leaning towards her, his grey eyes darkening.

The woman's chest rose and fell at a frantic pace and her eyes flickered beneath his stare. Presently she replied in a breathless voice, 'Yes, Phoebe does have magnificent hair.'

'And would you say it was too long, my dear? Too showy?'

The woman looked at Phoebe, at her lovely proud face and long auburn hair. She wished the girl had never come here. 'Perhaps a little . . . too long,' she muttered reluctantly.

Satisfied, he returned his attention to Phoebe. 'It seems we are all agreed,' he said with a handsome smile. Sensing that she was about to speak, he quickly asked, 'Are you settled in your room?' He was standing beside her now. The smell of his cologne was overpowering.

'Yes, thank you.' She met his gaze without fear, her nutmeg-brown eyes remaining guarded. He was a strange man, difficult to fathom. He had a gentleman's manner, a nice voice, and his smile was disarming. But she could not forget the letter he had sent to her mother.

'We are all very pleased to have you here with us,' he told her. 'I instructed your mother that you would need certain things . . . a bed, a change of clothes. Did you bring them with you?'

'Yes.'

'I trust you made your own bed and tidied the room yourself?' His smile deepened, coaxing her to return it, but she could not. She wanted him to move away. His nearness was offensive to her.

'I did all those things,' she answered, her head high and her gaze unflinching.

'And now . . . you must be hungry?'

'I am very hungry . . . yes.'

'Hmm.' He walked away, hands clasped tight behind his back. As he wended his way across the room to the top of the table, each step he took was slow and deliberate. When he reached the carver he swung round, his knuckles white as they gripped the curved top. The smile had gone from his face and his grey eyes were like tiny stones glittering in the daylight that spilled in through the window. He did not address Phoebe then. Instead he turned to his wife, saying in a voice that was barely audible, 'You also had my instructions, did you not?'

'Of course, and I did as you said.'

'Yes, yes. Don't worry, my dear.' He saw the damning effect his words were having on her, and saw too that Phoebe was paying the utmost attention. For what seemed an endless moment he stared at his wife and then smiled at her, smiled at Phoebe, and saved his broadest smile for Margaret. 'Your mother does have a tendency to amuse me,' he laughed, throwing his arms out and bringing his gaze back to Phoebe. 'That's a good thing between a man and his wife, wouldn't you say?'

When Phoebe nodded, he looked again at his wife. She was trembling. His voice cut into the atmosphere like a blade. 'You failed to see that the girl was washed and suitably dressed before you brought her to the table, my dear,' he said with a wide smile. 'But no matter! The two of you can attend to it right away.'

'She didn't forget,' Phoebe interrupted. 'My aunt told me to wash before I came down. It's my fault. I was so busy tidying up, I just forgot.' She could have told him how there was no soap or towel in the washroom, but then her aunt might be held to blame after all.

Phoebe's outburst had startled him. Turning to his bemused daughter he said, 'Well, well . . . it would seem that your cousin is a spirited little thing.' To his wife he said, 'Take the girl away, my dear. Scrub her well. Choose her a dress that looks less like a sack and . . .' His eyes roved over Phoebe's wild auburn hair. 'Never mind. There's time enough for other matters,' he said at length.

Ushering Phoebe towards the door, the flustered woman assured her husband, 'I'll have her back at the table in no time at all . . . you won't recognise her, I promise.'

His eyes widened and he shook his head slowly from side to side. 'Oh, didn't I explain, my dear? I'm sorry . . . I must have forgotten. You see, Margaret and I can't wait tea for you,' he went on with feigned surprise. 'I'm afraid you must both go without food tonight.' His smiling eyes dwelt on Phoebe's disbelieving expression. 'Of course you may enjoy a hearty breakfast in the morning, provided you present yourself in a suitable manner.' His manner abruptly changed as he continued in a more serious voice, 'Before the family attends Church, you and I must have a little chat, my dear. There is a great deal you need to be made aware of if we are to live in harmony under this roof.' His smile returned. 'For now, though, you must go with your aunt.'

'But I'm hungry! I've had nothing to eat since this morning.' Phoebe felt her aunt's fingers digging into her arm. She sensed the woman's fear and it made her even bolder. 'And I've already told you . . . it were my fault not hers. Why should *she* be punished as well?'

His smile was wonderful. His grating voice betrayed nothing of his anger. 'My, my! It seems you have learned nothing yet.' He straightened his tall formidable figure and stared at her for a moment, his grey eyes narrowed to dark seething strips. She was not afraid. He sensed that in her and knew his task would be hard. In that slip of a girl, bold, unusually beautiful and equally as determined as himself, he was reminded of his own sister; the same wanton spirit, the same wild rebelliousness that needed to be tamed now just as it was all those years ago.

But, even more disturbing, he saw a defiance in this girl that had never existed in her mother. Raw, unashamed defiance. His insides burned with rage and his hands itched to grab the poker from the hearth and lay it across her back. But he was a gentleman. He must never forget that. It would not do to let this wayward girl strip him of his dignity.

Instead he smiled all the more, asking with injured innocence, ' "Punish" your aunt? Whatever do you mean, my dear? Oh but you're very much mistaken,' he told her, leaning nonchalantly against the back of the chair as though discussing the weather. 'Nobody's being "punished". The very idea! No, no. It's just a matter of convenience, you see. By the time you and my good wife return to the table, my daughter and I will already have eaten and Daisy will have cleared the remainder of the food back into the pantry. She will have washed the tea things and, I dare say, have gone home to her own family by the time you're made presentable. We can't have our routine upset just because you "forgot" to follow instructions, now can we?'

He turned his attention to the woman by Phoebe's side. 'You understand, don't you, my dear?' he asked meaningfully. She hesitated. He widened his eyes and half-opened his mouth as though to speak. But then she quickly nodded and his smile returned. 'Ah, there you are then.' He waved his hand in a gesture of dismissal. 'Off you go now. I have quite an appetite on me, and the meal has been delayed long enough.'

When Phoebe stood her ground, the smile slid from his face. 'Yes?' he asked sweetly. 'Is there something you want to say?'

Phoebe was given no chance to reply but was swiftly propelled out of the room and into the hallway. Before she fully realised what was happening her aunt had hurriedly closed the door behind them. Leaning against the wall, her face chalk white and her breathing erratic, Noreen maintained her vice-like grip on Phoebe's arm. 'Never do that again!' Her voice was pitched low in a hoarse whisper. 'As long as you live, don't ever challenge him. *Think* what you will, but never speak out. You mustn't goad him like that, child. D'you hear me?'

'But it ain't fair!' Phoebe's opinion of her uncle was confirmed by the fear she now saw in the other woman's eyes. Her first instincts had been right. 'I knew it. He's a bad man, ain't he?' she asked now, her lips tightening with disgust as she glanced at the dining-room door.

Fearful that Phoebe might take it into her head to stride back in and confront him, Noreen realised that it would only add to the girl's troubles if she was to know the truth about her uncle or to learn what had happened between her own mother and him sixteen years ago. For her own sake she must never suspect. Phoebe's life here would not be an easy one because her uncle had set his sights on moulding this girl to his own will. After witnessing what had happened just now in the dining-room, Noreen despaired for the fight still to come. She knew that Phoebe could never win. She knew also that she herself was too worn out and conditioned ever to be of any use to the girl and it was painfully obvious that Margaret would only enjoy Phoebe's humiliation. The plain facts were that Phoebe was a wild and spirited creature who would not easily succumb to her uncle's discipline, and unfortunately she did not have one single ally who might help her through. She was alone here. That was the awful truth.

Quickly regaining her composure and releasing her hold on Phoebe's arm, she vowed never again to let the girl see beneath her calm veneer. 'You must not blame your uncle too much,' she said firmly. 'He was quite right to dismiss us from the table. You for not being presentable, and me for not having made sure that his instructions were carried out.' Squaring her neat shoulders, she took a moment to smooth some imaginary wrinkles from her dress before demanding of Phoebe, 'Tell me, Phoebe, was there a towel, and soap, in the washroom?'

Perplexed by her aunt's swift change of mood, she answered with a question of her own. 'Why did you let him treat you like that?'

'I don't know what you mean, child.' Phoebe's direct question had been like a stab to the heart. For so many years she had managed to rise above the degrading life she was made to suffer. Edward Dickens was her husband. For better or worse she had exchanged marriage vows before God. It was her bounden duty to keep those vows. Besides, she thought wryly, if she were to leave here, where would she go? She had no money and no friends. It had suited her purpose to lead a solitary life. The only way she had been able to survive these many years was by pretending. She fooled herself into believing that in many ways she was stronger than he. She lived in the hope that her humiliation was a private one, and that no one else could possibly imagine what went on behind closed doors. That way her dignity was kept intact and life was at least bearable. Sometimes, when his work kept him away for long hours, her prison was even enjoyable.

Now, though, for the first time, she had been foolish
enough to allow someone a peep inside and she deeply
regretted it. She would not allow it to happen again!

Gathering what was left of her courage she told Phoebe,
'I can understand why your uncle grew impatient with
you, child. Don't you know that it's rude to answer a
question with a question? I asked you about the soap and
towel which should have been put in the washroom. Daisy
was given strict orders to attend to it as soon as she came
in this morning. Are you sure you looked carefully?'

Phoebe took a moment to search her aunt's face. She
was intrigued. One minute it seemed as though the poor
woman might confide some inner anxiety, then there had
been stark fear, and now her expression was bland . . .
almost as though a mask had been drawn over her face.
Phoebe blamed herself for her aunt's dilemma. She
realised with regret that her pointed question had been
both intrusive and hurtful. Would she never learn to guard
her tongue?

'I'm sorry, Aunt,' she said with a half-smile, 'I had no
right to say such a thing.' Dipping her chin and looking
up with appealing eyes, she asked softly, 'Am I forgiven?'

Noreen hardened herself against those dark eyes and
the sincerity that shone out. The girl must be brought to
heel. Either Edward would do it or she herself must. Far
better that *she* took the task in hand. With this in mind
she told Phoebe in a deliberately harsh voice, 'It's no
good turning your charm on me or anyone else in this
house. It won't do you any good, and the sooner you
realise that the better.'

'I'm sorry.' Phoebe had been here only a short while

but already she was desperately homesick. 'I know I've got a quick tongue, and I know I'm wilful and disobedient. I know too that I've got to change my ways if I'm not always to be in trouble.' In spite of the way her aunt had sharply rebuked her, Phoebe could not help but like her.

'Very well, child.' Shame rippled through Noreen but she would remain on her guard from now on. The girl had a way of touching a body's conscience.

A peal of laughter from the dining-room caused she and Phoebe to look at each other, the older woman knowing that her daughter was delighted at the scene that had just taken place and the young one wondering what kind of girl it was who could stand by and see her mother humiliated like that. Noreen was the first to speak. 'You'd best get washed and ready for your bed.'

'Ready for bed!' Phoebe was astonished. 'But it's early yet. Won't I be allowed to come down again tonight? It seems such a lovely evening.' She had a mind to wander the fields and explore a little while the sun was still shining.

'No. Your uncle will send for you in the morning. Until then you had better stay in your room and think about what I've told you.' She turned Phoebe round and the two of them retraced their steps to the attic. The sound of laughter followed them up the stairs. The woman kept her gaze on the girl. In a way they were both outsiders, she and Phoebe. A rush of compassion prompted her to say, 'If I'm harsh with you, it's only for your own good. Do you understand what I'm saying, child?'

'Yes, I understand,' Phoebe replied. Yet the only thing

she truly understood was the sinking feeling in her own heart.

While Phoebe ran the bath water, her aunt went to the big free-standing cupboard on the lower landing. From here she collected a towel and a bar of green tar soap. When she returned to the washroom she found Phoebe already stepping into the bath. Pausing in the doorway, Noreen watched her for a moment. She thought the girl to be cruelly beautiful; her slender figure had already blossomed into that of a woman – breasts small and firm with large dark nipples, skin with a smooth creamy texture, and legs that were long and graceful. For a moment Noreen was flooded with a strange regret. But then, when Phoebe saw her there, she rushed forward, saying in a crisp voice, 'Here we are then.' She draped the soft white towel over the back of the small wicker chair; its frayed plaited strands stood up like fingers.

Placing the bulky bar of soap on the edge of the bath, she told the girl, 'For the life of me I can't understand why Daisy didn't do as I asked! I must have reminded her at least half a dozen times to make sure the soap and towel were put here first thing.'

'Who's Daisy?' Phoebe assumed her to be the servant of the house, a poor soul with a great deal of responsibility by the sound of it.

'Daisy's the cook, maid, and everything else rolled into one.'

'She doesn't live at Dickens House then? *He* said she would be "gone home to her family" by the time we returned.'

'No. Daisy doesn't live in. She lives in Mill Hill with her husband and widowed mother. She does a very long working day here. Your uncle regularly inspects the house from top to bottom so she has her work cut out for her. Besides which he has a healthy appetite and is very fond of fine food, well presented.' She made a noise in the base of her throat and looked away with embarrassment. 'I'm afraid I'm not one of those clever women who can lay claim to every domestic talent, and I've never been what you might call a good cook. Daisy is splendid at her work . . . a Godsend. And I'm very lucky to have her.'

'Is she nice?' Phoebe sank lazily into the bath, sighing contentedly as the silky water lapped over her.

'Oh, Daisy's pleasant enough, I suppose. She never has much to say but she gets on with her duties and as a rule I never have to tell her anything twice.' Noreen shook her head and lapsed into momentary silence before saying in a hesitant manner that reminded Phoebe of the White Rabbit in *Alice in Wonderland*, 'I'm quite certain I told her about the soap and towel.' She bit her lip at the thought that it might be she who was at fault and not Daisy after all.

'Is she pretty?'

Noreen laughed at the idea. 'I don't think you could call Daisy pretty.'

'What's she like then?' Phoebe reached forward, clutching the soap in long slender fingers. It was hard to the touch. Dipping it into the water, she rubbed it against the skin of her lower arm, flinching when the hard edges scraped deep.

Noreen felt herself being sucked into conversation, drawn to the girl in a way that could prove to be dangerous. 'That's enough chatter!' she chided. 'You'll meet Daisy soon enough, I expect. For now, though, you'd best get washed and into your nightgown. Your uncle will want to see you first thing in the morning, and you need to be bright and alert.' She glanced out of the window, her gaze travelling across the meadows and resting on the far horizon. Without looking at Phoebe she said softly, 'He's very demanding, I'm afraid. There's a great deal he will want to know, and he'll keep you before him until his curiosity is satisfied.'

'I don't particularly want to talk to him. Besides, there ain't nothing I can tell him that he doesn't already know.' The lather spread across the surface of the water, making frothy pyramids that spluttered and burst when Phoebe absent-mindedly poked them with her finger. She wasn't looking forward to being summoned by her uncle and having to stand before him while he put her through an inquisition. 'I don't like him,' she declared simply, bending her head to scoop the water and splash it on her face. The lather was stiff and refreshing, and the piquant aroma of the tar soap pleasant to her senses.

'Whether you like him or not is immaterial, my girl!' her aunt replied curtly. 'Neither does it matter what you want or don't want. You'll do as you're told.' When Phoebe stared up at her in a curious way, she quickly added, 'You'll soon find out the way of things, I dare say.' She waited a moment, watching as Phoebe leaned forward to dip her long auburn hair into the water. The wetter it became, the darker it grew, floating on the suds in thick wavy coils. *It would be such a pity to cut it all off*.

It was six-thirty by the time Phoebe returned to her

room, wrapped in a towel and shivering violently all the way along the landing. The hard cold floorboards struck chilly against her bare feet. It didn't worry her that there was no carpet. She and her mother had grown used to living without luxury. But their little house seemed always to have been warm and welcoming while this place struck a chill to the bones. The sun might be shining outside but here in the higher reaches of this great old house it was bitterly damp.

Earlier, Phoebe had neatly folded her nightgown and placed it in the bedside cupboard; she took it out now and slipped it over her shoulders, threading her arms through the sleeves and trembling deliciously when the soft material settled against her skin. Afterwards she stood before the window, vigorously rubbing her damp hair and taking it between the towel one hank at a time. Soon the lustre returned, its brilliance quickening to life in a shard of sunlight that streamed in through the window. She felt good, fresh and alive, with her spirits revived.

'I don't suppose you possess a robe?' Her aunt glanced at the long winceyette nightgown, thinking how unsuited it was to someone of Phoebe's loveliness. But then, she thought, it might be as well that the girl had never known anything better. Phoebe had not been raised in the manner of a lady; not like Margaret who, in spite of her privileged upbringing, was a great disappointment to her mother. It gave truth to the old adage: 'You can't make a silk purse out of a sow's ear.'

'Are these all you have?' she asked now, glancing up at the meagre collection of garments hanging on the picture rail.

'Never needed more.'

'And you haven't got a robe?'

'Never had use for such a thing.' Like her mother, Phoebe had always dressed as soon as she was up and washed. 'My mam always used to say that robes were for lazy folk, and them as were tied to their sick-bed.'

Ignoring Phoebe's comment, her aunt suggested, 'No matter. I'll fetch you one. It wouldn't do for you to be seen from the window in your nightgown.'

'But I won't *be* in my nightgown! I'm getting dressed. Happen I'll go for a long walk . . . wander the fields before it gets dark.'

'No, Phoebe. I'm sure your uncle would rather you stayed in your room until he's had his little talk with you.' Satisfied that the matter was now closed, she told the girl, 'I'm taking your brown shift with me. It needs laundering.' Or throwing away, she thought. 'But I'll find you something else. I suppose my own clothes would not look too odd on you . . . but you're a young girl and my clothes are more suited to a middle-aged woman. Don't worry, I'm sure some of my daughter's will fit you. Lord knows, she has enough dresses to start a shop and she'll never wear half of them, I'm certain.' She glanced at the cream dress hanging in pride of place on the wall. 'Is that the only other one you have?'

'Yes. It's my best frock . . . my mother made it for me. Don't you think it's just lovely?' Phoebe's face shone with pride.

'It isn't very practical, is it?' Noreen collected the brown shift from the bed where Phoebe had placed it on returning from the bathroom, and going across to the door, glanced again at the cream dress. 'Of course you mustn't wear that when your uncle sends for you in the morning. He would not approve of your wearing such a fancy thing,' she said. 'But don't worry. I'm sure I can find something more suitable. As I said, your cousin will no doubt have a rummage through her wardrobe. She'll have something there, I'm sure, and how can your uncle object then?' Her only worry was that Margaret would refuse to help. She could be the most selfish creature on God's earth when she put her mind to it.

'No!' Phoebe was horrified. 'I'm not ashamed of my clothes. My mother worked hard on that dress. Even when she was ill, she wanted to see it finished. You can launder my old one if you like, and if you think I should wear a robe then I'll wear one, because I'm in a strange house amongst strange folk. But if I'm to be taken before *him* in the morning, then I'll go in that dress . . . or I won't go at all!' Suddenly it was important that the matter be thrashed out right away. 'I'd like to see him right now,' she said, her dark eyes flashing. 'I have a few questions of my own to put to him!'

The woman stared at Phoebe, her mouth open and her head shaking slowly from side to side in disbelief. In that moment she was both afraid and proud. Proud that the girl would not so easily sacrifice herself, and afraid because she was sure of what the outcome must be. She looked into Phoebe's fiery dark eyes and saw how her long slender fingers were clenched in defiance. She wished that it could have been different.

'That's impossible,' she replied calmly. 'Your uncle always retires to his study after the evening meal. Of course, Saturday is somewhat different in that we don't have a heavy meal. He dines in town with business colleagues on a Saturday lunchtime and so we have a light tea. All the same, his routine of retiring to his study doesn't vary. And he won't be disturbed under any circumstances.' She made a small tutting noise. 'Besides, it seems to me that you need a while to cool your temper, my girl. If you were to see him now, you'd likely say something you might come to regret.'

'I won't feel any different in the morning.'

'Oh, I hope you do because it would be a great shame if you got off on the wrong foot with him.' She lowered her voice and looked beseechingly at Phoebe. 'Don't pit yourself against him, child. You'll only come off worse.'

Phoebe took a huge sigh that seemed to thrust her head upwards and for a while as she gazed at the high rafters it seemed as though she had not heard her aunt's well-meaning warning. Presently she answered, 'I'm sorry. I don't want to make things difficult for you. Really.' She looked into the woman's face but it was devoid of emotion, like a rag doll which Phoebe had been given as a child. 'I suppose I have to learn not to let my temper run away with me?'

'If only you could.'

'I will try, I promise.' She gazed longingly out of the window. 'But it *will* be all right if I go out, won't it? I need to get some fresh air.'

'I'd rather you didn't.'

'Did he forbid it?'

'No, but . . . I know the way he thinks.'

'I won't wander away or anything if that's what he's worried about. I can't run back home to Bury because there ain't no "home" for me to run to, is there? You know as well as I do there's nowhere else for me to go but here.' She smiled, asking in a more subdued voice, 'Please, Aunt. I'm sure he can't mean to keep me in this room all evening?'

There was a long agonising pause during which her aunt looked about as though for a means of escape, then she answered reluctantly, 'You promise you'll stay in the grounds of the house?'

'I promise.'

'And you'll wear one of your cousin's sensible dresses when you see your uncle in the morning?'

'I promise I'll think about it.'

Another pause before: 'An hour then. No longer, mind. Your uncle will be out of his study by then, and it isn't wise to antagonise him further.' Even as the words passed her lips she regretted them. 'If he sees you out of your room . . . well, on your own head be it.' She knew Edward Dickens as well as she knew the lines on her hands. Over the years she had learned to tread warily. Now Phoebe had arrived and the storm clouds were gathering. She shook her head forlornly. If the girl was intent on meeting her uncle head on, then she for one would not be responsible for the consequences. She had her own cross to carry. 'I'll fetch a robe,' she said. In a moment she had gone from the room, leaving Phoebe to dress quickly before her aunt changed her mind after all.

A few moments later Phoebe was running down the wide staircase. She looked exquisite in the cream dress, her wild auburn hair dancing to her shoulders, with tiny delicate curls framing her heart-shaped face and a brightness about her that dimmed everything in sight. Below her she heard the grandfather clock chiming seven. And from above she heard another voice call out, 'Wait a minute.'

She paused to glance up at her aunt who had been leaning over the balustrade but was now hurrying down the stairs, clutching a candlewick plum-coloured robe, a look of great anxiety on her face. Having reached the step above Phoebe, she dug into the pocket of her skirt from which she produced a length of black shoelace. 'Tie your hair back,' she said, thrusting the string into Phoebe's hand. Her pale blue eyes roved the girl's luxuriant locks. 'Do as I say,' she urged when Phoebe made no attempt to carry out the odd request. Glancing about to satisfy herself that they were not being overheard, she warned in a quieter voice, 'Don't ever let your uncle see you with your hair flying loose like that.'

'But I *never* tie my hair back.'

'Please, do as I ask, child.' Edward's sinister warning had not escaped his wife. 'Her hair is a little long, don't you think?' he had said. She knew him well enough to suspect his grim intentions. 'Trust me. It's for the best,' she assured Phoebe.

Suddenly it all became clear. Phoebe remembered how her uncle had made particular mention of her hair. 'You think he's going to cut off my hair, don't you?' For the first time she felt a pang of real fear.

'I'm afraid I don't have anything so pretty as a ribbon,' was her aunt's evasive reply. 'In any case, the shoelace will serve you better. It won't draw so much attention.' She began her way back up the stairs. 'I'll put the robe

in your room. Remember . . . an hour.' When she saw
that Phoebe was watching her with a puzzled look, she
reminded her, 'Tie your hair back securely. DO IT
NOW.' At the top of the stairs she looked back to see
whether the girl had heeded her warning. When she saw
that Phoebe was still debating what to do, she pursed her
lips and shook her head slowly in that familiar way. 'It's
up to you,' she murmured to herself. 'Don't say you
weren't warned.'

At the foot of the stairs Phoebe paused a while, her
troubled brown eyes staring from one door to the other.
One must lead to her uncle's study, she thought. In her
mind's eye she pictured him slumped in a leather chair or
straddled over a settee while he slept off the effects of
his meal. The picture brought her no comfort; neither
did it incur any particular feelings of belonging. Edward
Dickens was her mother's brother but he meant nothing
at all to Phoebe.

Her curiosity was aroused when she saw that the dining-
room door was slightly open. Going cautiously across the
hallway, she peeked in through the chink between the
hinges, hesitantly pushing the door open when she could
see no one beyond. The room was empty now, the table
cleared of its bounty and laid with a cream linen cloth
depicting tiny cornflowers at each corner. In the centre
stood a huge fern in a bulbous willow-pattern pot. There
was a lingering odour much like the warm acrid smell that
emanated from Jessup's old pipe. Wrinkling her nose
Phoebe looked round the room, thinking how friendless
it seemed with its great towering furniture of darkest
wood and the incoming daylight muted by the heavy tap-

estry curtains at the window. She shivered, hugging her arms about herself as she backed out of the room.

Through the fanlight over the front door, she could see that the sun was still as bright as when she'd alighted from the old man's wagon. Her heart was first cheered by the memory of Jessup and then dashed when she realised he wasn't ever coming back to collect her. Suddenly the house crowded in on her from all sides. She had to get out! Outside in the fresh air and sunshine, where the world seemed less like a prison. Remembering the reluctant promise she had made her aunt and not wanting to waste one more minute she hurried along the hallway, but just when she was about to turn the huge crystal knob that would open the front door and let the sunshine spill in, she was startled by a deep rumbling sound that caused her to slew round. It had come from somewhere behind her.

Instinct drew her glance to the panelled door opposite the dining-room. In that same moment, a busy little figure emerged from the farthest room; through the wide open door Phoebe could see a broad pine dresser and a lovely old fire-range overhung with all manner of copper pots and pans. Clad in a wraparound pinafore, the woman was aged about thirty years, misshapen and lumpy, with a white mob cap and a profusion of brown flyaway hair protruding from beneath. Her broad high-cheeked face was not unattractive but not by any stretch of the imagination could it be called pretty.

Unaware of Phoebe's presence, the woman raised her fist and shook it at the nearby study door, saying in a low gruff voice, 'If my old fella snored like that, I'd pack me bloody bags and no mistake!' Swinging round, she caught sight of Phoebe and her mouth fell open with astonishment. It clamped shut with embarrassment before she remarked in the same gruff voice, 'Oh, begging your pardon, Miss.' Her face drooped with trepidation. 'Is there something you want?' she asked, nervously wiping her hands on her pinny and coming forward with purposeful strides.

'No, thank you,' Phoebe replied with a smile. So this was Daisy. She was everything Phoebe had imagined. 'I'm just on my way out.'

The woman's pea-like eyes widened. 'You must be the niece,' she remarked, scrutinising Phoebe from head to toe. 'Well, if there's nothing you want, I'll get off home.' With that, she swung round and went sharply back into the kitchen to collect her coat and disappear out of the back door before anyone could find an excuse to keep her there.

Thinking it might be wise to follow her aunt's advice after all, Phoebe tied her hair back with the shoelace. It would be foolish to antagonise her uncle.

She stood a moment on the step, raising her head to the sky and letting the sun play on her face, its warmth seeming to reach right inside her. It was wonderful! Skipping on to the path, she scanned the landscape . . . to the right were green fields as far as the eye could see, and to the left the lane coming off Preston New Road, down which she and Jessup had travelled only a short time ago. It seemed like a lifetime to her now.

She went slowly along the path, pausing to gaze on the myriad vivid blooms that bordered the walls and nestled beneath the bay windows. She wondered in passing who kept the gardens so lovely. At the gate she waited a moment, leaning across it and gazing straight ahead towards the farm where she had seen the two young men. The memory brought a smile to her face. Had they been two casual farmworkers or did they belong on the farm? she mused. Were they brothers or had they been strangers brought together by their need for work? She could still see them vividly in her mind's eye . . . each one handsome in his own way. She recalled how they had looked at her, particularly the taller of the two, a dark-haired, bold fellow who made her feel strangely uneasy. And yet it was the other young man who filled her thoughts, the one who had shown little interest in her, the one whose strong broad back was bent to his work, the one who had glanced at her as an afterthought, his handsome brooding eyes glinting in the sunlight, magnificent eyes, blue-black like the colours of a raven's wing.

There was no one in the yard now. No sign of any living soul; only the red and yellow chickens who frantically dipped their feathered heads to and fro as they freely strutted about, stopping occasionally to peck at the earth or scrape with their feet. Phoebe watched them for a while, fascinated by their comical antics. It was a new and absorbing experience for her. Back home in Bury the only chickens they ever saw were the ones hanging in the butcher's shop. She much preferred to see them in their own backyard, so to speak. There was something unpleasant about dead creatures being strung up for display. But then, that was how it had always been and who was she to question the way of things?

It was only a few steps out of the garden and across the lane but to Phoebe it was like being set free. She lost no time in covering the ground between the open fields and the house. Unaware that she was being watched, she climbed the stile and followed the well-trodden path that led across the field. As she came nearer to the spinney, Phoebe could see the lake beyond. It lay before her like a sheet of midnight, the sunlight playing on its surface giving the appearance of a million scintillating stars. She quickened her step, crying out when a young deer burst out of the spinney to leap across her path.

Margaret's envious eyes followed Phoebe until she was gone from sight. When suddenly her mother's voice spoke quietly in her ear, she was visibly startled. 'You won't be vile to her, will you?' Noreen asked, absent-mindedly collecting her daughter's discarded clothes and hanging them in the wardrobe.

Margaret laughed aloud. 'What makes you think I'll be "vile" to her?'

It was a moment before her mother replied, and when she did it was to plead: 'Look through your wardrobe and see if there's anything there that might be of use to the girl.'

'I don't need to look. There's nothing in *my* wardrobe to suit her!'

'But you will look, won't you, dear?'

'I don't think so.'

Noreen stared at her daughter, shaking her head and tutting. 'I don't understand you,' she said regretfully, glancing at the wardrobe whose doors were flung open to reveal a bulging collection of garments. 'There must be *something* there that you no longer need?'

'There isn't!' Margaret strode across the room and slammed shut the door. 'And even if there was, I'd burn it before I'd see Phoebe Mulligan in it.'

'I do believe you would.'

'You *know* I would.' She stood with legs astride, hands on hips and her face twisted in a darkly charming smile that put Noreen in mind of Edward. Sadly, their daughter had been taught by a master. 'Is there anything else you want?'

'No. There's nothing else.'

'Good. Then if you'll kindly leave, I can get ready to go out.' She sauntered to the door and opened it, her blue eyes glittering triumphantly. 'And remember, Mother . . . the brat is *your* problem, not mine!'

As Noreen hurried out of the room, she made the aside: 'You really are a hard madam, aren't you?' There was no answer. Only the sound of the door being firmly closed behind her.

'And you, Mother, are as soft as dirt!' Margaret uttered with contempt. Her mother did not hear. She was not meant to.

Phoebe had skirted the spinney and was now standing on the edge of the lake. It was a glorious evening, one that she was destined to remember for years to come. She had never seen anything so beautiful, and it seemed to her as though she had accidentally wandered into Paradise itself. The lake stretched before her, shimmering in the sunlight and playing host to all manner of creatures . . . on the far shore, cows stooped to their knees in search of a drink, there were long-necked birds and brightly coloured ducks paddling close by, and from some way off a slinky water-rat regarded her with bright curious eyes before slithering into the water and gliding away in a wash of ripples. The smell of blossom pervaded the air, mingling with the elements of earth and trees and water, a unique scent that heightened awareness and touched the soil. Exhilarated, Phoebe wandered at will. She had never seen anything so beautiful. Above her the birds were in full song, beneath her feet the grass felt like the softest carpet, and for one very special, magical moment, she imagined her mother to be walking beside her. The feeling was so strong, so real, she thought her heart would break.

Climbing the rise beside the spinney, she sat cross-legged on the mossy bank, her emotions in turmoil. In that lovely place, so far removed from anything she had ever known, she felt lost and so alone. She lay back, looking up at the heavens and wondering how her life would turn out. Closing her eyes against the sun's strong rays, she listened to the many sounds around her: the birdsong, the gentle splashing of the water below, mooing cattle in the distance, and the gentle sighing of the breeze in the treetops. Nostalgia lapped over her; bitter-sweet memories overwhelmed her senses. It had been a long, unforgettable day, one in which she had left behind all that was good and familiar and had been thrust into a world that was both strange and hostile. But not here, she thought. Not here in this safe, delightful place.

At first she thought the cry was that of a bird overhead, but then it soared away and the sound came again, shriller this time, a cry for help. Someone was hurt, and it sounded like the voice of a child.

Phoebe scrambled to her feet, frantically looking around. When the cry rang out once more, she realised it had come from the spinney. Running into the thicket she paused, her ears alert to every sound. When the small voice cried out again and again, Phoebe followed it to the source: a clearing in the heart of the wood where she found a girl of about five years, her foot caught tight in a trap.

'It's all right, sweetheart,' Phoebe assured the sobbing child. 'It's all right . . . I'll have you out of there in no time at all.'

She was a pretty little thing, with short fair hair and large green eyes. Her face was creased in agony and stained with tears; half crouched, she had both her arms wrapped round her leg, rocking backwards and forwards in a bid to ease the pain.

'All right, lovey.' Phoebe knelt to see the damage. The teeth of the trap had dug deep but the blood was too congealed for her to see the true extent of the damage. The child was sobbing uncontrollably now. Never having come across anything like this before, Phoebe wasn't sure what to do. She loathed the idea of leaving the child while she ran for help, and yet she couldn't just sit here until someone found them. There was only one thing to do, but it frightened her. Somehow she had to release the child's leg . . . prise the metal teeth away. Frantically, she searched round until she found a short stout branch.

'Hold on to me, sweetheart,' she told the child, smiling reassuringly when all the while her heart was pounding. She daren't explain what she was about to do for fear it might send the child into hysterics. Instead she ordered gently, 'Look away. Close your eyes and hang on to me for all you're worth.' It seemed as though the girl knew what Phoebe intended to do because she did as she was told, her sobs giving way to a bright little song to give herself courage.

'That's right, lovey,' Phoebe told her with an encouraging smile. 'We'll have you free in no time.' Taking a deep breath and without putting weight directly on to it, she sat astride the child's leg. Inching her fingers between the gaps in the teeth of the trap, she tried to prise it open. When the child screamed out she made herself go on while comforting the girl as best she could. Wedging the thin end of the branch under the snare, she prised it away from the skin, forcing it into the ground so that it formed a lever. Carefully, inch by inch, she widened the gap between the teeth and the child's leg until it was just possible for her to grip the serrated ring with both her hands. Then, with the sweat running down her face and the child's cries wringing her heart, she yelled, 'NOW! Can you slide your leg out?'

She could feel the iron ring slipping tighter through her fingers. 'Hurry! Hurry!' She felt a tremendous relief when the child did as she was told. Oh so slowly, not crying now but whimpering. The skin sucked away, leaving torn bloody remnants of flesh hanging from the sturdy slivers of metal which had pierced with frightening ease. The child was crying again, but it was a strange little cry now and she was violently trembling.

Hating the knowledge that she was increasing her pain, Phoebe urged her on. 'Good girl,' she said. 'Just a little more . . . a little further.' The blood was spurting now, splashing over Phoebe's cream dress and dyeing the earth dark crimson.

Just when she thought she could not hold the trap open another second, the child was suddenly free. The teeth snapped shut, splitting the branch asunder. With a cry, Phoebe cradled the girl in her arms. 'I've got to get you home, sweetheart,' she said softly. 'Put your arms round my neck and don't let go.' Clambering to her knees, she took the weight of the child across her breast. 'You're a brave little thing,' she said. 'Braver than I could have been.'

The child looked up, making an effort to smile but grimacing with pain. 'It hurts,' she murmured, her tiny arms tight round Phoebe's neck and her big eyes swimming with tears.

''Course it hurts, sweetheart!' Phoebe said, picking her way through the bracken. 'But you have to try not to think about it. Look . . . I have to get you home, and you have to show me the way, ain't that right?' When the child nodded, she went on, 'There you are then! You'd best give me directions, hadn't you?'

'I just live on the farm.'

'The farm, eh?' Phoebe realised she must mean the farm opposite Dickens House but feigned ignorance. It was important to keep the child talking, keep her interested, occupy her mind so that she didn't have time to think about her leg.

Desperately afraid for her, Phoebe quickened her steps as far as her burden would allow. The farm wasn't too far away, thank God. She felt angry. What kind of parent would let a small child wander these woods on her own at this time of night? And so close to the lake at that! She intended giving them a piece of her mind and no mistake.

In a moment she had emerged from the spinney, her back breaking, her face bathed in sweat. 'It's all right, sweetheart. We'll be home in no time,' she told the child. There was no answer, only a pair of stricken green eyes staring up at her. Like a hurt dog, Phoebe thought with a rush of compassion, 'We'll be home soon enough, lovely,' she said all the same. The thought was comforting to her also. She daren't think what her uncle would say if he were to see her in such a sorry state. But when she thought about what this little girl was suffering, she realised she didn't give a damn what he might say!

Phoebe didn't see the man, but he saw them the minute they broke from the cover of the trees. The sight of Phoebe and the girl, bloodstained and looking as though they'd been tarred and feathered, was a terrible shock. At once he came running across the field, shouting, 'God Almighty! AGGIE!' The girl stirred in Phoebe's arms; the sound of his voice brought a smile to her face, but she didn't have the strength to cry out.

Phoebe recognised the man straight away. Thankfully she stopped, leaning against a broad oak tree, holding the child close and waiting for him to take the burden from her. He had been carrying a shotgun under his arm and there was a plump rabbit hooked to his belt, but he put them both to the ground as he came up the bank in great strides. 'What in God's name happened?' he asked, his horrified gaze fixed on the deep bloody gash in the child's leg. Tenderly, he gathered her into his arms while Phoebe related how she had heard the girl cry out and had found her trapped in the snare.

His face dark with rage, he spun round. 'Are you telling me she was out in the spinney . . . on her own?'

Before Phoebe could answer he strode away, calling out over his shoulder. 'Thank God you found her.' He was travelling so fast now she could hardly keep up. 'And you . . . are you all right?' he asked. When she told him that yes, she was fine, he said curtly, 'I'm Hadley Peters . . . from the farm. You'd best come home with me, Phoebe Mulligan. It wouldn't do for your uncle to see you like this.' Turning away, he went at an urgent pace down the bank and along by the lake, all the while softly comforting the child and assuming that Phoebe was following. But she was not.

Cutting away to the left, she quickly climbed the stile and ran down the road to her uncle's house where she sped up the front path, fervently praying that no one had seen her. Safely in her room, she turned the key in the door. 'Thank the good Lord!' she gasped. 'They ain't seen me.'

Something was different, in the room. She glanced about. Hanging from the picture rail were two dresses, one black with a neat lace collar, the other a drab grey colour but quite pretty, with scalloped short sleeves and a belted waist. Waiting a moment to catch her breath, Phoebe went across the room, ignoring the black frock. Taking down the other, she held it against her, spinning round in front of the mirror and dancing with an imaginary partner. 'It don't look half bad,' she murmured, a smile lighting her dark brown eyes. She imagined the dress to have come from her cousin when in fact it was one which her aunt had rummaged from her own wardrobe.

Returning the dress to its place, Phoebe took the robe which her aunt had left then went on tiptoe across the landing towards the washroom. 'I'd best get myself washed and tucked up in bed before somebody comes snooping,' she told herself. 'But, oh, I'm that hungry, I can feel my ribs clattering against each other.' Even so, the thought of going to her bed and waking up to a new day suddenly seemed more inviting.

It was some time later when Phoebe heard the front door close. Curious, she went to the window and looked out. It was her cousin, dressed as though she was going to a party and looking very attractive in a pale blue dress and pretty white ankle-strap shoes. She paced up and down the path, one minute glancing at her watch and the next standing at the gate, stamping her foot as she stared at the farmhouse opposite. Finally she swung round and stormed back into the house, slamming the door and cursing aloud as she ran back to her bedroom. There was the sound of a door crashing shut and then a series of noises like things being thrown across the room.

'My! My!' Phoebe pulled the sheet over her head to shut out the noise. 'Ain't somebody got a temper?' she chuckled. And with her stomach rumbling hungrily, she tucked herself up and closed her eyes. 'Best get me sleep,' she muttered. ''Cause tomorrow, I've to face the "bad man".'

Chapter Four

'Sit down, child, and for goodness' sake, relax! I'm not a monster, you know.' Edward Dickens had summoned Phoebe to his study first thing on this Sunday morning. She stood before him now, wide-eyed and afraid, her mind running over the strange events of the night. Things had happened in the small hours, in the dark . . . things that had left her wondering whether she had really seen and heard them or whether they were no more than a terrible nightmare. Certainly now, in the brightness of a morning, everything seemed normal enough. The sky was less sunny than yesterday, being overcast with the threat of a storm, but after the intense heat of these past few days there was nothing ominous about that. No, there was nothing so different. Daisy, too, had seemed exactly the same as she had been yesterday, although she was a bit flustered after having climbed the many stairs to tell Phoebe, 'Your uncle's waiting for you in the study, Miss. You'd better make it quick because he doesn't like to be kept waiting.' And now here he was, beaming from ear to ear and doing his utmost to put her at ease.

'Now then, my dear.' He waited until she was seated. 'I hope you're going to be happy here.' He studied her hard. 'You really are very pretty,' he said. Suddenly he noticed. 'Ah! I see you've tied your hair back.' He smiled and regarded her a moment longer before his smile fell away. 'No doubt that was your aunt's idea, eh?' Without waiting for her to answer, he waved his hand in the air. 'No matter! No matter!' he grunted. 'All in good time. For the moment there are more important things which you need to be aware of. Firstly, today is Sunday, and as a rule we would be attending service as a family. However . . . I hope we can be forgiven if we each offer our own little prayer today.' He raised his face to the ceiling and sighed, at the same time rubbing the flat of his hand over his forehead. 'I'm afraid I don't feel all that well.' His attention wandered and for a moment Phoebe thought he'd forgotten all about her when he seemed to address himself. 'God help us, but the duties of a man can sometimes be a very great burden,' he murmured, his grey eyes rolling in his head and his chest rising higher with every intake of breath.

'My mother and I seldom went to Church. She said the good Lord would hear our prayers wherever we were.' Phoebe suddenly felt the need to say something although when he sat bolt upright in his chair and stared at her, she wished she had said something less controversial.

For what seemed an age he sat there, stiff and upright, his eyes hard and unblinking. Phoebe squirmed in her seat, not sure whether she should stay or go. 'My mother was a good woman, and a good Christian,' she said in a bold voice.

'A good woman, eh?' It was a question but not a question. He mused a while longer, the smile slowly returning to his strong features. 'Of course!' He nodded his head and, pushing back his chair, rose to his feet, leaning forward over the desk, his long thick fingers stroking the neat beard that shaped his chin to perfection. 'Whether she was or whether she wasn't makes no difference now, does it, my dear? Your mother no longer has the responsibility of making *you* into a "good Christian". That unenviable task has now fallen to me.' He straightened to his considerable height and began walking slowly round the desk to where she sat. 'I can see it won't be easy, my dear. There are too many distractions do you see?' He waited for her to answer, his hands clasped behind his back and his head bent towards her.

'Yes, sir.' Phoebe was curious as to what these 'distractions' were, but she thought it best to say as little as possible. Especially when, every time she looked at him, she could see him the way she had seen him last night. Or *thought* she had seen him. Just remembering made her heart turn over.

'Good! Good! Some rules and regulations then.' He walked a little further round her, touching her hair with his fingers as he went. 'Things you must be aware of, my dear,' he said. 'Rules and regulations, all of which must be obeyed. Do I make myself clear?'

'Yes, sir.'

'Like I said yesterday, this is an orderly house and nothing must be allowed to interfere with routine. Isn't that right, my dear?'

'Yes, sir.'

He laughed, a low breathless sound. 'There you are then. That wasn't too difficult.' His voice fell to a whisper. 'But there will always be those who step out of line from time to time, and of course it will be my sorry lot to deal with them.' He was standing before her now, leaning backwards on the desk and looking down on her. 'Do *you* have any intentions of stepping out of line, my dear?'

'I don't know what you mean.' Her brown eyes stared back at him, bold and unflinching. What did he mean? Why didn't he get to the point so she could go and get some breakfast? Surely he could hear her stomach rumbling?

He chose not to regard her comment. 'My poor misguided wife had the idea that I might extend Daisy's duties to include the tidying of your room. "Nonsense," I told her, "the girl is more than capable of tidying her own room. Unlike our daughter, Phoebe Mulligan has known nothing else but tidying up after herself! The very idea! We mustn't go too far against the teachings of her mother . . . although of course there are certain failings in her upbringing which will take a time to rectify. But we shall succeed. Given time and determination, we shall certainly succeed." That's what I told her, my dear, and of course she came to see the error of her ways. These things have to be dealt with most carefully, don't you agree?'

'I don't know, I'm sure.'

'Oh, well then . . . you must take my word for it. Since I received your mother's letter, I've given the matter a great deal of thought and you must trust me in all things. That won't be so hard, you know. I'm not an unreasonable man. I provide for my family and execute my own duties to the best of my ability. As head of this household, I shoulder the ultimate responsibility . . . well, it goes without saying, it isn't easy. It's never easy. I know what it's like to work hard, my dear, but you won't hear me complaining about my work. Oh, dear me, no. I wouldn't be where I am today if it weren't for the fact that I've worked hard . . . harder than most, I'd say. Do you fear hard work, my dear?'

'No, sir.'

'Of course you don't. And I've lost no time in searching round to find you something suitable to do. As soon as I was made aware of your deprived situation, I knew my first duty was to find you a worthy position. You do appreciate that I can't possibly allow you to live here without contributing to the upkeep of this household?' His voice held an injured tone.

'I understand, and I want to earn my keep. I wouldn't dream of living on charity. And I'm not afraid of hard work.'

'That's very commendable, my dear. There's nothing wrong with hard work . . . on the contrary, it builds character, I find.' He began walking round the room again. 'Take me, for example,' he went on proudly. 'My father . . . your grandfather . . . left me a small store in Blackburn town centre. A thriving little store, I must confess. But it had great unfulfilled potential, don't you see? Sadly, your grandfather was a man of small ambition, content to earn just enough to keep his family provided for. When I was old enough, he set me on . . . paying me a pittance while I toiled up to sixteen hours a day . . . delivering and collecting stock . . . keeping the yard swept and clear . . . serving, cleaning, fetching and carrying. There was no end to it! But I stuck it out. Oh, yes,

I stuck it out, because I knew that one day the store would be mine. *Mine*, you understand.' Phoebe was startled when he suddenly slapped his hand on her shoulder. 'I knew, do you see? I knew that one day I would be given free rein, and oh how I longed for that day to come! When your grandfather passed on, I set about making the name of Dickens known from one end of Lancashire to the other. Can you understand that, my dear? Can you understand how a man would be impatient to see his name glorified in such a way?'

He hurried to his seat behind the desk where he sat down again. 'Can you possibly understand how excited I was . . . after being held back for so very long?' His eyes resembled hard bright buttons as he stared at her, eagerly waiting for her answer.

'I think so.' She thought it best to agree and for the first time wondered if he was mad. Perhaps it hadn't been a nightmare after all!

'Oh, my dear, there was so much I wanted to do . . . so many directions I wanted to go.' He was growing more excited, drumming his fingers on the desk and rocking himself backwards and forwards. 'There were too many general stores . . . too much competition. But I saw a need. I watched and waited. Then, when the opportunity presented itself, I seized it with both hands. Within two years I had closed the general store and reopened it as a gentlemen's outfitters. It was an instant success . . . just as I knew it would be! I've never looked back my dear. Now I have shops in every key town throughout the North-West . . . each catering to the needs of gentlemen. Not just suits and coats but every accessory imaginable . . . top hats, gloves, scarves, canes and cravats. Everything and anything a gentleman could want, he can get it all in one place . . . Dickens' Outfitters. Of course, my prices preclude those of a lower class, you understand. But then, Dickens' Outfitters does have a certain reputation to maintain. Part of my success has been knowing what type of staff to take on. Do you understand?'

'Yes, sir.'

'Your cousin Margaret will be trainee manageress in my newest store which is shortly to open in Ainsworth Street. She's well turned out, very pretty, and has a good head on her shoulders.' He smiled with satisfaction, 'Besides which she's very ambitious, much like her father.' He chuckled. 'Matter of fact, it wouldn't surprise me to see her running her own business before long. My goodness! That would raise a few eyebrows, I'll be bound. Indeed, I've already told her that if she does well for me, I shall consider setting her up in her own fashion store – a project which is close to her heart. As you can imagine, I have great hopes for her.'

'Am I to be given a position in one of your shops then?' Phoebe's heart sank at the prospect.

'Oh, dear me, no!' He was visibly shocked. 'Oh no, my dear. I have something much more . . . suitable . . . in mind.' His mood had been buoyant. Now it was subdued. His smile though was charming as he leaned back in his chair, saying, 'You mustn't worry though. I have your well-being very much in mind.'

'When can I start work then?' The sooner the better, she thought.

'One week from Monday if all goes well,' he told her. 'But we won't talk about that now, my dear. Arrangements are not yet finalised.' He glanced at his pocket-watch. 'The purpose of this little meeting is to put your mind at rest. Of course you also need to be aware of one or two little foibles of mine, my dear. Namely, I do not take kindly to disobedience, nor do I want you bringing strangers into my house. I'm not partial to visitors at the best of times.' He regarded her dress, suddenly realising that he had seen it before. He had a memory for such detail. 'Ah! So your good aunt has seen fit to do something useful after all,' he remarked, adding, 'I have it in mind to send Margaret into town next week with a view to acquiring some sensible clothes for you.'

'Can I go with her?'

'I think not, my dear. Money is not easy to come by and I wouldn't want you to think you could squander it. But she has good taste so you needn't concern yourself.' He glanced at his pocket-watch again. 'You must be hungry. Breakfast is always served at precisely seven a.m. Twenty minutes from now. Go away and think about what I've told you. Oh, one other thing, my dear . . .' He lowered his gaze, pursing his lips and pondering awhile, then in a strange grating voice he told her, 'I strictly forbid you to wander about the house at night.' He raised his head. 'Do I make myself clear?' There was no smile on his face now. Only an odd, disturbing expression she had not seen before.

'Yes, sir.'

'Good!' He sprang out of his chair, his face all happiness and his voice filled with laughter. 'You're a bright

little thing. Off you go then. Have a word with Daisy and
see if you can make yourself useful.' He smiled at her as
she turned away, and was still smiling when she glanced
back from the doorway. 'Off you go! Off you go!' he told
her cheerfully. But there was something in his
manner . . . something that worried her.

'Your aunt doesn't want any breakfast. According to the
master she had a real bad night. As for Miss Margaret,
well, I expect she's taking advantage of the fact that her
father won't be attending table . . . sneaking a lie-in, I
reckon, and who can blame her, eh? Not me, that's for
sure. I only wish *I* was so privileged.' Daisy didn't look
up when Phoebe asked whether her aunt and cousin had
already been down to breakfast. Instead she kept her full
attention on clearing the table. 'And what with the master
locked away in his study, it looks like you're the only one
to have an appetite this morning.' She made a snorting
noise. 'Though, for all *you've* eaten, Miss, I might just as
well not have bothered cooking at all!' she said gruffly.

'Is my aunt poorly?' It had been a strange experience
for Phoebe, sitting at that long table all on her own, with
only Daisy rushing in and out, fetching that, taking away
this. 'Have you seen her this morning?' she persisted.
Daisy shook her head. 'Well . . . d'you know what time
Miss Margaret will come down?' Clattering the plates on
to the trolley, Daisy shook her head again. Flustered,
Phoebe began helping to gather up the condiments and
crockery. 'I don't suppose anybody would mind if I went
out after I tidied my room, would they, Daisy?' she asked.

If she had been at home in Bury, there'd be no question

111

of not knowing what to do. She would be waiting on her mam, and afterwards she'd boil the hot water and wash her all over and then they would have a long cosy chat when her mam would tell her all the things she might have done if only the good Lord had spared her a while longer. But all that was gone now, Phoebe reminded herself. Her mam had sent her here, and here she would stay until she proved herself to be a credit to the darling woman whose memory she could never forget. 'My uncle can't object to me going out for a walk, can he, Daisy?' she insisted. 'But first I'll go and see if my aunt wants anything.'

''Taint no use asking *me* what you should or shouldn't do,' Daisy retorted, moving the trolley closer to herself. 'And I'd be obliged if you'd leave the clearing to me,' she added haughtily. 'I don't want the master to think I can't do the work I'm paid for.'

'Oh! I'm sorry, Daisy,' Phoebe apologised, dropping the cutlery on to the trolley. 'I only meant to help.'

'Well, that's very kind of you, I'm sure. But times is bad everywhere, and jobs is hard to come by. My fella's just been put on short time and I've a widowed mother to take care of. So, you see, a body has to be careful.'

'I understand.' Phoebe could see the poor woman's point, in a roundabout sort of way. 'It's all right if I tidy my room though, isn't it? My uncle says I'm to see to that myself.' She was glad, too. At least she wouldn't feel quite so useless. Still, perhaps it wouldn't be too long before she started work. 'Monday week' he'd said. A week would soon pass and Monday week couldn't come too quick for her. All the same, she would have preferred to start tomorrow.

'If your uncle says you're to tidy your own room, then that's what you'll have to do,' remarked Daisy in a sulk. 'But it just goes to show what I mean. If all the gentry start doing their own cleaning and tidying, what's gonna become of the likes of me, eh? We'll be on the scrapheap, that's what! Or rotting in the workhouse.' She was shaking the teapot so vigorously that the tea squirted out of the spout and on to the starched white tablecloth. 'There! Now see what you've gone and made me do,' she moaned, frantically dabbing at the offending stain with the edge of her pinafore. 'If *he* sees it, I'll be out that door with my hat and coat on before I can get me breath. Oh dear me! Dear me!' She looked as though she was about to burst into tears.

'Is there anything I can do?' If it had been her mam or Dora who had spilled the tea, Phoebe would have rushed to help. As it was, she didn't know *what* to do.

'No! No! Get yourself off, Miss. Do as your uncle's told you. I can manage.'

Phoebe quickly departed from the room, but then she remembered something. She could hear Daisy still mumbling and moaning. Peeping round the door, she asked, 'Which is my aunt's room?'

Daisy was startled. She was frantic in case the master caught her in such a mess. When she saw that it was only Phoebe, she visibly relaxed. 'Up the stairs, Miss . . . the door on your left. It's directly over the master's study.' When Phoebe thanked her and made to go, she called her back, ashamed that she'd been so hard on the girl. After all, the poor thing had just lost her mam and everything. 'You look right pretty in that dress, Miss,' she said by way of compensation. 'It belonged to your aunt, didn't it? But she ain't worn it in a very long time.' She smiled broadly, nodding her head in approval. 'I don't reckon it ever looked so pretty on her, though. But you're not to say so or you'll get old Daisy in trouble.'

'Thank you, Daisy.' Phoebe was surprised to know that the dress was one of her aunt's. She had believed that it was given to her by her cousin. But it made little difference. Like Daisy said, the dress was ever so pretty. She assured the anxious woman now, 'And don't worry, I'm not given to telling tales.' Then she went up the stairs to find her aunt's room. She could tidy her own afterwards.

'That'll make a pleasant change, Phoebe Mulligan,' Daisy muttered, her eyes still on the door. 'Most folks is given naturally to "telling tales". Happen you're one of them special few as knows when to keep things to themselves. And that's more than I can say for your snooty cousin!' she added in a quieter voice.

By! There were things she'd seen and heard in this house that'd make a body's hair stand on end. Things that didn't bear *thinking* about, let alone telling. It was more than her job was worth, happen more than her *life* was worth, to carry tales away from here, though. They were a rum lot in Dickens House and no mistake. That girl Phoebe, though . . . she was different. A good sort, and if Daisy's snippets of information were right, the girl came from a background much the same as her own. She liked her and that was a fact. All the same, she wouldn't be so daft as to confide too much in her. Not when the poor little soul was already being cunningly squeezed under the master's thumb.

She shivered. 'What's going to become of you, Phoebe

Mulligan?' she muttered. 'Happen it would have been a godsend if you'd been taken with your poor mam, Lord rest her soul.' She made a hurried sign of the cross on herself and returned to her work with more enthusiasm.

'Who's that?'

'It's me . . . Phoebe.' She leaned close to the door. 'I've come to see how you are. And I wondered whether you might want anything?'

'You shouldn't have come, child.' Her aunt's voice sounded odd. 'I'm well. It's just a slight tummy upset, I expect. Now go away before someone sees you hovering at the door.'

'Are you sure you wouldn't like a cup of tea? Or mebbe you'd like me to read to you, eh? My mam always loved me to read to her. I even won a prize at school for reading.' Phoebe wanted so much to go in and talk to her aunt. She saw the day stretching long and empty before her and felt very lonely.

'There's *nothing* I want, child. Go away from the door. If your uncle sees you there . . . God forbid . . .' The voice faded away, then came back sharply. 'Do as I say. Leave me alone and let me rest.'

Noreen was seated by the window. She was in far too much pain to lie in bed. In that moment she would dearly have loved to let the girl in but she dared not. There was nothing to be gained from involving her niece in what was a very private matter. The soft receding footsteps outside the door told her that Phoebe was going. Sighing with relief she struggled out of the chair, walking stiffly to the door where she quickly sprang the lock. It wouldn't do for anyone to come in here. Especially not him! But then, he wouldn't bother her. Not now. Not for a while at least.

For the next hour Phoebe busied herself in her room. She shook the mat out of the window, swept the floor, made the bed, and even cleaned the windows. She had done most of it the day before, and the room wasn't dirty, but it was something to do, something to keep her occupied. Afterwards she took her cream dress into the washroom and tried to get the stains off it but they wouldn't budge. Suddenly she remembered the way her mother used to get stains out with salt. It didn't always work but it was worth a try. Leaving the dress soaking in cold water, she went back to her room and collected her long grey cardigan. Glancing in the mirror, she thought Daisy was right. The dress which her aunt had given her really did look pretty. The colour was a softer grey than her cardigan and the cowl neckline suited her. The skirt was full and dipped low to her calves in a swirling hem. Flicking a brush through her unruly hair, she suddenly recalled her aunt's warning never to let her uncle see her hair flying loose. She looked at it now, thick wayward curls springing down to her shoulders and beyond, wild and wilful as she was herself. Taking the black shoelace, she gathered the russet-coloured hair into a bunch and tied it loosely at the nape of her neck. That done she went downstairs. There was no sign of anyone. The house was deathly quiet. Even Daisy had gone.

Gingerly poking her head through the kitchen door, she made sure there was no one waiting there to surprise her. The room was empty but still she went about on tiptoes, knowing that her uncle was not too far away.

The kitchen fascinated her. It was huge, almost as big as the entire ground floor of the house in Bury. Extending across the whole width of Dickens House, the back wall contained three large windows overlooking the rear garden. The window ledges were cluttered with pot-plants . . . tall prickly cacti and spreading vines, short thick plants with many blooms, and even a Busy Lizzie creeping along the sill. Two of the walls were hung with all manner of artefacts: a bronze bed-pan, metal colanders and round ladles, copper cauldrons and pans of all sizes. Strung high across the ceiling were wooden racks piled high with all the things a cook might delight in, and amongst them a clothes airer hung with neatly folded linen. There was a huge pine dresser, and a long well-scrubbed table with eight chairs set round it, and a walk-in pantry that was almost as big as Phoebe's room.

'Well, I'm blowed!' she gasped, staggered at the sight of every wall covered in long broad shelves, and every shelf crammed with big earthenware jugs labelled 'Home-made Sarsaparilla' and 'Ginger Ale'. There were pots of preserves, dishes of cheese, hands of meat, and altogether enough food to make a feast for an army! The whole kitchen swam in a delicious aroma of newly baked crusty bread and warm aromatic spices. It put Phoebe in mind of the smell that often permeated her own mam's kitchen.

She might have been tempted to linger a while, and even to sample a few titbits, but a sudden sound from the adjacent room, which she knew to be her uncle's study, changed her mind. Collecting a packet of salt from the pantry, she made her way back up to the washroom where she sprinkled a generous measure into the bath, at the same time swishing the dress round and round to distribute the salt evenly. That done, she went back downstairs and returned the salt to its proper place before going out of the back door. There was some exploring to be done. Today her uncle had not made demands on her time, her aunt was confined to her bed, and her cousin had not yet made an appearance . . . even though it was already fifteen minutes past ten. It seemed she had the morning to herself.

The garden was lovely. Surrounded by high walls, it was laid with meandering paths of crazy-paving and round every corner there was a surprise . . . dense shrubberies and little secret alcoves where pretty blossoms peeped out of rock formations, a small pond containing little fat fish and a cluster of bird-houses that resembled a tenement. At the very bottom of the garden, where the arched door led out to the farmland beyond, Phoebe found a delightful little wrought iron bench set right back in the apple orchard. Thinking there could be no better way to while away the time she curled up on the bench, surveying the beauty around her and feeling at peace for the first time since leaving home. The clouds were shifting now and the sun was breaking through, warming her face and lifting her spirits. She felt as though she was the only person in the whole world. It was a good feeling, but not one that she would want to last forever. Not for the first time she wondered who it was who kept the gardens so lovely.

Sitting there in that peaceful secret place, her thoughts inevitably began to turn to home. She missed her friend Dora. Judd too. She missed them so much. After her mam died, Dora and her brother had been her strength, and Phoebe would never forget that. When the time was right, when she had been here long enough to feel secure, she intended to ask her aunt whether Dora could come to tea one day. She wanted her aunt to meet her friend, to see what a fine person she was. She wondered what Dora was doing now, right at this very minute? And Judd. What was *he* doing? As it was Sunday morning, she imagined Dora to be in the kitchen and Judd to be walking that loveable old mongrel that always seemed tied to his ankle, for it went wherever he went. Thinking of them now, sadness began to settle on her. Their familiar faces rose in her mind: Dora's round and blue-eyed with many dimples and a ready smile, and Judd's warm smiling eyes as brown as chestnuts and thick fair hair that was worn long enough to touch his broad shoulders. They were good people. Kind, caring friends. She had intended waiting until she had a whole week's news before writing to Dora but now she knew she couldn't wait another day. Her mind was made up! She'd brought pen and paper with her, and a small number of stamps, all of which she had found in her mam's belongings. So she would write to Dora this very day.

With that decision made Phoebe felt a deal happier. Now her mind turned to other things. She wondered how the little girl was. Had the doctor attended her at home or was she in the Infirmary? She hoped the wound was not as bad as it had looked. The idea of going to the farmhouse popped into her mind and grew until she could think of nothing else. She wanted to pay the little girl a visit but worried in case it might seem as though she was intruding . . . after all, she was a stranger to these parts and it might not be the done thing to go knocking on folks' doors without being invited. All the same . . . she *would* like to satisfy herself that the little girl was all right. What had he called her . . . Aggie? Yes, that was it . . . such a pretty name, Aggie.

It took only a matter of minutes for Phoebe to go back through the house and out of the front door. The house was still as quiet as the grave except for the grandfather clock striking the eleventh hour just as she walked past it and very nearly frightening the life out of her.

Halfway down the path to the farmhouse her nerve almost gave way. Coming to a halt beside the willow tree she half-hid herself behind it, staring at the house and wishing she had never even crossed the road. It was in the style of a cottage, with tall red-tiled gables, leaded light windows and a delightful crooked door with a lantern hanging over it. It was so picturesque, she loved it on sight. Unlike Dickens House, it had an air of love and warmth about it; a welcoming feeling that gave her the courage to go on. Tentatively, she rapped her knuckles against the hard oak door. Almost immediately she heard the sound of hurrying footsteps and wondered whether someone had seen her coming down the path. If they had seen her approaching the farmhouse, then they must also have seen her hiding behind the willow tree. She blushed with shame. What would they think of her?

When the door swung open it was to reveal a man of medium height and pleasant, if worn features. He had a short bushy snow white beard and a brown felt cap sitting on the back of his head at a jaunty angle, with hanks of unruly white hair sticking out above his ears. In spite of the white beard and ruddy complexion, Phoebe guessed he was about the same age as her uncle. There was a certain jolliness about him that made her feel instantly at ease. 'I hope you don't mind me calling,' she said with a smile, 'but I was wondering about the little girl . . . whether she's recovering, I mean?'

'Oh! If it ain't the little angel herself!' he answered in a broad Irish accent, his brown eyes crinkling in a smile that seemed to banish the years from his face. 'You'll be Phoebe Mulligan or me own name ain't Lou Peters. Why, would yer believe I was of a mind to come and see yer this very morning, to thank yer personal like.' He was dancing on the spot with excitement. 'Come in! Come in, why don't you? As a matter o' fact the little darling's been asking after you.' He flung the door wide open and ushered her into a tiny square hallway with wood-panelled walls and thick rush mats underfoot. 'This is the tidy end o' the house,' he explained with a laugh. 'All the mud and stuff comes in through the *back* door . . . straight off the fields and across the backyard, d'you see? Though o' course I allus insist on them two fella-me-lads taking their boots off afore they set foot inside.' Closing the door, he put his hand on her shoulder and propelled her forward. 'She's in the parlour . . . wouldn't stay in her bedroom, the little pixie!' He rolled his eyes. 'But she's mending fine,' he assured Phoebe. 'Oh, aye! Our Aggie's mending just fine.'

He was striding ahead now, down the narrow corridor whose every wall was decorated with framed pictures of hunting scenes and pretty landscapes. 'What did the doctor say?' Phoebe asked with concern. The deeper she went into this lovely cottage, the more at home she felt. 'She was very good, you know. She hardly cried at all.'

He laughed, pushing open a door that led off to the left. 'If yer saying she were brave, I'm not surprised 'cause she's a darling little thing. But she can be a right little madam when she's a mind to an' that's a fact.' As he waited for her to enter the room, he whispered in her ear, 'But I wouldn't swap her for the world. She's me little beauty, that she is! And we all love her to bits?' Well . . . two of us anyway, he thought with regret.

The room was small and bright with a spacious inglenook fireplace and pretty bay windows. At first sight it looked hopelessly cluttered with a small chest of drawers beneath the window, two wall cupboards crammed with pretty china jugs and a tall brass fender with a slipper-box at each side that straddled the fireplace like a pair of arms embracing. There was a deep wooden rocker either side of the fireplace, and a small settee situated directly in front; it was covered in pretty floral-patterned material and squashed into its depths was the little girl, lying to one side with her bandaged leg stretched out before her. On seeing who it was who had sent her father rushing to the front door, she called out excitedly, 'Oh! It's the lady!' Twisting herself round she peeped over the top of the settee. 'Sit here with me,' she urged, her face first smiling then grimacing in pain as she shifted along and patted the place beside her.

'Now then, me beauty, sit still like the doctor told yer!' came Lou's sharp rebuke. 'Or I'll have to carry yer right back to yer room, and there you'll stay 'til you can do as yer told!'

Pulling a wry face, the girl turned to Phoebe. 'Daddy's a fusspot,' she said. Her giggle was infectious.

'There y'are, Phoebe me girl . . . didn't I tell yer she could be a right little madam?' Rounding the settee, Lou wagged a finger at the child. 'You behave yerself now. I'll not have yer calling yer old father a "fusspot",' he warned, but his eyes were twinkling and the corners of his mouth were already turning up.

Phoebe found herself laughing. 'You're on the mend, Aggie,' she said. 'I can see that for myself.'

'Oh, aye. She's on the mend right enough. And there ain't no keeping her quiet neither.' Lou indicated the place beside the child. 'Yer might as well do like she says. Although you'll need to mind she don't nag yer to sleep.' He waited until Phoebe was seated beside the girl, then asked, 'You'll have a bite to eat with us, sure yer will, and a mug o' my strong tea?'

'Plenty of milk and a heap of sugar,' Phoebe replied boldly. Somehow it didn't seem as though they'd only just met. She felt as though she'd known him all her life. When he laughed aloud, saying, 'Wouldn't yer know it? A lady after me own heart,' she found herself laughing with him and the girl, delighting in it all.

'Right! So what'll it be, a cherry cake or a wedge of apple pie?'

Before Phoebe could reply a small voice piped up, 'Apple pie! And can I have some too, please? A great big piece. And Phoebe wants a great big piece an' all.'

'Well now, how can I refuse?' Taking off his cap with a flourish he waved it before him, bowing low and asking politely, 'And would the ladies like the cake on a silver platter?' He looked up in a wide-eyed servile manner, sending them both into fits of laughter. 'Right away, m'lady,' he murmured sheepishly, backing across the room and out of the door.

'Do you think my dad's crackers?' Aggie asked, her eyes big and shining.

'Well no, I don't think any such thing,' Phoebe replied in mock horror. In fact she thought Lou Peters was wonderful.

'Do you wish he was *your* dad?'

Leaning forward and whispering, Phoebe told her, 'I wish he was my uncle instead of Mr Dickens. I bet I'd have a lot more fun.'

'Is he miserable . . . your Uncle Dickens?'

'Sort of.'

'You can share my dad if you like. I won't mind.'

The door opened and in came Lou, pushing a trolley laden with a two-tier dish stuffed with cake and a pretty tea set patterned with crimson roses. 'What's that yer saying, yer heartless hussy?' he demanded. 'Are youse cutting me up like I was a slab o' cake?' His remark was addressed to the child but he glanced at Phoebe with twinkling eyes and winked merrily. 'Be Jaysus! Sure that's a terrible way to treat yer own faither, Aggie Peters!' he said in a broken voice. 'An' him nearly fifty year old an' all!' He sat heavily in the chair and buried his face in his hands. 'Sure yer don't love yer old daddy no more, that's what it is. You've found a new fella, ain't that the truth?' He peeped between his fingers at Phoebe, who was trying hard not to burst out laughing. She couldn't remember when she'd enjoyed herself so much.

'I DO LOVE YOU! I DO!' Aggie leaned forward, her

arms stretched out, pleading. 'Mr Dickens is miserable, and Phoebe doesn't have any fun, and she likes you . . . and . . .'

'And I love you too, me beauty.' He sprang out of the chair and grabbed her to him. 'Yer a darling, sure yer are, and yer old daddy's just playing tricks on yer.'

Squirming from his embrace, she laughed. 'I know.'

'Yer did not!' he objected with suitable astonishment. 'Yer thought I was gonna throw yer out on the street, now tell the truth an' shame the divil!' Aggie's answer was to throw her arms round his neck and clutch him tight. 'All right then . . . I believe yer,' he said. 'Now let's have some cake afore we frighten our special visitor away.' Seating himself in a rocking chair, he pulled the trolley close to him and began pouring the tea into the cups. After putting in the milk and sugar he handed one to Phoebe, his expression more serious as he told her, 'Everything aside, me dear, I can't thank yer enough for taking care o' my little darling. I'm more than grateful, yer must know that. If there's ever anything I can do in return, well . . . you've only to ask, that's all. Just say the word.'

'I'm just glad I found her when I did.'

He shook his head and stared hard at the girl. 'If I've told her once, I've told her a thousand times . . . don't go wandering off from yer own backyard. But will she be told? No, she will not!' Returning his gaze to Phoebe, he explained, 'I expect I'm to blame when all's said and done. I should keep a closer eye on her. But it ain't so easy as all that, d'you see? There's a farm to run, and we're all called on to do our fair share. The bulk of the work falls on my two sons . . . twins they are, twenty-six years old, although Greg was born some forty minutes afore Hadley.' His face darkened as he went on in a softer voice, 'Greg's a law unto himself. Being the firstborn he's the rightful heir to Peters' Farm and all that goes with it. Oh, aye . . . Greg's the eldest right enough. But it's Hadley who's the more responsible of the two.' He paused a while, quietly musing, then in a lighter tone continued, 'However, they work hard the both of them, that they do, and I help wherever I can . . . milking the cows and gathering the harvest alongside them. But since their mammy died it's been my lot to look after the house and mind our sons' welfare. I'm not so agile on the farm these days and we can't really afford to pay help. But I don't mind . . . took to the house like a duck to water, yer might say. I clean and cook and see to it that there's food on the table when the fellas have done a hard day's work. It's a busy life without much reward.

'Y'see, it's the *big* farmers who rake the money in, the lucky blighters who have upwards of five hundred acres and more. Peters' Farm ain't but two dozen acres all told; enough to keep two strapping fellas working like the very divil, but not enough to make them rich for their troubles. But we do all right, and I'm not complaining. It's a good life.' He reached up to collect a pipe from the mantelpiece and proceeded to light it.

Phoebe waited. She knew it was time for her to go but was loath to leave. 'I've never known anyone who owned land,' she said with wonder. 'It must be wonderful when you know that it's your own ground you're walking on.'

'Aye, Phoebe, it is that,' he agreed. 'My faither were a farmer, and his faither afore him.' He laughed. 'Be

Jaysus! Didn't the sparks fly when I told me old fella I were going to be a sailor!' He chuckled, puffing furiously on his pipe until the smoke billowed round him like a grey cloud. 'But I came back to the land. A man allus comes back to the land. It draws him somehow . . . talks to him like the soft whispering of a woman. But like I say, Phoebe darling, there ain't a fortune to be had by it. But then again, what would I do with a fortune, eh?' he asked happily. 'We don't go hungry. We've a lovely home to call us own, and we've all got best clothes hanging in the closet. On top of that, I reckon there's enough money coming in to guarantee a modest living for a much larger family when the time comes.' He winked. 'That's allus assuming that me two sons will want to settle here, and that Aggie grows up sound and finds herself a good man to take care of her when I'm gone. Oh, aye! I'm a busy, merry fellow who could never suffer idle hands.' He sighed wistfully. 'The busier you are, the less time you have to reflect on what might have been . . . ain't that right, Phoebe Mulligan?' he asked, the broad grin on his face exaggerating the multitude of deeply etched wrinkles.

'I hope to start work Monday week,' she told him proudly. 'I'll be glad of that because I don't like taking charity from no one . . . least of all from *him*!' Her disgust for Edward Dickens was betrayed in her voice. She could have bitten out her tongue. 'I mean . . . it ain't right if you look to others to keep you, is it?' she asked hurriedly. Although she had taken an instinctive liking to Lou Peters, she warned herself to be cautious. After all, she didn't really know him well enough to open her heart to him, did she?

If he had detected anything untoward in her comment,

he wisely made nothing of it, replying innocently, 'You're right, me beauty, there's nothing so rewarding as honest hard work. And it does me old heart good to bend me back alongside me two sons. But y'see how busy I am, don't yer? And with little Aggie being the impossible article she is, it's hard for me to watch her every hour of every day.' He tutted and looked at the girl in a sorry manner. 'I love yer more than anything on God's earth,' he told her, 'but I swear you'll drive yer old father doolally afore yer much older.'

'I only went looking for Hadley,' the girl protested.

'Aye, and you've got the poor divil feeling guilty now. Shame on yer, young Aggie. How many times has your brother told you never to come looking for him when he's out shooting? It's dangerous, child! And well you know it.' He carved a generous wedge of cake and plopped it on to the plate, giving it into her outstretched hand and telling her with a sudden smile, 'But I reckon there's been enough said about it now. Yer home safe and sound, thanks to the good Lord . . . and o' course thanks to Phoebe here. However, yer may not be so fortunate next time, so it's to be hoped you've learned yer lesson. No more exploring all by yourself, eh? Will yer promise yer old faither that?'

'I promise.'

He sighed with relief. 'And I'll make *you* a promise,' he said. 'I'll find yer something interesting to do about the farm. Something that'll keep yer from wanting to go off rambling.' He would have liked to see the girl's face light up but he wasn't surprised when she merely nodded and thanked him in a subdued voice. It was well known that women weren't excited by farming the land, at least not to the same extent a fella might be.

For the next hour, Phoebe and Aggie were entranced by the stories that Lou told with such enthusiasm and in such vivid detail; although Aggie had heard them all before, she listened with renewed rapture as he described his many adventures when he was a sailor and not much older than Phoebe herself. There were fierce fights at sea, shipwrecks and desperate starvation when the rations rotted in the hold. 'Many's the time a flogging took place on deck, in full view of the ship's company,' he related, chuckling when he described how, 'O' course, I was never punished meself, 'cause I never let meself be discovered doing anything that could have got me fetched afore the captain. Oh, aye . . . yer have to be cunning, sure yer do. There ain't nobody else to look after yer but yerself.'

He painted their imaginations with dreamy tales of far-off places and mighty oceans: 'So vast that it seemed like the whole world had been swallowed up and we were the last people alive, cast adrift forever.' He shivered. 'By! It were a frightening feeling, I can tell youse,' he said with great conviction, bowing his head and dwelling on the past until it threatened to overwhelm him.

Taking a long deep breath, he glanced at the child. 'Well, I'm jiggered! Will yer look at that now? Sure I've talked the little mite fast and hard asleep.' He chuckled. 'I'd best tuck her up in bed afore she opens her mischievous eyes and demands another wedge o' cake.' With loving tenderness he gathered the child into his arms, thanking Phoebe when she carefully wrapped the blanket around Aggie's small still form. 'Stay a while, me darling,' he asked her, 'and I'll be back afore yer can wink an eye.'

While he was gone, Phoebe tidied the plates and cups on to the trolley then plumped the cushions on the settee. No sooner was it done than Lou returned. 'Aw, Phoebe darling, yer shouldn't have done that,' he chided. 'Visitors should be waited on and pampered, not busy themselves tidying up the minute me back's turned.' His homely old face creased into a grin. 'You just sit there and look lovely and I'll fetch us a fresh brew.' Before she could say anything he had hurried away, taking the trolley with him and singing an Irish ditty at the top of his lungs. Phoebe realised that the kitchen must be adjacent to this cosy little parlour because she could hear him very clearly when he called out, 'She's sleeping sound. The little tyke never stirred once, not even when I accidentally knocked the candlestick from the dresser. I'm not surprised she's worn herself out, though. She never stops. When she's not chattering, she's hopping round the room looking for mischief, and given half a chance she'd 'a followed Hadley again this very morning.'

He came back into the room, holding a mug of tea in each hand. 'This'll warm the cockles o' yer heart,' he told her. Handing one of the mugs to Phoebe, he held the other in front of her nose. 'This one's mine,' he said with a wink. 'Go on . . . tell me now, have yer ever smelled anything so delicious?'

Taking a deep sniff, Phoebe reeled back, wrinkling her nose in disgust. 'What is it?' she asked. 'It smells just like paraffin.'

'Paraffin!' He was horrified. 'Away with yer, Phoebe Mulligan! It's only milk, sure it is. Our own fresh milk from the cow this very morning.' He eased himself into the rocker and took a great gulp of the liquid, afterwards smacking his lips with satisfaction and gasping, 'By! That's a grand drop o' stuff. But, o' course, it ain't *just* milk,' he confessed slyly. 'I've spiced it up just the teeniest weeniest bit by putting a measure o' good stuff in it . . . only the very smallest measure, mind,' he promised on seeing Phoebe's disbelieving face. 'When a body gets to my age, it needs something to keep it going, don't yer know?' She laughed, picking up her mug from the table and sniffing at it, prompting him to assure her, 'Well now, will yer look at her! God bless and love us, me beauty. Did yer really think I'd take the liberty of dressing yer own drink with brandy?' He roared with laughter. 'Sure it's too precious to waste on a young 'un like yerself!'

'I can't say I'm sorry about that,' she confessed. She knew what the booze did to folks because hadn't she seen the rowdy merrymakers rolling home from the Bury pubs of a Saturday night? And wasn't it common knowledge how Maggie Blair from Victoria Street kept a secret hoard of brandy in her kitchen cupboard . . . and didn't she wake up so sozzled one morning that she'd forgotten to dress herself? And wasn't it relayed from one end of Bury to the other how poor Maggie answered the door to the postman with nothing on but the skin she was born in? It was said how after that the posties used to throw dice to see who had the pleasure of taking Maggie Blair's post to her door – and when they fished her out of the canal some weeks later, she was still clutching a flask of brandy in her frozen fingers. And now here was Aggie's daddy swallowing the very same brew. Still, he didn't look like the sort who drank to excess. You could always tell them, with their bulbous red noses and bleary eyes.

'It's just grand to have a visitor,' he said. 'Since my old darling's been gone, life does tend to get a bit lonely. Oh, I've got the lovely Aggie, and I'm very glad o' that. And there's my two sons. But, well, I do miss me wife and that's a fact. A young lass like yourself though . . . I shouldn't think you know what it's like to be lonely, do yer eh?' At once his face fell. 'By! What a brainless idiot I am to say such a thing, and your poor mam only recently gone, God rest her soul! Will I never learn to think before I blurt things out?' He was genuinely distressed.

'It's all right. It doesn't hurt quite so much now,' Phoebe lied. Losing her mam had been the worst thing in her life, and though she had now come to terms with it, the memory of that dear little woman would always hurt.

'I know different than that,' he said softly. 'I lost me own mam many many years ago, but I've never forgotten her. Sometimes, when I let meself think back over the years, I don't mind admitting that the tears are not far away.' He sighed and his eyes grew moist. 'Aw, but yer so young to be left on yer own,' he said. ''Tis a wicked world, sure it is . . . a wicked, wicked world.'

'I'm luckier than most, I suppose. At least I have a home.' Phoebe found small consolation in that but she didn't want Aggie's father to think she was ungrateful.

'And how does he treat yer . . . this uncle o' yours?' He had his own opinions about Edward Dickens but it wouldn't do to let the world know. Nor would he want to be held responsible for turning this lovely girl against her own uncle.

'All right, I suppose.' She could have said she didn't like her uncle. She could have explained how even before she came to Dickens House she had set her mind against him because of that heartless letter he had written her mother.

'Ah!' Lou smiled, but it was a sad, knowing smile. 'Ye don't like him, is that it?'

'I don't really know him.' Phoebe wondered just how much she could trust her newfound friend.

'Certainly I meself don't know the fellow too well, since we moved to these parts only four years ago, but from what folks say, yer uncle has worked hard to get where he is. He's a very powerful influence, I'm told.' Replacing his cup on the fender he regarded her with a serious expression. 'Something's troubling yer, ain't it, me darling? Is it him? Is it that yer can't take to Edward Dickens?'

'Not really.' Phoebe hadn't realised that her feelings were so evident. But then, she felt at ease with this man. 'It's just that I don't seem to fit in somehow.'

'But there's yer cousin who can't be much older than yerself,' he reminded her. 'Surely yer have a friend in her, don't yer?'

'We ain't exchanged two words yet, and to tell the truth I think she resents me being here.'

'Surely not!' he protested. And yet he knew Margaret Dickens well enough to realise that Phoebe might just have hit the nail on the head. Certainly that young woman had caused enough trouble here in this very household . . . throwing herself at one of his sons and then making a brazen play for the other. Happen it was as well that she hadn't made a friend of Phoebe or she just might influence the girl to bad things. 'But what about yer aunt? Now there's a good kind woman if ever I saw one.' More than that, he thought with a warm rush of feeling. She was the only woman he had looked at in a certain way since his own dear wife had been taken. 'Yer aunt made yer feel welcome, I know,' he said with a nod of his head.

'Oh, yes,' Phoebe admitted readily. 'She's very nice.'

'There's something troubling yer, though, ain't there, me beauty? Yer not happy at Dickens House but yer will be. It's all so strange for now but you'll get used to it, you see if yer don't. I expect he's a hard man to please though, yer Uncle Dickens?'

Phoebe had to laugh. 'Impossible more like,' she said. 'So far I ain't been able to do a single thing right. But he's not punished me or nothing like that. It's just that, well . . . I get the feeling he'd *like* to, although he never says so. Truth is he smiles a lot and talks softly but there's something odd . . .' She visibly shivered. 'I'm not making any sense, am I?'

'Oh, but yer are! I know exactly what yer mean 'cause I've met the fella meself once or twice. At one time we delivered fresh eggs and meat to Dickens House . . . yer aunt took the order but yer uncle paid the bill.' He stroked his beard thoughtfully before saying, 'And yer right, Phoebe gal, he *is* a strange fella and no mistake. It's downright unnerving when he speaks in that soft whispering voice while staring right through yer with vicious eyes.' Afraid that he might be alarming her, he added, 'But we all have us funny little quirks and that's a fact. Yer uncle no more than most, I expect.' He didn't tell her he had long suspected something was very much amiss between Edward Dickens and his meek little wife. He wasn't yet sure of his facts but if the day ever came when he was proved right . . . Dear God! It didn't bear thinking about. 'You've been given a nice room in that big old house, have yer?' He felt it might be wise to change the subject.

'Oh, yes! It's a tiny little room but ever so pretty. Right on the front of the house, it is. The one with the dormer window. And I've got my own washroom.' At the house in Rochdale all they'd had was an outside wash-house with a wooden lavvy.

'There y'are then. Right at the top of the world, eh? I bet yer sleep like a good 'un?'

Phoebe shook her head. 'Not really. There were these noises. Strange, they were, like the sound of the wind slicing through the trees but different, if yer know what I mean.'

'Happen it *was* the wind whistling through the trees?'

'No. I thought about it afterwards. There were other noises too. It must have been a nightmare.' She didn't say how she'd dreamed that her uncle had opened her door, nor that she'd sat up in bed terrified to see him standing there, the light from the candle in his hand casting his face in an eerie mask. She had seen him so clearly. Large as life and so real. He was sweating and breathless, his shirt open to the waist. For what seemed a lifetime he had stared at her from the doorway, his bare chest heaving and the sweat dripping from his temples. Above all she could remember his eyes, small and hard, staring at her, just staring and staring. She'd wanted to scream but couldn't. Then he was gone. The room was dark and she was alone.

In the morning she had convinced herself that it must have been a nightmare. Certainly her uncle had seemed quite normal when he had summoned her to his study. The thought of him caused her to scramble out of the chair now. 'I'd best be going,' she said, her eyes glancing towards the mantelpiece clock. It was twelve-fifteen. 'They'll be wondering where I've got to.'

Like Phoebe, Lou hadn't noticed the minutes slipping away. 'Be Jaysus, will ye look at the time!' he exclaimed, his merry eyes popping with astonishment. 'The fellas won't be long afore they're in for a bite to eat, and there's me having such a lovely time gabbing.' He chuckled, leading the way out of the room and along the corridor to the front of the cottage, chattering all the way as though he'd known Phoebe these many years. 'Sure it's been that grand having yer here,' he told her as he opened the door. 'Now, yer won't leave it too long afore yer come again, will yer, me beauty?' He looked at her with affection. 'Yer a bonny wee thing,' he said, 'and yer don't deserve to be lonely. It wouldn't be right if yer didn't have someone to talk to when yer felt the need. I'm in yer debt, Phoebe Mulligan, and you've made a good friend in old Lou, bless yer heart. Me and mine will allus be glad to see yer in our parlour, I can tell yer that.'

'I count myself lucky for having met you and Aggie,' she told him sincerely. She really felt that in Lou Peters she had found a friend who would always be there for her. On impulse, she kissed him on the cheek. 'Thank you,' she said simply. Before he could recover from her unexpected display of affection, Phoebe had hurried out of the door. She wondered whether she had been too quick to condemn her new life because now her heart was lighter for having met that delightful fellow. 'Things may not be so bad after all, Phoebe Mulligan!' she told herself softly. 'Because you've got two new friends already.' She didn't count the two men because she wasn't yet sure of them, and more than that, couldn't see how or whether they might play a part in her life. She couldn't have known that even at that moment Greg Peters was lying in wait, eager to introduce himself to the vivacious creature who had just emerged from his father's house.

As she reached the top of the path, Phoebe looked back. Lou was gone and the front door was closed. She supposed he was tending to his sons' meals. It seemed odd, a man cleaning and cooking. But then, if they couldn't afford a daily, and Lou was better employed in the house than on the farm, what could be more natural than that he should take on those responsibilities? Phoebe smiled as she murmured aloud, 'He seems happy enough in his work!'

'Ah! Now you must be talking about my father?' The man's voice was low and attractive but it startled her. As she swung round with a small cry, Greg Peters stepped out of the hedgerow, his dark brooding eyes regarding her curiously 'You're far lovelier close up,' he said boldly. 'And you look much older than your years. What did Margaret say? Eighteen?' He laughed rudely, his eyes roving her figure and coming to rest on her face. He had not lied when he told her she was lovelier close up. In fact, he thought, she was the most beautiful creature he had ever set eyes on.

'I'm nineteen soon,' she corrected him haughtily, and

not without a measure of curiosity. This arrogant fellow had caught her off guard, but she quickly composed herself. She remembered him from yesterday when Jessup had passed the field where the two men were working. Phoebe thought he too was very handsome close up. When he continued to stare at her with interest, but made no attempt to converse, she was surprised to find herself growing uneasy and irritated. She was also painfully aware that he was taking very intimate note of her. Now when he insolently straddled the gateway, effectively blocking her escape route, she was quickened to anger. Raising her head, she looked directly into those confident eyes which seemed to see right inside her soul. 'You're in my way,' she complained, her firm quiet voice belying the tremor inside her. She had taken an instinctive dislike to this fellow but in spite of her instincts telling her he was trouble of the worst kind, felt intrigued by him.

'Surely you don't mean to go without first making my acquaintance?' he asked. When she took a moment to answer, he sat back on the gate, his large hands gripping the posts either side and his dark eyes raking her face, seeming to taunt her.

'Don't play games with me. You know who I am right enough!' she retorted. 'I expect my cousin Margaret's told you everything you need to know?' She gave more question than answer but he merely smiled so she continued with growing irritation, 'You must be Greg Peters and I reckon we've already made our acquaintance in a way, seeing as you couldn't take your eyes off me when I first arrived on Jessup's cart.' She cocked her head to one side and stared at him boldly. When he laughed aloud, she demanded to know, 'What's so funny?'

'You!' he replied. 'Well, not "you" exactly.' He tried to make amends because he liked her. He really liked her. Girls had never meant more to him than a good time: Love 'em and leave 'em and to Hell with the consequences, that was his motto. But this one was different somehow. He didn't want to take her in the same way he had taken so many women. He wanted this one to come to him of her own free will. There was something exciting about her, a certain quality and fierce pride that was new to him. He had deliberately offended her and now wanted to make amends. 'It's just that, well, I suppose I expected you to talk more . . . more . . .' He shrugged his shoulders, irritated to find himself momentarily embarrassed.

'More ladylike, is that it?' she asked. 'You expected me to talk more like my cousin Margaret?' She laughed. 'Well, I'm sorry to disappoint yer, but like my mam used to say . . . it wouldn't do if we were all alike now would it?' Defiantly setting her small square shoulders, she insisted, 'Now if you'll kindly move aside, I'll be on my way.'

He made no move and for an uneasy moment gave no answer. A curious silence hung between them until he replied softly, 'I'd much rather we talked a while longer.' His dark eyes bored into hers, softly intimating things that she found deeply disturbing. 'I really would like to get to know you better,' he suggested, leaning forward and causing her to look aside.

Phoebe realised that he had no intention of letting her pass. Ignoring his meaningful insinuations she made no reply but swung away with the intention of finding another path out to the road. Turning sharply, she almost collided with the young man who had carried Aggie home. 'Jesus, Mary and Joseph!' she cried, clutching at her throat. 'You fair turned me heart over.'

Greg Peters was angry at his brother's untimely arrival. Being too intent on striking up a relationship with the lovely Phoebe, he had not seen Hadley approaching. Now he glared at the other young man, saying in a growl, 'You do choose your moments. Phoebe and I were just planning on going for a walk.' He smiled at her. 'Isn't that right, my lovely?'

'No, it ain't!' she snapped, then turning to Hadley explained, 'I came to see how Aggie was, and the time just flew away. I was on my way back to Dickens House.' She was tempted to say this arrogant fellow had barred her way but had already sensed the bad atmosphere between these two, and the last thing she wanted was to come between brothers. 'Twins' was what Lou had said, and seeing them together now was something of a surprise. They were so very different! The arrogant one had dark shifty eyes and hair as black as coal, while Hadley's eyes were blue as the deepest ocean and his hair the colour of God's earth. Both men were tall and well-built, but while Greg was a few inches taller and more visibly muscular, Hadley was somehow commanding in stature, quieter in nature and far more sincere. 'I'm glad yer sister's mending well,' Phoebe told him. She felt safe and comfortable in his presence, much the same way she had with his father.

'And I'm glad you took the trouble to pay her a visit,'

he said. 'I know she's been asking after you.' He looked at the other man who was sneering at this pleasant exchange. 'Don't you think we've taken up enough of this young lady's time?' he asked grimly, stepping forward to come between them.

'Young lady is it?' came the sarcastic reply. Greg Peters levelled his gaze on Phoebe for a brief moment then laughing softly he turned away, striding down the path towards the cottage, whistling merrily to himself. His powerful figure was soon lost to sight as he wended his way round the side and through the shrubbery to the back door.

Cupping his fingers under Phoebe's elbow, Hadley gently propelled her towards the front gate. 'You mustn't let him worry you,' he said, glancing at the spot where they had last seen his brother. 'He likes to hear himself talk. Greg's always fancied himself with the ladies.' His features broke into a smile as he gazed down on her. In Phoebe's uplifted face he could see that of another young woman – a beautiful tragic soul who had haunted him these past years. A dark expression flitted across his face as he asked softly, 'He didn't hurt you or anything, did he?'

Phoebe laughed nervously, but it wasn't what he had said that made her nervous. It was the way he regarded her with those anxious blue eyes that danced like sapphires. She got the feeling that he wasn't really looking at her at all. Of the two brothers she liked this one the best, but still she found herself glancing towards the cottage, wondering about the other one. Each of these men disturbed her. Greg Peters turned her heart over in one way. His brother turned it over in another. Gathering her thoughts, she realised he was still waiting for an answer. 'Oh, no! There was nothing like that,' she reassured him. Then, suddenly bristling, retorted, 'Besides, I can take care of myself!'

'I'm sure you can.' He opened the gate and followed her through it, tactfully changing the subject. 'I haven't had a proper chance to thank you for yesterday.' Closing the gate behind him, he strolled beside her across the road then over the pavement and on to the front of Dickens House where they paused in the brilliant sunshine, she smiling up at him, he with one hand on the gate and the other on her shoulder. 'The doctor says she'll be fine and her leg will heal just like new.' When he returned her warm smile she was amused to see how his mouth curled up at one corner.

'I'm glad about that,' Phoebe told him. 'She's a grand lass, bright and cheeky. I like that in a young 'un.' According to her own mam, that was exactly how Phoebe herself had been as a girl.

'Oh, she's that all right. Cheeky as a wagonload o' monkeys and twice as mischievous,' Hadley agreed with a laugh, adding seriously, 'Aggie's a real delight, but did my father tell you what trouble we have getting her to attend school?'

'No!' Phoebe was astonished. 'I would have thought Aggie and school went together like a horse and cart. She seems so interested in what goes on around her. And that makes for good learning, don't it?' She could see from his expression that his sister's schooling was a matter of real concern to him. 'Has she said *why* she don't like school?'

'They say she's backward, that she can't seem to learn the letters.' He looked aside as though weighing a personal matter in his mind. 'It's a shame because, like you say, she's very bright . . . bright as a button. But she's not long started attending so I reckon they've been a bit quick branding her a failure. I've told them so in no uncertain terms. She'll be fine, I'm sure of it. Trouble is, now she's taken to inventing ailments so she can stay away.'

Lou Peters had explained the girl was 'not long turned five'. It seemed to Phoebe that there couldn't really be a problem, or if there was it wouldn't last long. 'I went to a Church school, and I remember how I hated the first few weeks,' she confessed. 'Like Aggie, I began to invent any excuse for not going. I wanted to stay at home and do the things I enjoyed instead of sitting on a hard bench for hours and gazing out of the window, wishing with all my heart that I could be anywhere else but there. It took me a long time to realise that I could learn things in school that I could never learn outside. My mam kept telling me that I should be grateful. In time I came to see that she was right. It got to be a real joy, learning letters and numbers. Being able to read words and to put yer thoughts down on paper is a special gift. Next time I see Aggie, I'll tell her that,' she promised. 'Show her what she's missing.' She met his concerned gaze with a mischievous wink of her eye. 'Aggie will beat it, you'll see,' she said. 'Just give her time.'

'Thank you for that,' he said softly. He looked at her as though seeing her for the first time. She was so young yet her words were wise, as though she had lived beyond her years. 'Of course you're right,' he said, nodding his head in agreement, 'Aggie will beat it, I'm sure. And I'll tell her what you've told me. For now, though, I'd best let you get off.'

He watched her go into the house before retracing his steps to the cottage. He thought that Phoebe was as lovely in nature as she was in appearance. And he reminded himself of how she had come to these parts as an orphan, alone in the world except for the Dickens family whom according to Margaret she had never known existed. It would be hard for Phoebe to adapt, and it would be painful. In spite of her forthright nature, and her adamant belief that she could look after herself, she was bound to be vulnerable during these difficult times. It was a sad fact of life that wherever there was a lame or lonely creature, there would always be predators. His brother Greg was a predator of the worst kind, a hard and selfish monster who took delight in using women to his own ends. Phoebe would be just another conquest, another casualty to be thrown aside when the time came. But not this time! Not Phoebe. Not if *he* could help it.

Hadley realised that Greg would have to be watched. It was obvious he'd taken to hankering after her. She couldn't know how he had ruined other lives then walked away without any regrets or conscience. Could she even begin to guess how he could ruin her life if he put his mind to it? Hadley wouldn't let it happen. 'You won't spoil this one's life!' he muttered angrily, looking towards the cottage and imagining his brother there. 'Unless it's over my dead body!' His face was set grimly as he went inside. In his heart he knew there would be tears and heartache before this was all finished, but even Hadley

144

could not know how prophetic were the words he had just now uttered.

Phoebe had taken two steps into the hallway when she was grabbed from behind and viciously swung round. 'You bitch!' Margaret hissed, pressing her against the wall and pinning her there. 'I saw you with him! Smiling up at him like a lovesick cow. Don't ever make up to him like that again or I'll slice your face from ear to ear.' She stared at Phoebe's shocked brown eyes. 'Do you hear what I'm saying? DO YOU?' she demanded in a harsh voice. Her hands wound themselves round Phoebe's small white throat, her thumbs squeezing hard into the soft flesh.

'Get yer hands off me!' Phoebe struggled in the vice-like grip, half choking as the fingers locked tighter round her throat.

'DID YOU HEAR WHAT I SAID?' Margaret's face was thrust forward, blue eyes glittering. 'Stay away from Hadley, I'm warning you.'

Phoebe was defiant. 'I'll talk to whoever I like,' she said. Her voice emerged in a strange guttural sound.

'Not to *him*, you won't! Hadley Peters is mine.' The baby doll features leaned closer, grimacing with sadistic delight. 'I'll give you just one warning, cousin dear . . . if I see you talking to him again, I'll make sure my father knows about it. I don't think he'd like it if he knew how you were flaunting yourself at the young men from the farm. Did you know that when he got your mother's letter his first instinct was to send you to the workhouse?' She smiled with glee at the look of horror on Phoebe's face.

'It still isn't too late, is it?' she asked spitefully. 'Oh, I could stir up a deal of trouble for you, Phoebe Mulligan. I could tell my father things about you and Hadley Peters . . . thing that might change his mind about having you here after all.'

'Lies, you mean?' Phoebe gasped. She had her fingers locked round her cousin's wrists, trying frantically to pull the hands away from her neck. The pain was like a red hot needle down her throat. A thought suddenly occurred to her. Why was her cousin only *threatening* to put her in her uncle's bad books? If Margaret hated her as much as she obviously did, why wasn't she already on her way to the study to stir up this trouble she'd promised? For a minute Phoebe was puzzled, but then, like a bolt from the blue, she saw the reason. 'Of course,' she said. 'You won't go to your father about me talking with Hadley Peters because there might be *other* questions, eh? Questions you wouldn't want asked. Questions about *you* and Hadley. Your father don't approve of that young man, does he? If he thought for one minute that you fancied Hadley Peters, it'd be *you* in trouble, wouldn't it?'

She felt the fingers relax and took a deep breath. 'That's it, ain't it?' She saw the colour drain from her cousin's face and chuckled with satisfaction. 'You and Hadley, eh? And yer father don't know or he'd turn the world upside down!' She raised her head and stroked her fingers down her throat. It hurt like the very devil.

Straightening her shoulders and drawing herself to her full height of five foot two, Phoebe looked the other woman straight in the eye. 'I don't want your man,' she said, adding with contempt, 'though I think he might be too good for the likes of you. My meeting with Hadley Peters was nothing for you to get worked up about. I just went to the farm to see how the girl was after her accident yesterday. I've got no designs on yer fella, Miss High and Mighty, so yer needn't worry.'

She saw the look of relief in the baby blue eyes and knew she could never like this young woman who had come at her out of the shadows like a coward. 'For your information I ain't got designs on nobody. But I'll tell you this – if I *had* got a fancy for Hadley Peters, which I ain't, you telling me to keep away would only make me all the more determined to have him. And think on this while you're at it. I might be answerable to your father, more's the pity, but I ain't answerable to *you*, so just remember that. And remember this as well – I ain't one to go running to your father with tales and gossip, but if yer ever lay a finger on me again, I'll chop the bugger off, so help me!'

'How dare you speak to me like that?'

'Because I don't like you, and that makes me bold!' Phoebe was beginning to enjoy the situation which had happily turned to her advantage. 'I'm stuck here in this house and you're stuck here with me, ain't that the case?' she asked pointedly. When all she got for an answer was a dark scowl, she answered her own question, 'Whether we like it or not, you and me have got to tolerate each other, ain't we? Happen you could stir up a deal o' trouble for me with your father, but it seems I could do the same for you if I took a mind to it. I won't,' she promised, 'not unless I have to. Not unless you make me.' She didn't like threatening but liked being threatened even less.

Cold hard eyes stared back at her, bright with hatred. 'You should never have come to this house. You're not one of us and never will be.'

'Look, I didn't want to come here, and I won't stay a minute longer than I have to, I can promise you that.' At the moment she was totally dependent on her uncle, but there would be a time in the future when that wouldn't be the case. Things would change, she would be older, and with the help of the good Lord, life would take a turn for the better. That day couldn't come soon enough for Phoebe. Regarding the other woman she said coldly, 'I think we've both said enough. So you'll excuse me if I go and see my aunt?'

As she turned to leave, Margaret's voice made her pause. 'Stay away from him, and keep out of my way while you're living under this roof. You've made an enemy of me, Phoebe Mulligan, and you'll come to regret it. I'm too much like my father to forgive easily.' She laughed then, a cruel sinister sound. 'We don't suffer fools gladly, and we're not afraid of meting out punishment, in whatever form.'

Phoebe turned, measuring the other woman's face with quizzical eyes. 'What d'yer mean?' she asked. There had been something about that veiled warning that raised the hairs on the back of her neck. She was only just realising that she must never underestimate the vile depths to Margaret Dickens' character.

'Ask your aunt. She knows,' came the sly answer. 'Oh, but she won't tell. She knows better than to tell.'

Noreen Dickens remained in the chair, her face turned

to the window. She could hear Phoebe calling, asking whether she was any better. 'Would you like me to come and sit with you awhile? Happen I could read you a story?'

She didn't answer. There was nothing to say. Time would pass and she would emerge from this room, just as she had done on many occasions before. The scars would fade. The memory would dim. Until the next time. The next time . . .

She shivered, hugging herself in the warm sunshine that danced in through the window. She felt sorry for the girl outside the door, but she couldn't feel sorry for herself. Too much time had slipped away. Too many days and too many long empty nights. *Life*. Life had slipped by. But not for the girl. Not for Phoebe. All the same, she was trapped here. Like Noreen, she was trapped in this house. Maybe there was still a chance for the girl though? But her own chance had long gone, and with it her courage.

She drew the curtains and shut the daylight out. With slow careful steps she eased herself into the bed, painfully pushing down beneath the sheets. In a few moments she would be asleep and it wouldn't be so bad. Until next time. *Until next time*. The words echoed in her tortured mind until the last ebb of slumber bore her gently away.

Phoebe heard her aunt moving about. 'I'll call on you later,' she promised, disappointed that her aunt had not seen fit to want her company. She ran up the stairs to her own room where she knelt before the window and watched the world outside. A great sigh bubbled up from

149

somewhere deep inside her. There was a sadness in this house that she couldn't fathom. A kind of despair.

'It's a puzzle,' she murmured to the tree outside her window. 'A real puzzle.' In that little house in Bury there had been poverty and at times a deal of worry. There had been sadness too when her dad was taken from them, and her own inconsolable grief at the recent loss of her darling mam. But it was a different kind of sadness that existed in this house.

'Happen it's because there was love in my little world,' Phoebe told herself now. 'Or maybe it's having too much too easy that corrupts a family . . . makes a body hard and selfish.' She didn't know what spoiled the atmosphere in her uncle's house. She only knew that there was something unhealthy here, lurking beneath the surface like the shadows in a darkened street. Yet she wasn't frightened by it. She was only sorry, and curious.

Going to the small cupboard which had only recently graced her own bedroom at home, Phoebe took out some writing paper and a pen, then returning to the window placed the items on the sill and knelt in the same position as before. Taking a moment to gather her thoughts, she began writing.

Dear Dora,
I expect Jessup told you I arrived safely. I was going to leave it a whole week before writing because I didn't think there would be much to tell. But I'm feeling a little bit homesick just now, and I've been thinking a lot about Bury, and remembering what special friends you and Judd have been. I miss you both.

Anyway, Dora, you'll be pleased to know that I've already made three friends here. Yesterday I went for a walk and found a little girl caught in a trap . . . a wicked thing that was probably meant to maim some helpless creature. Anyway, I managed to free her just as her brother arrived to carry her home.

Today I went to see how she was getting on and she was mending well, so the doctor said. Her daddy is a lovely little man with a mop of white hair and a grin that stretches from ear to ear. He's that funny, and so friendly. He puts me in mind of a little goblin. His name's Lou Peters, a widower with two sons, Greg and Hadley, twenty-six-year-old twins, but they're not a bit like each other really. Hadley was the one who carried the girl home. I met him again today and he walked me back to the house. He's nice and very handsome.

My uncle is really strict, and my cousin Margaret is very pretty but has a nasty, selfish streak. It's plain to see that she's been dreadfully spoilt. My aunt doesn't have much to say for herself. She's a timid little thing. I like her. I don't know why, but I feel sorry for her. She's poorly just now, but I hope she'll soon be well enough to come out of her room.

I'm to have some new clothes tomorrow, and I'll be going to work on Monday week. I'm really looking forward to that because there isn't much to do here. The countryside is lovely though, Dora, and like I said I've made three friends so maybe it won't be so bad after all, eh?

Is everything all right with you and Judd? Please

remember me to him, won't you? I'll write again next week.

Love from,
Phoebe xx

She didn't say anything about Greg Peters or about the nightmare. She didn't want Dora worrying about her, and anyway, she wasn't sure how to explain the way Hadley's brother had made her feel, the way he had both frightened and intrigued her. Nor could she sensibly describe that awful nightmare that had seemed so real: the strange swishing noises in the dark, and the small muffled cries that touched her heart with pain. And how could she tell of the way she had seen her uncle standing wild-eyed in her bedroom doorway, dishevelled and dripping sweat? She kept these things to herself because she couldn't really expect Dora to understand, not when she didn't understand them herself. The more she thought about it, the more she had come to believe that it was either a figment of her imagination or a product of some dark terrifying dream. She wouldn't tell Dora. She wouldn't tell anyone. No! These were things best forgotten, pushed to the back of her mind, or better still thrust out altogether.

She hoped her letter to Dora betrayed nothing of her deeper anxieties. Furthermore, Phoebe had already made herself three promises. Firstly, she would avoid Greg Peters whenever possible. There was something about that darkly handsome fellow that spelt trouble. Secondly, she would keep on her guard where Margaret was concerned. And thirdly, if Lou was in agreement, she would use her spare time in teaching Aggie how to read and write. The thought alone brought a rush of pleasure to

Phoebe's heart. Besides, the days would soon roll away, and it would be Monday week before she knew it. There was her new work to look forward to, and then she could prove her worth to her uncle and aunt.

As Phoebe went down the road to post her letter she thought about Aggie and the happy hours she might spend in the little girl's company. It would be grand if she could encourage her to learn. Now there was a jaunty spring to her step as she broke into a rendering of 'When Irish Eyes Are Smiling', a song her mammy had dearly loved. Suddenly her life had taken on a new meaning and her heart was lighter than it had been for many long weeks.

Judd came into the parlour, the grime of work still on him. Since the Corporation had made him up to working foreman, his responsibility had trebled. He was still part of the gang that maintained the tram-lines or dug up the roads and filled in the craters made by the incessant movement of horses' hooves and motor-vehicles which were multiplying at an alarming rate. Soon the motor-vehicles would outnumber the trams and horses and his work would increase tenfold. Times were changing fast and a man must be ready to change with them. There was much resting on his shoulders but he liked it that way. He was always the last to leave his post but didn't complain. It was his work and he was paid good money to oversee the safety of each and every traveller. The men respected him, and he prided himself on a job well done. It was his conscientious attitude and attention to detail that had sent him quickly up the ladder of promotion.

All the same, on this Thursday night his back ached

like the very devil was riding on it, and his stomach growled with a great emptiness. As he came into the parlour his brown eyes popped open with surprise because there was his sister Dora seated at an empty table with her back bent over some piece of paper.

'What's that?' he asked, his voice betraying surprise that the table was not yet laid, although there was a delicious smell of steak and kidney pie oozing out of the kitchen. 'Somebody's last will and testament, is it?' he asked teasingly, rubbing his fists into his eyes and blinking the weariness away. 'Left you a fortune, have they?' he laughed good-naturedly.

Dora was always dreaming about being left a fortune which was curious because she didn't know anybody who even possessed one. When she appeared not to have heard him he shook his head and went, still chuckling, into the scullery where he took the big black kettle from the gas-ring and shook it. There was a good measure of water in it, no doubt for a fresh brew of tea.

'I'll use this for my wash,' he called out. Still no answer, so he tipped the water into the pot sink. It was just right, not too hot and not too cold. Undoing the upper buttons of his shirt he slid it down to his belt before proceeding to wash every inch of his body from his head to his waist, working up a tarry lather and whistling merrily as a man likes to do at the end of a very long, hard day's work.

Judd was a fine figure of a man, his broad chest and sinewy back tanned by the ferocity of the midday sun. He stood before the sink, half-stooping, his feet apart and his thick fair hair dipping into the bowl. Scooping up the water with capable hands, he doused the hair until it shone black, then taking the bar of tar-soap rubbed it into his scalp, working the lather with his fingers and methodically moving his hands down his face and neck. This was the time of day he liked the best, when he could wash away the sweat and feel the trickle of water against his skin. It was a good feeling.

'It's from Phoebe.' Dora rushed into the scullery and began bustling about, collecting plates and cutlery from the cupboard and taking them to the table, then coming back to open the oven door and see whether the pie was nicely browning. She felt guilty because the dinner wasn't already on the table. She was flustered and so she chattered. Her round face was red and she almost dropped the pie when her tea-cloth caught on the door of the oven. 'Oh dear. I'm sorry, our Judd,' she apologised while rushing in and out. 'Only I got my nose stuck in that letter and I forgot all about you.' She made one more trip with the condiment set then hurried back into the scullery to tell him breathlessly, 'There! Dinner's on the table.' When he reached out, eyes screwed up and his face dripping with water, she guided the towel towards his hand. 'And your clean shirt's on the back of the chair there.' She pointed to the ladder-backed stand chair in the corner of the scullery. He nodded. He knew the routine.

'What would I do without you, eh?' he asked, rubbing the towel over his thick wayward locks. He laid the soiled shirt on the drainer from where Dora collected it. 'I'll put this in the wash basket,' she said, 'then I'd best put the kettle back on. I expect Dad'll be wanting another brew.'

'I'll take it up, Dora.' He wiped the excess moisture from his broad brown chest and quickly slid the blue-checked shirt on. 'I'm going up now,' he said. 'How's he been today?'

'He's been fine, our Judd . . . just fine. But it's no good you going up just now, 'cause he's had his dinner and he's hard and fast asleep.' She peeked at her brother's disappointed face. 'It's best to let him sleep. He didn't have a good night, as well you know . . . seeing as you had to go in to him more than once.'

'He were disturbed right enough.' Judd recalled how his father had kept him for a good hour, talking, just talking. 'Did the doctor come by?' he asked. 'I called in to the surgery on my way to work.'

Dora nodded. 'Dad's all right. No better, no worse.' She didn't want to tell him how the doctor had said: 'Your father's mind has begun to wander, I'm afraid. The slightest infection, well . . . it's best that you should know.' Lying in bed had badly weakened the old fellow's heart and it was showing the strain. 'Have your dinner first, our Judd. Then happen he'll be awake and you can have a chat with him. He'll like that.'

'I'll just go and make sure he's all right.' Brushing past his sister he went two steps at a time up the stairs and into the front room where his father was fast asleep. Looking down on his wan face and listening to that rasping sound that came with every painful breath, he knew in his heart that it would take a miracle for his father to recover completely. Still, as Dora had said, he seemed no better, but no worse. He supposed that was all they could hope for. He leaned forward, gently gripping the long gnarled fingers that had once been sturdy and work-worn, the nails blackened with dust from the coal-pits.

He had been beautiful once, broad of chest and possessed of thick fair hair much the same as Judd's. He'd laughed with joy and cried with despair like any other man, and he'd loved his woman with a fierce possessiveness that had turned to fury when the good Lord saw fit to take her all those years ago. The wounded passion raged inside him like an inferno, burning and shrivelling everything good. Soon he was scarred and empty, wanting only to join his beloved Mary.

Standing there, looking down on the pitiful remains of that once handsome man, Judd could not stem the tears. They trickled down his face and into his mouth, salty on his tongue, opening wounds that crucified him. In his mind's eye he saw his parents together. They had been wondrously happy. He could remember it all so clearly. He studied the gaunt face a moment longer, searching for the man, the other man, the man who had been his father. Only a trace of that man remained. 'I love you, Dad,' he murmured. Somehow, more than ever, it was important that his father should know that. There was no answer, only the harsh breathing and a silence that closed in on him, a cruel silence that spoke volumes. Raising his face to the ceiling Judd inhaled deeply, steadying his emotions, preparing to face his sister. Before he went back downstairs he must rid himself of all sorrow. Dora had more than enough to contend with, without him sitting opposite her wearing a grim face. Quietly, he closed the door and went down the stairs. Later he would come back and sit awhile to let his father reminisce while he himself thought more deeply on the past. Sometimes it was good to dwell on the past because only then could you truly appreciate the future. He thought of Phoebe. There had been a time when he thought she would be his future. But that was another sadness.

'Still asleep, is he?' Dora was seated at the table, waiting to serve the meal. Now, when he sat opposite her, she took one of the two plates set before her and began cutting into the pie-crust.

'Sleeping like a babe,' Judd told her, taking the plate from her hand and helping himself to potatoes from the dish. 'What else did the doctor say?' he asked, frowning.

Dora was a moment giving her answer. Laying her fork on the plate, she gently chided, 'You're not to worry, our Judd. I've already told you what he said. Dad's about the same.' She wasn't lying, but she wasn't revealing everything the doctor had told her. Later she would have to tell Judd exactly what was said, but not now. Not yet. There would be time enough. 'How did it go today?' she asked in an effort to change the subject. It wasn't good for Judd to be constantly fretting about his father. There was nothing he could do. Nothing any of them could do. She had come to accept that, and so must he. And when the time came, he had nothing to reproach himself for. There was no finer son anywhere, and no finer brother.

'Same as always,' he replied between mouthfuls. 'The weather's creasing, though. The bosses don't particularly like us stripping off but a man can't work in that heat without the feel of a breeze on his back.'

'Are you going out tonight?'

He shook his head. 'No. I'll finish my meal, then I'll sit with Dad a while.'

'You could meet up with a few mates.' It worried her

that he rarely went out, except maybe on a Saturday when he went down to the pub where the other gangers congregated.

'No.'

'I've got a few bob . . . haggled with the butcher and made a saving,' she said. 'You're welcome to it, our Judd.' All work and no play was no good to man nor beast.

'What!' He stared at her then helped himself to another potato. 'Are you saying that I should squander the coppers in your purse? D'you think I'd see you haggle to save a few bob so I can chuck it over the pub counter?' He said it in a light-hearted manner but she knew he was deadly serious. 'Keep your money for better things, Dora,' he told her. 'If you're shrewd enough to save from the housekeeping I give you, then you deserve to buy yourself a new hat or something.'

'But you're so generous,' she protested. 'And you do like a pint now and then, don't you?'

'Aye, I'll not deny it.'

'But not tonight?'

'No, lass. Not tonight. I'm not a man for going out drinking in the week, you know that. Saturday night's a different matter because I don't have to get from my bed at five o'clock on a Sunday morning.' He laughed. 'Hey! You're not trying to get rid of me, are you, Sis? You haven't got a fellow tucked away somewhere, have you . . . waiting 'til my back's turned so you can have your wicked way with him?' He peered at her with accusing eyes and laughed aloud when his words made her giggle with embarrassment. Having finished his meal

159

he leaned back in his chair, folding his arms above his head and stretching out his long legs beneath the table. After a while he picked up the newspaper which Dora had placed beside his plate. He flicked disinterestedly through it before replacing it on the table.

'There's still talk of French troops withdrawing from the Rhineland,' he remarked, his eyes drawn to the letter which Dora had been reading. He wanted so much to ask after Phoebe but he was afraid that something in his voice might give him away. 'There's things brewing across the Channel and that's a fact.'

'There's enough excitement going on in *this* country, our Judd,' Dora told him. 'I'm blessed if they aren't still kicking up an almighty fuss about the length of women's skirts. Some folks seem to think that while hemlines rise, morals are bound to fall. Stuff and nonsense! Now the doctors are saying that we'll suffer all manner of ill-health if we don't keep our hems to the ground . . . we're all about to get "puffy legs" because we've let the daylight see 'em, that's what they're saying! Did you ever hear such claptrap?'

Judd laughed aloud. 'Well, us fellows don't mind, I can tell you that,' he admitted. 'It's a treat to see a pretty well-turned ankle.'

It was true, though. The Church was up in arms about 'the immorality of women'. Maybe they had some cause to be shocked because it seemed to have happened overnight . . . young women dancing the night away in skirts almost up to their knees, laughing carefree 'flappers' piling into fancy motor-vehicles and encouraging reckless young men to tear along the road at speeds of up to thirty miles an hour. His thoughts drifted back to Phoebe and he couldn't take his eyes off the letter. He found himself imagining its contents. Was she well? he wondered. How was she coping with her new life? Had she mentioned him? Was she lonely? He couldn't bear it any longer. 'That letter,' he began hesitatingly, forcing his voice to sound matter-of-fact. 'You say it's from Phoebe?' The very mention of her name raised all kinds of excitement in him.

'That's right.' Dora beamed with happiness. 'Thank God she seems to be settling in without too much upset. She's already made three friends? Ain't that grand?' She clapped her hands with glee. 'Phoebe'll be all right, I just know she will. Poor little bugger, she's had such a rough time of it. A little bit o' good fortune is long overdue if you ask me.'

'What else does she say?'

'Here. Read it for yourself while I clear the table.' She stood up and pushed the letter towards him. 'She mentions you in there an' all.'

As he opened the letter, Judd was acutely aware that Phoebe had written these words which he was now reading. No, not just words but thoughts, *her* thoughts, made in her heart and transcribed to the page by her own fingers. He could feel her on the paper. He could see her in his mind's eye, as vivid and real as though she had just entered the room: her small perfect figure; auburn hair spilling over her shoulders; that familiar face, exquisite yet strong, full mouth and that wonderful smile that could light up a room. He could see it all, and his heart ached because of it. He bent over the table, shoulders hunched

161

and his head resting on his hands. He felt closer to her than ever. As he read the letter, his pleasure turned to pain. Who was this man Hadley? 'Nice' Phoebe called him . . . and 'handsome'. There was a certain warmth about the description which made him jealous. But then he sharply reminded himself that Phoebe did not belong to *him*, more was the pity. Besides, he was probably reading more into her words than was meant. Phoebe was barely eighteen, while this Hadley fellow was twenty-six years old and probably married into the bargain. He wondered whether Hadley had a fancy motor-vehicle.

'She seems all right, wouldn't you say?' Dora had returned with a tray which she set down on the table. 'She's getting new clothes and starting work Monday. Happen this fresh start will turn out for the best after all, eh?' She slid the half-empty pie-plate on to the tray and waited for his answer.

'Aye. Happen it will.' He didn't look up. Instead he kept his gaze fixed on the open letter. There were things in it which bothered him, disturbed him deep down. 'Like you say, it's good that she seems to be settling in all right. After what she's been through, it can only get better.'

'Reading between the lines, her uncle is a domineering fellow and I don't reckon she likes her cousin much. That one sounds like a right madam!'

'Well, it seems as though Phoebe has her to rights, and besides she can look after herself.' He was beginning to feel angry and didn't know why.

'Did you see where she mentions *you*, our Judd?'

He nodded. 'Aye.'

'Said we were her friends, that she'd been thinking

about us all the while. Did you see that?'

'Aye.' He looked up then, smiling into her bright blue eyes. 'She'll never have no better friend than you, lass,' he told her with affection. And nobody who loves her more than me, he thought.

'I'm sure she knows that, our Judd. Now then, if you've finished with the letter, I'll put it safely away. It's got the address and everything where she is, and I intend to write back this very evening.' She had been on her way to the scullery but paused and glanced back. 'Is there anything special you want me to tell her?'

'I don't think so.'

'Right then, I'll just send her your best wishes.' She went on her way and was soon humming a melody to the sound of clattering dishes.

In the parlour, Judd took his pipe and baccy pouch from the mantelpiece. When his pipe was lit and he was seated in the black horse chair beside the empty firegrate, his mind remained on Phoebe. He didn't really know how long he'd loved her. It seemed like always. They had grown up together, him and Dora and Phoebe, living in each other's houses, playing on the cobblestones and scouring the marketplace after closing in search of good pickings. They'd swapped hoops and marbles and traded daydreams, they'd laughed and fought together. He even recalled when she was just a baby in a cradle and he a boy of five. Now she was going on nineteen and he was twenty-four, and their childhood was gone forever. *She* was gone forever. No! He couldn't think like that. He mustn't.

All those years . . . And in all that time he had never

guessed that love was creeping up on him. He hadn't known how he felt until that day when he'd seen her leaving on Jessup's wagon. He'd wanted to run after her and tell her how much he loved her, how he had *always* loved her. But he couldn't. She had been through so much, it wouldn't have been fair to burden her with such a confession, out of the blue like that. She had never given any indication that she saw him as anything other than just a friend. It would have embarrassed her. She might even have laughed at him. But no, she would never do that. All the same, his instincts told him to hold back. Better to have her as a friend than not at all. And so he suffered his love for Phoebe in silence. One day perhaps, one day in the future, he might summon the courage to tell her how he felt, but not yet. Not until he was sure that she wouldn't reject him. If that day ever came, he would be the happiest man on God's earth. But he despaired of seeing such a day because he knew in his heart that Phoebe did not love him in that way, and probably never would.

Suddenly his need for her grew like a lead weight inside him. Troubled anew, he went from the parlour to the front door where he stood on the threshold, legs astride, pipe in mouth, his fond gaze looking first up the street, then down its entire length. It was here he and Phoebe had played and laughed together, grown together, come to know each other like brother and sister. That was it . . . they were like brother and sister, and she would be shocked to know he felt any other way. The cobblestones in the road were just the same as when his sister and Phoebe had skipped on them, jutting from the ground like shiny wet loaves and worn thinner by the tread of many feet; the flagstones on the pavement were grey and crooked just like they had always been, and the gas-lamps where they had lassoed their ropes and swung round and round stood strong and straight, just as when he was a boy. Time had marched on but these things remained the same. Nothing else in the street had changed. Only him. And Phoebe. And his need for her.

Newly-weds were moving into the little terraced house where Phoebe had grown up. He had seen the young man carry his wife into their first home. He had heard them laughing, happy and excited about their new life and their plans for the future. He imagined them lying in bed at night, content in each other's arms, and was filled with a terrible longing, wishing it could have been him and Phoebe in that little house, she in his arms and the two of them so very much in love. But it wasn't to be.

He wondered what she was doing at that very moment. Not for an instant did he believe she might be thinking of him. Dora's voice cut into his reverie, telling him his father was awake and asking for him. 'All right,' he called back. 'Tell him I'm on my way.' He looked up to the sky above the chimney tops. Somewhere, not too far away, that same sun was shining on her. 'Don't forget me, Phoebe, my lovely,' he murmured softly. He closed his eyes on the memory of her face, letting it flood his heart for one special moment. Then he straightened his back, squared his shoulders, and went quickly back inside.

Chapter Five

Phoebe examined herself in the mirror. 'You'll do,' she said, hands on hips and twirling about. 'Though I say so myself, Phoebe Mulligan, you've made a good job of this dress.' Then she added with a chuckle, 'Though I don't reckon your cousin would agree.'

The dress was one of the garments that Margaret had purchased in Manchester last week, and which Edward Dickens had described as 'serviceable'. When Phoebe was given the garments she despaired about having to wear them. There were two skirts, one brown and one blue, and a white blouse that would pair with both. There was also a dress which she had chosen to wear today. It was blue with white spots on it, baggy sleeves to the wrist, and like the skirts had been two sizes too big. When she tried it on, the neckline sagged below her collar-bones and the voluminous skirt trailed to her shoes. Phoebe's reaction was one of horror but her uncle soon told her in no uncertain terms to: 'Thank your cousin for taking the time and effort to shop for your wardrobe, my girl. But, mind! I intend to deduct sixpence from your pay-packet every week until the entire amount is repaid.'

Phoebe soon realised the futility of protesting and instead closeted herself in her room and got to work with needle and thread, grateful for the sewing skills her mammy had taught her. She shortened the two skirts to just below the new fashionable calf-length, reduced the waist to her own size twenty-two, and made two belts from the excess material. The blouse needed only one alteration, and that required snipping a piece out of the collar and realigning it, so that it fitted snugly round the neck. The dress had warranted the most attention, but the result was astonishing. She admired it now, looking in the mirror and thinking how peeved her cousin would be to see the difference. It fitted as though it had been tailored for her. The sweetheart neckline was now neat and pretty, the sleeves snug and tapered in just below the elbow, the waist fitted perfectly and the skirt clung at the hips before falling to the hem in deep swirling ruches. It was a delightful dress and Phoebe loved it, though not as much as she loved the one her mammy had made for her. The hem was modestly short and the cornflower blue background suited her vivid colouring handsomely.

She had made a matching ribbon which she now tied round her hair, bunching the springing locks into the nape of her neck and making a large extravagant bow that suitably restrained the disobedient curls. One more twirl in the mirror, one glance around the room to satisfy herself that everything was spick and span, and then she was ready. Taking her black handbag from the cupboard, she went in haste down the stairs and out of the front door where her uncle was already waiting.

'Quickly, girl! Quickly!' Edward Dickens stood beside his prized black Ford motor-vehicle, his fingers drumming on the open passenger door and his booted foot impatiently stamping the pavement. 'Move yourself, girl.' He snatched the fob watch from his waistcoat pocket and glanced down at it, snorting as he thrust it away again. 'I should have been gone from here fifteen minutes ago,' he snapped, carefully taking off his trilby and placing it in the back of the car. He had on his best black work suit, his shoes polished like mirrors and his tie drawn up so tight that he had the look of a man being choked.

'But it's only ten past six,' Phoebe protested. Monday week had arrived at last and here she was, at some unearthly hour, being taken into Blackburn town where she would be introduced to her new employer. As she closed the front gate her stomach was turning somersaults. It was a special day in more ways than one because today was also her nineteenth birthday. No one knew, and that was the way she wanted it.

'Don't answer me back,' her uncle retorted, 'and I'm only putting myself out this once to make sure you get there. From tomorrow you'll travel on the tram-car like everyone else.' His accusing stare was designed to unnerve her as she hurried towards him. He had been secretly impressed when she had presented herself in the dining-room this morning. There was an eagerness about her that quite took him by surprise. But it would never do to let her know that, Oh no! Judging by her impudent remark just now, it was clear that Phoebe Mulligan still had a great deal to learn. Just as he had first suspected, she was wayward of spirit and undisciplined. During this past week he had given her just enough rein in order that he might assess her character. His suspicions were confirmed. She had too many opinions about too many matters that did not concern her. She was too curious, too confident by far, and possessed of an irrepressible nature that she had no right to.

There was no doubt in his mind that she needed to be brought to heel. He would need both patience and cunning to eliminate the bad elements in her character. It was not going to be an easy task, and he was not strong on patience. But he must bide his time. There was an old saying of which he was very fond. 'Give them enough rope and they'll hang themselves.' That was exactly what he intended. To give her enough rope and hope she would hang herself. He dropped his chin to his chest and secretly chuckled. He was quite enjoying this little game of cat and mouse. She wouldn't be quite so bright and eager when she saw what he had in store for her this morning. Phoebe Mulligan was not here to be cossetted. She was here to earn her keep, and to learn humility. Today was only the start.

Leaving the passenger door open, he went to the front of the car where he stooped to the radiator and drove the starting handle home, all the while deviously observing Phoebe as she came at a run along the pavement. In spite of himself he had to admit that she was indeed a very attractive young woman. *Too* attractive, he thought. Too shapely of limb, and all that titian-coloured hair. Of course! He reminded himself again that he must do something about that mass of hair although she had taken to tying it back and distracting his attention from it. All the same it was very remiss of him, especially as she was about to be installed in a more public place. But then, he'd had so much on his mind of late, what with one thing and another, more particularly this new establishment and all the responsibility that went with it.

As he stared at Phoebe, he was reminded of his own late sister. Jessica had been about the same age as Phoebe when she . . . when he . . . He sharply dismissed his dangerous thoughts. Things of that sort were best forgotten. He turned away, fixing his attention on the car. He was angry with himself. Angry with his sister for dying and foisting her daughter on him. What right had she to raise the past and torment him anew? Disgust and venom filled his heart. 'Damn you to Hell, Jessica!' he muttered, thumping his fist against the bonnet. But he couldn't rid himself of the memories, and couldn't still the hate and bitterness inside him. And now all of this was levelled at Phoebe.

The engine was turning. Drawing the starting handle out he went quickly to the car, putting the handle on the floor at the back and himself in the driving seat. 'For goodness' sake, get in!' he told Phoebe. She had caught sight of someone at an upstairs window at the farmhouse, thinking for a moment that it might be the girl. 'I said GET IN,' her uncle demanded angrily. 'What the devil do you think you're playing at?'

The car gently swayed as Phoebe clambered in. He did not look at her, but he could smell her presence, fresh and pleasant, like blossom after rain. Even when she spoke, asking where she was to work, he did not answer, dared not look. Instead he remained stony-faced, stiff and upright in the driving seat. Phoebe realised he was punishing her for some reason, maybe for keeping him waiting, though she suspected his reasons went deeper than that. He's a strange man, she thought, her spirits beginning to dip. But then she remembered it was her birthday, and today was the day when she would gain a degree of independence. She wouldn't let him ruin it. She wouldn't let *anything* ruin it. There was great excitement in her, a wonderful feeling of accomplishment and challenge. In her heart she believed her mam was up there in the Heavens somewhere, watching, willing her to do well. With renewed determination she turned away from her uncle's sour face and settled back into the seat, shivering when the hard leather struck cold against her back.

As the car began moving slowly down the lane and along the main Preston New Road, Phoebe made herself imagine the place where he was taking her. Had he changed his mind and decided to install her in his new shop? she wondered. Was she to be trained in the same work as her cousin? Or had he secured her a position in an office . . . she was good at figures, and her handwriting was impeccable. He knew all that because he had tested her on these very things last week. He knew also that she was an excellent reader, and that she was quick to learn. An office clerk. The idea grew on her. Whatever position he had in mind for her, Phoebe was determined to put her heart and soul in it. She had things to prove, and he had already told her he put great store by hard work.

It was a lovely morning. Already the sun was filling the sky. The fields stretched away into the distance, covered by the late-night dew and shimmering like a silver sea in the warmth of a new day. 'Ain't it a grand morning, Uncle Dickens?' she asked in a bright voice. When he merely grunted, she shrugged her shoulders and concentrated on enjoying her very first ride in a motor-car. It was noisy and draughty and the vibrations rippled up her spine. But it was also wonderfully exhilarating, and she loved it.

The market-hall clock was showing six-thirty as Edward Dickens drove into Ainsworth Street. Already the town was awake. Hordes of cotton mill workers huddled together, pushing towards Cicely Bridge, their flat caps like a sea of twill and their snap-cans clinking in rhythm with the stamp of their iron-rimmed clogs on the pavements. The streets were alive with the sounds of a town at work: the clip-clop of horses' hooves and the rumble of cart-wheels on the cobbles; newsvendors yelling out the latest headlines at the top of their lungs; a beshawled old woman offering 'Cockles and whelks, fresh this morning'; and above the din, the sirens from the numerous mills intermittently shrieked.

The lights from the many street lamps were now extinguished but they lined the pavements like smart grey soldiers in salute, proudly wearing the emblem of the Lancashire Rose on their shoulders; like the church spires they held themselves aloof from the bedlam below. The tall mill chimneys belched out their fumes and the grey-black vapour settled like a dark cloud over the whole town, blotting out the sun and filling the air with specks of charcoal that irritated the throat and stung the eyes. Blackburn was no different from any other mill town, no better and no worse. Here Phoebe felt at home because she had lived all her young life beneath the wail of those same sirens. She was a mill town girl and proud of it.

As they passed the grand new store on the corner of Ainsworth Street, Phoebe looked up to see sprawled on a board above the window: DICKENS' GENTLEMEN'S OUTFITTERS. In that moment when her uncle slowed the car she was thrilled. He *was* going to train her in his new store after all. 'What do you think to that?' he asked, turning his face towards the establishment, his chest bursting with pride. 'There isn't a store to touch it, not in the whole of Lancashire!' he proclaimed.

'It's very smart,' she admitted. The store straddled the corner. One panoramic window looked out on to the maze of streets and the other faced the railway station, market and boulevard. It was in a prime position and there was an air of superiority about it that overwhelmed every shop in the vicinity.

Phoebe was surprised and disappointed when her uncle drove on, along Ainsworth Street and down by the boulevard. He turned left, up a small incline and into a narrow ginnel where a row of bent and crooked shops seemed to sink into the pavement. Suddenly Edward Dickens eased the motor-car to a halt, edging it into the kerbside and telling Phoebe, 'Look sharp, girl. We're here.'

He flung open the door and got out with great fuss and ceremony. Collecting his hat from the back seat, he placed it on his head at a sombre angle and waited for her to disembark. 'I shall expect you to conduct yourself with decorum at all times,' he told her with a curious grimace. 'It wasn't easy securing this position for you so I hope you value it.' He slewed round when a man of medium height and pleasant features emerged from the shop.

'Ah! Mr Quinn, my good man.' His tone was false and his manner curt. Returning his attention to Phoebe he declared impatiently, 'Mr Quinn is your new employer.

Mark well what I've told you,' he warned. 'I can't linger here. I must be on my way, I'm late already.' He cast an accusing glance at her. 'I'll be back here at six this evening so mind you're ready and waiting.' To the man he said, 'You will of course inform me of any misdemeanour or disobedience?'

The man nodded but said nothing although he reserved a small encouraging smile for Phoebe. Together they watched the car draw away down the narrow street. Quinn made a homely-looking figure in his brown leather overall, and she looked sadly out of place in her posh blue spotted dress.

Curious, Phoebe cast her gaze up and down the street. The pavements were barely wide enough to walk on and the jutting roofs almost touched each other. Even now at this early hour there were children playing on the cobbles, some rolling their hoops and some casting stones from the back of their hands to see which way up they might land. Others were chasing each other, squealing with delight as they fled this way then that. The buildings were one long parade of ancient shops, dilapidated yet picturesque; there was a confectioner's and a butcher's, a baker's and an ironmonger's, a pawnshop with three huge brass balls hanging above the door, a tobacconist's and two second-hand shops, one selling clothes and the other furniture. There were others whose nature was not immediately apparent from where Phoebe was standing. Mingled smells permeated the air . . . freshly baked bread, dry snuff, wet fish, ripe fruit, tobacco, and others that were not so easily recognisable but which assailed the nostrils and clogged the throat with their pungent

presence. 'That's the leather you can smell.' Mr Quinn
had seen Phoebe wrinkling her nose. 'You'll get used to
it,' he promised with a warm ready smile.

Feeling oddly at home in his presence, she laughed. 'I
hope you didn't think I was pulling a face. It's just
that . . . well, it stinks a bit, don't it?'

He leaned back his head, perfectly proportioned on
straight wiry shoulders, and laughed. His fine short-cut
brown hair was neatly combed, and his whole countenance exuded contentment; he was not much taller than
Phoebe, but somehow seemed to tower above her. For
what seemed an age he continued to regard her with
honest green eyes, then he said in a voice that betrayed
surprise, 'You're not at all like I expected.'

'Oh? And what *did* you expect?' When her uncle had
first left her here she had felt lost and forlorn, disappointed that he had not taken her into his own store.
Now, though, she felt more content than cheated. The
children playing in the street, the humble shops, and this
man who was to be her employer . . . they were her kind
of people. That was what she was used to.

'Oh, I don't know. Someone older perhaps,' he admitted. 'Certainly I didn't expect anyone quite so lovely.'
His smile broadened and she thought him somewhat
attractive in a mature kind of way. 'Must be my lucky
day,' he said, clicking his tongue in a gesture of approval
then shouting, 'Whoah! Watch out!' when a marauding
child knocked into him. 'Little blighters,' he told Phoebe
good-naturedly, adding with a sorry expression, 'They're
not mine, I swear.'

'Whose are they then?' Phoebe couldn't see any dwelling houses hereabouts.

'Oh, they live here in Lord Street . . . in the rooms above the shops,' he explained, pointing to the upper windows which were dressed with pretty net-curtains. 'We're not grand folk who travel from the outskirts of town,' he went on, 'we're shopkeepers every one, and live and work in these premises.' There was a certain pride in his voice and a hint of amusement in his green eyes as he looked at her.

'Of course,' Phoebe apologised, surprising herself when she then boldly asked, 'Do *you* have a family, Mr Quinn?'

'Not "Mr Quinn". please. Marcus is the name,' he said, thrusting his hands into the pockets of his overall and eyeing her with interest. 'No, I don't have a family.' He laughed, but it was a hollow sound that spoke of underlying pain. 'Shameful, wouldn't you say? A man in his early forties and still not wed?' The smile slid from his face and he looked aside, watching the children at play. He did have a love once. Just once. Only she went away.

'There's nothing shameful about not being wed,' Phoebe told him in a firm voice. 'I expect you ain't met anyone you want to spend your life with. And there's no sense getting wed just for the sake of it, that's what I say.' She had taken a liking to Marcus Quinn and sensed his loneliness. 'I'm Phoebe Mulligan,' she said, offering her hand in friendship. 'If you'll tell me what you want me to do, I'll get to work,' she said in a brighter voice.

'Very well, Phoebe Mulligan,' he mocked gently, 'Let's go inside.' He made a gesture towards the doorway of the quaint little shop with its bullseye windows. 'If it's work you're after, you'll not be disappointed because I'm warning you, it's piled right up to the ceiling.'

Phoebe was fascinated. Marcus took her on a tour of

his cherished premises, from the front shop area where the customers were served to the rooms above where it would be part of her duty to make the tea: 'At precisely ten-fifteen in the morning, and half-past two in the afternoon. And we'll have cream cakes on us birthdays.' She told him it was *her* birthday today, but that he must not make it widely known. And, 'You'll have to wait until the next one before we have cream cakes . . . that's if I'm still here,' she added hastily. After all, it wasn't her intention to stay for too long. Once she'd proved herself to her uncle, Phoebe was convinced that he would trust her with greater responsibility.

The front shop area was the largest room of all, being some fifteen feet square. There was a panel-fronted counter in one corner with shelves behind, and other shelves covering every wall from floor to ceiling. They were crammed with boots, shoes and clogs of every size, description and colour; bunches of this beautiful hand-made footwear hung by waxed leather laces from the shelf ends and even dangled from the ceiling beams. It was impossible for a body to walk tall and straight beneath or they would become hopelessly entangled. Phoebe wondered whether this was the reason Marcus had a slight stoop to his shoulders.

The back room was the workshop where shoes were repaired and made. In the centre was a short stout bench arrayed with tools, including two sizes of hammer, a strong set of pliers and a dish filled with shiny brass tacks. There were boots and clogs in various stages of creation, and a pot of creamy liquid that might have been glue or might have been polish. In any event, it exuded a smell that tickled the nostrils and stung the eyes. Pulled up to the bench was a stool with a round red cushion tied to its surface, and close by was a hobbling foot with a gentleman's boot stretched tight over it. There was a trestle beside the bench which was draped with a length of brown beaten leather. All around the room similar trestles bore layer upon layer of skins in varying quantities, some natural brown and others dyed in muted shades of red, blue or black. A peculiarly warm acrid smell hung in the air, thick and invasive, seeming to fill every crack and crevice. But there was a homeliness about the place, and Marcus Quinn's steady reliable personality was stamped everywhere on the careful layout of his work-bench which spoke of loving hands, on the plain no-nonsense curtains that hung at the windows, on the shiny kettle that rested on the tiny gas ring, and on every piece of solid oak furniture that made this delightful little place a real home.

There were three rooms above the shop: a tiny sitting room and scullery combined, with a washroom squeezed between these and the bedroom; this was the only room that Phoebe was not shown into, and rightly so, for it would have greatly embarrassed both her and her employer.

'There you are then,' he declared, leading her into the rear yard. 'You've seen my kingdom. What do you think? Are you staying or can't you wait to run down the road after your uncle?' He paused outside a barn door. 'I hope you'll want to stay though,' he said softly. 'I know it isn't much of a place for a young lady to spend her days, especially as I can pay you only twenty-five shillings a week, but it's good honest work and you'll get to meet some grand folk . . . have a natter like . . . see what makes the world tick.' He smiled and the years fell away from him. 'What do you say, Phoebe? Will you stay?'

'I've got no choice,' she said with a wry little smile, but when she saw that he was disappointed, told him, 'and even if I had, I don't suppose for one minute that I'd go "running down the road" after my uncle.' The reason being that she wouldn't want to give him the satisfaction. But she kept that bit of information to herself.

'Well then, this is the barn,' he said, proudly showing her inside the small stone building. 'This is where I keep the skins. It's cool, do you see?'

Phoebe set one foot inside and shivered violently. 'Freezing more like!' she said, drawing away.

'It has to be cold because the skins need to be kept fresh.' He pointed to a pile of raw skins piled on to a trestle in the corner. 'They're delivered here, and I take them into the shop as and when I need them.' He then went on to detail the process of boot and clog making, from the raw skin to polishing the finished article. It was plain to Phoebe that he took a great pride in his work and strangely enough as he talked she felt her own interest growing – especially when he promised her a pair of shiny black patent shoes. 'Given time, you should be able to make them yourself,' he said with conviction. She laughed at that.

He found her a brown overall much like his own and helped her to tie it on. 'You don't want to spoil them,' he said, looking at her best pair of black ankle-strap shoes. She didn't want to hurt his feelings by telling him that she'd been looking forward to working in a smarter place than this, so she took the stout pair of blue clogs he gave her and, though they weighed like a ton on her small feet, nodded eagerly when he asked whether they were all right. Surprisingly enough, they were extremely comfortable. 'Right then,' he said, taking stock of her in her brown overall and spanking new clogs. 'The first job of a morning is to show the world what we've got to sell.' Reaching up to the beams, he unhooked a string of boots which he gave to Phoebe, then another which he gently put around her neck, then a third and a fourth string, this time of brightly coloured wooden clogs which he strung across his own shoulders. 'Remember always to put out the clogs and boots . . . never the shoes. Boots and clogs are for ordinary folk. Shoes are for gentlemen,' he explained as she followed him outside and watched him hang the articles across his shop window.

'But why can't we put the shoes out?' she asked, taking the loads from round her neck and handing them up to him.

'Because gentlemen don't often find their way down Lord Street, and because I only ever make such shoes to order.' He looked at her quizzically. 'Didn't your uncle tell you that I supply him? That I'm contracted to sell my gentlemen's shoes to him and to no one else?'

Phoebe shook her head. 'He didn't even tell me where I was coming to work,' she said, frowning.

He nodded. 'Ah, well, I suppose it's not for me to question the likes of your uncle,' he said, shrugging his shoulders. 'No doubt he has his reasons.'

'I expect he's told you all about me?' Phoebe wondered how much more secretive her uncle had been. 'I expect you know I'm an orphan . . . that I was sent here because my mother wanted it?' She cast her eyes down. 'I don't think he really wants me at Dickens House.'

In no time at all the footwear was hung, making a splendid show which was designed to attract would-be customers to part with their hard-earned brass. Satisfied, Marcus went back into the shop and Phoebe followed. He turned then to tell her, 'There's no need for me to know your business.'

He didn't reveal what Edward Dickens had told him: 'Phoebe Mulligan is wild and wilful, unladylike I'm afraid. My sister has left her in my charge and it's my duty to place her in work of a kind that will tax her energies and banish any thoughts she might have of being a "lady" in a gentleman's house. I don't want any special favours shown her. On the contrary, I expect you to work her until she's bone tired. I demand that she earn every penny of her wages which of course I shall deduct from our weekly business transactions. Now then, Mr Quinn, bearing in mind that I pay you a great deal of money for the shoes I purchase here, and notwithstanding that you had no previous plans to take on an assistant, does this little arrangement between ourselves cause you any problems?'

Like Phoebe, Marcus was left with no choice. Edward Dickens was a very influential man, and though he could purchase no finer shoes for his establishment than from Marcus Quinn's cobbling shop it would not have been wise to go against his wishes. Besides, there was the other reason. One which was closer to Marcus's heart. One which he could never reveal to either Phoebe or her uncle.

And so the arrangement was made, wages were agreed,

and Phoebe was delivered here on this Monday morning, unaware that her new employer had his own misgivings. Now, though, knowing that she was Jessica's girl, and having seen and spoken with her, Marcus realised that Phoebe was a blessing in disguise. Certainly his days would be much brighter for her delightful presence. As for Phoebe being 'unladylike', Marcus thought her uncle must be blind!

'Phoebe Mulligan, y'say?' The toothless old woman shivered and wrapped the threadbare shawl tighter about her. 'It's cold in 'ere! Allus bloody cold in this 'ere shop.' She was a sorry-looking creature with grey dishevelled hair and the hem of her skirt dragging along the floor. She waited for Phoebe to confirm that yes, she *was* Phoebe Mulligan, then in a suspicious tone said, 'Aye, that's what the cobbler told us last week . . . new assistant by the name o' Phoebe Mulligan, that's what 'e said.'

Screwing her face into a multitude of wrinkles and regarding Phoebe with beady bloodshot eyes, she went on, 'Yer belong to that fella as keeps the posh shop on the corner, don't yer?' She leaned her elbows on the counter and set her old mouth in a grimace. 'Dickens, ain't it? Edward Dickens . . . Gents' outfitters, would yer believe?' She laughed aloud. 'Yer can call it whatever yer likes, m'dear, but it's still a shop. That's all it is . . . just a shop.' She held out a gnarled hand, opening it to reveal a small green ticket. 'Me boots 'ad better be ready,' she warned. 'The buggers have been here long enough!'

Phoebe plucked the ticket from the old woman's palm and carefully scrutinised it. 'It's my uncle who owns the shop on the corner,' she said with a chuckle, 'though I don't know as he'd like it being called that.' All the same, the old woman was right, she thought, a shop was still a shop when all was said and done. She turned away, holding the ticket in one hand and running the other along the top shelf. This shelf was stacked with brown paper bags heaped one on top of the other, all tied with string and all having different coloured tickets attached. After matching first the colour and then the numbers on the tickets, Phoebe drew the parcel down. 'There you are, luv,' she said with a bright cheery smile. 'That'll be sixpence.'

'Sixpence!' The old woman thumped her fist on the counter. 'That's daylight bloody robbery!' she exclaimed, snatching the brown paper parcel and thrusting it into her hessian bag. 'I shan't pay and that's that,' she cried, turning to hurry away.

'Now, now, Mavis, we don't want none of your tantrums.' Marcus had watched the transaction from the doorway of his workshop. He came forward at a smart pace to put his arm round the old one's shoulders, drawing her to a halt. 'Shame on you,' he said kindly. 'Trying your old tricks on my new assistant . . . thought you wouldn't be tumbled this time, did you? Thought Marcus was safely out of the way, did you, eh?' he asked. His voice had taken on a serious note, but there was a twinkle in his eye. 'You old rascal!'

At this the old woman chuckled and swung her bag into his groin, 'Marcus Quinn,' she said with a loud tut, 'I'm buggered if yer ain't got eyes up yer arse!'

'Language, Mavis. Not in front of this young lady,' he chided, glancing at Phoebe who was enjoying every minute.

'Oh! "Lady" is it?' The old woman came back to the counter to examine Phoebe anew. She roved her eyes from the ribboned hair to the proud handsome features, and the warm, nutmeg-brown eyes that returned her stare accusingly. 'Yer don't look like him. That fella Dickens . . . he's yer uncle, y'say?' Phoebe nodded. 'Hmmm.' The old woman looked at Marcus and back again at Phoebe. 'That one's a tight-fisted old sod!' she muttered. 'An' he's a miserable old bugger . . . ain't got the time o' day for folks such as meself.' Still muttering, she dug deep into the hessian bag. 'An' you're as bad, Marcus yer old bugger,' she told him, 'I'll pay yer bloody sixpence . . . though it won't leave me with a penny left to see me through the day,' she complained in a sulky voice.

'I'm sorry about that, Mavis. But we all have a living to make,' he told her firmly. When he saw Phoebe was visibly surprised at his remark, he put a finger to his lips in a warning.

'Bloody capitalists. Yer all the same . . . see an old woman starve, yer would,' came the sharp rebuke. Still muttering, she took out her purse and opened it. Marcus had seen it all before but Phoebe's eyes popped at the sight. The purse bulged with half-crowns, shillings, and even a guinea or two. She tipped the lot on to the counter. Phoebe had never seen so much money all at one time. 'I ain't got no sixpences,' the old woman grumbled, 'so you'll 'ave to wait 'til I come in next time.' She crammed the coins back into the purse and dropped the purse into her bag.

'All right,' Marcus agreed. 'But we'll keep the boots here until then.' He dipped his hand into the bag with the intention of retrieving the brown paper parcel.

'Yer bloody won't!' Snatching the bag away, she put it on the floor between her legs and covered it with her long skirt. Then she reached into her shawl. There was a clinking of coins and a few choice words before she produced a shiny sixpence which she slapped on to the counter, at the same time telling Phoebe, 'An old woman ain't safe nowhere these days . . . robbed at every turn. It's *you* that should be ashamed, yer buggers, not me!' With that she picked up her bag and went at a smart pace out of the shop, leaving Marcus chuckling and Phoebe wondrously bemused by what she'd just witnessed.

'I thought she was a penniless old tramp.' Phoebe hurried to the door to watch the old woman go down the street.

'That's what she wants you to think,' he said. 'Old Mavis is a rogue . . . a loveable old rogue, but a rogue all the same.'

'But she shouldn't be carrying all that money around with her.' Phoebe was well aware there were worse rogues than Mavis stalking the streets.

'She knows that. And Lord knows folks have warned her often enough. But she's a law unto herself is old Mavis.' He laughed out loud. 'I'll tell you what, though. I wouldn't like to be the fellow that makes a lunge at her . . . he'd be in for a surprise and no mistake.' He nodded towards the door. 'She's been around a long time . . . knows how to take care of herself.' He glanced up at the big round-faced clock that hung above the door. 'Time we had a tea-break.'

Phoebe had been enjoying herself so much that she hadn't realised how quickly the time had flown. The shop had been busy since opening and she hadn't even been able to watch Marcus at work. 'Does it quieten down a bit now?' she asked, making her way across the room to the workshop.

'For a while,' he said. 'It'll be a steady stream from now until noon, then there's another rush when folks pop in during their lunch-break. Afternoons is brisk enough,' he warned, 'but you can cope right enough, lass.' He smiled at her. 'You're a grand little worker and no mistake.'

'And you're a grand employer,' she teased. 'So I'll get off and make you that mug of tea.' She went at a skip into the back-room, and from there up the stairs to the scullery.

In a surprisingly short time she returned to the shop with a neatly set out tray containing a teapot, milk and sugar bowl with a spoon and two earthenware mugs. She was surprised to see the front door shut and the 'Closed' sign hanging there. Marcus returned just as she was pouring out the tea. 'Happy Birthday,' he cried. Placing a white cardboard box on the counter, he flung open the top to display two rather large cream cakes covered in chocolate and oozing strawberry jam. 'Well, you surely didn't think I was going to let your birthday go unnoticed, did you?' he asked with a grin.

'You *are* a rascal . . . just like old Mavis said,' Phoebe

laughed. There was a lump in her throat and the tears were not too far away. 'Oh, Mr Quinn . . . *Marcus*!' she corrected when he wagged a finger at her. 'What a lovely thing to do.'

'You like cream cakes, don't you?'

'Love 'em.'

'Right then. So I'll go and get us a plate each and we'll tuck in before Mavis comes back and snatches them from under our noses.'

And that was exactly what they did. Phoebe sat on the stool behind the counter and Marcus sat opposite, on a chair brought from upstairs. The 'Closed' sign remained on the door until every last crumb of cake was gone and the mugs were drained dry. Afterwards, Phoebe insisted on washing up and he went back to his work-bench, in between bobbing up and down to serve the odd customer. The shop was suddenly busy just before closing with folks collecting repairs or purchasing clogs for work. The hands of the clock went round and all too soon it was time for Phoebe to get herself tidied up ready for home.

'Do you think you'll like working here with me?' Marcus seemed anxious. He watched her take off the brown overall, pat her dress neatly about her and run a comb through her magnificent auburn hair before securing it into the nape of her neck again. As he looked on her, waiting for her answer, he smiled. But it was a sad little smile. She had brought a new presence into this dreary little shop, a brightness that lit even the darkest corner. And only now did he realise how lonely his life had been. He would have liked a daughter, a daughter like Phoebe. As he gazed on her, a great sorrow filled his heart and he was forced to look away.

'Shall I tell you the truth?' she asked, going to the window and sitting on the seat there, her eyes turned towards the evening sky and her view marred by the rows of clogs and boots that made her skyline. When he didn't answer straightaway, she looked round. He was hunched on the stool, his gaze cast to the floor and a faraway gleam in his eyes. Suddenly he looked up. 'Mr . . . *Marcus* . . . shall I tell you how I felt when I first saw this little shop?' she persisted.

'Go on then,' he urged.

'I was disappointed at first,' she confessed. 'I really believed that my uncle was going to train me up in his big posh store. I honestly thought I was going to be meeting all the gentry who come from far and wide to buy at Dickens' Gentlemen's Outfitters.' She laughed, and he was made to laugh with her when she said, 'Old Mavis was right . . . it *is* just a shop. And what's more, I don't reckon I'd be any happier there than I've been here today.' She came to the counter and leaned her elbows on it. Resting her head in her hands, she told him in a softer voice, 'Of course I'm going to enjoy working here. You've taught me a great deal, Marcus. How to keep the ledger and customer accounts, what makes a good sale, and how to deal with irate folk when they've been given two odd boots.' They laughed at that, remembering how the railway porter came rushing back into the shop complaining that he'd been given one black boot which was his, and a cream lace-up ankle boot which: 'If the bloody missus clapped eyes on it, it would spark her into thinking I've a bit on the side!'

'You didn't need no training,' Marcus told her now, ''cause you're a natural learner. Tomorrow I'll show you how to take stock, and how to sort good leather from bad.'

'And can I watch you work?'

He looked at her long and hard. 'Better than that,' he promised. 'You can tap the brasses round the clog rim.' Shaking his head at her obvious enthusiasm, he said, 'I never would have believed that a lass could take such an interest in how a pair o' boots go together.'

'Ah! It isn't just that though, is it?' she pointed out. 'It's the whole *business* . . . buying the leather, selling the merchandise, book-keeping, and getting the satisfaction from watching your trade grow.' She leaned forward, turning his heart over when her smile led him back over the years. 'Does that answer your question?'

Recovering himself, he chuckled. 'I reckon I'd better watch out, Phoebe Mulligan, or you'll be making off with all my secrets and setting up in business against me.'

At that she imitated old Mavis, cocking her head to one side and saying in a screeching voice: 'Shame on yer, Marcus Quinn, that's what I say . . . shame on yer!' They were still laughing when the door was flung open and the formidable figure of Edward Dickens straddled the threshold.

At once the atmosphere changed and an ominous silence descended. He stared at the pair of them, his eyes hard and curious, his expression at first puzzled then angry as he glared at Phoebe. Without a word, he put out his arm and jerked his thumb towards the black car parked outside in the road. Quickly gathering her bag from the counter, she whispered an urgent 'Cheerio' to Marcus, then brushed past her uncle going straight to the car and climbing inside, her eyes turning back towards the shop.

The door was still open and her uncle remained there, a large solid shape, still as a statue, staring inside. Leaning forward, Phoebe could see Marcus. The two men simply stared at each other; not a word was exchanged. A moment later her uncle returned to the car, stony silent, his chin thrust out in defiant fashion as they went at a slow bumping pace down the cobbled road and into Ainsworth Street.

'We had this strange old woman in the shop today,' Phoebe said in an attempt to explain their laughter. 'I was mimicking her when you came in just now.' An awkward silence fell between them and she was afraid that Marcus Quinn would be held to blame. 'I weren't doing no harm. It was the end of the day and I've worked hard since the minute you dropped me off this morning.' She sighed. 'I know I shouldn't have been larking about, but . . . it weren't Mr Quinn's fault.'

Her uncle turned to her then, a swift sideways glance that warned her she'd said more than enough. 'Whether I like it or not you are a member of my household,' he said in a low cutting voice, 'and as such, I expect you to conduct yourself with suitable dignity at all times. Do I make myself clear?'

Phoebe reluctantly nodded. She hoped he didn't intend to assign her to some other employer. 'It really wasn't Mr Quinn's fault,' she said sincerely. 'And it won't happen again, I promise.' When he gave no answer she folded her arms and slid deeper into the seat, resigning herself to the fact that he was already making other plans for her. It seemed that nothing good ever lasted; at least not in her experience.

* * *

Marcus locked the door and pulled down the shutter. The streets was always busy at this time of day, the men were home from work and the children spilled out in numbers to play until the last vestige of daylight. As he made his way to the back of the shop where he satisfied himself that all was secure, Marcus was occupied with thoughts of Phoebe's uncle. He'd fully expected to be torn off a strip or two after being caught laughing together with Phoebe. Instead her uncle had stood in the doorway just staring at him with those hard glittering eyes, accusing yet not accusing, and for those few moments when he might have said all that was obviously on his mind, said nothing at all. Then he had angrily slewed round to depart the premises, slamming the shop door behind him.

'You're a strange fellow and no mistake, Edward Dickens,' Marcus muttered as he climbed the stairs to his sitting-room. 'But for all your stony silence you managed to get your message across. It's forbidden to get on familiar terms with any member of the Dickens family, however humble she might be or however unwelcome in your splendid household. Oh, and above all there must be no laughter! Oh, dear me no. Only hard work and small reward. I know what you were saying, even though you didn't actually *say* it.'

As he came into his bedroom and passed the dressing mirror, he looked into it with a smile, saying with a laugh and a pull of his forelock, 'Oh, yes, I got the message, Mr Dickens . . . *sir*.' In a moment though, his mood was more sober. Like Phoebe he wondered whether she would be allowed to carry on working in his shop. He hoped so. He certainly hoped so.

Seating himself, he stared into the mirror at his own image, at the thin features, the quiet green eyes and neatly combed brown hair that was already showing signs of greying. 'It's too late for you, Marcus,' he whispered. 'You missed your chance, and now you're too old . . . still too much in love with *her*.' Opening the top drawer he took out a framed photograph, which he had deliberately hidden when he knew that Phoebe was coming to work here.

For a long moment he gazed fondly at the picture there of an attractive young woman of Phoebe's age with sparkling eyes and the same auburn hair. 'Oh, Jessica,' he moaned, shaking his head from side to side as though to shut out the memories that still haunted him. He smiled sadly. 'Your daughter was here today, did you know that? Your daughter, Phoebe. She was *here*, in my shop. We worked together and we laughed together.' A long painful sigh came from deep inside him. 'Oh, Jessica. To think she could have been *ours* . . . yours and mine.' Tenderly he stroked her face, remembering and loving her still. 'You shouldn't have deserted me,' he murmured. 'We needed each other, you and I.' His voice grew harsh. 'But he wouldn't let you love *anyone*, would he? Your brother Edward doesn't approve of love . . . or laughter.' He groaned aloud. 'Oh, Jessica! Jessica! *Why didn't you let me tell him?*'

He remembered that certain summer some eighteen years ago when he had pleaded with Jessica to let him go to her brother and tell him how they wanted to marry. They were both so very young, and so much in love. He was blind, but not Jessica. She knew all along that it could never be. Looking back now, he realised how impossible it all was. He a humble cobbler's apprentice, and she the sister of an up and coming business man, a someone who was already making his mark in this town and beyond. Jessica lived in fear of her brother. She broke off her relationship with Marcus, pleading with him not to contact her or even to let it be known that they had been seeing each other. He gave her that promise and he had kept it ever since. Soon after that she had gone from Blackburn and he had never heard of her again – until a few weeks ago, when news of her death had reached his ears. In that moment his heart had died inside him. There had been no other woman in his life since the lovely, gentle Jessica. There could be no other love for him, no real purpose in his dreary existence.

But then, Phoebe had entered his life, bringing sunshine and laughter with her. Phoebe, blessed with the same warm quality he'd adored in her mother. 'She's done you proud, Jessica,' he told the photograph. 'She's a delightful creature, full of life and possessed of your special beauty, though not quiet and shy like you,' he said in a bemused tone. 'She has such vitality. A certain spark that won't so easily be put out.' His expression hardened. 'But he's determined . . . your brother, wielding his authority, ruling her with the same iron hand.' As he put the photograph away, he chuckled. 'Somehow, though. I've got a feeling he won't find it so easy. Not *this* time!'

The fire had really taken hold. Raking together the few

remaining leaves and bracken, Noreen tossed them into the incinerator and watched the curling black smoke as it writhed upwards through the trees. The only peace she found was out here, in this garden which she cared for with tenderness. When her daughter's voice called out to inform her: 'You'd better come inside. Father's home,' she threw the rake down and went with slow reluctant steps across the lawn towards the house. There was no joy in her heart at her husband's return, only indifference and a latent feeling of dread.

'She's in trouble,' Margaret greeted her at the door, her face wreathed in a smile as she moved aside to let her mother pass.

'What do you mean? *Who's* in trouble?' Noreen paused on the step, looking up at her daughter's delighted face, and even before the answer came, she realised.

'*Her!*' came the retort. 'Who do you think?'

'You mean Phoebe?' Noreen brushed by, quickening her steps as she did so. Even the feel of her daughter's arm against hers made her flesh creep. She was so much like her father.

Margaret gave no answer. The moment her mother was out of sight, she ran down the steps and across the lawn towards the spot where Noreen had been gathering the leaves. The fire was still crackling, intermittent flames leaping out of the smouldering debris. She glanced back at the house then, satisfied that she was not being watched, slipped her long manicured fingers into her skirt pocket. Slyly, she withdrew the large square envelope. It was addressed in bold capitals:

Phoebe Mulligan,
c/o Dickens House,
Preston New Road,
BLACKBURN,
Lancs.

Unable to resist just one more look, she opened the envelope and surreptitiously slid out the card. Keeping both it and the envelope close to her body, she looked down with a sly expression, at the same time reading in a whisper:

Happy Birthday, Phoebe. I'm sorry I didn't write back straightaway, but I was taken with a bad bout of 'flu and kept to me bed. I'm on the mend now, though, so don't worry. Me and Judd are glad you've found some new friends. It seems that you're settling in all right, bless your heart. It's a shame that your cousin isn't so friendly, but never mind, eh? If I know you, you won't let it bother you too much.
    Don't forget to keep in touch, bless your heart.

Lots of love,
Dora and Judd

With a quick angry movement, she crumpled the card and threw it on to the fire, then the same with the envelope. She watched them blacken and curl; she watched the dark circles spread over the paper until each article was engulfed. Then, laughing, she ran back to the house.

As she passed her father's study, her enjoyment intensified when she heard him addressing Phoebe in forbidding tones. He was warning her that any further flippant behaviour of the kind he had witnessed earlier would result in severe punishment. 'Take this as the final warning, and be mindful that I shall be watching you very closely from now on.' He then informed her that she had, 'forfeited any part of your wages for this week'. With that he dismissed her: 'Go and wash up for dinner, and think yourself fortunate that I don't confine you to your room on this occasion.'

Phoebe stood before him, her hands demurely joined and her eyes cast downwards. She had made the mistake of trying to defend herself at first, and it only served to make matters worse. Now she thought it best to let him believe how she was immensely sorry for the events of the day.

Adopting a humble countenance appeared to have been a wise decision because now his temper had suddenly improved, although she would not be allowed to leave until she had been well and truly reprimanded. So she remained in this contrite position, listening to his droning voice and thinking about her old friends Dora and Judd, and wondering why Dora hadn't replied to her letter. Still, not to worry, she told herself. Dora never was one for being quick off the mark. She'd give it another few days then she'd write again.

On leaving the study, Phoebe was confronted by her cousin who had been waiting at the foot of the stairs. 'You'll never learn, will you?' she told Phoebe. 'When are you going to realise that you're not wanted in this house? That you're only here on sufferance?' With one hand on the banister and the other toying with her yellow hair, she taunted, 'Doesn't it bother you that you're a burden? That you're common and poor? Don't you realise you're a disgrace to this family?'

There was a strange excitement in her face as she waited for Phoebe's answer. When it came, it wiped Margaret's smile away. Phoebe told her in a calm dignified voice, 'I'm beginning to realise a great many things, and there ain't a single thing I can do about any of them – for now at least. But I'll tell you this . . . every time you open your mouth I know it isn't *me* that's "common" or a "disgrace". It's *you*.'

She stepped forward, saying in a mock refined tone that sounded remarkably like her cousin's, 'Now, if you'll allow me to pass, my dear, I really must make myself presentable for dinner.' With a confidence that belied her churning stomach she went on up the stairs and into her room where she leaned against the closed door with her brown eyes raised to heaven. 'Watch yourself, Phoebe gal,' she murmured softly, "cause you've made a bad enemy in that one. And now she's got her knife out for you.'

Chapter Six

The month of June had passed all too quickly. July had proved to be even more glorious, but now that too was almost at an end. All day the sun had beaten down, scorching the earth and curling the blossom, without even the slightest breeze to give relief. Now, in the late hours of a hot sultry evening, the lake lay flat and smooth like a sheet of dark glass with the moon's reflection seeming like a child's ball balanced on the surface. Somewhere a dog barked, and then the silence settled once more, eerie and clinging. The farmhouse was in darkness. All was quiet. The only light to be seen for miles around was the light emanating from Noreen Dickens' bedroom. Through the window the shadow moved, *his* shadow, and she crouched in the bed, not daring to move, hardly daring to breathe. The closer he came, the more her heart beat with terror. *He* had done that to her; slowly and deliberately over the years, *he* had pressed her spirit down until now there was no fight left in her, no ambition, no will to change this empty thing she had become.

'Don't be coy, my dear, you know how that infuriates me.' Edward Dickens stripped away the last of his undergarments and laid them, meticulously folded, across the back of a chair.

As he moved stealthily towards the bed, he caught sight of his naked form in the wardrobe mirror. 'After all,' he murmured sweetly, pausing to admire the well-built figure and slightly rounded stomach, 'you must agree that your husband is a fine figure of a man.' He turned full frontal to the wardrobe, breathing in and swelling his chest so that he seemed to fill every inch of the mirror. He thought himself to be a handsome fellow; his thick hair that had once been black as night was now marbled with streaks of grey, but he thought the greyness lent a certain elegance to his bearing; the neat beard shaped his chin perfectly, following the contours with trimmed precision. He was not unaware that his strong features still commanded the odd admiring glance. He was immensely proud of himself, deliciously mindful of the corpulent and erect member that signified his manhood. His every nerve ending was at screaming pitch and, like a spoiled child, he longed to be cosseted, to be loved until he ached, to be wantonly used then thrown away, to be teased and tormented until his soul was in agony.

When his passions were roused like that, he was filled with a destructive and all consuming glory; possessed of a desperate urgency to satisfy that passion. For months it would lie dormant, but then, some small inexplicable thing might awaken it; the turn of a woman's pretty ankle, an intimate smile that was not meant for him, a stranger's glance, or the conclusion of a difficult business deal. Whatever the reason, when the passion came on him, there was no peace until it was quenched. Often, that same passion gave him the insatiable madness of a beast, but it was only momentary. Sadly, it was over all too soon, but until then he delighted in himself, savouring the promised enjoyment and his own prowess. 'Yes, you're very fortunate,' he told his wife in a soft soothing voice. 'Few women have so handsome a husband.' A moment longer his piercing grey eyes appraised the image, then he proceeded towards the bed, his footsteps padding menacingly on the carpet.

When he slid in beside her, she trembled violently, biting her lip until the blood spurted into her mouth. She made no move, but lay there, impassive, knowing that he would take her on this night, just as he had taken her on other nights, viciously, selfishly, without love or feeling. In that moment when he turned her over, she stretched out her arms, gripping the bed on either side, her unflinching gaze meeting his magnificent glittering eyes. She prepared herself to be brave. Oh, yes, she could be brave without him knowing it. If he knew, he would only punish her all the more. His eyes crinkled into a devilish smile, mirroring her own reflection, pale and distorted in those grey shimmering depths. 'You won't disappoint me, will you, my dear?' he murmured. She remained silently staring, willing her spirit to flee from that place and dreading the moment when he would lay his flesh upon hers. He sensed her reluctance. It excited him beyond endurance.

Gently, he laid her out before him, ravaging her quiet dignity and loathing her because of it; he caressed the small well-shaped breasts and the dark round nipples, and as always he was pleasantly surprised at their firmness. With supreme tenderness he opened her thighs and pressed himself down into her, crying out with each invasive thrust, probing her mouth with his tongue, biting, tasting her fear, wanting to devour her. Still she remained silent, unyielding. He felt an insane desire to hurt her. He wanted so much for her to take part in his enjoyment. He tried to love her, to feel some kind of affection for her, but he could not. It infuriated him that he could never reach her. He could not accept that she was superior to him. His loathing heightened. He would teach her . . . punish her. *He must!* Her quiet sobs penetrated his thoughts. Smiling, he looked down at her face. She was turning away. 'No, no, my dear,' he whispered. 'Look at me. You must look at me,' With rough grasping fingers, he turned her face towards his; her tears spilled over his hand, damp on the sheet. He fell on her then, wrapping his arms tight about her, drawing her into him, exploring her very soul. There was no love between them. Only her pain, and his fear, and a sinister dark hatred.

The attic was unbearably hot. Phoebe had slept fitfully, but now something awakened her so that she sat bolt upright in her bed. Someone, or something, had cried out. Disturbed and curious, she climbed out of bed and went to the open window, where she leaned out and listened intently. But no, she could hear nothing now. 'Some poor creature caught in one of them awful traps,' she said with disgust. Tomorrow she would have a word with Lou about it. After all, he must have his suspicions about the fiend who was setting them.

She stayed by the window a while longer, gazing out across the night sky and thinking how magnificent it all was. She had been here just over a month now, and still she didn't feel as though she really belonged. She had come to love old Lou very much. He made her laugh, and was a good father to Aggie. She smiled then, thinking of the little girl. Phoebe's greatest joy had come from teaching Aggie how to read and write. Just one hour every evening and the child's progress had been remarkable; she was quick to learn, and now she was beginning to get excellent reports from school. Phoebe was very proud of her. As far as her job at the cobbler's shop was concerned, Phoebe was delighted when her uncle allowed her to remain there. 'But mind . . . I'll know if you abuse my trust,' he had warned with that teasing smile she had come to be wary of. But she had grown to love her work. Marcus had taught her so much. In the time they had known each other, she and Marcus had become steadfast friends. Now she could not envisage working with anyone else.

Tomorrow was Saturday, and she'd promised to take Aggie into Blackburn town. 'I shan't even be able to drag myself out of bed unless I get some sleep,' she muttered wearily, climbing back beneath the sheets. In a moment she had fallen into an uneasy slumber. She was restless in the stifling heat of the room, and her subconscious was still disturbed by the cries which had woken her earlier.

In the room beneath Phoebe's, the young woman lay in her bed, her blue eyes wide open and raised to the ceiling. Like Phoebe, she had been awoken by the cries. But *unlike* Phoebe, she was not tormented by thoughts of night creatures and snares. She had heard those same sounds before, often, and each time they had prevented her from sleeping; not because they touched her conscience or troubled her, but because they excited her in a way she could not explain.

Now, she lay awake, listening for the pitiful sounds to

come again, for she knew they would. The windows were open and the curtains flung back; the room was lit by moonlight, soft hazy fingers of light that traced the shadows and contours of her face. There was no sleep in her now. Swinging her legs out of the bed, she opened the drawer of her bedside cabinet. It took a moment of fumbling until her fine shapely fingers alighted on the silver cigarette case there. With trembling hands she placed a cigarette between her lips. Another moment to find the elegant lighter before quickly putting the flame to the end of the cigarette. Greedily inhaling, she blew out the smoke in a series of small puffs, timing each one carefully and watching them disperse in the light of the moon.

When the sobbing began again, she listened a while. Then she stubbed the cigarette out in the crystal ash-tray, swung herself back into bed and slithered deep beneath the sheets, only her face visible above the bedclothes. It was an attractive face whose features, in the garish light of the moon, bore an uncanny resemblance to those of her father. Especially when she smiled, as she did now. A sigh, a low secretive chuckle, and then she turned over to resume her contented slumber

In the morning, rain poured from the skies with a vengeance, billowing grey clouds hung low and pregnant, and the sun hid its face as though in shame. It was ten minutes to seven when Phoebe came into the dining-room. Daisy was there, having just brought a fresh pot of tea to the breakfast table. 'I heard you making your way down, Miss,' she said, her face unsmiling as she waited for Phoebe to seat herself. 'Now then . . . what takes yer fancy this morning?' she asked. 'Will it be eggs, bacon and tomatoes?' She cocked her head to one side, regarding Phoebe. 'Or d'you mean to be awkward and fancy some'at I haven't got?' She pattered across the room towards the door, standing there, hands on hips, looking decidedly impatient. 'I haven't got all day, Miss,' she grumbled.

'I'll just have toast and marmalade, if that's all right,' Phoebe said, 'I'm not very hungry.'

'Toast and marmalade!' Daisy tutted loudly. 'That's not much of a breakfast if you don't mind me saying so, Miss.' She came back to the table, face crestfallen and injured voice demanding, 'What's the matter with my eggs and bacon then? Fresh tomatoes too. Straight from the market on my way here this morning they were.' She let out a huge sigh. 'I don't know why I go to such trouble, I'm blessed if I don't!'

'Oh, Daisy, there's nothing at all wrong with your eggs and bacon,' Phoebe warmly reassured the dear soul, 'I'm just not hungry, that's all.' She felt tired and somehow troubled, although she wasn't quite sure why. She thought it might be the sound of that creature in the night. 'I didn't sleep well,' she added as though that might soothe the irate Daisy.

'Bad night, eh?' Daisy peered into Phoebe's face, noting the dark circles beneath her brown eyes and drawing a conclusion that gave her a deal of curious satisfaction. She'd seen the very same shadows under her own sister's eyes when she was with child; though her sister denied it to the very end. 'What caused that then, d'you reckon, Miss?' she said cunningly. 'Why was it that you couldn't sleep?'

'It was so hot, Daisy, and when I did finally get off to

sleep, I was woken by these cries . . . like an animal in pain. I mean to find out who's been setting them traps in the fields. Dreadful cruel things they are, Daisy. You know how little Aggie was caught in one, don't you?'

Daisy nodded. 'Aye, you've told me often enough, Miss,' she replied thoughtfully, her mind racing. 'Cries, y'say? What sort o' cries? Where d'you reckon they came from?' It wasn't the mention of traps that had caught her attention, and now she put other spiteful thoughts out of her mind. Suddenly she was even more interested in these noises that Phoebe spoke of. But even as she opened her mouth to pursue the conversation, she swiftly cautioned herself. It was dangerous to talk of such things. 'No!' she cried, just as Phoebe was about to elaborate. 'I can't waste my time here, Miss. I've work to do, and no time for talking nonsense with you, if you don't mind me saying.' There were certain things she didn't want to know, and there were things she *already* knew that she wished she didn't. She must have been staring at her master's niece in an odd way, because Phoebe asked in an anxious voice, 'Are you all right, Daisy?'

Squaring her shoulders, she hastily replied, 'Yes, yes, . . . of course I'm all right, Miss.' She hurried away. 'I'll get your toast and marmalade.'

'I can fetch it myself if you like.'

'You will not!' Daisy called over her shoulder. 'You know very well how the master feels about things like that. It's *my* job to put out the breakfast, and I'll thank you to remember it.'

All the same, Phoebe followed her into the kitchen. 'Am I the first one down?' she asked.

Daisy slammed the pot of marmalade on the dresser-top, squinting sideways at Phoebe in a disapproving manner. 'Wait at the table, Miss,' she insisted, 'I'll have your toast afront of you before you've finished your first cup of tea.' She glanced towards the door, fearful that Edward Dickens might suddenly appear. 'By rights you shouldn't be in my kitchen, Miss,' she told Phoebe in a disgruntled voice. 'And you're not helping me. Remember that, Miss . . . if anybody wants to know, you tell 'em, you're *not* helping poor Daisy!'

'All I want to know is whether I'm the first one down,' Phoebe said affectionately, 'I wouldn't dream of "helping" you against your will.'

'Go back to the table and I'll talk to you when I fetch your toast and marmalade.'

'Honestly, Daisy!' Phoebe shook her head in disbelief as she went out of the kitchen to resume her place at the table. Daisy was a peculiar soul and no mistake, she thought with some amusement.

Phoebe was on her third cup of tea when Daisy came bustling into the room with a generous helping of toast and a dish of marmalade dressed with a tiny silver spoon. 'There y'are, Miss,' she said, beaming from ear to ear and placing the articles before Phoebe. 'Now then . . . the master's been up and gone since five-thirty this morning.' She gave Phoebe an odd look. 'Come to think of it, Miss, aren't *you* required at the cobbler's shop this morning? I would have thought it were one of Mr Quinn's busiest days.' She knew the fellow well. 'He's a nice bloke is that Mr Quinn,' she said now with a smile wrinkling her face. 'A real gentleman if ever there was one.'

'He is,' Phoebe agreed wholeheartedly, 'and I'm not required this morning, Daisy, because the shop is closed on account of the plumbing which decided to erupt yesterday afternoon. The whole place was in Bedlam, and the fellow who came out said it would take a full day's work to put right the damage. According to Marcus it's going to cost a pretty penny.'

'Heavens above, whatever next!' Daisy was delighted. So! It was 'Marcus' now, was it? And, unless she was very much mistaken, Phoebe's lovely brown eyes had an extra sparkle in them when she mentioned the fellow's name. Well, would you credit it, eh? They did say as how some folk were attracted to the oddest types. Surely, though, *this* young woman couldn't have an eye to Marcus Quinn? Oh, he was a splendid enough fellow she couldn't deny that, but well . . . Phoebe was such a beautiful little thing. Likely she could have any young man she set her cap at. Oh, but then it wouldn't do to forget how she had come to this house destitute, and it was as plain as the nose on your face that nobody really wanted her here, not even the mistress. Wait, though! Happen the master's niece wasn't so innocent as a body might think. After all, Marcus Quinn was a good catch when all was said and done. What did it matter if he were old enough to be her father? What! Latch herself on to him and she'd be comfortable for the rest of her days, that she would.

Daisy was so taken with having 'discovered' a secret, that she found herself breaking into a little song. Now then, *here* was a snippet of gossip that could only benefit her reputation. There was nothing better than a good helping of scandal to liven up a body's existence. By!

There were plenty of folk down her street that would give their eye teeth to be working in this house, because wasn't there enough gossip here to keep them all going till Christmas? All the same, it was a great pity that she couldn't talk about certain things. She wasn't so daft that she'd risk her livelihood for the chance of a good gossip. But, oh, Phoebe Mulligan and Marcus Quinn. Now *there* was something a body could get her teeth into. Come to think of it, wasn't there a rumour once before, regarding the very same fellow and *Phoebe's own mother*? True, it were a long time back and a lot of water had flowed under the bridge since then. But she recalled something . . . a whisper here and there? Oh well, happen not.

'And what about my aunt?' Phoebe asked patiently, secretly amused at how Daisy's attention seemed to wander in the middle of a conversation.

Daisy was brought back with a bump. 'Oh!' she cried, going bright red in the face when she realised that Phoebe had been watching her. It was a good job she couldn't read her mind, Daisy thought with alarm. 'The mistress is already fed and now she's out in the potting-shed,' she said, rolling her eyes to heaven and forcing a chuckle. 'Her and that blessed garden, Miss. I understand that when she first came to this house the gardens were a bit of a mess. It took her a while, but she got 'em round and, well . . . you can see for yourself what a grand job she's done.' Her manner was altogether more pleasant now. 'As for Miss Margaret . . .' She pulled a face of silent disapproval. 'There's been no sign of her at all. Having a lay-in, I expect,' she added, thinking how that posh madam had done nothing to deserve a lay-in. If anybody deserved such a luxury, it was *she*! Up at the crack of dawn, rushing her life away, and all for the price of survival. 'D'you want any more tea, Miss?' she asked grudgingly. 'I know how you likes your tea of a morning.'

Phoebe shook her head. 'No thank you, Daisy,' she said gratefully. In fact, she could have managed a fresh brew of tea but she didn't want to send the poor woman into another panic.

'Right then, Miss,' Daisy was obviously relieved. 'I'll get started on the washing-up. You eat that toast before it goes cold. *All* of it, mind,' she coaxed. If she had to say which member of this family was the easiest to get on with, it would have to be Phoebe. But then, she reminded herself, this young woman wasn't really a member of the family. More like a lodger, that's what she was, poor little bugger.

Once Daisy had gone from the room, Phoebe stared at the mound of toast, thick chunky slices, beautifully browned and so extravagantly buttered that it oozed over the crusty edges, dripping down the sides to form little yellow pools on the plate. She couldn't eat it! No amount of cajoling by Daisy would entice her to take even one bite. After all the palaver and fuss that Daisy had caused, Phoebe had gone right off the idea of toast and marmalade. But it was more than her life was worth to leave it now. Looking around the room, she spied the morning newspaper on the sideboard where her uncle had placed it. Quickly, before Daisy came back, she took the newspaper and wrapped the toast inside. No sooner was that done, than she heard Daisy coming along the hallway. Stuffing the newspaper up the back of her grey cardigan, she quickly got out of the chair, ready to make a hasty retreat.

In that moment, Daisy rushed into the room, her eyes popping open as she stared at the table, 'My word, Miss!' she exclaimed, 'Whatever have you done with all that toast?' Without waiting for an answer, she smiled broadly. 'There! I knew you'd enjoy it,' she said. 'My old fella's the very same . . . he can't resist a slice or two of Daisy's buttered toast.' She beamed on Phoebe. 'Fresh baked bread and new butter,' she declared proudly. 'It'll do you the world of good.' She was still beaming when Phoebe made a careful exit, not daring to turn away, but going out of the room backwards while Daisy set about clearing the table. 'Oh, you naughty thing' she cried. 'You've never even *touched* the marmalade . . . and after Daisy went to such trouble spooning it from the pot.' When she looked up, Phoebe was gone. It would be much later before she realised that the master's newspaper had gone too. Phoebe had squashed it into the bottom of the midden, buried beneath the day's rubbish.

Phoebe always kept her room spick and span so it didn't take long to tidy it now. The main task on this Saturday morning was changing the bed. She had found the freshly laundered linen in a neat pile outside her room, put there by either her aunt or by Daisy, she assumed. Before going down to breakfast she had brought it in and placed it on the chair. Quickly now, she set about stripping her bed and making it up again, turning the top sheet back so that it showed the crisp white pillowslip beneath; her mam always said that a newly-made bed should seem both clean and inviting, and that was exactly the way Phoebe's bed looked now. That done, she shook the mat out of the window and went quickly round the few items of furniture with a duster and polish, until the whole room smelled of lavender.

The only photograph Phoebe had of her mother was tattered and old; Jessica was never one for having her picture taken. In fact she had said: 'I've only ever had three pictures taken in my entire life – one when I was sixteen, one when I was married, and the other with you when you were an infant.' The wedding photograph had been a bad likeness of both Phoebe's parents; it was faded brown and badly cracked across both faces so that they were hardly recognisable. Reluctant to throw it away, Phoebe had it safely tucked away in the portmanteau beneath the bed. She had no idea where the first picture had gone because the one she had on her mantelpiece was of her and her mam together. She would always cherish it. There was her mam in a white dress, seated on the best parlour chair with her shining hair combed back and dressed with a lovely mother-of-pearl clip. On her lap sat the bonniest baby with big brown eyes filled with love laughing up at her mammy.

She had never seen the picture of her mam when she was only sixteen, and her mother would only say in a tone that made Phoebe think she had regretted mentioning it in the first place, 'Oh, it got mislaid, I expect. Forget about it, dear.' When she was packing up to leave the house, Phoebe had searched high and low for that other photograph, but it was never found.

Taking the framed picture down from the mantelpiece, Phoebe told the silent smiling face that was much like her own, 'Well, Mam . . . Marcus Quinn says I'm doing well at the cobbler's shop. I've managed to stay out of my uncle's bad books for two whole weeks, and that spoiled cousin of mine ain't caused me no bother lately.' She frowned, thinking hard and recounting certain incidents that told her Margaret was still out for her blood. 'She's a bad 'un though, Mam, so I'll have to watch her all the same. For all I know, she might be cooking trouble up right at this very minute. I wouldn't put it past her, that's for sure. Besides, they always say a rattlesnake makes more noise just before it sinks its poisonous fangs into you.' She came up in goose bumps at the very thought. 'Ooh, it don't bear thinking about!'

She laughed softly, saying, 'Don't you worry though, Mam, because I've got that one's measure and no mistake.' On impulse, she kissed her mother's image. 'I hope I'm doing you proud, Mam,' she murmured. 'I'm trying so hard.' She glanced round the room, holding out the photograph. 'See that . . . not a speck of dust to be seen. All my clothes washed and ironed, and I've even made little cotton coveralls to keep them in so the dust don't settle on the shoulders. I can't have a wardrobe because your brother says it costs good money which he's not prepared to spend on my account. And even if *I* could save enough to buy a second-hand one, there ain't nowhere up here to put it. I'm not likely to get another room, am I, eh? So there you are . . . we do the best with what we've got, ain't that what you always say, Mam?' Carefully replacing the photograph, she added with a wink, 'I'm off to see Aggie now, so mind you behave yourself.'

With that, Phoebe departed the room, making certain

the door was securely closed behind her. She had wondered about asking if she might have a new lock fitted. The old one had grown rusty long before she arrived and it had never been replaced. But there was no point in asking for a new one because she knew what her uncle's answer would be. There was a bolt on the inside, and there was no reason for her to believe that anyone would interfere with her few belongings. All the same, she hated leaving her room open to all and sundry. In this big unfriendly house, this little attic room was her only real sanctuary.

On a day such as this, when the heavens opened and threw down a deluge, Phoebe had only her dark jacket and long grey cardigan to protect her from the weather. Preserving the smart little jacket for best, she had opted to wear the long grey cardigan over her white blouse and brown skirt.

'You're never going out without a mackintosh on, Miss?' Daisy had been washing the breakfast things when Phoebe came into the kitchen. 'By! You'll get soaked to your skin!' she declared, wiping her hands on her apron and going to the back door. 'Here, put this on,' she said, plucking a coat from one of the old garments kept on the door-pegs for such a purpose. 'It might be a good idea if you waited for the rain to ease off a little, don't you think, Miss?' she asked without too much concern. Her job was to feed the family and to clean the house they lived in. That was where her duties ended, but Phoebe wasn't such a bad little thing and it would be a pity if she were to catch her death.

'Thank you, Daisy.' Phoebe took the coat and put it

round her shoulders. 'I'll try and dodge the raindrops,' she said with a chuckle, lifting the coat over her head and opening the door with the intention of launching herself at a run into the garden. The puddles had settled at regular intervals all along the path with drops of water dripping incessantly from the overhanging boughs; from where she stood Phoebe could see that the shed door was open, although there was no sign of her aunt. The rain was driving from the east and so there was no danger that it could find its way in through the open door. Besides, it wasn't cold; if anything it was humid and the rain was a welcome relief.

'Humph!' Daisy dug her arms into the soap-suds and rattled the crockery with a vengeance. 'Please yourself,' she said huffily. 'It's none of my business when all's said and done.'

'Thank you all the same,' Phoebe called as she surged out of the back door and along the path, skipping and swerving to avoid the puddles, crying out when a branch flicked across her shoulders and showered its watery burden all over her.

Noreen had been watching from the window. When she saw her niece approaching she opened the door wide, remarking with surprise as Phoebe came in at a run. 'Whatever possessed you to come out in this weather?'

'Same thing as possessed *you*, Aunt,' Phoebe replied with a friendly smile as she threw the coat off and shook herself like a dog, laughing when her aunt quickly stepped away.

'It wasn't raining quite so hard when I left the house,' replied Noreen. 'Anyway, what is it you want?' She returned to the old rocking-chair in the corner, gently pushing on the floor with her toes and making the chair dip back and forth in a slow methodical manner.

'I just wanted to talk to you, that's all.' These past weeks, Phoebe had tried desperately to make friends with her aunt but it was an uphill struggle. There was a seemingly insurmountable barrier between them, and it was a source of deep regret to Phoebe. She looked at her aunt's face now, a pinched grey face, devoid of light or happiness. On that occasion when she had been taken poorly, Noreen had stayed in her room for almost a week, refusing entry to anyone; even Daisy was made to leave the tray outside the door, when it would be taken in some moments later, reappearing some time after that with most of its contents gone. 'We never talk, do we, Aunt?' she said, hanging the damp coat on the door-nail and seating herself on an upturned wooden crate.

'What's there to talk about?' asked Noreen. She didn't look up. She was afraid that Phoebe might see the pain in her eyes.

Phoebe shrugged her shoulders. 'I don't know,' she said honestly; her aunt was a difficult person to converse with. 'Happen you could tell me whether you're pleased with me . . . or whether there's anything I do that annoys you? There's Aggie and her schooling. Or I could tell you about my job at the cobbler's shop . . . you've never asked, Aunt.' It was a great disappointment to Phoebe that her aunt had never shown the slightest interest. With a candour that startled Noreen, she asked, 'You knew my mam, didn't you? We could talk about her. I'd like that.'

'I don't need to know how you're getting on at work,

Phoebe. You'd be the first to know if your uncle was displeased with you . . . and I would be the second. Obviously you haven't got yourself into any trouble, and it would pay you to keep it that way.' Phoebe's reputation had gone before her, and even now there were times when her fiery temperament came to the fore; there was a degree of animosity between Phoebe and Margaret that had not gone unnoticed. By and large though, Phoebe seemed to have it all under control. Certainly, her cousin had not found it easy to get under Phoebe's skin; a point which had only served to further antagonise her.

'I haven't done anything to upset you, have I?' Phoebe insisted. There *was* something, she just knew.

'No, of course not, child.'

'Somebody has upset you though. Is it *him*? Has my uncle upset you?' She shocked herself by asking such a thing. She hadn't meant to. It just came out as though it had been simmering below the surface, waiting to break free. But why should she think such a thing? In all the time she had been in this house, she had never once seen bad blood between her aunt and uncle; no more so than with any other couple. So *why* had she said such a thing now? No wonder her aunt seemed so upset.

'My! You do have a vivid imagination,' came the sharp retort. 'Whatever do you mean? What on earth makes you think I'm troubled.' She gave a small laugh. 'The very idea!' Gripping the slender curved arms of the rocking-chair she dug her toes against the floorboards and pushed hard, sending the chair back and forth frenziedly, almost as though the very mention of her husband had let loose a devil inside her. 'What possessed you to say

217

such a thing?' she demanded, bringing the chair to an abrupt halt, her blue eyes surprisingly hard and hostile as they raked Phoebe's face.

'I'm sorry. I shouldn't have said that,' the girl admitted. 'It's just that, well . . .' She sighed aloud. 'I'm really sorry.' If she was to go on, she would only get herself in deeper and so she quickly changed tack, turning her head to gaze out of the window at the tree tops. 'Even in the rain the garden's so beautiful,' she murmured.

She had been surprised to learn that it was her aunt who kept the garden in such good condition. It showed a side to Noreen that bore out Lou Peters' opinion. 'She's a fine woman,' he'd declared once after supping a pint of the best. 'Wasted on him she is . . . wasted!' There had been bitterness in his voice, enough to make Phoebe wonder whether the irrepressible Lou had a secret yearning for her aunt, but he wouldn't be drawn further, only saying with a laugh, ''Tis a fact that the drink loosens a man's tongue and gets him hanged.' But he *had* said it, and Phoebe was curious now.

'Happen I can help you in the garden when the rain stops?' she asked. She felt herself being shut out as always when she tried to get close to this timid, private creature. For a moment then she was lost for words, casting her gaze around the shed and seeing it for what it was – a sanctuary. 'Do you want me to go?' she asked sadly.

Noreen looked up, searching Phoebe's face. There was a kind of terror in her pale blue eyes, and when she smiled, as she did now, it was almost as though she was apologising for what she was. Deep inside, there was another person, hiding, shrinking from the light. She didn't say anything then but slowly shook her head. She stared a moment longer before looking away. 'No,' she said in a whisper, 'you can stay if you want to.'

In that moment when her aunt had looked at her, Phoebe had seen what the other had tried so desperately to hide . . . fear, a deep weariness of life. 'Mr Peters says you've done wonders with the garden,' she said. Mention of the garden brought a light to her aunt's eyes that was a relief to see.

Noreen settled back in the rocking-chair, gently tipping it back and forth, nodding her head with every movement. 'Mr Peters is a nice man,' she said, relieved that the subject was changed. It had startled her when Phoebe made such a remark concerning Edward. There was enough shame in her cowardly heart without harbouring the fear that their ugly scenes might have been overheard. A chill trembled through her when she thought about the man who was her husband. *One of these days she might have to kill him!*

'I thought I might go into town later.' Phoebe had seen the woman's features harden and the strange look that had come into her eyes. It frightened her. 'Why don't you come with me?'

'No. You go along and enjoy yourself, child.' The blue eyes were smiling now, but the sadness was only veiled. 'Do you have any money?' She knew how mean her husband was.

Digging into her cardigan pocket, Phoebe drew out a clutch of silver coins. 'Four shillings,' she said, but there was a tinge of disappointment in her voice. After a month at Marcus Quinn's shop, she really thought her uncle would be more generous; especially as Marcus had given her a glowing report.

Noreen stared at the coins. She wasn't surprised. 'I suppose we all have to be grateful for small mercies,' she said cynically. 'Mr Quinn doesn't pay you direct then?'

'No. My wages are paid directly to my uncle each week. That was the way he wanted it when the arrangements were made, so Marcus told me.' The last thing Phoebe wanted was to cause trouble. 'I ain't all that bothered though,' she said honestly, 'because I don't really need much money. I'm fed and housed, and I've enough clothes to last me a while yet.' She laughed then. 'Although I'd be a liar if I didn't say I was disappointed. It would be nice to have a few extra shillings to save. It's always a good idea to plan for a rainy day, that's what my mam used to say.'

It was then, in one of her rare moments of affection, that Noreen reached out to take Phoebe's hand in her own. 'You're a lot like your mam,' she murmured. 'You miss her very much, don't you?'

Phoebe hung her head. 'I try not to. It don't do no good.' She lifted her head and there were tears in her eyes. 'But, yes . . . I do miss her. I miss her a lot.'

'Of course you do, child. It's only natural.'

'Have you seen that photograph of her? The one in my room?'

'Yes. She was a very attractive woman.'

'There's another photograph of her on her own, but I couldn't find it. Mam said it was lost years ago.'

'Things do get lost. I shouldn't worry. The one you have is delightful . . . mother and baby.' She smiled.

'Take care of it always,' she said. Yes, she had seen that photograph, and she had looked at it long and hard. In spite of everything Jessica had never starved her child of love, and the child's devotion was evident in her striking brown eyes. There had never been such love between herself and Margaret. Her daughter had always turned to Edward, and he to her. For some reason beyond her understanding, Noreen had always known that she was an outcast to them both.

'Of course I'll cherish it,' Phoebe said, then surprised the other woman by asking pointedly, 'You didn't ever see that other picture did you? The one of my mam on her own?'

'I hardly knew her. She wasn't likely to show me any pictures of herself.' Noreen's reply was not a lie, but it was tantamount to one for she *had* seen the picture which Phoebe referred to. What was more, she knew who had it now. The affair between Marcus Quinn and Phoebe's mother had been hushed up, for reasons best known to Edward. But, before Jessica went away, she confided certain things to Noreen; things that would have been better kept secret. It was then that she revealed her love for Marcus Quinn, saying, 'He has a photograph of me. I have nothing of him but memories. Pray for me, Noreen, pray that I'll be strong. Because for as long as I live, I must never again see or talk to him.'

'Oh, listen!' Phoebe sprang from the chair. 'It's stopped raining.' Going to the door, she stuck out her hand, catching the drips that ran down the roof and trickled over the doorway. 'Will you let me help you with the gardening?' she asked again. 'I would really love to.' Turning round to look at her aunt who had come up behind her, she added, 'We didn't have a garden where we lived. You stepped straight out of the front door on to the pavement, and there was only a small flagged yard at the back.'

'There's little we can do now . . . not while the ground is still wet,' Noreen stepped outside, lifting her face to the sky. 'Later,' she said, 'I'll find you something to do.'

'And you won't come into town with me?' Phoebe hoped she might have changed her mind.

'No. You get off now.' Turning away, Noreen went back inside the shed. This time she closed the door and bolted it from the inside. Even one visitor was too many in her secret place.

As Phoebe went away up the path, she forced herself to think of other matters. Her aunt was so obviously a private woman, one who would not change overnight and maybe never would. But then Phoebe asked herself a question that brought her up sharp. Who was *she* to decide whether her aunt's behaviour was such that it should change? And back came the answer: she had no right at all. What her aunt chose to do or not to do was her own affair. 'It ain't none of your business, Phoebe Mulligan!' she told herself in a firm voice. 'You're only a lodger in this house, and it would serve you well to remember your place.'

The clouds were lifting and the sun was already breaking through as Phoebe skirted the house and made her way across the road to the farm. Maybe Lou would allow her to take young Aggie into town. It would be grand, her and Aggie, browsing over all the posh shop windows and maybe taking a pot of tea and a cream cake in that delightful little café next to the marketplace. After that, she could take Aggie and show her the cobbler's shop where she worked with Marcus. The thought cheered her no end.

There was no answer at the front so Phoebe went round to the back of the farmhouse, tapping on the door there and pushing it open at the same time. Lou had told her never to knock, but to: 'Walk in at any time, me beauty. We don't want you standing on ceremony 'ere.' But Phoebe didn't feel right about just walking in so she always tapped the door first to let them know she was on her way. Usually Aggie's small voice would cry, 'It's Phoebe!' But on this occasion she was greeted with that particular silence that told her there was no one at home. 'Lou!' she called down the passageway. 'Aggie! Are you there?' Still no answer.

She went from the parlour to the kitchen, then to the foot of the stairs where she called again. Retracing her steps to the back door, she looked in the place where all the wellington boots were normally lined up. They were all gone. 'Out across the farm,' she murmured. 'Now, where would Aggie be?' She clapped her hands together as the answer came. 'Of course!' The girl didn't care for being left in the house when everyone else was out working on the farm. Since her leg had healed, she had taken to climbing right up to the top of the hay bales in the barn and there she would sit, reading her books and occasionally watching her father at work below. Then, when she had finished her reading, she'd climb back down again, take up a broom and sweep out the old barn, while her father praised her for the good girl she was.

It was only a few steps from the house to the main yard and from there to the barn. In no time at all Phoebe was swinging open the big old doors. There was no sign of Lou or anyone else come to that. 'Aggie, are you in there?' She ventured further into the darkened interior. The barn was huge. There were no windows, only two skylights high up where Aggie usually sat, and the incoming light from the great doorway. Phoebe loved the smell that pervaded the old barn, a dry musty odour that spoke of sweat and animals and new-mown hay. Tilting her head back and peering upwards, she called again, 'Aggie!'

'She's not here.' Greg Peters stepped out of the shadows.

'God almighty!' Phoebe was more angry than frightened. 'What the hell d'you think you're playing at . . . creeping up on a body like that?' Her throat had gone all dry and her heart was thumping as though it might leap straight out of her chest.

His expression was one of complete surprise. 'Oh, I'm sorry. I didn't mean to frighten you,' he lied with a devastating smile.

'Well, you *did*!' she retorted. Somehow, whenever she and Greg met, it always ended up in a sparring match. Over these past weeks, though, he seemed to be going out of his way to be pleasant. But that only made her all the more suspicious.

'Like I say, Phoebe . . . I didn't mean to frighten you.' He leaned against a post. 'You've done wonders with Aggie,' he said, his gaze fixed on her face. 'I've watched you . . . seen how she responds to you. You shouldn't be working in a cobbler's shop. You're a natural teacher, anyone can see that.'

She laughed then. 'Well, fancy that, coming from you of all people. You said yourself I was no lady,' she accused, 'and how could a common thing like me become a teacher?' She had never forgiven him for looking down on her in that way, but then he wasn't the only one.

'I was wrong.'

'Oh?' His answer had shaken her. For a moment she was lost for words, then with a mock curtsy she said bluntly, 'Whatever have I done to earn such approval, sir?'

Her manner angered him. She had a way of belittling him, a way of getting right under his skin. However hard she fought against him, he wanted her all the more. Phoebe would not be won either by flattery or force, he knew that. Inside, he ached to hold her. Something told him that she was weakening towards him; behind that fiery and aggressive façade, there was a soft and yielding creature, as hungry for love as he was. Why couldn't he reach her? What was it about her that churned him up inside? 'Aggie's away over the fields with her daddy,' he murmured now, coming towards her, covering the ground between them in easy strides. In the half-light, with her long auburn hair cascading in deep loose waves about her shoulders, and her sparkling brown eyes wide and accusing, she looked exceptionally lovely. There was a wildness about her that excited him, and yet she was possessed of a certain innocence that set her aside from all other women he'd known. Right from the start Phoebe had raised emotions in him that were both astonishing and frightening. He'd never really been in love, and he wondered whether that was what he felt as he looked on her now. 'What is it that makes you want to fight me?'

he asked, his voice unusually gentle, his quizzical gaze holding her there.

'Huh!' Phoebe's feet wanted to run from that place but something stronger held her back. 'I don't want to fight you,' she replied coolly, when all the while her heart was beating rapidly. 'I don't know what you mean.' He was close now . . . too close. When he'd first stepped from the shadows, Phoebe had reeled back to press herself against the wall of the barn. Now, she could feel the wooden beams against her shoulders and he was only an arm's reach in front of her. There was a stable wall to her left, a block of straw to her right, and no way out but forward.

'Move yourself!' she said boldly, squaring her shoulders and preparing to push past him. But he was big and far stronger than she. Besides, she had no wish actually to touch him in her effort to break through. Phoebe was under no illusion that if he wanted to detain her there was little she could do about it, although her sharp eyes had already picked out a long-handled rake leaning against a railing not too far away. If needs be, she wouldn't hesitate to stick him with it. 'Did you hear me? I said move yourself!' she insisted, her eyes glittering angrily. When the only move he made was to bring himself nearer to her, she was gripped by a strange excitement.

'You don't really hate me, do you, Phoebe?' he asked in a sincere voice.

'No, I don't hate you,' she replied. Greg was Aggie's brother and Lou's son. How could she let herself hate him?

Her answer had pleased him. It was a beginning, although he could still sense her hostility. 'Then how *do* you feel towards me?'

'I don't feel anything towards you,' she lied. She wasn't sure exactly what it was that she did feel but there was certainly something. And it was a source of anxiety to her.

He smiled. 'Yes, you do,' he said confidently. He came closer then, stretching out his arms and putting them one either side of her. Resting his palms flat against the wall, he bent his head down, leaned forward and kissed her full on the mouth. Delighted when she stiffened beneath him yet made no move to push him off, he grew bolder; sliding one arm round her slim waist and the other round her shoulders, he drew her into him, a fever burning through him as he tasted her softness, the moist fullness of her lips. In that moment he knew beyond all doubt – he was in love.

Clasped in his arms, all of Phoebe's instincts warned her to pull away, to get out of there. Greg Peters was a bad lot. In her heart she knew he was trouble. But his arms were oddly comforting and his kiss had kindled something in her. Until this minute she hadn't realised how lonely she was, or how desperate for love she had grown. She had no one. No one to call her own, no man to share her life with. For a while she ignored her own instincts and clung to him, returning his kiss with all her lonely heart, melting to the warmth of his body, and wanting him so much . . . so very much.

'Phoebe!' Aggie's voice cut through the air. In that instant she realised her shame. Desperately she pushed

Greg away, and because he too had been surprised by the girl's shout, he made no resistance. Instead he went quickly in the opposite direction, without even a backward glance. Soon he was lost to sight, and it was as though he had never been there at all.

'I'm here, sweetheart.' Surreptitiously patting her hair in place and straightening the creases in her skirt, Phoebe emerged from the gloom. She was filled with shame at what had taken place here. It would never happen again, she vowed, lonely or not. She would wait for the right man to come along. There would come a day when she would find happiness and true love. But it certainly wouldn't be with the smooth-talking Greg Peters! His brother Hadley, now, that was a different matter altogether. But then, he was smitten by Margaret, wasn't he? All the same, there was no harm in living in hope, was there? Phoebe asked herself. She wasn't altogether certain whether she loved Hadley in that way, but her heart did a little skip whenever she was close to him.

'I was up on the top field with Hadley and we saw you come into the barn.' Aggie chatted excitedly as they made their way back to the house. 'Daddy's gone into Preston for some tractor parts and he won't be back for a while yet.' She was thrilled when Phoebe suggested that she accompany her into town, racing away to ask Hadley and telling Phoebe that perhaps he could come too.

Phoebe followed, thinking she would have liked nothing better than for Hadley to go into Blackburn with them, although of course it was highly unlikely. As she came towards the farmhouse where Hadley was waiting by the back door, her mouth was still bruised from Greg's passionate kiss and her heart burned with shame. And if she thought that none of it showed when she came face to face with Hadley, she was mistaken.

Some short time later, Phoebe and Aggie set off towards the tram-stop on Preston New Road. As she went, Phoebe glanced up at her cousin's bedroom window. The curtains were still drawn. 'Lazy bugger!' she muttered beneath her breath.

'What did you say, Phoebe?' Aggie was skipping along beside her. The few coins she'd got from Hadley were chinking in the pocket of her red dress, and her eyes were shining with the excitement of her first real adventure this weekend.

Phoebe cursed herself. Swearing was not nice at the best of times, but swearing in the company of someone like Aggie was unforgivable. 'I was just thinking out loud,' she said.

'What?' insisted Aggie. 'What were you thinking?'

'Oh, I was just thinking about the lovely time we're going to have in town.'

'And you're going to show me the cobbler's shop where you work, aren't you, Phoebe?'

'I am that,' she replied proudly.

'It's a shame Hadley couldn't come with us.' Aggie could never hide her love for him.

'Not to worry,' Phoebe told her.

'I expect we could have asked Greg, but . . .' Aggie wrinkled her nose in disgust. 'But we wouldn't have any fun with him because he's too miserable.' The tram could be seen coming down Preston New Road, so the two of them broke into a run. Aggie resumed her conversation just as the conductor was giving them their tickets. 'Do you like Greg?' she asked Phoebe in a rather loud voice. 'He likes you, I know he does, 'cause he watches you all the time when you're not looking.'

Acutely aware that every passenger on the tram was eagerly awaiting her answer, Phoebe felt the blush spread from her neck right up to the roots of her hair. 'Well, I never!' she remarked, pointing out of the window and distracting the girl's attention. 'Will you look at that?' In the field just beyond the road a huge floppy-eared hare sat bolt upright, staring at them as they went by. Phoebe was thankful when it proved enough to take Aggie's mind off the subject of Greg.

Hadley stood his ground. 'You're a bastard!' he said, clenching and unclenching his fists, and suppressing the desire to launch himself at the cunning, smiling face before him. 'You'd better take this as my last warning. Next time I'll have to give you a leathering,' he promised.

Greg threw back his head and roared with laughter. But when he saw the look in his brother's eyes, he grew more thoughtful. He might be forty minutes older and somewhat bigger in size, but he knew that Hadley was by far the stronger. 'Out with it then,' he demanded. 'What are you getting at?'

'You know well enough. I saw you running from the barn only minutes before Phoebe came out the other end.' His narrowed eyes blazed at the other man. 'If I thought you were intent on making a play for her . . . if I believed for one minute that you meant to play havoc with her life . . . So help me, Greg, I'd swing for you!'

'So! You saw me come out at one end of the barn, and Phoebe from the other,' Greg scoffed. 'I'm telling you, I didn't even see her in there.' He laughed, a soft low sound that enraged the other man. 'You're imagining things,' he said. 'Besides, she's not my type. I like them a bit more experienced.'

'Aggie's mother wasn't "experienced", was she?' There was real hatred in Hadley's voice, and regret, and something akin to sorrow.

'Blast your eyes!' Greg surged forward, then stopped himself. 'That's all in the past. There was an agreement never to mention it again. A new life, we said. For the girl's sake.'

Hadley forced himself to stay calm. 'You're right. That was what we agreed, and I'll abide by it. Only because I would hate Aggie to discover the awful truth.' He loved the girl as though she was his own. 'But mark my words,' he warned, 'I won't stand by and see you destroy Phoebe's life. She's good and decent and deserves better than a swine like you!' When Greg smiled again, this time with the look of a man who had got his own way, Hadley went on in a voice that trembled with rage, 'Lucy Soames was about the same age as Phoebe. It's too late for that poor soul, but I promise you this – if I so much as see you within ten feet of Phoebe, all agreements arc null and void and I'll shout your filthy secret from the rooftops.'

'So you'd shame Aggie too, would you?'

'No. She'd be long gone, to a place where you and your tainted ways couldn't hurt her.' He stared at the man who was his brother, and he wished it wasn't so. After all this time he still couldn't forgive him. 'Damn you!' he hissed before breaking away, his fists still clenching and unclenching, and a deep regret in his heart that he could not mete out the punishment so long deserved.

The sun was setting. In the soft light of a dying day the man fell to his knees. With immense tenderness he placed the pink carnations before the headstone. Tears rained down his weather-worn face and for a moment he could not speak so great was his pain. His vision was blurred as he looked on the black granite stone, silently reading the words written there. When his strength of heart returned he waited a moment, picturing her in his mind as a precious infant, a child, then as a girl only just blossoming into womanhood. His agony was unbearable. 'I'll find him,' he vowed. 'I promise, here in this churchyard, where God is my witness, I WILL FIND HIM!' There was hatred in his heart then, and a desire to kill. He prayed the Lord to forgive him but asked that he also understand.

The daylight was fading fast and still he stayed: living with her, laughing and crying with her. He had been away these many years, a jailbird who had brought both shame and tragedy on his family. But now he was a free man – free from the confines of a prison cell but not from the thing that haunted him. He could never be free from that . . . not until the wrong was righted. Not until the deed was done.

When the last vestige of daylight melted into the darkness, he went away, a sad and lonely figure, stooped at the shoulder and crippled at heart. 'I won't forget,' he promised the moonlight. 'And I won't rest until he's found!'

After a while only the night creatures could be heard, rummaging through the undergrowth. The churchyard was silent and the moon picked out his flowers, and the headstone, and the name written there:

LUCY SOAMES
Beloved daughter of John and Ada
1901–1920

Chapter Seven

'Aw, come on, Phoebe, can you honestly see me at a barn-dance?' Marcus straightened his back and groaned. He had been seated at his work-bench for almost three hours and his bones seemed to have stiffened into a crooked position. 'I'm grateful to you for asking, though.' He put down the pretty cream-coloured ankle boot and stretched his legs beneath the bench. 'I'm not sorry these are finished,' he sighed, glancing at the last of a pair which had taken over a week to complete.

'They're so beautiful,' Phoebe said, collecting the dainty boots in her hands and gazing at them from every angle. 'You're so clever, Marcus.' She had watched him this past week, constantly bent to his work, tapping and shaping, polishing and fussing, until the boots began to take on a life of their own. They were a splendid example of his unrivalled skill as a shoemaker, and the prettiest things Phoebe had ever seen; created in the softest leather and dyed a perfect shade of cream, they were gathered into a ruffle at the ankle, the slender heel gracefully curved and the tiny round buttons set from instep to ankle with painstaking precision. 'I hope the lady in question realises the work and love you've put into them,' she said now, reverently replacing them on the bench and wondering whether there would come a day when she might own such a pair of expensive boots. She thought not.

'So do I,' Marcus said with a broad grin. 'So do I.' He looked up at Phoebe and his heart was warmed right through. 'Now then, where's the boss's mug o' tea?' he asked with feigned authority. 'I hope I don't need to remind you that a cobbler can't work unless he's well fed and watered.' And he had worked non-stop since first light that day. September was the month when children were kitted out with new clogs for school, and the better off folk were shedding their summer footwear in favour of sturdier boots that would keep out the cold.

'The kettle's on, M'Lord,' Phoebe said, curtseying in a servile manner and making a flourish with her arm.

'Give over,' Marcus said in a laugh. 'What am I going to do with you, eh? You're incorrigible.' He bent his legs and raised himself off the stool, stretching his arms above his head and flexing every muscle that had cramped during the course of the day. 'Put the "Closed" sign up, lass,' he said. 'We'll keep the blighters out 'til we're good and ready to let them in.'

'I should think so too,' Phoebe agreed. 'You've earned the right to have your lunch in peace.'

'And so have you,' he reminded her. On this Saturday, they had been inundated with customers. 'I don't know how I managed without you, I really don't,' he told her. 'You're a natural businesswoman, that's what you are, Phoebe Mulligan,' he said proudly. 'What's more, you have such a winning way with the customers.' And with me, he thought with mingled joy and sadness. You have a winning way with me too. There was much on his mind when he told her now, 'I couldn't do without you, that's for sure.' Realising how serious his voice had sounded, he added with a smile, 'So if you should be tempted to leave me for some posh shop down Ainsworth Street, I'd be lost.'

Phoebe had been on her way across the back-room towards the stairs when his words pulled her up sharp. 'If you're referring to Dickens' Gentlemen's Outfitters, you needn't worry,' she declared. Phoebe had long ago decided that her uncle had no intention of employing her at his precious store, especially now that Margaret was installed as trainee manager. 'Anyway, I wouldn't go there if I was asked,' she added with a wry little smile, 'There's no call for common folk like me in such an establishment. I'd only be out of place.'

'Don't put yourself down, Phoebe.' Marcus hated hearing her talk like that. 'With you behind the counter, your uncle would sell more merchandise in a day than he's ever sold in a month!' She laughed then, and he thought the sound filled the shop with sunshine, 'Go on, then. Away and brew the tea while I clean up.'

Later, when they were seated opposite each other across the counter, Marcus picked up the thread of their previous conversation. 'I mean it, Phoebe,' he said. 'I really don't know what I would do without you if you decided to look elsewhere.' He hoped his voice sounded suitably casual. He didn't want to risk frightening her into doing the very thing that he would move heaven and earth to prevent, although he knew there must come a day when her ambitions would take her from him. She was too quick and talented to be held back for long. 'You've gained real business acumen, and now you've the experience to make you an asset anywhere,' he said reluctantly. 'There's no doubt that you could demand a better wage than I pay you.'

She was hurt. Replacing her cheese sandwich in her lunch box, she asked, 'Do you really think I would leave you for more money?'

'I wouldn't blame you.' Secretly he was thrilled at her words. 'After all, opportunities abound for a young lady such as yourself . . . bright, intelligent and eager to learn.'

'Bless you for that,' she said. Marcus always saw her as a lady when certain other folk saw her only as an intruder. 'I've got no intention of leaving you,' she assured him. 'I'm happy here. I love the work, and enjoy meeting the people. Besides, even if I did earn more money, it would only go to my uncle. I'd still get the same four shillings at the end of each month.' She shrugged her shoulders. 'So, you see, you're worrying over nothing at all.' She picked up her sandwich and examined it carefully. Unlike her cousin Margaret she wasn't given a midday meal allowance. Instead she had to make her own sandwiches every evening. She really didn't mind so much, but that morning when she went into the scullery to collect them, there was an army of ants all over the shelf in the pantry. Her screams had brought everyone running. Daisy was beside herself, crying how she was always most careful to keep the pantry a haven from insects; she even offered to make Phoebe a fresh batch of sandwiches: 'Just in case one of the blessed pests have found its way in.' The master wouldn't hear of it. 'Even were she to eat one, it wouldn't harm her,' he said. Afterwards he and Margaret could be heard sniggering together in the dining room.

Lunch was quickly eaten and the shop was reopened the exact moment the market-hall clock struck the half-hour after twelve. Already there were three customers waiting at the door. 'Come on, lass!' Mrs Dewsbury was the butcher's wife, a large red-faced personage with enormous hands and feet, the former hidden in gloves of best kid and the latter squeezed into expensive black patent shoes two sizes too small. When the door opened she was the first to barge her way past Phoebe, surging into the shop with all the grace of a ten-ton elephant. 'About time too!' she snapped with a toss of her bleached head. 'I swear your lunch-breaks get longer and longer. I've been waiting outside for three-quarters of an hour.'

Marcus was on his way back to his bench. 'Now, now, Mrs Dewsbury' he chided, 'we've only been closed for half an hour . . . same as always.' He didn't bother to turn and look at her. Mrs Hilda Dewsbury was never a pleasant sight at the best of times.

'Stuff and nonsense!' she roared. 'Three-quarters of an hour, I tell you,' she insisted. Swinging round to face the other two customers, a slight old woman and a red-headed lad of about sixteen, she demanded, 'Isn't that right?'

'Don't ask me, missus,' the lad replied, making hard work of chewing a treacle toffee and showing it in various stages of mastication inside his mouth. 'I ain't getting involved in no arguments. Gets yer in trouble, does that. So leave me out of it. You fight yer own battles,' he said cheekily.

'And I've been sent to fetch my husband's work boots,' the old one said, looking from one to the other as though for reassurance. 'He wouldn't like it if I caused any trouble.'

'Quite right,' Phoebe declared. It would seem that Mrs Dewsbury's reputation had gone before her. 'Now then, what can I do for you?' she asked the pouting woman who had been out to cause a rumpus.

'You can do nothing at all!' came the haughty reply. 'There's a new man cobbling shoes at the market. I'll take my custom there from now on.'

Phoebe didn't care for the old windbag but knew what a troublesome gossip Mrs Dewsbury was, and if she were to put her mind to it there was no doubt she might persuade one or two of the weaker amongst her husband's customers to follow her example and boycott Marcus Quinn's shop; no doubt they would return once they discovered that he was the best in Blackburn but there would be good relations and valuable revenue lost in the meantime. With this in mind she put on her brightest smile. 'D'you know what, Mrs Dewsbury,' she said. 'I've a feeling you could be right . . . we just might have been a teeny weeny bit late in opening the doors today.'

'I knew it!' The indignant Mrs Dewsbury bristled from head to toe.

'Ah, but you see, it was really *your fault*.' Phoebe let the smile fall slowly away. 'Or at least . . . your husband's.'

'Whatever do you mean?'

'Well, y' see, Mrs Dewsbury, as a rule Mr Marcus here,' she glanced at her employer who was standing between the two rooms, greatly bemused and curious to know how she might get herself out of this dilemma ' – well, he wouldn't dream of going over his half-hour break. Today, though, he had one of your husband's meat pies, and he was enjoying it so much that he completely forgot the time.' Her sorry brown eyes never once left the woman's face even though she knew the other two customers were highly amused by her ploy and she couldn't have looked them in the eye to save her own life.

Mrs Dewsbury positively swelled with pride. 'Well, fancy that,' she mumbled, plucking at the feathers in her fancy hat and extravagantly preening herself. 'Of course, I'm not surprised. They do say my husband makes the best pies in the whole of Lancashire,' she said. Her smile was frightening as she beamed on every one in turn. 'That's Dewsbury's butcher's,' she told the other two customers. 'You can't miss it . . . it's the one right on the corner of Penny Street.' She then took out two enormous clogs from her shopping bag. 'They need new irons,' she informed Phoebe. 'I'll be back Friday afternoon.' She would have shown a smile to Marcus but he was in the back-room, keeping well out of sight, with his hand pressed tight over his mouth, terrified that the laughter would bubble over before she was gone from the shop.

'The clogs will be like new,' Phoebe told her, wondering how anyone could walk in a pair of barges.

'Oh, I'm sure!' Mrs Dewsbury remarked. 'I have every confidence in Mr Quinn. After all, isn't he the best cobbler in Blackburn, my dear?' A rubbery grin to one and all then she was gone in a grand display of fat and feathers, leaving an outburst of laughter behind her.

The remainder of the day passed without incident although there were enough customers for Marcus to declare, 'I can't say I'm sorry it's Sunday tomorrow.'

'I don't like Sundays.' Phoebe didn't look up from tidying the counter. 'All that kneeling and praying . . . and it ain't as though it's in a proper Church either. I wouldn't mind that. Me and my mam used to go to Church. But we meant it when we prayed . . . not like *him*. He must be the biggest hypocrite under the sun.' It had been a real shock when first Phoebe had been told to, 'Get yourself suitably attired for Church' . . . only to find that her uncle's church was no further than the long room upstairs in Dickens House. Directly above the kitchen and running the whole length of the house, this room was stripped bare except for one darkwood pew which was positioned before a lectern in the shape of a huge eagle with outstretched wings. From here Edward would address the entire household, including the reluctant Daisy; the service would be a long prolation of fire and brimstone when the master would vigorously condemn the 'evil doings of mankind', and the whole event would end in a sobering hymn, in which everyone was expected to 'raise the roof and send your soul to Heaven'. Phoebe was convinced that any 'evil doings' were done by him alone, and that no matter how loud and lusty he sang, his soul wouldn't even get so far as the sooty chimney-pots.

At five-thirty the little shop was 'ship-shape and Bristol fashion', as Marcus would say. Phoebe secured the ribbon in her hair and draped her long grey cardigan over her small straight shoulders. It was time to go. 'Have you thought any more about the barn-dance next Saturday?' she asked. 'Oh, Marcus, do say you'll come,' she urged. 'You'll enjoy yourself, I promise. Besides, Dora and Judd have been invited, and I do so want you to meet them.' Ever since Hadley invited her to the end of harvest barn-dance, Phoebe had counted the days. More and more she had come to think of Hadley in a way that she knew could only bring heartache. But there was no dictating matters of the heart, and as long as she didn't let her feelings get out of hand, there'd be nobody hurt.

Marcus shook his head. 'Of course I'd love to meet your friends, you know that,' he said. 'But as for flinging myself about in a barn-dance.' He chuckled at the very idea. 'I don't know,' he murmured. His heart longed to go, but his head warned against it. 'I've never been to a barn-dance before. I might make a complete fool of myself.'

'No, you won't!' Phoebe protested. 'I've never been to a barn-dance either, but there can't be much to it. According to Hadley, the fiddlers play and the man calls out the steps.' She swung round, laughing. 'It'll be fun.'

'It might be fun for you, young lady,' he teased, 'but *I'm* not eighteen anymore.'

'Give over!' She laughed. 'Anybody would think you were old. I expect you could show everybody up if you put your mind to it.' She collected her bag from the counter and fastened the top button of her cardigan. 'Don't say you're not coming, Marcus,' she pleaded. 'It's a whole week away yet. Think about it some more. I really want you there.' She had grown very fond of him.

He was more a friend than an employer. And he was so much fun, she actually looked forward to coming to work.

'All right, I'll think about it,' he promised. 'Now get yourself off home.' He turned away, pretending to tidy the box of leather patches. He hated Saturdays. It seemed a lifetime before Monday morning when she was here again. When she called out 'Bye then', he merely nodded. The door swung to and the little shop was quiet once more. He went to the window and peered out. Phoebe was running down the street, her long auburn hair glittering in the sunshine of a wonderful summer's evening. Soon it would be autumn, and then the winter would sweep in with a vengeance. He hated the long bitter-cold days. He hated the loneliness of his existence. His feelings for Phoebe confused him. All he knew was that she had brightened his life in a way that made it all worthwhile.

Phoebe ran all the way down to the boulevard. At the bottom of the road she paused to get her breath. 'Good, the tram ain't in yet,' she gasped. Last week she'd missed the six-thirty tram and been suitably punished. 'Don't expect to come into this house at any time you feel fit,' her uncle had announced in full fanfare. 'We do not wait at table for the likes of you.' In great ceremony, with her cousin and her aunt looking on . . . one delighted and the other sympathetic but trying not to show it . . . she was despatched to her room without dinner, forced to eat the remains of her cheese sandwiches. And if he'd known she had them in her bag, she wouldn't have been allowed *them* either.

The square was teeming on this Saturday evening. It seemed to Phoebe that all life congregated here. People in a hurry poured out of the railway station. There were smart and upright businessmen in black suits and trilbys; other men, stooped and weary, making their way back from various factories, flat caps pulled down and heavy-booted feet trudging their way home. There were groups of giggling young women, and families clustered together as they wended in and out of the moving trams. And all around the noise rose up like the hum of a million bees in flight.

'Hello, dear.' The voice was breathless. 'Just got out by the skin of my teeth today. The old sod kept finding other things for me to do.' The woman was familiar to Phoebe because she always came rushing out of the hotel at the same time every day and together, she and Phoebe would walk to the tram-stop. They boarded the very same tram and throughout the journey to St Silas' Church where she disembarked, the poor harassed woman would describe her day as a kitchen-hand at the hotel, in such fine detail that Phoebe knew everything there was to know about the place and the people in it. She'd already taken a dislike to the proprietor who, according to the woman, was a real slave-driver. 'She follows me about, wiping her fingers along the banisters to check for dust and measures the cleaning fluid every morning.'

Nevertheless, with short-cropped dark hair and chubby features, the woman was as round and bouncy as a foot-ball. 'My goodness! It's busy tonight,' she declared, ner-vously shadowing Phoebe as she made her way through the tangle of traffic and surging bodies. 'Can't hardly hear yerself think!' she complained in a voice deliberately pitched to rise above the newsvendor's shouts. Just then a black motor-vehicle drove past within inches of them, giving the woman a nasty fright. 'Noisy, smelly things,' she yelled, shaking her fist as it went merrily away across the tram-tracks. Addressing Phoebe she demanded irately, 'What's wrong with horse-drawn carriages, that's what I'd like to know? Horses have been good enough these many years . . . and now we're beginning to be plagued with these dreadful dangerous monsters choking the air with fumes and noise!'

'It's progress.' Phoebe stepped up the small kerb into the tram-stop. There were four others already waiting: a harassed woman with two children who were fighting each other, and a sour-faced gentleman of senior years. Occasionally he glared at the children when their mother wasn't looking and for a while at least they fell silent, hiding behind her skirt and peering at the man with curious eyes.

'Progress, eh?' The woman gave a snort. 'Well, it isn't for the better, that's for sure!' she grumbled. Give me the old ways any time. Next thing you know, there won't be a tram nor a horse-drawn cart left in the whole of Lancashire.' Shaking her head, she muttered and mumbled. When the tram came she climbed on in front of everybody else, still muttering and mumbling. All the way up the steps to the top deck, she muttered and mumbled, and throughout the twenty-minute journey to St Silas' Church gave her views without restraint. At the church she clambered off the tram and waddled away down the street, leaving everyone feeling all the more miserable for having caught the same tram; and though they remained silent throughout her tireless tirade, there wasn't a soul there who didn't agree with her views.

At twenty minutes to seven, Phoebe alighted in Preston New Road and ran all the way up the lane to the house. In the distance, she could see Lou and Aggie walking towards the field with the two labrador dogs bounding away up front. She shouted a greeting, jumping up and down to attract their attention. Aggie saw her first and gave a shout, but it was too far away for them to converse, so they exchanged waves with Phoebe and each went their own way. There would be time enough later to chat about things in general.

Margaret passed her in the hallway. She didn't speak. She hardly ever spoke these days, unless it was to pass a caustic comment. Since their last confrontation, Phoebe had been careful to keep out of her way. When trouble found her out, she could look after herself as well as anybody else, but she wasn't the sort to go looking for it.

Upstairs in her room, Phoebe pushed the door to and slipped the bolt. Sighing, she went to the window and looked out, as always her eyes seeking the farmhouse opposite. She wondered where Hadley might be. He was a strange fellow, she thought. During the evenings when she went to help Aggie with her schooling, Hadley would be seated by the fireplace, bent over his newspaper, seemingly oblivious to Phoebe and the girl poring over books in the window-seat. But then Phoebe would look up to see him staring at her, and her heart would turn over. He hadn't said anything, nor at any time had he given her cause to believe that she was anything more than a friend to him. True he was always delighted to see her, and he made her exceptionally welcome whenever she went to

247

visit, but then so did everybody else, she reminded herself. All the same he seemed to smile at her in a particular way, and always went to great pains to see her to the gate on leaving.

'What are you doing to me, Hadley Peters?' she asked now, her gaze growing fonder the more she stared at the farmhouse and imagined him inside.

In her mind's eye she could see him, stooping to avoid the low beams as he came in the parlour door then seating himself beside the fireplace, long legs stretched out and his untidy hair falling over his eyes so that he must keep flicking it back in order to read the paper. On the occasions when she looked up to meet his gaze he would seem incredibly shy, smiling at her then nervously shifting his gaze. Within minutes he would go from the room, suddenly to reappear to walk her to the gate when it was time for her to leave. 'Better not let Margaret see you walking me to the gate,' Phoebe murmured, leaning forward on her elbows and twining her long locks round her fingers. 'Else we'll *both* be in the doghouse!'

She thought about the relationship between Hadley and her cousin. It was a strange to-do. Certainly he cared for her, that was plain to see, and she was besotted with him. From her window, Phoebe had seen them together on various occasions: sometimes walking the fields, other times just standing back from the gate in intimate conversation. Last Friday evening the two of them had come home in a taxi-cab and kissed goodnight right outside this very front door. It seemed to Phoebe that they were getting bolder and less worried about what Margaret's father might say if he caught them together.

'When a fellow's got somebody like Margaret Dickens hankering after him, what makes you think he'd want *you*?' Phoebe murmured. 'Ask yourself that, my girl . . . then happen you'll stop imagining things.' She laughed. It didn't mean anything even if he *was* flirting with her because all fellows were born flirts however much they might deny it. Anyway, she reminded herself, she was probably exaggerating Hadley's interest in her; though he did seem to be always watching over her, and that was a fact.

Suddenly her mind was charged with thoughts of another, more familiar face, a quiet hard-working bloke with the most honest and straightforward nature you could imagine; Judd was the kind of man any girl might fall for . . . strong handsome features and a charming smile that came straight from the heart. Phoebe had seen him grow from a boy to a man and was immensely proud of him. She loved Judd in a very special way. All her life he had been like a brother to her. Now she was eagerly awaiting a letter from Dora telling her that yes, they would be delighted to come and join in the fun. They didn't even need to worry about catching a late night tram because Lou had arranged for them to stay overnight at the farmhouse. It was over a week since Phoebe had written telling them they were invited. If she didn't hear by Monday she would write again. The post couldn't be trusted. Look how her birthday card from Dora had gone astray!

'Stop your dreaming,' she told herself sharply, 'else you'll be late down for dinner and *he'll* be after your blood.' Swinging away from the window, she crossed the room and stood before the dresser mirror. What she saw was a young woman who had blossomed since coming here. The reflection of a girl with strong classic features and forthright brown eyes presented a lovely picture. Even so there was a weariness about her in that moment, because, although Marcus made her work seem more like a pleasure, it was nevertheless very tiring to stand on your feet all day. Most of the customers were helpful cheery folk but there were always the ones whose aim in life was to be as difficult as possible. Throughout the course of a week Phoebe had to deal with a fair number of such creatures and, by the time Saturday evening arrived, it was beginning to tell on her. 'You ain't bad though, Phoebe gal,' she told herself in the mirror, a smile wreathing her lovely face. All the same, there were faint shadows beneath her eyes and a tiredness about her countenance that belied her enthusiasm. 'All right,' she admitted, pulling a wry little face, 'you *could* do with a lazy bath and a good night's sleep, I won't deny it.' Sighing loudly, she plucked the ribbon from her hair and at once it spilled over her shoulders, thick and rich, its warm russet colour seeming to infuse a glow into her pale features. Bending her head forward, she dug her fingers deep into the tangled mass, running her two hands its whole length, then flicking it upwards so that it settled against her head like a glorious halo. It felt so good.

After all these weeks she still daren't venture out without her hair tied back. She hadn't forgotten her uncle's words nor the curious way he stared at her now and then; although, unlike when Hadley stared at her, it was *she* who was forced to look away. Her uncle posed a puzzle to her. His smile was sweet and his tongue smooth as silk, and yet there was something about him, a kind of menacing undercurrent, that always made her wary. She shivered aloud, strangely disturbed by her own thoughts.

Determined not to attend table even one minute late, Phoebe had the lazy bath she'd promised herself then cleaned her teeth, brushed her hair and put on her blue polka-dot dress. 'There you are,' she told herself, 'it's remarkable what a soak in the tub will do for a gal.' She laughed then, looking up at her mother's photograph. 'Better watch it, Mam, or they'll be carting me off,' she said. 'I'm beginning to talk to myself.'

After tying her hair back with the broad blue ribbon which she'd made herself, Phoebe thought she was presentable enough to make her way downstairs. A glance at the bedside clock told her that it was five minutes to eight. She didn't want to be too early going into the dining-room, but more importantly she did not want to be late. Firmly closing the bedroom door behind her, she went down the stairway at a leisurely pace. On reaching her cousin's room, Phoebe could hear her moving about inside. 'Huh!' she snorted. 'It won't matter if *you're* late, will it. Daddy's little darling!'

As it happened, Phoebe was wrong on this occasion. When she entered the dining-room her aunt was already there, fussing over the table and tolerating Daisy's complaints about, 'Them blessed potatoes from the top farm . . . go mushy in the water they do . . . and they don't make nice crispy chips neither!'

'Have you told the master?' Noreen was reluctant to interfere in such domestic issues. She did not command the purse-strings and, according to her husband, was 'not sensible enough in these little financial matters'.

'Well, o' course I have, Ma'am . . . but the master insists it's *me* that's at fault. It isn't, though,' she protested in a harsh whisper in case he should overhear. 'If you don't mind me saying so, Ma'am . . . if he will buy the cheapest, nastiest potato he can find, then he mustn't expect me to work miracles.' She threw out her chin and rammed her clenched fists on to fleshy hips. 'I'm no genius and never said I was,' she declared in a sulk.

'I understand, Daisy, I really do.' Noreen straightened up from her usual task. She had been placing her husband's evening newspaper just within his reach, but not so close to his plate that he might spill his soup on it. 'But you know how shrewd Mr Dickens is regarding money.'

'Aye, I'm well aware of that.' She rolled her eyes to the ceiling. There wasn't a single soul in the whole of Blackburn who didn't know Edward Dickens for the skinflint he was. 'But I'd be that grateful if you'd talk to him about going back to Lou Peters for his spuds. Will you do that for me, Ma'am?' she pleaded. 'There isn't all that much difference in the price, and Lou Peters' goods is far superior.' She let out a strange little noise that might have been a sigh, but then she might have been clearing her throat to make the following profound statement. 'A carpenter's only as good as his tools, and a cook's only as good as her potatoes . . . if you follow my meaning.' That bloody Edward Dickens would be the first to complain if the food wasn't to his liking.

'I can't promise anything, Daisy,' Noreen apologised. 'But yes . . . I'll see what I can do.' She never imagined for one moment that her husband would pay mind to what *she* had to say.

Daisy was grateful all the same. 'Thank you,' she said, waddling away. 'I'd best get off to the kitchen and make sure the soup isn't spoiling . . . or that'll be something else I'm taken to task over.' She really did sigh then, long and loud.

'Poor Daisy.' Phoebe went straight to the dresser where Daisy had laid out the desserts . . . a pretty scalloped dish of banana trifle; two plates on columned stands, one containing a lemon meringue and the other dressed with individual cakes, each baked in its own frilly little case. Suddenly Phoebe was very hungry.

'Go to your place, Phoebe,' her aunt told her, ignoring her sympathetic comment concerning Daisy. As Phoebe went to the farthest end of the table where she stood behind her chair in the way her uncle had instructed, Noreen bestowed on her a weak smile. 'Good girl,' she said. 'We don't want any bad tempers round the table, do we, eh? Your uncle will be here at any minute.'

She glanced nervously towards the door. At that moment the hallway clock struck eight times, each strike resounding through the house like the call of doom. On the final stroke Edward Dickens appeared at the door and the whole room felt as though it had just been plunged into shadow.

He stood there for what seemed an age, his hard grey eyes going from one to the other, coolly roving the room as though seeking some poor unfortunate soul who might have been hiding in the darkest corner. He remained so for a good five minutes, his hands clasped behind his back, his chest taut and legs slightly apart. The silence was thick and foreboding. He stared at his wife who lowered her gaze then at Phoebe who had her back to him but could sense his gaze on her. It made the hair stand up on the back of her neck. Then he stared at the dresser and its meticulously displayed contents. He drew in a great noisy breath and waited a moment longer while the clock on the mantelpiece ticked into the unnerving quietness.

'Where is she?' he asked, in such a soft voice it made Noreen glance up to make certain he had spoken at all. He smiled on her then, a slow, deliberate smile that drained away any ounce of courage she might have mustered. 'I do believe you're failing in your duty, my dear,' he murmured, coming into the room. 'Surely you should make it your business to see that your daughter is present at the table at the appointed time?' He was standing beside her now, peering into her eyes, his face suddenly set like stone.

'I'll get her at once.' Like a frightened animal Noreen scurried out of the room.

'Ah!' Edward's smile became a grin, the thick fleshy lips parting to display a splendid set of teeth. He watched his wife hurry from the room then bestowed a gentler smile on Phoebe. 'Hmmm,' he muttered, nodding his head. 'It pleases me to see that you at least are acquiring a degree of good sense.' It was a rare compliment that made her decidedly uneasy.

Patting both hands across the mound of his stomach, Edward made a satisfied noise while taking up his place at the head of the table. He stared at the door. The clock

ticked on, and somewhere out in the garden a bird began
singing. You wouldn't sing if you were in here, Phoebe
thought, secretly wishing the floor would collapse right at
the spot where he was standing. She was acutely aware
of her uncle's long thick fingers drumming on the table.
She knew his eyes were still on her but did not intend to
gratify him by looking up. Instead she kept her gaze fixed
on the rose-pattern of her china plate and prayed that
her aunt would be back shortly; she didn't care whether
Margaret was with her or not.

'Your mother was exceedingly beautiful. You could be
her standing there.' His remark caused Phoebe to jerk up
her head in astonishment. In all the time she had been in
this house, he had never spoken of her mother in that
way. In fact, there had been times when Phoebe had
desperately wanted to discuss her mother with him but
always he had avoided the subject, even grown agitated
whenever she broached it. Her aunt was the same.

'Was *this* her place?' she asked hesitantly. 'Did my
mother sit here for her meals? Is that why you allocated
this chair to me?' She had always thought it strange that
he should have placed her at the head of the table
opposite him. She had suspected that his real reason was
so that he could watch her every expression throughout
the meal. She couldn't know now that her words had
struck him to the very heart.

'Where in God's name are they!' He struck his fist on
the table and Phoebe felt the tremor that ran through it.
'Hell and damnation!' he exploded, then seeming curiously astonished by his own undisciplined outburst, gave
a sigh that swelled his chest and brought him to his full

considerable height. 'Tell Daisy to bring in the first course,' he instructed Phoebe in a calmer voice. His smile was magnificent.

A few moments later Daisy had served the soup and still there was no sign of the two women. Phoebe was desperately uncomfortable, especially as her uncle kept lifting his face to beam at her in a dreadful manner. 'Delicious soup,' he exclaimed more than once, slurping his way through it and occasionally pausing to dab at his beard with the napkin. 'I must commend Daisy on her excellent cuisine.'

In that moment there was a flurry at the door and in rushed Margaret with her mother trailing behind. 'I'm sorry, Father,' she said brightly. 'The truth is I just fell asleep . . . you know yourself it's been a very tiring week.' She went to him and threw her arms round his neck in an embrace. 'And you're an old slave-driver,' she added boldly, 'so you've only got yourself to blame.' She put her nose in the air and sniffed. 'Something smells good,' she said, making a ceremony of seating herself at the table. Relieved that the matter had passed without uproar, Noreen also crept to her place and quickly sat down. It had been the devil's own job getting the sulky young woman out of her bed.

Having heard the mistress and her daughter come down the stairs and into the dining-room, Daisy soon appeared with the tureen of piping hot soup. Sensing the fraught atmosphere, she prepared to serve it and make haste out of there as fast as her legs would take her. But then *his* voice caused her to drop the ladle back into the broth. 'No, Daisy,' he said. 'Take the soup away.' While everyone looked at him, he went on, 'You may also clear away all but mine and Miss Mulligan's places.'

Margaret was aghast. 'Whatever do you mean, Father?' she demanded.

He kept his eyes down for a moment, deliberately antagonising her, then looking to Daisy he said in a controlled voice, 'Have you grown deaf, woman? You have your instructions. Now be about your business, before you're sent packing as well.'

Margaret looked round in astonishment when her mother quietly departed the room; that poor woman had known her husband long enough to realise that later, in the dark hours when the world slept, someone would be made to pay for this. She prayed it would not be her.

'If we're made to go . . . why isn't *she*?' The irate young woman glared at Phoebe with glittering eyes.

'Oh, my dear, you surely don't intend to question my judgment?' His steel grey gaze met hers and she read the message it conveyed. In all of her life Margaret Dickens had never been afraid of her father but in that moment when she came too close to that side of him which was always reserved for others less fortunate than herself, her selfish heart was jolted. Without another word, she wisely followed the hapless Noreen into the hallway from where they parted in separate directions; Noreen to the sanctuary of her shed at the bottom of the garden, and Margaret to her room where she would lie sulking and hating Phoebe all the more.

'Come on! Come on! Enjoy your meal, my dear.' Edward made an extravagant gesture with his arm. 'Spoil yourself,' he said. 'From what Mr Quinn tells me, you deserve it.' He smiled and smiled again, and his smile was so pronounced that his eyes were closed and his face was squashed from forehead to chin as though a great weight was pressing from either end at once.

At that point Daisy brought in the main course, placing the meat dish directly before him and lifting the lid to reveal a sizzling leg of gammon, brown and crisp, and beautifully dressed with honey and pineapple. 'Splendid!' he cried, tucking his napkin more firmly into the neck of his shirt. 'Splendid! Splendid!' He leaned forward to grasp the carving implements.

'My word, Daisy, it certainly smells delicious,' he remarked, leaning forward and twitching his nose at the rising steam. 'You've surpassed yourself, my dear,' he told the beaming maid. 'Surpassed yourself indeed!'

While he set about carving the enormous joint, Daisy plodded out of the room then plodded back with a huge deep dish separated into several different sections, each containing an equal portion of yellow cabbage, tiny red carrots, bright green peas, and a mound of turnip mercilessly mashed with milk and butter before being lovingly shaped into a small pyramid. 'Tuck in, my dear,' Phoebe was told and did the best she could under the circumstances, although every mouthful threatened to choke her.

Throughout that dreadful and unforgettable meal she was made to endure the sight of her uncle constantly smiling at her, occasionally flattering her with regard to her work at the cobbler's and pointing out in flowery terms what a 'sensible and industrious fellow' Mr Quinn was. The more wine he drank, the more eloquent and loud her uncle became, sniggering at one instant and roaring with laughter the next; all the while thrusting more food into his mouth which he then proceeded to chew with the utmost vigour.

'What!' he demanded when Phoebe asked for permission to leave the table. 'You've eaten no more than would keep a sparrow alive.' He flung himself back in his chair and glared at her with popping eyes. 'I do hope it isn't my company that's urging you to leave,' he said meaningfully, while drawing the flat of his hand across his forehead to wipe away a film of glistening perspiration.

'Honestly, I couldn't eat another mouthful.'

'A pudding then? I'm certain I can tempt you to a pudding?' His eyes widened and his eyebrows made wide comical arches above. His face was reddened by the wine, and made redder still when Phoebe refused. 'Dear me. I could have sworn I'd persuade you to try Daisy's remarkable apple pudding,' he said in a ridiculously childish voice.

'I'd like to leave the table, sir,' Phoebe insisted. If he didn't soon dismiss her, she was sure she might tell him what was really on her mind . . . that he was a drunken pig who disgusted her to the core.

'What do you think of your employer, my dear?' He had a special reason for wanting to know, and if Phoebe had guessed it she would have been shocked.

'He's a good man.'

'A good man, eh?' Suddenly his mood was more serious. 'Tell me, my dear . . . do you find Mr Quinn to be pleasant company? What I mean to say is, do you find him . . . attractive?'

Phoebe was puzzled by his questions. 'I don't know what you mean,' she said. 'He's very kind, and well respected by everyone who comes into the shop.'

'But . . . do you find him *attractive*, my dear?' He meant to know. He *had* to know. Deep down the feelings were creeping back, and that was dangerous.

'I've never looked at Mr Quinn in such a way,' she confessed.

He chuckled. 'Is that so?' he asked, tapping his teeth with the prongs of his fork and regarding her through curious eyes. 'Well now, you do surprise me.' Since that first day when his sister's daughter had been despatched to him, he had formulated a plan, a devious plan, which he hoped would 'kill two birds with one stone'. Not a single day had passed without his keeping this delightfully cruel little plan at the forefront of his mind. Now, when he silently took stock of her heart-shaped face and expressive dark brown eyes, he thought again that Phoebe was incredibly lovely. She had a presence about her that could stir a man deeply. Jessica had been lovely also but not like her daughter, not in the same way. Phoebe could light a room with one tiny glance from those wonderful eyes while Jessica's beauty had been quiet, more reserved. Phoebe was still a gem in the making . . . an uncut diamond. 'I did love your mother, you know,' he uttered in a whisper that startled himself.

'Did you?' Phoebe's voice was hard. 'Then why did you write her such a cold unforgiving letter?' When she returned his gaze she held her head high, her eyes condemning him.

Phoebe's harsh words stabbed him to the core, raising

memories that were too much for him to cope with at that moment. The wine had heightened his pleasure, sharpened his pain. The more he looked on Phoebe, the more she put him in mind of his sister. Suddenly his mood darkened. 'Go on. Get out,' he ordered. 'Get out of my sight!' And before he might change his mind she took him at his word and went quickly from there. Sometimes he could be so pleasant that she blamed herself for not seeing the goodness in him . . . after all, he hadn't turned her over to the workhouse, had he? But then, there was a certain look in her uncle's eyes that put the fear of God in her.

Noreen had locked herself in the shed. No amount of cajoling by Phoebe would persuade her to open the door. Eventually, she gave up trying and made her way round the house to the front gate, then from there to the farmhouse. It was fifteen minutes past nine, a glorious evening when the twilight emerged like a creeping shadow and the daylight was soon swallowed up. The moon played hide and seek in a silver-streaked sky, and as she walked across the road, Phoebe marvelled at the strange silence all around; on every side there were creatures – in the air, in the undergrowth – probably listening to her every footstep and remaining still until she'd passed. As they intended, she didn't see them. But she knew they were there just the same. She could feel their presence . . . sense their fear. It was a weird and eerie sensation, knowing that in the quiet street, lit only by a single lamp, she was not alone. And knowing it, she quickened her footsteps.

The door swung open to reveal Lou Peters with a newspaper clutched in his hand and his spectacles perched on the end of his nose. 'Well, well, if it isn't the very lass herself!' he remarked with a broad grin.

Seeing that he must have been enjoying a quiet moment in which to catch up on all the local news, Phoebe at once apologised. 'Oh, I didn't mean to disturb you,' she told him in a sorry voice. But if the truth were told, she was more sorry for herself than for Lou because she really needed someone to talk to.

'Away with yer, woman!' he cried. 'What! Yer a sight for sore eyes and that's a fact.' He pulled a wry little face. 'Aggie's tired herself out though. She's been helping her brothers to stack the hay in the barn, and now she's fast and hard asleep in her bed,' he explained. 'Oh, but here's a lonely old soul who'd love yer to come in and share a brew with him.' He gave a canny wink and a nod of the head, at the same time throwing the door open and ushering her inside. When, groaning, Phoebe explained how she'd seen enough food and drink to last her a lifetime, he suggested heartily, 'Well, there ain't nothing to stop yer from whiling away an hour or so with me, is there? And the pair of us having a chin-wag into the bargain. What d'yer say to that, me darlin'?'

'I'd say it's just what the doctor ordered,' replied Phoebe with a bright smile to match his own.

A few moments later they were seated in the parlour, exchanging tales about the week and talking eagerly of the forthcoming barn-dance. 'It'll be grand,' said Lou. 'We can all put on our best bib and tucker and enjoy ourselves 'til the cows come home. I'm really looking forward to it.' He rubbed his hands gleefully and settled back in his chair, quietly regarding her and thinking how she never seemed to have any fun. 'How are you, me beauty?' he asked with concern. 'How's it going at the house?'

'Oh, it ain't too bad,' she said, and the grotesque image of her uncle at the dinner table loomed into mind. 'I'm looking forward to Saturday as well. It'll be lovely to see Dora . . . and Judd,' she added hastily. Yes, it would be lovely to see both of her old friends.

'You miss them badly, don't yer?'

Phoebe nodded, her thoughts wandering back to the days when she was really happy. Would she ever be that happy again? she wondered.

'Was Judd yer sweetheart?' Lou wanted to know. 'You've told me about your friends, but you've said nothing at all about a sweetheart. A girl as bonny as yourself . . . I reckon yer must have had a sweetheart,' he teased.

Phoebe had been stirred by his suggestion. She and Judd? The very idea! 'No, he wasn't my sweetheart,' she replied softly. Somehow, though, the thought had warmed her through and through.

'Is he handsome?' Lou persisted.

Phoebe nodded. 'Yes, I suppose you could call him handsome.' In fact Judd was really good-looking.

'A nice bloke, is he?'

'The best.'

'Well now.' Lou thought a while. 'Does *he* have a sweetheart?'

Phoebe laughed at her friend's curiosity. 'No, he

doesn't have a sweetheart. Well, not that I know of.'

'Hmm.' He chewed his lip and regarded her curiously. 'A handsome likeable young fella and he hasn't got a sweetheart?' He continued to observe her closely. 'D'yer think maybe the poor soul's hankering after someone he can't have?' he asked meaningfully.

'I'm sure I wouldn't know,' Phoebe said thoughtfully. Suddenly Lou's words had set her thinking about Dora's last letter. 'Judd's that moody lately, you'd think he were in love,' she'd written. 'The girl that gets him will be a lucky soul,' Phoebe said now, and for some reason felt a pang of regret at the thought of Judd walking down the aisle with some stranger.

What the devil's wrong with you, Phoebe? she asked herself, thinking how she must be suffering regret that their childhood was over and they were all grown up now.

'And what about you, me beauty?' Lou asked. 'Have yer found yourself a good man yet?' He knew that Phoebe worked like a dog all week, and for a mere pittance. He also knew that a considerable amount of her time was spent in taking care of herself at home; apart from her meals she did everything for herself . . . kept her room spick and span, did all her own washing and mending, and took a great pride in it by all accounts. On top of that, she helped her aunt in the garden, and religiously set time aside for little Aggie's lessons. Consequently, she left herself precious little time for socialising.

'Give over, you old devil,' Phoebe retorted good-humouredly. 'You know quite well the fellow hasn't been born that can match up to you, and *you* absolutely refuse to wed me, isn't that the truth?' Her brown eyes twinkled as she cocked her head to one side and stared at him in a melancholy fashion.

'Aw . . . yer full o' the ol' blarney, sure y'are,' he laughed, shaking his head and thinking what a darling she was, and how this Judd must have been blind not to see that.

'If I can't have you then I don't want nobody,' Phoebe kept a straight face, until he threw his newspaper at her, then she fell back in the chair laughing.

'Aw, I'm sorry, me darlin',' Lou told her, 'I've no right at all to ask such questions. And I swear I'll not ask again.' It would have done his old heart good to have seen Phoebe and Hadley together; he didn't like Margaret Dickens. He believed that spoiled young woman was a bad choice for his son to have made. Hadley was certainly head over heels in love with the pampered young lady, that was plain to see. Still, there was no harm in wishing that he would come to see her for what she really was.

'I should think so too! Just so you know . . . I ain't got no sweetheart and I don't want none,' Phoebe lied, at the same time wondering what he'd say if he knew she had a hankering after his own son Hadley.

'Well, all I can say is, it's a good job I'm too old in the tooth or I'd take yer dancing meself this very night, sure I would.' He winked and her spirits were lifted straightaway. 'I'll tell you what though,' he added mischievously, 'I intend to have me fair share o' dances at the do next Sat'day . . . we'll have us an Irish fling to top 'em all, I can promise yer that, me beauty.' Springing out of the chair he took her by the waist and spun her round and round until he was too dizzy to stand, whereupon he fell on to the settee, gasping and breathless.

'All right then,' he conceded with a chuckle, 'happen I'll settle for a respectable waltz.' He leaned forward to collect the newspaper which was lying crumpled on the carpet. As he gathered it into his hands and his eyes alighted on a certain article, a look of horror came over his face. Straightening his back, he sat stiffly on the edge of the chair, his hands trembling as he scanned the print. 'God Almighty!' he murmured, and his face was ashen.

'Are you all right?' Phoebe had seen the colour drain from Lou's face and was afraid for him.

For a moment he gave no answer, only stared at the paper in his hand, gripped so hard that his knuckles were stretched taut and bloodless. 'Sorry, me darlin',' he started in a small voice, but then he seemed to compose himself, going on in a brighter tone and with a half-smile that was meant to allay her fears, 'O' course I'm all right . . . except I might have pulled a muscle or some'at.' He grinned then. 'Serves me right for flinging meself about like that. I forget I'm not as young as I used to be.'

'Is there anything I can do?'

'No, no,' he protested. 'Only, it might be best if I get to me bed.' He pulled a sorry face. 'Would yer mind, darlin'?'

Phoebe was soon on her feet. 'You're sure there's nothing I can do?'

'Don't worry yerself. It's some'at and nothing,' he assured her. 'A good night's sleep an' I'll be as fit as a fiddle. I've had it before. It comes and goes.'

Satisfied that it was nothing too serious, Phoebe left him searching for the liniment and bemoaning his 'poor old limbs'. 'I'll pop in and see you tomorrow,' she promised.

Closing the door behind her, Lou hurried back into the parlour, all signs of his affliction miraculously gone. As he went by the kitchen he glanced at the open shotgun rack. The Enfield was missing! 'Damn and blast the bugger!' he cursed. His strictest instructions were that all four shotguns should be securely locked away at the end of each working day. Seizing his topcoat, he prepared to go out in search of Greg, all kinds of fearful thoughts running through his mind as he recalled the newspaper advert. 'It's starting all over,' he murmured. 'Is there no peace to be found because of him?' Flinging the back door open he strode into the night, but then remembered the child sleeping upstairs. Aggie! He glanced up at the bedroom window. He couldn't leave her sleeping alone in the house. There was no telling what might befall her.

And so he came back into the kitchen, took off his coat and waited, impatiently pacing to and fro across the parlour carpet and constantly peering through the window into the darkness. 'You'd best get home soon, yer bugger,' he groaned. 'The devil's on yer heels an' this time he means to run yer to ground. And God help us but I'm afeared he'll take the rest of us with yer!'

Edward Dickens settled back in his chair and unfolded the newspaper on his lap. The advert seemed to leap from the page:

If anyone knows the whereabouts of Gregory Peters, formerly of Appleby, would they please contact Mr J.

Soames, Soames' Farm, Green End Lane, Appleby, Cumbria.

All contact will be kept confidential and any useful information will be suitably rewarded.

'Well, well!' Edward Dickens flung the newspaper to the floor and thrust himself out of the chair. Going to the cabinet, he retrieved a batch of old bills from the bottom drawer and began excitedly shuffling through them. 'There! I knew it,' he cried, singling one out. It was a bill from Peters' Farm for the delivery of 'One sack of potatoes, and a half-crate of prime cabbages'. The original typed heading read:

Peters' Farm,
Wood Lane,
Appleby,
Cumbria.

'Gregory Peters, eh? . . . formerly of Appleby?' Turning his head thoughtfully to regard the newspaper lying crumpled on the floor, Edward stroked his beard and chuckled to himself. He further scrutinised the bill, noting how the entire heading was run through with a pen and replaced with Lou Peters' present address. 'This is a puzzle and no mistake,' he addressed himself softly. But then he liked puzzles. On the other hand he had no liking for Hadley Peters. It irked him to see how that young man had wormed his way into Margaret's affections.

'I'm sorry, Margaret my dear,' he sighed, 'but if this proves to be the opportunity for me to be rid of a certain young man once and for all, then I would be failing in my duty if I didn't pursue it to the bitter end.'

He carefully replaced the bill then returned his attention to the newspaper and to the advert which he quickly tore out and continued to study for a few moments more. 'Well, Mr J. Soames, I do believe you and I should have a little talk,' he said, nodding his head in agreement with himself. 'And soon. Yes, very soon,' he decided. But first he had promised himself a nap for the affairs of office were very tiring. Afterwards he would think all the more on how he might approach this little dilemma.

Chapter Eight

'There she is! Look, there's Phoebe!' Dora was already at the door of the train, waiting for it to stop. At the sight of her friend standing on the platform she was beside herself with excitement. Thrusting her head through the open window, she waved and shouted to catch Phoebe's attention, then almost lost her balance when the train slowed to a halt in violent fits and jerks. 'Phoebe!' she cried, spreading her legs wide to keep upright and thrusting her head out of the window. 'Yoo hoo . . . Phoebe!'

When the breeze caught her hat and sent it spinning along the platform, she found herself being snatched back from the window by a pair of strong determined arms. 'Oh, our Judd!' she moaned. 'You'll have to get it back. That were my best hat.'

'You can think yourself lucky it wasn't your *head* that was whipped off,' he told her firmly as she struggled to return to the window. 'Come away from there.' He kept a hold on her until the train had juddered to a halt, then picked up the overnight valise and pushed the door open. 'Mind the step,' he warned. If ever there was a woman who was accident prone, it was his sister.

Phoebe had heard Dora's voice above the screech of the train whistle and now she stood back, her eyes roving the carriages for the dear familiar face that was momentarily lost to her. A great billowing column of steam rose from the engine, engulfing everything and everyone in a grey mushrooming cloud, then suddenly there were people everywhere, appearing out of the ghostly gloom and hurrying in all directions: folk leaving, folk arriving, some waiting to greet the disembarking passengers, and others there to ply a trade. Phoebe ran between them, eyes peeled so she wouldn't miss Judd and Dora. All week she'd waited for five-thirty on Saturday to arrive. And now it was here, and she could hardly contain herself. 'Dora! Oh, Dora!' she cried now on spying the short dumpy figure emerging on to the farthest end of the platform. It had been weeks since they had seen each other and there was so much to talk about, so much to tell.

As Phoebe ran the length of the platform she thought Dora looked exactly the same: the same walk that was more of a waddle, the same bright cheerful face and bobbed fair hair, the same . . . always the same, thank God! Throwing herself into Dora's arms, Phoebe hugged her and danced her about a bit, then clung to her and cried, 'Oh, Dora, it's wonderful to see you!' And Dora clung to her, and they embraced and laughed and cried and made such a fuss that people regarded them with envious little smiles.

'Don't throttle me then,' Dora said breathlessly. 'Or I shan't be able to tell you all the news, shall I, eh?'

'What news?' Phoebe was instantly curious. It was only then that she saw Judd making his way towards them. She would have gone to him and hugged him in the same way she had hugged Dora but something stopped her. He looked the same, handsome as ever, not tall yet not short, his fair hair still tumbling over his ears and touching his shoulders, and he was smiling in that lop-sided way she knew so well. His face lit up when he caught sight of her and his hazel eyes smiled with pleasure. Everything was the same but *not* the same. Judd seemed different somehow yet she couldn't quite decide what was different about him.

Intent on watching Judd's expression as he came closer, pressing through the crowd that surged forward, Phoebe hadn't realised that a girl was actually walking with him until she heard Dora say, 'This is Shirley. Remember I wrote and told you about her?' When Phoebe seemed taken by surprise she asked anxiously, 'It *is* all right, isn't it? I mean . . . your friend *did* say she could stay as well, didn't he?'

Phoebe was quick to assure her, 'Of course it's all right.' She hadn't forgotten. Since Dora had told her about the young woman who'd 'set her cap at our Judd', Phoebe had been most anxious to make her acquaintance. After all, Judd was like a brother to her and she had almost as much interest in his welfare as Dora. 'Hello . . . I'm Phoebe. Glad you could come,' she told her, extending a hand in greeting. The young woman was every bit as lovely as Dora had described, with dark hair and soft grey eyes and a figure that seemed more mature than her eighteen years. She was dressed in a summer suit of palest green, with black patent shoes that had a higher heel than Phoebe had ever worn.

The young woman didn't answer her greeting. Instead, she inclined her head, shook Phoebe's hand warmly, smiled in a kind friendly manner, then looked up to Judd as though for reassurance. 'She really is lovely,' she told him in a murmur. 'You didn't exaggerate.' There was a hint of regret in her voice.

Putting the bags to the ground, Judd placed his hands on Phoebe's shoulders, gazing down on her upturned face, his quiet smile enveloping her. 'It's good to see you, Phoebe,' he said. 'And how are you . . . really?' he asked in a soft voice that excluded the other two women.

Phoebe felt uncomfortable yet warmed by his touch. There was a moment when she seemed lost for words, when their eyes met and she couldn't see the boy she had grown up with; all she could see was the man and she was confused. 'I'm fine,' she replied, and when she hugged him all confusion was gone. 'Oh, Judd! I'm so glad you decided to come after all,' she said, kissing him on the cheek and not knowing how she sent his heart into somersaults. 'Dora said you might not come, and I did so want you to be here.'

'Oh, and why's that?' he ushered Dora and the young woman before him, then followed at a leisurely pace, smiling down on Phoebe and waiting for an answer to his question.

'Why do you think?' she demanded laughingly. 'Because I want to show you off of course.' She glanced at the young woman who seemed anxious that Judd and Phoebe should not be left too far behind. 'She's very pretty,' Phoebe observed with a wink. Then, teasingly, 'Is she your girl?' She needed to know.

Judd paused, looking down on her with feigned indignation. 'Phoebe Mulligan, I'm surprised at you,' he tutted, beginning to walk on. 'Such personal questions. How would you like it if I asked you about your young man?' he added craftily.

'I ain't got a young man,' she retorted, but her mind was filled with images of Hadley.

'I find that very hard to believe.' He smiled then. Her answer had pleased him but he did not care for the fact that she still saw him as a brother. He was a man caught between two women . . . Phoebe who would be horrified if she knew how he felt towards her and Shirley who made no secret of the fact that she would love to be his wife.

They were at the kerbside now. 'Stay here,' he told the women. 'I'll get us a cab.' As he strode away, Dora engaged Phoebe in excited chatter about the coming weekend. She didn't see how Phoebe's brown eyes kept turning to where Judd was talking to a cab-driver. But the other young woman saw. And she wondered.

Lou was delighted. 'So these are yer friends, Phoebe darlin'?' he said, his face glowing as he looked from one to the other. 'Come away in,' he invited, snatching the bags out of Judd's hands. 'I'll have the kettle brewing in no time at all, sure I will. Yer must be tired after yer journey. Soon as ever you've had some'at to eat, I'll show you yer rooms. Nice they are . . . look out over the fields they do. Later I'll take yer round the farm. It isn't too big but it's home. My two sons are out across the top field and won't show their faces until tea-time,' he chattered on, ambling down the passageway to the parlour. They all followed him, Phoebe and Aggie directly behind, then came Dora and Shirley, and now Judd, happy that Phoebe had found such good friends, and looking at her longingly as she laughed with the little girl who held her hand and smiled up contentedly, a wealth of love flowing between the two of them.

'By! There's gonna be such a grand do tonight,' Lou told them, kicking his legs in the air and shouting out. He chatted and laughed and made them feel as though they had known him all their lives. No one could have guessed that beneath his happy façade he was a worried man. Only Greg knew. He also knew better than to talk to anyone about it. As yet Hadley was unaware of the advert which signalled a new threat to their peaceful existence. The newspaper had been conveniently lost.

Time was running short and Phoebe had much to do. After they had all spent a happy twenty minutes with Lou and Aggie, getting to know everyone, she decided she must leave. 'You'll be all right with Lou,' she told Dora, 'and I'll be back before you know it.' She glanced at the mantelpiece clock; it was already seven p.m. There was nothing else for her to do now but get herself ready. All week she and Aggie had been helping to prepare the food, and everything was 'ship-shape' as Lou might say.

'That's right, me darlin',' he interrupted, 'you get off now. Thanks to you and the young 'un, everything's laid out properly and we're ready for the charge. Folk will start arriving at eight, and every manjack of 'em wants to meet yer,' he said with a twinkle in his eye. 'Me and Aggie have talked so much about yer, we've whetted their curiosity.' He addressed himself to Judd. 'Phoebe's a grand lass, sure she is. Did she tell yer she's taught our

Aggie how to read and write when the teachers had given up the ghost?'

'She did mention it in one of her letters but she made little of it as I remember.' He looked at Phoebe and was proud. 'But you're right, Lou,' he said quietly, 'Phoebe is a grand lass.' He was unaware that the young woman seated beside Dora was regarding him very closely.

'Give over!' Phoebe protested. 'Aggie's a natural learner.' She felt herself blushing beneath Judd's fond gaze, 'I'd best be going,' she said, rising from the chair and leaning over to plant a kiss on Dora's chubby face. 'I'll be back within the hour,' she promised. 'Will you be all right?'

'Of course she will be,' Lou said. 'Go on. Get off and leave these good folk to me.' He looked at Judd, saying, 'If yer want, there's just time to show yer round the ol' place . . . though o' course we won't be able to go across the fields just now. Happen we'll do that tomorror afore yer go back.'

Everyone seemed keen on having a quick look round and so Phoebe chose that moment to take her leave. There was a spring in her step as she crossed the road to Dickens House. It was grand having Dora and Judd here. She wasn't so sure about the young woman though.

Noreen was on her way into the kitchen when she heard the front door opening. She spun round, a look of fear on her face, but when she saw that it was Phoebe, her whole body relaxed. 'Oh, it's you,' she said, coming back along the hallway. 'Your friends arrived safely, did they?' she asked, but wasn't all that interested. There were other things on her mind.

'Oh, Aunt, it's wonderful to see them,' Phoebe replied,

her brown eyes shining. 'Dora hasn't changed a bit.' But Judd has, she thought.

'That's nice, dear,' Noreen acknowledged in a stiff voice as she began to move away. 'You'll have a lovely time tonight then. I've heard people say that the Harvest Dances are always special.' She had never been to one herself although she would have liked to. The truth was her social life had come to an end on the day she was married to Edward Dickens.

'Why don't you come too?' Phoebe had asked the same question only a few days ago. The answer was no then. It was no now. 'It's only across the road after all . . . and you never go anywhere,' Phoebe urged.

'No, dear.' Noreen turned away. 'Your uncle would absolutely forbid such a thing.'

'But he won't be here, will he?' Phoebe had come to know his habits well. On Saturday night he went into Manchester, and in the small hours would come home the worse for drink. 'He wouldn't even know. Who's to tell him?' she asked. 'I certainly wouldn't and Margaret daren't . . . especially when she'd be in trouble for going herself.' So far they'd all been most careful not to mention the Harvest Dance in his presence. If he knew, he would be sure to forbid *any* of them attending it.

'I won't be going, and that's an end to it,' Noreen told her firmly. 'And if I were you, Phoebe, I'd be very quiet about the whole affair.' She glanced round furtively as though expecting her husband to jump out of the wood-work. 'Walls have ears,' she warned. With that she went away at a hurried pace, through the kitchen and on into the shed where she would spend the greatest part of this summer's evening, listening to the strains of the fiddle as they wafted towards her on the breeze, and in her frightened lonely heart she would regret the vows she had taken long ago. But most of all she would loathe the man who had squashed her spirit and used her until there was nothing left.

Phoebe came down the stairs at ten minutes to eight. She had taken great care to look her very best tonight and the result was stunning. Her figure was shown to perfection in the exquisite cream dress her mother had made; her lovely face was glowing, her brown eyes sparkled, and her wild auburn hair tumbled loose about her shoulders in a cascade of natural deep waves.

Margaret was on her way upstairs. Seeing Phoebe making her way down, she deliberately set herself so that neither could pass the other without difficulty. 'My! My! We have gone to a lot of trouble to make ourselves glamorous,' she taunted. 'Oh, but I forgot. You're entertaining friends, aren't you?' She sniggered. 'I'm certainly looking forward to meeting them.'

'Really?' Phoebe feigned astonishment. 'I wouldn't have thought you'd waste your time because you see they're my kind of people . . . honest hard-working folk who I grew up with. I'm surprised you'd want to be seen in the same room.' She was on a higher step, looking down on that surly creature, and it gave her a good feeling. 'But, unlike me, they are civilised, so I'm sure they'll have no objections to meeting you,' she said with an infuriating smile. 'Especially as you have so few real friends of your own.' She watched the colour rise in the other woman's face and she knew she had hit home.

'You're a bastard!' The words were spat out. 'One of these days you'll rue having made an enemy of me.' Her vivid blue eyes were hard and vehement as she continued to stare at Phoebe. 'Watch out for me, Phoebe Mulligan,' she hissed, 'I don't forgive. And I don't forget.' She then roughly pushed Phoebe aside and continued on up the stairs, her fists clenched together and her face a mask of fury. She was seething with hatred, and all of it directed at Phoebe.

Phoebe went on her way, wondering not for the first time whether she'd been wise to antagonise her cousin. There was something particularly vindictive about Margaret Dickens. 'A chip off the old block,' Phoebe chuckled as she went out of the door. She delighted in the fact that Margaret was also keeping secrets from her father. Only the other night there had been a dreadful row that kept the whole household awake beyond midnight. Someone in town had let it be known that Margaret was still keeping company with Hadley Peters, in spite of her father's issuing strict instructions that she was not to see him anymore. This was the stick with which Phoebe could beat her. Margaret knew that. It rankled with her. And it also thwarted any devious plans of her own to cause Phoebe harm.

Just as Lou predicted, the dance was a grand do. He had many friends and colleagues in the farming community, and they were already arriving when Phoebe and Dora strolled through the big barn doors: the men looked comfortable in their cords and plain dark shirts, and the women had dressed for dancing, the younger ones living up to the latest fashion with scalloped skirts just below

280

their knees, and the older ones revealing only glimpses of their ankles.

'What d'you think, Dora?' Phoebe extended her arm, effectively encompassing the scene before them. She was naturally proud of the way it had all come together after the hard work put into it. The barn was decked out in streamers and balloons, every wall stacked high with hay to keep out the evening chills, and the lanterns hung low from the rafters, the flickering flames throwing soft halos of light all around. At the far end of the barn a makeshift stage was built out of compressed straw with flat planks of wood laid out to form a strong smooth surface; this would house the fiddle-player and the caller who would send them dancing across the floor in tune to the merry music.

Four long tables were laid end to end along one wall, each covered in a white sheet and set with enough food for a banquet. There was crispy roasted pork, fresh fish caught and cooked that very day, slices of other meats, and wicker baskets of crispy rolls beside pretty little bowls of freshly churned butter. There were dishes containing beetroot and pickles, sausages and hard-boiled eggs; bowls of rosy apples straight out of the orchard, and other bowls of trifle, fruit salad, and potent punch. Two wooden barrels stood one either side of the farthest table, and in between were large earthenware jugs of ginger ale, sarsaparilla, soft drinks and cider. There were great pint mugs and glasses of every description. The tables bowed in the middle with the weight of it all.

'I've never seen anything like it.' Dora had come into the barn and stood open-mouthed, staring at the spectacle laid out before her. 'It must have cost a fortune,' she gasped.

'Not when you think about it,' Phoebe told her with a chuckle. It pleased her to see how Dora was enjoying it all. 'The fish came out of the river, the fruit came off Lou's own trees, and the meat came from his farm. Aggie and I helped him to prepare it all, so he didn't have to pay for no outside help. And there you are.' She linked her arm with Dora's and propelled her forward. 'The fiddler and the caller don't come for nothing, but they'll take part payment in food and drink, and we can all help to clear away in the morning.'

'Are you happy, Phoebe?' Dora had seen how she was with the little girl, and her affection for old Lou was obvious. She was glad of that. But there had been something in Phoebe's letters that spoke of unhappiness. Dora had come here with the intention of getting to the bottom of it and had told Judd as much. She had also voiced her suspicion that there could be a man involved, and her instincts told her it was one of Lou's son's. Certainly Phoebe had written in glowing terms of the one called Hadley. But then they had met him only a few moments after Phoebe left the farmhouse, and it turned out that he was deeply involved with Phoebe's cousin Margaret. 'Is there something you want to tell me?' she asked in a concerned voice.

'I'm not sure what you mean,' Phoebe replied thoughtfully. Earlier, Dora and Judd had expressed a wish to meet her aunt and uncle, but so far she had managed to put them off.

'Oh, I expect it's me just being silly,' Dora told her.

'It's just that . . . I got the impression from some of your letters that all was not well.' She stopped and looked Phoebe straight in the eye, saying, 'If there was something wrong, you would talk to me about it, wouldn't you?'

'You're imagining things.' Phoebe laughed, thinking how perceptive her old friend was. She had tried hard not to betray certain things in her letters, like her feelings for Hadley when all the time she knew he was Margaret's fellow, or the way her uncle made her frightened even while he was smiling at her, or the awful loathing her cousin had for her. Then there was her aunt, a timid creature who had taken to hiding in the shed more and more; Phoebe often wondered whether that poor soul was losing her mind. There was something else too. Lately she had begun to wonder where her life was leading; she was increasingly dispirited and restless. More than anything, she was lonely. Even when she was laughing with Lou or chattering with Aggie, she still felt incredibly lonely.

Somehow she couldn't talk about her fears to anyone except Marcus. He was always there, always caring, ready to down tools and shut shop at a minute's notice. He knew how she felt about Hadley but never judged her. She was grateful for that. She had confided things in Marcus that she could never confide in anyone else. He was a wonderful person, very much part of her new life for she spent most of it with him in his little shop, from morning till night, six days a week. She had come to know and respect him. In a strange way she saw him as being closer to her than anyone else. She loved Dora, and felt immense pride in the man Judd had become. These two would be very special to her for as long as she lived. But when she needed a shoulder to cry on, it seemed always to be Marcus who was there. Her heart warmed as she thought of him now. Looking about, she searched the barn for him. 'I wonder if Marcus has arrived yet,' she told Dora. 'I do so want you and Judd to meet him.'

'And when are we going to meet your aunt and uncle?' Dora returned. 'Will they be here tonight?'

'Hardly!'

'When do we get to meet them then?'

'Not tonight, I'm afraid. Happen in the morning,' came the reluctant reply. The thought of introducing Dora and Judd to her uncle turned Phoebe's stomach. Her instincts warned her against it. 'He's gone into Manchester and won't be home until the early hours,' she explained. 'After lunch tomorrow he'll be straight into his study, and woe betide anybody who disturbs him. But there might be an opportunity in the morning,' she said, rolling her eyes. 'To be honest, Dora, you wouldn't be missing much if you didn't meet him at all,' she confessed in a harder voice.

'You still don't like him, do you?' Dora had read between the lines of Phoebe's letters, and suspected that all was not well in Edward Dickens' house.

'No, I don't.' Phoebe might have added that he frightened her but thought better of it. After all, he had never really done anything to warrant that kind of fear.

'And your aunt?'

'As I said in my letters, she's more to be pitied than blamed, poor thing.' Phoebe shook her head. 'She keeps herself to herself. But I think you'd like her.' In an effort to change the subject, she indicated Judd and Shirley deep in conversation at the far end of the barn. 'Does she love him?' she asked.

'It looks like it. She's round the house at every opportunity, and it isn't me that's the attraction, that's for sure.'

'What about Judd? Does he love her?'

'Well, he takes her out to the pictures and the like.'

'Do you think they'll get wed?'

'It wouldn't surprise me.' Dora had a few questions of her own to be answered and now she asked, 'What about Hadley Peters? You haven't gone and fallen for him, have you, Phoebe? Not when he's promised to another. You must know that only makes for heartache. Now his brother on the other hand . . . Greg, well, he's every bit as handsome, don't you think? Footloose and fancy free as well, by all accounts.' She giggled. 'He waylaid me earlier on . . . seemed very interested in you. If you ask me, Phoebe gal, I reckon you've only got to click your fingers and he'll come running.' She nudged her friend playfully. 'Don't tell me you don't find him attractive?' she insisted.

'He's all right, I suppose,' said Phoebe. She didn't see any point in explaining she thought Greg was too handsome and arrogant for his own good. The fiddler started playing then and Phoebe's foot started tapping. In no time at all the caller was urging everyone to 'Take your partners' and soon the party was underway. Phoebe was glad of that, because for now anyway Dora's probing questions could remain unanswered.

The evening seemed to fly away. Phoebe danced with Judd, then she whirled with Lou, and now it was coming up to ten o'clock and Aggie was spinning her round and round to the merry tune of the fiddler. 'Hey! You'll have me too dizzy to stand,' Phoebe laughingly told her. 'How about if we go and get ourselves a drink?' she suggested hopefully, sighing aloud when Aggie nodded her head in agreement then groaning when she added cheerfully, 'We can dance right away after though, can't we, Phoebe?'

It was Lou's turn behind the bar. 'Well now, look at the pair of youse,' he chuckled. Then, to Phoebe, 'I don't know which of yer is worse an' that's a fact.' He handed over two glasses, one containing cider and the other a small measure of sarsaparilla which he gave to Aggie, at the same time telling her, 'Another half-hour, me girl, then yer daddy's taking yer home sure he is.' When she grumbled he told her sharply, 'No arguments! The deal was that yer should be tucked up in bed before ten . . . and I've already given yer one reprieve. Half an hour, I say, then it's home to yer bed before folks start getting rowdy.' He winked a merry eye at Phoebe. 'And you go easy on that cider, me beauty,' he warned. 'It's potent stuff, and if I recall you've had more than one already.' All the same, he was delighted that she was having such a good time. Lord only knew she didn't have too much gaiety in her young life.

'Oh, so you're keeping a beady eye on me, are you?' Phoebe said, wagging a finger at him. It was true though. This was her third glass of cider and already she was feeling as rosy as a ripe apple. 'Don't you worry about me, sweetheart,' she said, her brown eyes dancing. 'We're having a wonderful time.' She flung her arms out and cuddled the girl. 'Ain't that right, young 'un?' she asked, planting a kiss on the child's eager face.

Lou roared with laughter. 'Sure yer incorrigible, the pair on yer,' he declared, turning his attention to other customers who were shouting above the music to make their voices heard. 'Don't forget what I said, Aggie,' he called when Phoebe and the girl headed back to the dance floor. 'Half an hour, then I'll be looking to take yer home.'

'Attention everyone, please.' The voice sailed above the din. 'Look this way, folks.' Almost at once the din subsided, with only a slight disturbance from those who were impatiently waiting at the bar. 'Look, Phoebe. It's Hadley!' Aggie began jumping up and down when she saw him standing beside the caller with his arm round the waist of Phoebe's cousin. The two of them were smiling on the sea of upturned faces, waiting to choose their moment. Suddenly silence descended and there was an air of excited anticipation.

Phoebe didn't hear the announcement, at least not word for word. Her thoughts were in turmoil. In her heart she had already sensed why the two of them were up there on the rostrum. They were happy, and they were in love. Any fool could see that. Suddenly the place erupted with folk cheering and clapping. 'Oh, Phoebe, they're gonna be married!' Aggie was beside herself with delight. 'Hadley's gonna get married!' She flung herself into Phoebe's arms. 'I can be bridesmaid, can't I?' she wanted to know. Suddenly that was the most important thing in the world to her.

'I'm sure you can, sweetheart.' Phoebe swallowed the pain in her throat and hugged the girl hard. 'How could they refuse?'

The music slowed to a sentimental melody. Dancers

left the floor and drifted to the bar. Others took their place, soon lost in each other's arms, the older ones remembering how it used to be, and the young ones filled with hopes for the future. There was nothing better than news of a wedding to tug at the heartstrings.

Phoebe led the girl to where Dora was sitting. Phoebe's friend had never been one for dances and so far nothing could persuade her out of her chair. But no sooner had she and Phoebe exchanged two words than she was grabbed by a ruddy-faced farmhand with a pot belly then whisked on to the floor before she opened her mouth in protest. 'No! I can't dance!' she could be heard shouting as the two of them stumbled through the moving couples. His answer was to encircle her waist with both arms and push her round the floor as though she was a wheelbarrow to be shifted. Even with a sorry heart, Phoebe had to laugh.

'Can we ask Hadley . . . about me being bridesmaid?' Aggie insisted, addressing her question to Phoebe but staring with big eyes towards the dance floor. Like Phoebe she was fascinated by the sight of Dora being crushed in the big man's arms.

'We can't ask them now,' Phoebe declared, 'but there'll be time enough tomorrow.' All enthusiasm for the evening had gone. She had a mind to make her way home. Her brown eyes gazed at the couples locked in each other's arms. It seemed as though the world and its lover were out there on the floor: Margaret was gazing adoringly at Hadley, and there was Judd, smiling and handsome, holding his girl tight while she buried her head in his shoulder. Two couples, two men who had touched her life in different ways. Just then Margaret's gaze searched her out and she smiled, a slow satisfied smile that told Phoebe she was still an outsider. She looked away. For the first time in her life she felt a real pang of envy.

'Where's your other friend?' Aggie asked, kneeling on the floor and looking up with bright quizzical eyes. 'Daddy said you could bring him tonight, didn't he?'

'Who's that, then?' Phoebe was only half listening. She wondered whether Lou had been right about her having had too much cider because suddenly she felt light-headed.

'You know who.' Aggie sighed and rolled her eyes heavenwards, looking for all the world like a little old woman. 'Mr Quinn, that's who.'

'Oh, you mean Marcus!' Phoebe had looked for him earlier but so far there was no sign of him. She glanced round the room at the dancers, then the little groups of people standing round the perimeter. She looked towards the big open doors and scanned the bar. Marcus Quinn was nowhere to be seen. 'He promised he would be here,' she told Aggie in a small voice, her heart sinking with disappointment. She had so much wanted to share this evening with him. And now, when she felt so low, he might have cheered her up. Marcus was much more than her employer. He was her dear friend, and she loved him. 'He'll come, I'm sure,' she said with conviction. 'I expect something's delayed him, that's all.' She wasn't to know that Marcus had made an appearance some half hour earlier and had quickly departed when he saw her laughing with Judd.

'Come on now . . . yer time's up,' Lou had come to

collect the child. 'I've left the bar in capable hands,' he told Phoebe, 'so I'll not be back tonight.' He had seen how Phoebe gazed on the dancing couples and suspected she had eyes only for Hadley. He saw how suspiciously bright were those sad brown eyes and said nothing. He wondered whether Phoebe's recent loss of her mother had made her extra vulnerable, and would have moved heaven and earth to see her walking down the aisle on Hadley's arm. In his heart he knew that Phoebe was a better woman than Margaret Dickens could ever be. But there was no accounting for love, and there was nothing he could do. 'Goodnight, me darlin',' he whispered with a merry wink of his eye. 'I'll see yer on the morrow.'

'Goodnight, Lou,' she returned. 'It's a lovely party.' Catching the child into her arms, she hugged her close. 'Goodnight, sweetheart,' she whispered. 'Go along with your daddy now.' Addressing the man, she said, 'Happen I'll not be too long before I make my own way home.'

'Aye,' he said fondly. He looked at the tears shimmering in those magnificent brown eyes, and noticed her glowing face, and for the first time saw the child in her. 'And happen that won't be a bad idea. Like I said, I reckon you've had one cider too many, my beauty,' he chuckled. Then, grabbing Aggie by the hand, he went on his way.

Greg Peters leaned against a timber strut, his dark eyes intent on Phoebe. There was a yearning in him, a deep uncontrollable yearning that haunted him night and day. He had taken many women, and had never loved. But he loved now. And it hurt. News of his brother's announcement had greeted him the moment he came through the door, but it came as no surprise; Hadley was the marrying kind. He was also a fool who couldn't see what was right under his nose. Phoebe had a hankering after him, and he hadn't even noticed.

'Goodnight, Greg.' A sleepy voice sounded in his ear. Aggie didn't look for a kiss. She was just a little afraid of her big brother.

'Going so soon?' Ignoring the girl, Greg turned to his father.

'It's time the child was in bed.' Lou's answer held hidden undertones. 'But then, *you* wouldn't know about that, would you?' For what seemed an age the two men stared at each other, and there was something weighty between them. It was a moment before Lou snapped in a low harsh voice, 'Have yer no bloody sense? Come away from the door, you fool. And keep yer eyes skinned!'

'Don't concern yourself about me, old man.' There was savage contempt in Greg's eyes.

Lou made a noise in the back of his throat, at the same time shaking his head and glaring a moment longer. Then, with a cursory glance, he swept the child into his arms and strode angrily into the darkness.

Phoebe wished the night away. Alone and dejected, she watched the dancers a while longer, smiling back when they deigned to smile on her and laughing a little to see Dora thoroughly enjoying herself. Everyone was coupled up, smiling and happy. Judd and Shirley moved round the dance floor close in each other's arms, until the music stopped and a fair-haired young man approached Shirley for the next dance. Suddenly, Phoebe realised that Judd was making a beeline for her. She couldn't face his pity; it wasn't fair that he should feel obliged to dance with her. Quickly, she slipped away.

From his vantage point Greg watched her every move. He saw the young man searching for her, and was delighted when that same young man was quickly taken back on to the dance floor by his pretty companion. Going to the bar he collected two tankards and a jug of cider. Once outside the barn he took a small flask of brandy from his pocket and poured the contents into the cider jug. Then he went looking for Phoebe, determined that this night would not end in disappointment.

She hadn't meant to wander so far away from the barn but the lake was unusually beautiful and the night was sultry. Entranced, she sat on the grassy bank, listening to the sounds of nature; the gentle ripple of the water, the rushes brushing against its surface, and the small splashing sounds when the water creatures crept from their hiding places to slink away as hunters of the night. The moon was high in the sky and the stars seemed so far away in that vast mysterious space. Here, in this lovely lonely place, Phoebe realised how empty her life really was. Oh, she had her friends and thank God for them. But she had no one of her own, no one left to love. Both her parents were gone. There was no man who she might plan a future with, no real purpose any more. 'Away with you, Phoebe Mulligan!' she chided herself. 'It ain't as though you're old and withered. There's time enough for you to find someone of your own.' She didn't hear the soft footsteps approaching, and when he spoke she spun round, her eyes big and frightened.

'I know how you feel,' he murmured, sitting beside her.

When she made as though to rise, he pressed his hand on her arm. 'Please . . . don't go,' he implored. In the moonlight his eyes were like dark fathomless pools. 'I'm lonely too,' he said softly, adding with a cynical little laugh, 'though I don't suppose you believe it.'

'You're right. I *don't* believe it!' Phoebe retorted. All her instincts warned her to flee. But something else enticed her to stay. He was devilishly handsome and she would be a liar if she said she wasn't flattered by his attention. Besides, she *was* lonely, and what harm could it do to sit and chat a while?

He saw her relax and knew his ploy had worked. 'Life can be so cruel, don't you think?' he asked, sidling up to her.

'What d'you mean?' His black eyes were all enveloping. She could feel herself warming to him. Be careful, gal, she told herself. This one's a devil in disguise.

'Oh, Fate, if you like. You and me.' He smiled. Perfect white teeth against a sun-browned face, and those eyes, dark as night, smiling on her, disturbing her deeply. 'You and Hadley. Me and Margaret.' His words whispered of secrets.

Phoebe stared at him? 'What are you saying?' In her heart she knew he had guessed her affection for Hadley. But him and Margaret? That was a shock.

Her astonishment excited him. It would keep her here, where he wanted her. 'I loved her once,' he lied. '*I still do.*' The smile slipped from his face and he stared at the ground as though in deep painful thought. 'It didn't work out. She saw Hadley as the better man,' he said. It wasn't all lies because he had come nearer to loving Margaret than any other woman he'd ever known. But they were too much alike. It had been a turbulent alliance that had burned itself out.

Phoebe was astonished by his revelation. Certainly she would never have guessed. 'Does Hadley know?'

He shook his head, returning her gaze. It was a moment before he spoke. 'No,' he said presently. 'And he never must.' He wasn't concerned for Hadley's feelings, but afraid of the consequences should Hadley discover the truth: that his girl had spent many a night in his brother's arms. 'It was all too brief. Not worth causing heartache over.' Though there had been a time when he would have delighted in taunting Hadley with his conquest, Margaret saw it another way, and he offered no argument. It served his purpose better to remain silent. That way, Margaret got the man she'd set her cap at, and he was left to play the field without any complications. Secretly, though, it gave him a lift every time he saw the two of them together, knowing that he had bedded her many times.

'You're bastards, the pair of you!'

'You don't really believe that, do you, Phoebe?'

'He should be told.'

'And then what? Margaret adores him, you must see that for yourself.' Personally, he suspected that selfish little creature was totally incapable of adoring anyone. 'Hadley's obviously besotted with her.' He shook his head. 'You're wrong. It wouldn't achieve anything if he were to be told that Margaret and I were once lovers. It was a while back now . . . and, besides, she's made her choice. It's Hadley she wants for a husband. There's been nothing between us for some time now. It's over . . . in the past . . . an affair of the heart that came to nothing.'

He smiled at her, shaking his head slowly from side to side, his voice soft and persuasive. 'Oh, Phoebe . . . Phoebe, you're such an innocent. Would you really want me to tell him and spoil his happiness?'

'I don't know.' Doubts were beginning to creep in. 'I suppose it would cause upset all round,' she reluctantly conceded. 'I reckon he'd half kill you, and serve you right!'

'And what do you think that would do to our father . . . to see his sons at each other's throats? Of course the marriage would be off, and for what? Like I said, what happened was wrong, I know. But it was over a long time ago.'

'But you said you still love her.' Phoebe wasn't entirely convinced, but saw the sense of what he was saying. What point would there be in raking over old ashes and turning an entire family upside down? 'How can you be sure it won't flare up again . . . after Margaret's wed?' The thought was horrifying to her.

'Because she has no feelings for me, and because I know when to concede to the better man.' The words tasted bitter on his tongue. Hadley would *never* be a better man than he! He could see how he was winning Phoebe over to his way of thinking. 'It happened, and now it's over. Let it stay that way,' he urged. Suddenly he wondered if he'd gone too far. His reason for confiding in Phoebe in the first place, was merely to convince her that he was every bit as lonely as she was. God forbid that she should actually reveal any of this to Hadley! He forced his most devastating smile. 'You do agree with me, don't you?'

'Happen I do. To a point.' Phoebe wondered at his

reason for confiding all of this to her. 'But you're still a pair of bastards!' she told him.

He laughed. 'A lonely bastard though.' He let her think on that for a moment before talking of other things, cunningly engaging her in conversation that took her mind off the weaknesses in his character. They talked of family, of the world and its hardships, of love and losses and loneliness. The longer they talked the closer they seemed to come, and the more Phoebe asked herself whether perhaps he was not quite the monster she took him for while *he* secretly congratulated himself on his own deviousness. The night grew darker and the moon played hide and seek with the wispy grey clouds. The breeze heightened, and the strains of the fiddle wafted towards them. 'It's a beautiful evening,' he murmured, gazing up at the sky and feigning admiration. He had placed the jug and tankards behind him. Now, he brought them forward. 'What say we toast the couple's health, eh?' he asked. 'If you ask me, I reckon Hadley's marrying the wrong woman, but there you are. Love makes strange bedpartners.'

Phoebe didn't answer. There was a deal of anger in her still. And regret. And heartache. But in all of that she was mellowed by this man's soothing company. She called herself the worst kind of fool. What in God's name made her fall for a man who was promised to another? She should have had more sense. But then, like Greg said, and quite rightly: Love made strange bed-partners. In any case, how could she be sure it even *was* love? She was no expert on the subject that was certain! She watched as he poured a measure into the tankards. Handing one to

Phoebe he said, 'To Hadley and Margaret!' When she hesitated he chided cunningly, 'Surely you'll drink to their happiness?' He pressed the tankard into her hand, at the same time raising his and saying cheerfully, 'To Margaret and Hadley.' He slyly regarded her out of the corner of his eye, congratulating himself when she lifted the tankard to her lips and took the smallest sip.

The fiery liquid burned her throat and sent her into a coughing fit, but at the same time it instilled a warm comfortable glow inside her. She sipped a little more. It was good. It lifted her spirits and drowned her loneliness. 'I'd best go and rescue Dora,' she said, then surprised herself by giggling. 'She's been a good friend to me, and I love her dearly.'

'And her brother? Judd, isn't it? Has *he* been a good friend?'

'Of course. He's always watched out for me.' She recalled the time when they were children, laughing and fighting with each other. She recalled the way it had been then, and the way it was now. She recalled the girl in his arms and felt a pang of regret. Why did it all have to change? Judd had been like a brother to her, and now things could never be the same again. But everything changes she thought, and regret stabbed her heart. 'I love them both dearly,' she murmured, choking back the tears. 'I always will.' There was a strange mood on her now. One minute she wanted to laugh, and the next she felt like crying and couldn't understand why. 'I don't know what I would have done without them,' she said with great sincerity, turning her serious brown eyes on him. 'They're my real family, don't you see?'

'Then it's only natural that you love them,' he replied, returning her gaze and thinking how truly lovely she was. He wanted to crush her in his arms but knew that if he moved too quickly, the moment would be lost forever. 'What about the Dickenses? Are you happy there, Phoebe?' His voice was deliberately caring. He was well practised, while she was yet of a tender age and charming innocence.

She shook her head. 'No,' she said simply, tipping the tankard to her lips and taking a gulp of the soothing liquid. She began to think she might have been wrong about Greg.

'Edward Dickens has certainly earned something of a reputation,' he confessed. 'I can imagine he must be difficult to live with?' She laughed at this and he sidled closer. 'But surely your aunt is of a kind, gentle nature? Certainly my father often passes the time of day with her. Apparently they share the same passion for gardening.'

'It's the love of her life. She has few friends and no one ever visits the house.' She pictured her aunt sitting in that isolated shed. 'She's lonely too,' she said, twice dipping her finger into the tankard and licking it clean. She felt warm all over.

'Loneliness is a terrible thing,' he remarked. Then he leaned forward and whispered in her ear, 'But *we* needn't be lonely.' She looked at him then, and he was more handsome than any man had a right to be. 'Dora will wonder where I've got to,' she said. When he gazed at her like that, she shivered inside. Her head was beginning to spin. For one hazy minute there she could have sworn it was Hadley who sat beside her, whispering soft and

298

lovely things in her ear. She longed for a man's arms round her. She had never known that joy. 'I must be going,' she said lamely. Her heart was beating furiously.

'Must you?' he asked, stroking her face with the back of his hand. 'You're very beautiful, Phoebe . . . did anyone ever tell you that?'

'No.' In all of her young life, no one had ever told her that in such a way.

'Oh, but you are,' he murmured. 'You're the loveliest creature I've ever seen.' He didn't lie. She turned away then, confused, but happier than she'd been for a very long time. 'A man could easily love you,' he went on seductively. '*I* could easily love you.' He slid his hand round her throat, touching her ear, tracing her lips. He sensed her loneliness, and like the predator he was played on it, gently, persuasively, using all the powers of his worldly charm. And as he poured out his heart to her, he left the tiniest part of it in her possession. 'I *could* love you,' he whispered sincerely. 'Oh . . . so easily.' He felt her resolve melting. Encouraged by her confusion, he pressed his mouth into her hair, marvelling at the wonderful abundance of wild curls blown about her face by the incoming breeze. She excited him like no other woman.

Now, when he roamed his hand down her throat to the point of her breast, Phoebe stiffened, softly moaning. His mouth was on hers, soft and warm. It was good, so good to be wanted. His arms were strong about her and she melted into him. It took but a moment to discard her dress. The night was cooler now but his flesh burned against her. His mouth pressed harder, demanding, wanting, raising the same want in her. No more loneliness. No more regrets. Only a sense of belonging. Above her the stars twinkled and winked. Beneath her the grass was velvet down. She opened herself to receive him, and when he pushed into her, cried out. There was bitter-sweet pain, then a glorious sensation that rippled through every inch of her body. Her heart pounded and she clung to him. His lips were moist – on her mouth, on her shoulder, in the curve of her throat. His tongue followed the curve of her breast, encircled her nipple, wet and delicious, raising every kind of emotion in her. The night remained eerily silent but for soft moans of passion, growing to an all consuming rage, hungry, urgent. All the stars burst at once, filling the sky with a blinding crescendo of silver sparks. Another moment, then he was gone, and she was crying. Desperately afraid. Mortified with shame.

It was two o'clock in the morning. The man swaggered down the road, unsteady on his feet and merrier than he'd been in a very long time. Oblivious to everything, he raised his voice in a bawdy song, throwing his arms about as though he was conducting a great orchestra. He didn't see the motor-vehicle until it was almost on him.

'Hey!' he yelled, stricken white and spreading his hands in the air. 'Are yer trying ter kill me or what?' he demanded, lurching towards the gentleman who climbed out of the driver's seat to glare at him. 'Yer bloody fool. Yer very nearly ran me over!' His frightened shouts echoed along the darkened streets. 'Yer should be locked up . . . put where yer can't do no bloody harm.' Waving his fist in the air, he grew braver with the knowledge that he was still alive. 'I've a good mind ter report yer,' he threatened, drawing closer to the other man.

'Get out of my way, or I might have a change of heart and make a proper job of you,' came the surly reply. Edward Dickens had come away from the gambling tables with a lighter wallet and a heavier heart. Losing a considerable sum was irritating enough, but it hadn't helped his temper when he failed to find a bed-partner to compensate. Oh, there were cheap slags and whores aplenty, but he was a man of taste, and would rather settle for nothing at all than for second best. And so he was in a foul mood which just might have been tempered by murder of a kind. When the hapless fellow ventured ever nearer with a mouthful of sharper abuse, he warned in a voice to frighten even the bravest of men, 'It would pay you to be on your way, you drunken fool!'

But the fellow's brains were pickled by the booze. 'Oh, aye?' he taunted. 'Well, happen that's just where I'm going, matey.' He regarded the other man with renewed curiosity. 'Yer a crusty ol' bugger, ain't yer? But yer won't dampen my spirits, because I've had a bloody good night, and I'm sorry fer you if yer ain't. Garn, yer miserable old sod!'

Something about the man's bearing caused him to peer closer. 'Well, I'm buggered! It's Edward Dickens, ain't it? The fella as sells clothes ter the toffs?' When the other man strode away, he called after him, daylight dawning in his befuddled brain, 'I expect you've been doing some celebrating of yer own, then?' He chuckled. 'An' who's ter blame yer, eh? Not me that's fer sure. 'Cause it ain't every day a fella's blessed with such good news, is it?' He started on his way again. 'I've got three of me own an' I can't get rid of 'em nohow, more's the pity!' He launched into a sad rendering of an old Irish ditty to raise his flagging spirits. Soon he could be heard from one end of Preston New Road to the other and it didn't bother him at all.

But something he had said left Edward Dickens greatly bothered: 'I expect you've been doing some celebrating of your own . . . It ain't every day a fellow's blessed with such good news, is it?' Slinging off his coat and scarf, he made his way straight to the study where he poured himself a deep measure of best whisky. 'Drunken bastard!' he muttered, sinking into the leather chair and stretching out his legs. 'What did he mean, though? Why would I be celebrating? "Blessed with good news" the fool said.' It irked him that he couldn't make head nor tail of it.

Shaking his head, he frowned until the wrinkles in his forehead deepened to crevices. 'Drunken bastard!' He glared at the door as though seeing the man there. 'Pity I didn't run the wheels right over your useless head,' he snapped. He felt incredibly weary tonight. 'Muggy bloody weather!' he snarled, swigging half the whisky down in one go. 'To Hell with it all.' There was something worming in him, something that wouldn't let him be, a feeling of growing horror and a certainty that one day he would have to pay for his sins. The thought put the fear of God in him, so much so that he couldn't rest. He downed the remainder of the whisky. 'What's wrong with you, man?' he reprimanded himself. 'You're getting to be afraid of your own shadow!'

But it wasn't his shadow that he was afraid of. Oh dear no. It was something far more substantial than that!

'Damn your eyes, Jessica,' he moaned. '*You* did this to
me. I was putting it all behind me, beginning to forget.
And then you had to go and die on me, damn and bugger
you! *Why did you send her here?* Was it to haunt me?
Did you want to punish me, is that it?' There was such
fury in him, such inexplicable loathing. 'I did it for you,'
he whispered. 'I did it because I loved you, can't you see
that?' He rested his elbows on the chair arms and slumped
like an old, old man. 'I couldn't let you marry him,' he
groaned. 'You were always too good for the likes of
Marcus Quinn.' He chuckled then, but there was no mirth
in his laughter. 'You never did forgive me, did you? All
those years gone by, wasted, and still you can't forgive
me.' He dropped his head to his chest and cried like a
baby. 'Oh, Jessica . . . Jessica! Did you have to send her
here? You knew I couldn't refuse. But you were wrong
to do that, my dear. Don't you see? I can't love her. I
can't bear her to be near me. It's like a knife in my heart.
Oh, my poor, lovely Jessica . . . if you thought to punish
me in this way, then it was wicked of you. And so wrong,
my dear. Oh, so wrong.'

His restlessness took hold of him like a tangible thing,
driving him to his feet again, making him pace the floor,
up and down, up and down, a caged creature seeking a
way of escape. He wanted things, bad things, things that
were not his to take. 'No . . . NO!' His cries were awful.
Upstairs Noreen heard and was mortally afraid. Margaret
heard too, but then she had heard before and tonight she
had a wedding to think of. Nothing else mattered.

Edward Dickens stretched himself to his considerable
height, frantically running his hands through his hair and

grabbing at his temples, trying desperately to still the teeming devils inside him. But they were persistent. So persistent. He returned to the desk and helped himself to another measure of whisky. He would drown the clawing demons that wouldn't let him be. But they'd be back tomorrow. They always were.

The dawn came quickly, streaking the night sky with brilliant shards that blossomed into daylight. The world was awake, the sun overlaid everything in a gossamer haze, and one finger of morning invaded Phoebe's room, disturbing her from a fretful night. Later, the events of that night would reap their own terrible consequences but for now, she dreaded only this day, one she would have cause to remember with a far deeper sense of terror.

Turning towards the window, she blinked her eyes. Sighing deeply, she turned away, and buried her head beneath the bedclothes. She had no wish to get up, no desire to wash or dress or show herself downstairs. Folding her hands in a gesture of prayer, she laid her face down on them, her eyes open now, and still red from crying. She was lonelier than ever. Only now she didn't know which was worse . . . loneliness, or shame.

The night had seemed never-ending, filled with sounds that made her tremble. She had heard the cries that rang through the house in the early hours when she had lain awake, unable to escape her fears in slumber. She was at the window when her uncle drew up in his motor-car and witnessed the angry exchange of words between him and the irate fellow who had almost contributed to his own end. Later, when she had bathed for the umpteenth time, wanting to wash away the shame that clung to her, she had heard the cries. Just one word repeated twice: 'NO . . . NO!' but it had chilled her to the bone. At first she'd wondered whether it was some unfortunate soul caught in the realms of nightmare but then she realised it was her uncle's voice. No doubt news of his daughter's betrothal had raised the devil in him and he was laying down the law. After all, Edward Dickens was not a man to be defied, and Margaret had gone against his express wishes. All the same, though, it was a weird lament, and one which only added to her own bad dreams.

Phoebe threw back the covers. Already the room was warming to the morning sun. A peep at the clock told her it was quarter to six. She couldn't have had more than three hours' sleep because she had still been kneeling by the window searching into the night for some kind of peace when the downstairs grandfather clock struck three a.m. 'Come on, Phoebe gal,' she told herself now. 'It ain't no use lying here wishing it hadn't happened . . . because it *did*.' And how she prayed to God that it hadn't. Closing her eyes, she sought to erase the memory from her mind. It was no use. Slowly, as though the weight of the world rested on her shoulders, she got out of bed, wrapping her robe tight about her slim form and padding to the window on bare feet. With quick angry movements she flung back the curtains and slid the window open to look out.

The sky was bright. The grass was green, and the starlings sat along the rooftops just as they always did. The dry warm smell of new mown hay teased her nostrils, and somewhere in the distance a dog was barking. In spite of herself, she smiled. The world appeared to be exactly the same. But it wasn't. Phoebe knew the world could never be the same again for as long as she lived. Her gaze wandered to the farmhouse opposite, then on to the roof of the old barn. Far off, the lake shimmered and sparkled. Beautiful. Sullied. Knowing her secret. Suddenly she felt the hairs on her arms stand up and she shivered violently. The incoming breeze had turned spiteful. Regretfully, she closed the window.

Going to the door, she made certain it was bolted. It wasn't enough just to glance, she had to push the bolt home just that bit further, afterwards trying the handle and satisfying herself that it couldn't be opened from the outside. She stayed by the door, listening, curious, waiting for a noise . . . *any* noise that would tell her she wasn't alone in this cold unfriendly place. But all was silent. Deathly silent. The house was asleep.

She went back to the bed and sat with her head aching as if it was pressed down by a great weight. One dark thought, one awful realisation, paraded through her mind again and again. Last night she had lost her virginity. That was all she could think of, and the pain was tenfold. 'I shamed myself . . . and I shamed you too, Mam,' she whispered. She was aware of her mother's soulful eyes looking down from the mantelpiece, accusing her, saddened by what had befallen her foolish daughter. Phoebe imagined her mother in the room with her. It brought her both comfort and dread. Yet she couldn't look up. She couldn't look into that darling face. Even now she wasn't certain how it happened. 'How in God's name could I have let it?' she asked herself, hating every inch of that body which she had handed over so willingly. 'In the whole of my life I've never so much as touched a drop of drink.' But now it had brought about her downfall. 'There's no one else to blame but myself.' 'The devil's brew' her mam had called it, and by God she was right. And the 'devil' was Greg Peters in disguise!

Phoebe stared up at her mother's picture. 'Oh, Mam, what am I to do?' she asked forlornly. 'I've done wrong and I'd give anything to put it all right again,' she went on in a whisper, afraid that someone might be listening to her shameful confession. 'How can I go out there and face everybody? They'll all know, 'cause they'll see it in my face.' She laughed a little, tossing her head angrily. 'They were right, weren't they, Mam? When they said I was no lady . . . they were right.' She gazed a moment longer into her mother's eyes and her heart weighed like lead inside her. All her tears were shed now. They were not the answer. They never were. She had learned that a long time ago. When life chose to cause upheaval and chaos, there was only one thing to do and that was to stand tall and straight, facing it head on. She prayed she had the courage to do that.

For the first time since dragging her way home last night, skulking out of sight so she wouldn't be detected, Phoebe felt her strength returning. 'I won't give him the pleasure of seeing me brought down,' she said, going to the mirror and staring at the dishevelled creature there. 'I can put on as brave and proud a face as anybody.' But she didn't *feel* 'brave' or 'proud'. She felt dirty and cheap . . . used and discarded. They were not very pleasant feelings and she despised him. But she despised *herself* even more! 'Look at you, Phoebe Mulligan!' she demanded. 'What do you see, eh?' Leaning forward she examined the girl in the mirror: the same brown eyes, albeit sadder, the same wild abundance of auburn hair, and the same calm classic features. But, like the world outside, they were *not* the same, and now they never would be. Not to her at any rate. The image told her something else too. It told her that a girl had gone to the barn-dance but a *woman* had returned. 'It don't make you any better for that, Phoebe Mulligan,' she said scornfully. 'And it don't hide the shame that made you so.'

It was four minutes to eight when she entered the dining room. She presented a bright fresh picture in her white blouse and blue summer skirt; she had scrubbed her teeth until they sparkled, and her hair shone like an autumn halo around her quiet face. Her smile though was subdued, and her eyes shadowed by a sleepless night. Her aunt had been the first one to arrive. She turned to smile as Phoebe came into the room. 'Hello, dear,' she said, quickly returning her attention to the task of arranging daffodils in a china vase. 'Did you see Margaret on your way down?' Noreen hadn't forgotten what had happened the last time her daughter chose to be late to table.

'No.' Coming to stand beside her aunt, Phoebe went on, 'I didn't see anyone at all.' She was fascinated to see how very clever her aunt was with things of the earth, how daintily and exquisitely she placed each and every flower until the whole arrangement was a thing of splendour; the vase was best white china, bulbous at the bottom and slender at the top, and the daffodils formed a perfect bouquet. 'I wish you'd been there last night,' she said now. Maybe then the awful thing wouldn't have happened.

Phoebe's pain must have betrayed itself in her voice because Noreen turned to regard her with quizzical eyes. 'You know your uncle would never have permitted such a thing,' she said thoughtfully. 'He's not too fond of Lou Peters, or any of the family come to that.' Her thoughts turned inwards, to the time when she met Lou Peters along the lane, and he had flirted outrageously with her. On that day she felt more of a woman than she had in many a long year. 'Personally I think Mr Peters is a delightful man,' she dared to admit. Her gaze grew intense. 'Are you all right, dear?' she asked, suddenly aware of Phoebe's pale features and troubled brown eyes.

'I'm fine,' Phoebe lied, an embarrassing pink flush coming over her face. 'I'm just a bit tired, that's all.' She realised with astonishment that her aunt appeared quite unaware of her daughter's exciting 'news', and Noreen's next comment confirmed her belief.

'I expect Margaret was there last night? I've a feeling she's defying her father's instructions to stay away from that young man.' She tutted softly. 'Foolish girl. But then, you young ones are all the same . . . partying and fun before a good night's sleep.' She seemed instantly regretful that she had classed Phoebe and the selfish Margaret in the same mould. 'Still, I don't begrudge you your moments of happiness, dear,' she said, fondly touching Phoebe on the shoulder. 'God knows you haven't got much to celebrate about your life in this house. You do work very hard, and it has been a while since you saw your friends.' She glanced at the door. 'But you mustn't mention the barn-dance in front of your uncle, dear,' she pleaded. 'He doesn't hold with such things.' She smiled then and Phoebe saw the beauty beneath. 'What about your friends then . . . did they enjoy themselves?'

Phoebe laughed. 'They had a wonderful time.'

'That's nice, dear. But they're going home today, aren't they?' Phoebe had been full of their visit, eager to talk about it days before she even knew they would accept.

'Yes. Lou's taking them in to Blackburn station.'

'I expect you can't wait to get over there this morning?' Noreen smiled a rare smile which lit up the whole of her face. 'I'm really glad you have such good friends,' she said softly. Phoebe looked so sad this morning, probably because her friends were leaving soon. For a fleeting moment Noreen felt the strongest urge to take her in her arms and hold her as she knew her mother must have held her. Noreen had forgotten what it was like to embrace another human being, and was so very lonely. Suddenly there was a slight sound at the door, and even before she turned her face to him, she knew it was her husband. In a furtive whisper she warned Phoebe, 'Say nothing in front of him. *Say nothing!*'

In his usual authoritative manner Edward Dickens remained at the door, staring at the two women and half-smiling as they made their way to the table. When they were standing behind the chairs at their respective places, he came forward, striding across the room with slow decisive footsteps, his head up and his hard grey eyes searching the room for any little thing that might cause him to give vent to his bad temper. Swinging round at the head of the table, he gripped the chairback with strong fists and continued to observe the two women. Noreen fidgeted but looked away but Phoebe stood tall and straight, meeting his gaze with quiet defiance. Her shame burned inside her like a beacon, but she would not let him know it. She would not let anyone know it.

'I do hope I won't be called on to inflict punishment,' he sighed, glancing at the mantelpiece clock and noting that it was only a minute to go before eight o'clock. He smiled, turning to beam at one then the other. 'It's a dreadful thing . . . to inflict punishment on one's own,' he said meaningfully. 'Especially on the Lord's Day.' He inhaled loudly, filling his great chest with air and drawing his mighty frame to its full considerable height. His expression grew grim. Only the ticking of the clock broke the unbearable silence . . . tick, tick, tick, spending the seconds, bringing the hands nearer and nearer to when it would chime out eight pretty tinkling chimes. Phoebe glanced at her aunt and her heart went out to that poor frightened woman. 'Would you like me to go and call her?' she asked boldly, daring to smile at him.

At first he appeared to be astonished. But then his every feature relaxed into a wide horrifying smile as the clock struck its first chime, echoing as it did the louder chime of the grandfather clock in the hallway. His eyes looked beyond Phoebe and there was delight in his face as he spoke. 'Ah! Margaret, my dear,' he declared, lowering his voice to chastise. 'You do like to try your father's patience, don't you? I would rather you didn't cut it quite so fine, my dear.' His meaning was unmistakable. But then his eyes softened as she breezed into the room and made straight for him, her blue eyes twinkling and her painted lips drawn back in a smile.

'But I'm not late,' she reminded him. 'You can't say that.' She came to where he stood and raised her face for him to kiss. He did not disappoint her.

Soon they were all seated and Daisy was plodding back and forth in her usual unhurried fashion. Phoebe wondered what could be wrong with the amiable little woman, because she looked grim-faced this morning, not her usual self at all. As for Phoebe, she wasn't the slightest bit hungry and so picked at the bacon on her plate, dreading the moment when her uncle would announce that breakfast was over and it was time to make their way upstairs. The moment came all too soon. 'It would appear you have all replenished yourselves,' he said, rising from his chair. 'Now it's time to replenish your souls.' Without another word he went from the room and they all followed . . . first Noreen, then Margaret, and last Phoebe.

As she approached the foot of the stairs, Phoebe peered into the kitchen. Daisy peered back and frowned, clamping her mouth tight and turning her eyes upwards in despair. Her despair heightened when the master called out, 'Leave it, Daisy. Don't keep the good Lord waiting.' Her mouth opened as though she was about to reply but then she sighed, threw her dishcloth down and took up position behind Phoebe. 'I ain't got time for this,' she was heard to mutter. 'There's too much work still to be done . . . floors to be scrubbed and dishes waiting to be washed. And I can't see the good Lord doing it for me, I can tell you that!' she complained. Edward Dickens stopped and looked down at her, and she was struck silent.

As they went up the stairs and along the landing, a feeling of the ridiculous came over Phoebe and it was all she could do not to laugh. There they all were, traipsing up the stairs like a procession of chicks behind their mammy, and not one of them in a position to refuse the whim of this man who loved to be obeyed. Phoebe wondered about his true motives. Nobody loved the good Lord more than she did, because it had been part of her upbringing to know the strength and forgiveness of the Maker. Yet, right from the very first time she had entered the room which her uncle described as the 'Praying Room', she had sensed a bleakness there, a certain cold emptiness that denied the Lord's presence. She sensed it now as they filed into the solitary pew, remaining on their feet while he positioned himself before the lectern. 'Be seated,' he instructed, then wasting no time, launched into a sermon that warned of 'the evil around us' and 'temptation that creeps up and takes us unawares'. And while his voice droned on, Phoebe turned her thoughts to the 'temptation' of Greg Peters. She asked the Lord's forgiveness and wondered what would become of her.

It was an hour later, at fifteen minutes to ten, when Phoebe came into the morning sunshine. She took a moment to breathe the fresh clean air. There was something very unhealthy about that 'Praying Room', she thought. Not for the first time it crossed her mind that Edward Dickens was a man of many dark secrets; a man who had designed that room not for the replenishment of other souls but for the purging of his own spirit. It was a strange thought. But then, she thought, her uncle was a strange man.

Feeling as though she'd just been let out of prison, Phoebe ran all the way to the back of the farmhouse, her eyes watching out for Greg and her spirit prepared for an unnerving encounter. As it happened, he was nowhere to be seen. There was no one in the house, and as she came back into the sunshine Phoebe cupped her hands round her mouth. 'Lou! Dora!' she called as she hurried towards the big barn.

'Well, bless yer heart!' Lou appeared like a leprechaun out of the gloom, seeming tiny and insignificant beside the huge open doors; he had on a green woollen trilby with a short pink feather protruding from it, and his homely face was creased into a broad grin. 'Sure yer a darlin', what are ye?' he asked, coming to greet her. 'Yer always as good as yer word,' he said. 'And I'll not deny I'm glad of every pair of hands I can get this morning. They're all inside, with the exception of young Shirley, who seems reluctant to leave her comfortable bed so early of a morning.' He chuckled. 'Nice enough girl, but a bit delicate by my reckoning.' Thrusting his fists into his pockets, he groaned, 'You've never seen such an unholy mess in all yer life!' he told her. 'And I feel terribly guilty, taking advantage of you and yer friends.'

'Nonsense!' Phoebe told him. 'It's all part of the fun.' She glanced about. 'And where's Aggie?' she wanted to know.

'Ye might well ask. She's still in her bed, fast and hard asleep, the little devil.'

In a moment Dora had appeared and her face lit up at the sight of her friend. 'Oh, Phoebe!' she cried, running to grab her in chubby arms. 'I can't recall ever enjoying myself so much . . . the barn-dance . . . and that young man!' Her face blushed a brilliant shade of pink. 'He's promised to write to me. Happen he'll even come to visit . . . Oh, Phoebe, what fun! I didn't get to bed 'til the early hours.'

Much to the amusement of Lou, who hurried alongside, she grabbed Phoebe by the arm and propelled her towards the barn, all the while gabbling excitedly about the young man and how she had been enthralled by the entire evening.

Suddenly her voice fell. 'And where did *you* get to?' she demanded. 'I searched high and low for you.' She giggled. 'Sneaked off with a young fella of your own, did you?' she asked, with a sharp nudge and a mischievous wink. 'Who was it? Come on, Phoebe Mulligan! Tell your old friend what you got up to,' she insisted. She knew it wasn't Hadley because he was still dancing with Margaret when Dora had called it a night. 'Did your employer turn up . . . Marcus Quinn? Was it him you went off with?' she wanted to know. Tact was never Dora's strong point.

'Leave the lass alone,' Lou interrupted kindly. 'She went home to her bed, isn't that the case?' he asked her, deliberately throwing her a lifeline but secretly curious as to whether there was any truth in what Dora was implying.

Phoebe laughed, hating to lie and choosing instead to turn the tables on her inquisitive friend. 'We're not all fortunate enough to find a handsome young man who promises to write and happen visit,' she teased. 'And, no, I did not sneak off with Marcus.' She shook her head at the thought. 'The very idea!' she declared, adding with regret, 'I wonder why he didn't turn up.' If only he had, she thought. If only he had she might not have done what she did. There was a dark mood pressing down on her and she mustn't let that happen. 'Right! Let's get on,' she suggested, surging forward and taking Dora with her. 'The sooner the barn's cleared up, the more time we'll have together . . . and you can tell me all about your young man,' she teased, making Dora giggle. Phoebe had known her long enough to tell that this young man would be just a passing phase. Dora was not the marrying kind.

When Lou protested that 'Us men can manage all right. There's no reason why you and Dora can't take yerselves off right now', Phoebe answered by rolling up the sleeves of her blouse and energetically launching herself into the work. She and Dora swept the discarded food from the tables into rubbish bags, carefully collecting the cutlery and crockery which was then ferried to the house and washed before being packed into the cupboards. In the barn the men set about clearing the ground underfoot. Judd and Lou folded the tables and replaced them in the loft; Hadley dismantled the stage and carted away the empty beer barrels, and soon it was as if there had never been a party there at all.

'You're a very special person, do you know that?' Phoebe had been rehanging the brooms in the rack at the rear of the barn when Hadley came up to help. She spun round to find him looking straight into her surprised brown eyes. His smile was devastating. 'Some lucky man will be blessed with a fine wife in you one day,' he told her, leaning down to kiss her warmly on the forehead. Without another word he strode away, leaving her confused and, strangely, a little angry. She wondered about her feelings for him. Something in her had died, and she didn't know what. After last night she wondered whether she would ever again feel the same about anything.

Judd's heart fell like a stone inside him as he watched Hadley bend to kiss Phoebe's upturned face. As a man he knew there was nothing but gratitude meant on Hadley's part but he still couldn't be certain about Phoebe's feelings and so kept close his own love for her.

Margaret arrived just as the work was finished. It took only one glance for Phoebe to see that she had gone to a great deal of trouble with her appearance. Gone was the dreary face that had stared at her across the breakfast table. Her yellow hair was curled into a bounce, and she had changed into a very fetching sky blue dress that highlighted the vividness of her eyes. 'Oh, Hadley, if I'd known you were hard at work I would have been here much earlier to help,' she said, her voice all sweetness and light and her smile shameless. She would have drawn him away without passing the time of day with anyone, but he took her by the hand and introduced her first to Dora and then to Judd. 'These are Phoebe's friends,' he explained. 'And now they're *our* friends.'

'Pleased to meet you,' she said, even indulging in a shaking of hands all round. Her gaze lingered a moment on the handsome Judd but she hardly noticed Dora who enthusiastically held on to Margaret's fingers, shaking them up and down, and bubbling over with congratulations on the 'romantic announcement'. Afterwards, Phoebe's poor opinion of her cousin plummeted even further when she saw her surreptitiously wipe her hands on one of the folded tablecloths, her face dark with disgust as she glanced at the exuberant Dora who was telling one and all that she would 'never forget what a wonderful time I've had!'

Shortly afterwards Hadley and his love wandered away, deep in conversation. Margaret had led him to believe that she had spoken to her father and everything was all right. But when Hadley insisted that he call on his future father-in-law, she slyly dissuaded him as usual, claiming that: 'Daddy's up to his neck in matters of business.' And so, yet again, she managed to keep the two men apart.

Aggie arrived to take the effervescent Dora on a tour of the lake. Lou and Judd wandered off, discussing the merits of government, until Shirley appeared, when Lou made his way back to the house, leaving the couple to wander away together. Aggie was full of excitement, wanting Phoebe to go with her and Dora on a tour of the top field. 'You can see the whole world from there!' she told Dora, and how could their visitor refuse to go with her after that? 'But you'll have to wait a while because there's still a few plates and things to wash,' she explained, looking to where Phoebe was gathering the remaining odd pieces to be found scattered about the barn.

'That's all right, Dora,' Phoebe assured her. 'You and Aggie go ahead. I'll catch up as soon as I've finished.'

Dora was greatly tempted. Time was running short and she had seen so little of the farm. 'You're sure now?' she asked.

'Go on,' Phoebe urged, then glancing at Aggie she insisted, 'Stay on the footpath, won't you? Don't go near the lake.' The banks were dangerously steep in places. Returning her attention to Dora, she explained, 'It won't take long before I'm finished here. I'll see you both in a while, eh?'

Dora laughed as Aggie grabbed her by the hand. 'Come on,' she urged, tugging her towards the barn door. 'Else it'll be time for you to go, and I want to show you our special places . . . Phoebe's and mine.' The two of them went out of the door, laughing and excited, and Phoebe's heart was warmed by the sight. If only it could stay like this, she thought. But it couldn't, and soon her friends would be gone. She tried not to think too hard about it.

While Phoebe worked, going from one corner of the barn to the other, she had the strangest feeling that someone was watching. Twice she paused in her labours to rove her anxious gaze round that great empty place, and each time she laughed at her own fears. 'You're getting to be afraid of your own shadow, Phoebe Mulligan,' she told herself, beginning to sing as she went, and casting her mind to other things such as Judd and his girl. It would certainly be an odd thing to see him wed. Shaking the thoughts clear, she dwelt on the matter of her cousin and the uproar she was convinced lay just around the corner. It was painfully obvious that Edward Dickens knew nothing of his daughter's total commitment to Hadley. 'You're too good for her,' she murmured, pausing to gaze towards the farmhouse where she had last seen them heading.

'And what about you, Phoebe?' The quiet voice came out of the shadows, making her swing round in alarm. Greg Peters was on her before she could make a move.

Crushing her to him, he murmured, 'Surely you don't still prefer him to me? Not after last night?' His eyes were dark as the shadows and his voice was heavy with passion. 'I could love you,' he whispered. 'You know that, don't you?'

'Take your hands off me!' Phoebe warned, summoning every ounce of her strength to fight him off. But he was strong. Too strong for her.

Cupping her chin with long hard fingers, he turned her face to look up at him. 'You and me . . . we could make a future of sorts.' He laughed and it chilled her to the bone. 'You liked last night, didn't you?' When her answer was to sink her teeth into his hand, he pulled her roughly to him. 'You little wildcat!' he said breathlessly. 'You're all woman though . . . I like that.' He lowered his head and smothered her with kisses. She couldn't breathe. Clenching her fists, she pummelled them again and again into his chest. But he was like a man possessed. He meant to have her and no amount of struggling on her part would deter him.

Her mind quickened. Pretend, she told herself. Fool him. It's your only chance. She stroked his face, surprising him. His eyes gazed down on her, alive with lust. 'Not like this,' she said softly, loathing him. 'Wait. They're not far away.' Her heart leaped when she felt him relax his grip. A look of puzzlement crossed his features, then an expression of sheer delight. 'Why not *now*?' he asked, nuzzling her ear. 'What if I can't wait?' He moaned and took her to him, the force of his kiss bending her head back. She found herself struggling again. Desperate, she kicked out. There was a loud cry and she wasn't even certain whether it was she who had made it.

A fleeting shadow passed between them and she felt herself being flung aside. In the half-darkness the two men grappled. Then came a crunching blow and one man stood over the other. The atmosphere was charged with hatred. She recognised the other man. 'Judd! No!'

Unlike him, Phoebe had seen the knife in Greg's hand as he writhed on the floor. 'Leave him be,' she yelled, flinging herself between the two men; there was no doubt in her mind that Greg would run the knife through Judd's heart without a minute's hesitation. 'It's all right,' she insisted, forcing her voice lower, its calmness belying the fear and turmoil inside her. She was shocked by the whiteness of Judd's face, the contempt and disbelief there. 'It's all right,' she repeated, putting her hands on his chest. She could feel the broad taut muscles there. The sinews in his neck quivered as he bent his face to hers. 'What are you telling me?' he asked, looking down on her grimly. 'Are you saying you *weren't* fighting him off?' There was pain in his eyes and she misunderstood.

When Phoebe hesitated the other man leaped to his feet. Locking her in an embrace, he pressed her to him, leering at Judd and boasting, 'You must be blind, man! Me and Phoebe were having a bit of fun, that's all.' He sniggered. 'A lovers' quarrel.' He glanced down at her. She could feel the knife-handle digging into her thigh. He smiled wickedly. He knew why she had intervened and it only added to his enjoyment. 'Isn't that right, Phoebe?' She didn't answer immediately. His smile slipped away and she sensed the threat; felt his hand drop to his side. Suddenly nothing mattered but that Judd should be safe.

'That's right,' she murmured, and her heart sank at the shattered look on his face.

He stared at her and nodded his head slowly, the truth sinking in. 'I'm sorry,' he said, his features remaining hard and unyielding. 'You must think I'm a complete fool . . . bursting in like that. It's just that, well . . . I thought . . .'

Phoebe shook her head. 'You weren't to know,' she said brightly. 'It's all right. There's no harm done.' Secretly she thought, You're still alive, thank God. She hadn't wanted Judd and Dora to go, but now she wanted them to leave as soon as possible. She walked with him to the door, making conversation and allaying his fears. Greg followed.

When Judd was safely on his way, Phoebe let her suppressed emotions spill over. She was overwhelmed by such fury that it frightened her. In that moment when Greg came up behind her to place his hand on her shoulder, his soft taunting laughter was more than she could bear. 'You're a clever little bitch,' he said. 'Couldn't bear the thought of him being stuck in the ribs, eh?' He groaned with a deep-down need that had only been heightened by the deception. He began to paw her. 'Or did you suddenly want me as much as I want you?' His fingers slid down her blouse.

Her fury lent her an almighty strength. Swinging round, she brought her bunched fist up and smashed it into the side of his face, sending him reeling backwards, more with shock than pain. When it seemed he might spring at her, Phoebe stood her ground, her brown eyes glittering dangerously as she told him in a quiet dignified voice, 'If you ever lay a hand on me again, I swear to God . . . I'll kill you!' She stood there, legs astride, her fists clenched by her sides and her whole body bristling with loathing. There was no fear in her now. Only a terrible anger that seemed to consume her. She couldn't take her eyes off him. There was murder in her heart. Ashamed of her own feelings, she turned and walked away, slowly, deliberately, taunting him now. And he watched her go, laughing softly, but this time he made no attempt to follow.

The three of them viewed the world from the top field and then all returned to the farm by way of the lake. 'It's so beautiful,' Dora gasped, her entranced gaze skimming to the far-off willows. 'Much more than I could ever have imagined.' Phoebe's letters had lovingly described the landscape, but in reality it was magnificent. They stayed a while longer, and they talked of Dora's young man and spoke excitedly of when they might get together again and mulled over things close to both their hearts. Aggie played close by, and Phoebe told Dora how much she loved the delightful little girl. Then Aggie persuaded them to play hide and seek and everyone had a wonderful time before they made their way back down to the farmhouse.

Phoebe took Dora and Judd to meet her aunt. Everything was nice and polite, and Noreen apologised because her husband was ensconced in his study and, according to instructions given earlier, was not to be disturbed under any circumstances. Secretly, Phoebe was glad about that.

Soon the best part of the day had gone and it was time for Dora and Judd to leave. 'Look after yourself, lovey,' Dora said, tears falling down her face when Phoebe gathered her in her arms. 'Oh . . . I'll be thinking of you every minute,' she promised. 'Every minute, I tell you!' Sniffling into her handkerchief, she climbed on to the wagon, her sorry eyes gazing back at the barn and her mind picturing the young man there. She hoped he would write because she would be counting the days.

Now it was Judd's turn. Being so close to Phoebe was almost more than he could bear. That business in the barn was still too strong in his mind. More than ever he was convinced that she could never be his. 'Take care of yourself,' he said softly, reaching down and kissing the top of her head. Dear God, he thought, how can I not take her into my arms? But he couldn't. He daren't. And so he looked on her lovely face and his love grew tenfold. Suddenly he was gripped by a moment of madness. 'Phoebe . . . I . . .' His heart shook inside him when her warm brown eyes smiled into his, stirring him deep inside.

'Let it be, Judd,' she whispered, suspecting he was about to apologise for what had happened earlier. He sighed and raised his head, looking up to the heavens, grappling with what was in his mind and in his tortured soul. 'Goodbye, sweetheart,' he murmured, smiling on her now. 'If you ever need me . . . either of us . . . you know where we are.'

'I do,' she said, and was thankful that he had not pursued the matter of her and Greg Peters although she realised how hard it must be for him not to warn her off such a man. Ever since her father died, Judd had taken it on himself to look out for her, and now he was trying hard to let go. She didn't know how to tell him that it wasn't easy for her either. Just now she had sensed his

pain and loved him all the more for it. But there was
something about him that confused her. Always she had
looked on Judd as a brother, but now he was changed
somehow; growing away from her. It was a sad but
moving realisation. Behind him Phoebe could see the
young woman, impatiently waiting, wanting him. For
some inexplicable reason, she resented that.

'Take care of yourself,' he murmured, squeezing her
small hands in his. 'And don't let it be too long before
we see you again.'

'I won't,' she promised. Something in his manner
touched her deeply. 'I'm lucky to have you both as
friends. God bless.' She hugged him to her, clinging to
him, desperately needing him to stay yet wanting him to
go.

'We'd best be off.' The young woman stepped forward
and at once Phoebe knew how dearly Judd was loved.
Freeing herself from the strong protective arms that had
encircled her she whispered in his ear, 'She's a lovely
girl, Judd.' Then, in brighter mood, 'I expect there'll be
another announcement soon, eh?'

He smiled in that familiar lop-sided way she had come
to know so well. 'I don't think so,' he said quietly, shaking
his head. Phoebe was both surprised and relieved. 'Away
with you,' she said laughingly, accompanying him to the
wagon and repeating her goodbyes to one and all. She
then watched him help the young woman on to the cart,
afterwards climbing up beside her. In another few minutes
they were going down the lane and out of Preston New
Road. The sun was shining and the afternoon was pleasantly warm but Phoebe's heart was suddenly cold. She

had wanted to go to the station with them but Judd had persuaded her not to. 'Better to say our goodbyes here,' he explained. Though he didn't add that he might have been tempted to say more than was wise if she had been sitting beside him all the way.

Aggie had stayed in the front garden, playing with the dogs. It was much more enjoyable than seeing the grownups on their way. Now, though, she was eager to have Phoebe all to herself. 'Let's take the dogs for a walk,' she suggested. And Phoebe was only too thankful to take advantage of this. At the top of the brow, she paused and looked back. They were gone and she didn't know when she might see them again. Ahead of her Aggie was shouting for her to: 'Come on, Phoebe.' She ran after the child. But her heart was down there, travelling with her two friends, Dora . . . and Judd.

Daisy's mood was definitely much brighter. In the kitchen she went about her task of preparing dinner with a devious little smile on her face, telling herself every now and then, 'There's going to be a wedding . . . ooh!' She made extra pretty patterns in the pie pastry and clapped her hands together. 'Nobody loves a wedding more than old Daisy,' she declared, grinning from ear to ear. 'And nobody bakes a grander wedding cake,' she boasted, giving a little twirl and almost losing her balance. 'But it'll cost you, Edward Dickens,' she promised. 'You can rely on that!'

Phoebe had no appetite. Too much had happened these past few days, and none of it good. But she was amused when Daisy kept winking at her. She wondered what could have brought about such a change in the little woman's mood. At breakfast Daisy had gone about her duties with a face down to her knees, and now she was positively bursting with affection. 'There's plenty of apple pudding left if anybody wants a second helping,' she told them, looking up and down the table at everyone in turn, her face squashed into the most ridiculous grin.

'No, thank you, Daisy.' Edward Dickens had also noticed her happy mood and he found it most embarrassing. 'I think we've all had our fill,' he said. 'You may bring the coffee in.' He turned to his wife. 'By the way, my dear, you haven't forgotten I shall be leaving very early in the morning?'

Noreen couldn't bring herself to look at him but she hadn't forgotten. How could she? Ever since he'd told her he would be away for two weeks she had lived for the day of his going. 'No, I haven't forgotten,' she said, keeping her gaze from him and collecting imaginary crumbs from the table.

'I'm not looking forward to it,' he lied. 'These business conventions can be uncomfortably long and tedious, my dear.' He made no mention of the clerk he would be taking with him, a young woman of pleasant appearance and voracious sexual appetite. Nor did he reveal the other matter which he meant to pursue. He had the advert safe and sound, and had discovered enough to convince him that the Peters had a greater enemy than he. When Noreen still did not return his gaze, he grew impatient. 'In case you might be interested,' he said cynically, 'once the conference is at an end, I shall travel south to investigate the possibility of spreading my wings, so to speak.

There are numerous opportunities opening up there. Specialised menswear is a market that's hardly tapped, and I mean to exploit any and every opportunity to expand Dickens' Gentlemen's Outfitters, you can depend on that, my dear.' He rubbed his hands together at the prospect, staring at her harder when she deliberately kept her gaze averted. 'My dear, whatever ails you?' he asked in a bitter-sweet voice. 'I do hope you wish me good fortune in my travels . . . after all, it is my hard-earned money that puts the food in your belly and the clothes on your back.'

Noreen looked up then but there was no answering smile. 'Yes, I *do* know, dear,' she said curtly, as always a little afraid.

Puzzled by her manner, he played his fingers on the table, staring at her, then at Margaret, and finally fixing his gaze on Phoebe. 'I expect you to be on your best behaviour while I'm gone,' he said sharply.

'Of course,' she replied demurely, causing him to regard her with suspicion.

'Hmm.' He roved his eyes from her to Margaret and suddenly his smile was warmer than a summer's day. 'I'll find something precious for you on my travels,' he promised her lovingly. Not once since his darling child was born had he ever returned from a trip without an expensive treat for her. 'Remember what I told you though . . . you may assist Mr Hetherington in his managerial duties, but only when he requests it. I applaud your ambition but you're not yet ready to assume any top level responsibility.' He saw she was about to protest and stopped her at once. 'Mr Hetherington is in total charge.

Do you understand that, my dear?' The corners of his mouth had drooped and his expression was forbidding.

'As you say,' she reluctantly conceded. She had been secretly hoping that her father's absence would be the stepping stone to greater things for her. Already she was becoming bored with the menial tasks he had set her. Unlike him, she did not see the merits of 'starting at the bottom'.

In that moment Daisy returned, still wearing the silliest grin. 'Ah, Daisy. Thank you.' He bestowed a smile on her and when she seemed reluctant to pour his coffee in her usual customary manner asked impatiently, 'Is something the matter?' He had seen her grinning like a Cheshire cat and thought she must be going out of her mind.

'Not at all!' Daisy said, still beaming from ear to ear.

'Well then, kindly fill my cup and take yourself off to the kitchen. We have family matters to discuss here.' Time and again he had taken the trouble to impress upon this woman the dangers of forgetting her place but Daisy was a fact of life and he must be patient, especially as he paid her very little for her labour and she complained even less.

'Oh ho! "Family matters", eh?' she giggled, lifting the coffee pot and pouring the hot brown liquid into his dainty china cup. 'Beggin' your pardon, sir,' she added hastily, thinking she had unwittingly shortened his temper, 'only I'm that excited.'

'Excited?' He lifted his hand in horror to indicate that she was in danger of filling his cup to overflowing. 'There *is* something ailing you!' he snapped. 'You appear to have taken leave of your senses. Have you come into money or what?'

'Oh, no, sir.' She moved along the table, offering coffee to one and all. 'It's just that, well, you won't forget, will you, sir? I do the best wedding cake in the whole of Blackburn . . . in the whole of *Lancashire* if you don't mind me saying.' She inclined her head towards the horrified Margaret. 'Oh, Miss, I'm that pleased for you. If it hadn't been for Molly Armstrong whose son played the fiddle at last night's barn-dance, I might never have known. Congratulations!' she cried, beaming at Margaret whose face had dropped and whose eyes were tightly closed.

'Shut up, you fool!' she hissed through her teeth. But there was no stopping Daisy when she was in full flow.

'I can do all the catering . . . known for it, I am,' she insisted. 'I expect there'll be a considerable number of guests seeing as your father's a pillar of the community.'

'Daisy!' Phoebe was the first to speak, and the tone of her voice, together with a discreet shake of the head, warned the maid that she would do well to leave the room without delay. A quick anxious look round the table at their mortified faces sent her on her way as fast as her short legs would carry her. 'I've done it again,' she muttered, hurrying from the room. 'When will I ever learn to keep my mouth closed?'

'I've no appetite this morning.' Noreen sought to dispel the fraught atmosphere. 'If you'll excuse me, I'll get about my household duties.' She made as if to rise from the chair but was stopped by one forbidding glance from her husband. Dreading the scene that might follow, she

330

cowered back, lowering her gaze to the tablecloth and counting the stitches in the rose pattern. She thought about her precious garden, willing herself away from that table and into the unique privacy of her little shed. And still her spirit was not calmed.

Phoebe sat quiet and still, waiting, knowing that it would only be a moment before he spoke. She thought Margaret a fool. It was inevitable that her father would find out, if not from Daisy then from another source. In this instance Hadley could not be blamed. More than once Phoebe herself had heard the two of them, late at night beneath her window; Hadley would be pressing for a meeting with her father and Margaret would be going to great lengths to dissuade him.

'Well, my dear?' he began in the softest, kindest voice. He neither smiled nor scowled nor even looked at her in that instance. He merely gazed ahead, holding his coffee cup in one hand and a stark white napkin in the other, alternately sipping and dabbing, sipping and dabbing. Phoebe was mesmerised. There was something deadly fascinating about him, something comical yet darkly terrifying. 'You have something to tell me, I think?' His voice was stiff now. Slowly he brought his steel grey gaze to bear on her

Swallowing hard, Margaret looked up. 'I would have told you,' she said frantically. 'I had it in mind to tell you this very day.' She cast a hate-filled glance towards the door. 'Damn and blast that bloody woman!' She spat the words across the room and thumped her fist down on the table. 'Must *they* be here, Father?' She threw a cursory glance at her mother and then at Phoebe. 'After all . . . I don't have to answer to them, do I? This is between me and you.' In her boldness, she was confident that he could refuse her nothing.

Addressing Phoebe with savage contempt she ordered, 'Leave us. Now!' Phoebe made no move. She resented the other woman's arrogance. Besides, she was experiencing a wicked delight in being able to witness Margaret's discomfiture. In answer to the instruction she merely smiled and settled deeper into her chair.

The other woman was incensed. 'You heard what I said.' Her voice trembled with rage. 'Get out! Both of you.'

'Now, now, Margaret,' her father chided with astonishing charm. 'You presume too much, my dear. No one leaves this table until I say so.' He sat straight and stiff, his expression giving nothing away. For what seemed an age he glared at his daughter. 'Am I correct in thinking that you have promised yourself in marriage to Hadley Peters?' His voice trembled.

Margaret searched his face, looking for any sign of compassion or weakness. She was disappointed. 'I mean to marry him,' she confessed. 'And nothing you can say or do will make me change my mind.'

The silence was like a wall between them. Phoebe sat still, her fists clenched, her only concern being for Noreen who was visibly trembling. With his next words Edward shocked them all. 'Would you sign the young man's death warrant, my dear?'

'What in God's name do you mean?' There was real fear in Margaret's voice now.

'Before I see you marry this man . . . *any man* . . .

there would be murder done.' He sounded calm but there was insanity in his eyes. He saw how his words had affected her and was pleased. Now, when he spoke, his smile was magnificent. 'There, my dear. You see how you have spoiled my meal with your foolish whims and fancies?' He took up the napkin and feverishly dabbed at the corners of his mouth, delicately wiping his moustache and replacing the napkin with a flourish. 'Of course there can be no marriage.'

'I WILL MARRY HIM!' She sprang to her feet, thrusting the chair away, her blue eyes vivid with fear as she faced him across the table.

'No, my dear,' he growled, rising from his seat, 'you will not. Now let that be an end to the matter.' He would have gone to her then but she fled from the room and so he leaned his great frame upon the table. Spreading the palms of his hands to support his weight, he dropped his chin into the thickness of his neck and sighed. The heart-felt sigh seemed to shrink him before their eyes. Then he lapsed into a silence that was unnerving to the two women still seated. He hung his head in despair and sighed again; afterwards he raised his head. Addressing Phoebe in subdued tones he ordered, 'Get out!' Flicking a contemptuous glance towards Noreen, he snapped, 'And take her with you.' He didn't actually look at his wife nor she at him but she wasted no time in putting a distance between them.

Outside in the hallway Noreen leaned against the wall, her face as grey as the ceiling. 'We'll all live to regret that foolish girl's actions,' she whispered.

'It isn't your fault,' Phoebe reminded her. 'He can't

hold you to blame for what Margaret does.' She took the little woman's hands into her own and was shocked by how cold and trembling they were. She recalled her uncle's words, and how he had spoken of murder, and her heart was chilled. 'What will he do?' she asked. Phoebe's instincts warned her that something dreadful would come of it all.

Noreen's answer was to draw away, going down the hallway and through into the back garden as though the devil was on her heels. Phoebe followed. 'What will he do?' she insisted as they made their way towards the orchard. She was stopped dead in her tracks when her aunt spun round to say in an odd matter-of-fact voice, '*Why . . . he'll do exactly as he says, my dear.*' And before Phoebe could recover from the awful implication of those words, she hurried away to seek the sanctuary of her shed and to lock herself in where no one could reach her.

It was almost midnight. Disturbed by what she had seen and heard this day, Phoebe couldn't rest. At first when she came to her bed she was bone-tired. Then she couldn't sleep. And now she was past being tired altogether. She lay still and thoughtful in her narrow bed, her wide brown eyes turned towards the night sky beyond her window. Some hours before it had been uncomfortably warm in this tiny room and so she had left the window open a chink. Now, though, the night breeze had freshened, gathering the dampness from the higher ground and cooling the valley below. Phoebe shivered, huddled beneath the bed-covers.

I could do with another blanket, she thought, tucking the clothes in around her. She toyed with the idea of going to the laundry cupboard on the floor below, but if it was cold in her room, it would be even colder outside it. The wind began to howl, finding its way in through the open window and whipping the curtain ends high into the air. The candle-flame flickered and danced, making weird shadowy patterns on the wall.

Phoebe turned this way and that but still she couldn't get warm, and couldn't force herself to go to sleep. Climbing out of bed, she hurried across the room, a chill striking up through her when her bare feet touched the cold lino. As she stretched forward to close the window she was aware of two figures standing by the gate. In the light from the street lamp, Phoebe recognised them. It was her cousin . . . and Hadley. They were arguing. Impulsively, Phoebe drew back, but made no attempt to close the window. Instead, she listened.

'I must talk to him, Margaret.' Hadley was gripping her by the shoulders and was obviously angry. 'I've listened to you for too long. You shouldn't have led me to think he knew of our plans.' He groaned aloud. 'God almighty! *Any* father would be furious. I begged you not to make the announcement until I'd spoken to him.'

'It wouldn't have made any difference,' came the defiant retort. 'We're getting married whether he likes it or not. I'm old enough to know what I want. And I want you.'

'All the same, I wouldn't feel right if I didn't try to heal the rift between you. It's best if we don't set a date . . . not until we've put things right with your father.'

'We're getting married in two months' time, and to Hell with him!'

'No.' He was adamant. 'There's no hurry. If it means

335

making peace between us and your father, we'll put the wedding back.' He dropped his arms to his sides. 'You go in now. It's late,' he said, reaching out to open the gate. 'It's a pity your father's away for the next two weeks. The sooner we get this over the better.' He looked up at the house. 'No matter,' he told Margaret angrily. 'It will just have to wait until he gets back.'

'I'm not putting the wedding back, Hadley.' Her voice rose sharp and decisive.

'Like I say, I'll talk to your father on his return.' When she would have protested further, he kissed her lovingly. 'It's too late to argue,' he told her, and the tone of his voice was enough to quieten her. Another kiss then they parted company, she going quickly into the house and he returning to the farm.

From her window, Phoebe watched Hadley's tall handsome figure as it crossed the road. At the gate of Peters' Farm he turned and glanced over to satisfy himself that Margaret was safely inside the house. Then he swung away and was soon gone. 'She'll bring you nothing but trouble,' Phoebe warned out loud. 'What's more, I'll bet a week's wages she won't stay faithful to you, even after you're wed.'

She was convinced that her cousin was using Hadley as a stick with which to beat her own father. 'That spoilt madam can't love *anybody* for five minutes at a time!' she whispered harshly, slamming the window shut and going back to her bed. And still she couldn't sleep, so she tossed and turned and listened to the sounds of the old house as the wind blew against it, making it whisper and sing. She had a mind to go down to the kitchen and make herself a cup of tea, but knew her cousin might be loitering there so dismissed the idea. After a while she began to feel sleepy, to dream, and soon to slumber.

It was Margaret's voice that woke Phoebe. But it was her uncle's that kept her awake. Intrigued, she went to the door and put her ear to the panelling. Sure enough, it *was* him, and he was uncomfortably near. 'Open the door, sweetheart,' he was pleading, over and over. 'Don't be angry. I only want to talk to you.'

'Jesus, Mary and Joseph!' Phoebe backed away from the door. *He was asking her to open her door to him.* But then he said something that calmed her frightened heart. 'Margaret . . . open the door, there's a good girl.' Curious now, Phoebe went out on to the landing and peered over the banisters. Edward Dickens had stooped outside his daughter's room, trying to see in at the keyhole. He was dangerously unsteady on his legs and tapping the door with a half empty whisky bottle. 'That Peters fellow isn't half good enough for you,' he said in a sweet voice. 'There's no man on earth good enough for you.'

'Go away. You're drunk!'

'Oh, my dear, I know it. The thought of you . . . in his arms . . . his bed!' He was crying now, long racking sobs that echoed through the house. 'I can't let you do that to me. You do understand, don't you?' Silence greeted him. He called again but she gave no answer. Stumbling against the door, he pleaded, 'I'm only doing what's best for you.'

Again no answer. His pleading became a threat. 'I won't be disobeyed! Not by you. And not by *her*. She was the same . . . I had to make her see. Oh, but I did love Jessica . . . just as I love you. But she wouldn't listen.' He jerked a thumb up to where Phoebe was leaning over the banister. 'That bloody girl! She's too much like her mother, with her bold ways and that proud beauty. Sometimes when I look at her . . . dear God!'

He began to cry, raising his fists and pounding them against the door. 'Temptation is a terrible thing. Margaret. Do you hear what I'm saying? Those two, like peas out of the same pod. And now you. I never thought *you* would be the same. But then Jessica was your aunt . . . I tend to forget that.' He was laughing now, a horrible grating laugh. 'I should have known the same bad blood runs in all of you.' He stumbled away, but not before trying the door once more and kicking it hard when he found it to be securely locked against him. 'I'm not finished yet,' he warned. 'And you'll not marry him, I promise you that.'

Phoebe felt as though she'd been slapped in the face. The way he had talked about her darling mam! In a way that made her blood curdle. Why did he hate her so? What had split them up all those years before? What did it all mean? Curiosity rose in her again. As before, it deepened to anxiety. 'There's something bad here,' she murmured, 'something really bad.' And as she returned to her room Phoebe swore to get to the bottom of it all. Tomorrow she would broach the matter with her aunt, and wouldn't be so easily put off. Not this time.

The window was closed and the room didn't strike quite so cold now. It was such a small area that even the presence of one human being lent it a degree of warmth.

With her body more comfortable, but her mind troubled by her uncle's strange behaviour just now, Phoebe took a while before she went off to sleep. But, in all the uproar, she had done the one thing she had vowed never to do. *She had left the bedroom door unbolted.*

'To Hell with all of them!' Downstairs in his study Edward Dickens tipped the whisky bottle to his mouth and drained it dry. 'D'you hear what I say?' he demanded, shaking a fist at the ceiling. 'You won't get the better of me, you buggers.' He burst into a fit of the giggles, but then his mood took a sombre turn. Going to his desk, he took out his treasured photograph of Jessica, looking at it, holding it to his chest and talking to it as though it could hear his every word. 'You did it to torment me, didn't you?' he asked. 'You sent her here to punish me?' He was crying now, sobbing until the tears flowed down his face to make small wet patches on his shirt. 'Oh, Jessica . . . Jessica! How could you do that?' His agony was unbearable.

He sank into the chair and stared at the photograph a while, staring and thinking. Thinking and crying. Suddenly his anguished thoughts cleared and he could see it all. The force of his realisation was such that he was made to struggle from the chair and pace the room, up and down, a jubilant mood on him now. 'I KNOW WHY YOU SENT HER,' he cried, laughing. 'Of course. You didn't do it because you wanted me to suffer, did you, my lovely Jessica? You've placed her in my care so that I can guide her on the right path . . . just as I guided you. Oh, and I've let you both down, haven't I? All these weeks.' He hugged the photograph to his breast, wrapping his arms round it and rocking from side to side. 'The girl *is* rebellious, Jessica,' he said, nodding his head feverishly. 'And she's devious too. Oh, she isn't *outright* defiant but I know what goes on in her mind. She's too silent . . . too sullen. Oh, yes, I know what she's thinking right enough. Just as I knew what *you* were thinking.' He chuckled merrily. 'You needn't worry though, Jessica. Now that I know what it is you want me to do, you mustn't worry.'

With the greatest reverence he replaced the photograph and made his unsteady way out of the study and into the kitchen. 'I've put it off for so long but now you see how even Margaret has turned against me? Ever since your daughter came into the house, I've struggled and fought with myself. And now I see what I must do.' Going to the desk he took up the lamp, cursing when his hand touched the hot glass.

The hallway was partly lit by the lamps which were positioned at each post of the staircase. Swaying with the alcohol he'd consumed, he went into the kitchen. There was a series of noises suggesting he might be searching for something, and then a few minutes later he reappeared, without the lamp but carrying a metal object that glistened in the artificial light. At the foot of the stairs he waited a moment, one hand gripping the banister and the other thrust in his pocket, still gripping the object. He took a further moment to compose himself. 'It's time,' he murmured, starting forward. 'It's time.'

Upstairs Phoebe was in a restless sleep. But the day had worn her down and she would not easily have woken. Slowly he came up the stairs, stumbling, stopping, pressing on, always pressing on. In her bedroom, Noreen turned over, disturbed by what she took to be the sound of the elements against the walls of the house. She woke with a start. Sitting up in her bed, she listened. No. There was nothing. Her nerves had been shattered by the sound of her husband pleading to be let into his daughter's room. She knew the signs. She had suffered it all before. Margaret was made out of the same hard mould as her father. She was more than capable of looking after herself. Lying there in the dark, Noreen's thoughts turned to Phoebe's mother, Jessica, and for one agonising moment she was plagued with guilt. Jessica had been a lady, and she was vulnerable. Men like her brother Edward would always prey on such as her. 'I could have been a better friend to you,' Noreen murmured now. Disillusioned with herself, she deliberately thrust the thought from her mind.

Outside her room Edward stood motionless, moving on only when he thought she would not perceive his presence. Satisfied, he continued past his daughter's room, his eyes closing rapturously when he pictured her in her bed. Sighing, he continued on up the stairs to the top landing. To Phoebe's room. 'It's all right, Jessica,' he whispered, 'don't be afraid.' In his drink-fuddled mind, he imagined his sister to be waiting for him there.

Phoebe slept on, unaware that her bedroom door was being gently pushed open. He came inside, his breathing harder and his heart beating like a wild thing. Sidling towards the bed, he stroked her long auburn tresses, caressing the beautiful coiled locks between his fingers and sighing within himself. She stirred. Alarmed, he drew away, his eyes gazing down at her lovely form. In her restlessness, she had thrown off the blanket, and only the sheet covered her breasts; exquisite rounded mounds pushing up from beneath. Oh, how he longed to touch them, to caress the softness of young warm flesh, to feel its silkiness against him. But no! Later. There would be time enough. For now he must do what he had too long neglected. Her pride, her wantonness, the symbol of her wickedness, must be destroyed.

Carefully, he took the scissors from his pocket, long devilish blades designed for mayhem. Lock by lock he began, softly snipping, turning each lock with delicious enjoyment, ruthlessly savaging the magnificent mane. Soon, the pillow was littered with dismembered strands, crimson dark against the pale linen. She stirred again. He couldn't stop. Not now. The fever was on him.

Phoebe was in the throes of a terrible dream. Her mother was calling her but she was nowhere to be seen. The leaves were falling all around, long brown shapes, falling over her body, making a strange clicking sound as they fell. Her mother was calling, but Phoebe couldn't find her. She was frantic. A sense of horror took hold of her. She began struggling, but unseen hands kept her pinned down. Her eyes flicked open and she saw him. SHE SAW HIM! Her screams rang through the house. With every ounce of strength she tried to fight him off but he was incredibly strong, like a thing possessed. In the half-light she saw his face – crazed, insane. 'Don't fight me,' he pleaded. 'Please, Jessica . . . don't fight me now.' He began tearing at her clothes, his hands all over her, hurting, wanting. 'NO!' Lashing out, she felt her nails score his skin. Tiny droplets of blood splashed down her fingers. His anger exploded. He was shouting now, cursing, tearing at her like a madman. She had been taken unawares and now there was no escape. Her screams rang out again and again. He was on her now and her senses were darkening.

On the lower landing, the women had heard Phoebe's shocking screams but they made no move. The young one hid herself beneath the clothes but the other was out of her bed, pacing the floor, torn apart by the awful thing she knew was taking place. She wasn't surprised. Since the first day Phoebe had come into this house, it had been only a matter of time . . . only a matter of time. The screams had stopped now but the silence was even more deafening. Suddenly she was running. Shouting. 'LEAVE HER BE, YOU BASTARD.' Fear had drained away and in its place there was nauseating horror. Haunted by Phoebe's shouts for help, it was the same horror which lent wings to her feet and gave her a strength she had never known she had.

Phoebe saw her aunt burst into the room and her heart leaped inside her. His hand was clamped over her mouth, suffocating her, the long thick fingers digging into her skin. Every inch of her body was bruised and hurting. Another minute and he would have her at his mercy. She saw her aunt pick up the brass candlestick. When it came down on the side of his head, she felt the shudder ripple through him. He made a strange gurgling sound as he slithered away. Then she was in her aunt's arms, sobbing, clinging to her as though she would never let go. Out of the corner of her eye she could see his large grotesque form spreadeagled on the floor. She was desperately afraid. 'It's all right, sweetheart.' Her aunt's voice was soothing to her unravelled senses. 'He won't hurt you. I won't let him hurt you.' She felt herself being rocked, and knew her own pain was nothing compared to the agony of this woman.

'Have you killed him?' The whisper issued into the room shockingly. Margaret stood at the door, a lamp in her hand and a look of glee in her bulbous blue eyes. She dropped her gaze again to the still figure lying on the floor.

The awful realisation of what she had done seemed suddenly to strike Noreen. Her hand flew to her mouth and she stared at the limp figure of her husband. Falling to her knees, she passed her hand over his face, leaning her ear to his mouth. 'He isn't dead,' she said with great relief. Remembering made her bold. 'But he should be,' she murmured. 'If there was any justice in this world . . . he should be.' She raised her eyes to those of her daughter and as their gazes locked, she murmured, 'Do you know what he meant to do here this night?' Her features hardened, and the startled young woman could never recall seeing her mother look at her in such a way. 'Your father . . . the highly respected Edward Dickens . . . DO YOU KNOW WHAT HE MEANT TO DO HERE THIS NIGHT?' she demanded in a low trembling voice. Pointing to Phoebe, who was still quietly sobbing, clutching the blanket to her half-naked form, she insisted, 'Look at her. See what he's done. Thank God I was in time!' She couldn't bear to think of the consequences if she hadn't taken her courage in her hands. Her emotions were in turmoil. She was filled with a crippling sense of shame and, strangely, a peculiar sensation of pity for the man who lay only inches away, his temple grazed by the sharp edge of the candlestick. The trickle of blood seemed ridiculously small when compared to the mighty loathing with which she had wielded the instrument. 'He won't die,' she said, and a well of laughter bubbled up inside her. 'He's too wicked.'

'You'll be punished for what you've done,' Margaret told her viciously. She ventured further into the room to stare down at her father with morbid curiosity. Her thoughts ran ahead. It was a pity her mother hadn't killed him, because with Edward dead there would have been no one to oppose her marriage to Hadley. At once she was mortified at her own thoughts. He was her father and she loved him. Her mother's words finally infiltrated her mind. DO YOU KNOW WHAT HE MEANT TO DO? And yes, she did know. Jealousy darkened her heart. 'It's your fault, you bitch!' she hissed, glaring at Phoebe. 'You should never have come here. Now *she'll* suffer for it, you can be sure of that.'

'Help me to get him to his room.' Noreen sought to distract her daughter. There was too much bad feeling in this house. 'Quickly!' she urged in a hard voice, and more astonished than offended, her daughter helped to carry him down the flight of stairs and into his bedroom. The smell of stale booze and the extraordinary weight of his considerable frame was unpleasant to them both. His occasional groans and bouts of cursing told them that he was not badly hurt. After setting him on the bed, his daughter assured herself that he was more drunk than dying and then promptly departed, leaving her mother to tend the wound on his temple. But she couldn't resist one more cruel jibe. 'He'll punish you. And I, for one, won't care.'

The grandfather clock was striking three in the morning. Though still badly shaken, Phoebe was partially recovered from her ordeal. She had lingered in the bath, washing away the marks of his hands on her. The wounds were superficial, but there were others that would not so easily be washed away. But she felt better, not quite so tainted. He had not penetrated her, and Phoebe would be forever grateful to her aunt for that. Now, freshened by the hot soothing water and dressed in a clean nightgown, she realised how truly fortunate she had been. While Phoebe had been bathing, her aunt had changed the bedclothes, surreptitiously gathering the remnants of the auburn locks and placing them in a bag which she put outside the door.

In the candlelight Noreen saw the real mutilation that had taken place. 'Your beautiful hair,' she moaned, putting her hands around Phoebe's face and forcing those fierce brown eyes to meet hers. 'Don't fret though,' she whispered lovingly, 'your hair will grow again.' She glanced at the angry marks along Phoebe's neck and down her arms. 'And they will heal,' she promised. Shaking her head in disbelief, she said brokenly, 'But what he tried to do . . . what he would have done if I hadn't . . .' Her voice collapsed in a sob and she clasped the girl to her. 'I should have told you,' she murmured harshly. 'Can you forgive me?' Her whole body seemed to vibrate as she began to sob, tenderly stroking Phoebe's hair and rocking her back and forth. 'Forgive me,' she kept repeating. 'Please forgive me.'

Phoebe made no answer, too overcome, still in shock. Deep down there was a terrible raging anger but as yet it could find no outlet. After a while she drew away from her aunt's arms. 'I'll never forget what you did for me,' she said softly. It was all like a dream, but horribly real. Too real. 'What will happen to you?' she wanted to know.

'Nothing, child,' Noreen answered confidently, although in her heart she knew she would be punished just as Margaret had promised. 'He was drunk. Tomorrow he won't remember a thing,' she lied. She studied Phoebe's unhappy face as she told her in a low urgent voice, 'Tomorrow he'll be gone, and won't be back for two weeks.' Suddenly her fingers gripped Phoebe's face as she warned harshly, 'You must make plans to leave this house, child. Leave it, before it's too late.' She glanced furtively about her. 'Your uncle is a dangerous man . . . far more dangerous than you could ever imagine. Tonight . . . what he did . . .' she gasped as though her heart had been stabbed through. 'It won't end there,' she warned. 'You must get away, I tell you. Put as much distance between yourself and him as you possibly can.' She grasped Phoebe by the shoulders. 'Do you understand what I'm saying?'

'Is he insane?' Phoebe seemed not to have heard. Instead she voiced the question that had been playing on her mind since she'd seen his face above hers, seen those awful eyes looking at her in a way that would always haunt her . . . grey and hard as slate they were. Deranged.

'You'd best try and sleep now, child.' Noreen looked

at the small sorry figure, at the way Phoebe was hunched in the bed with her knees drawn up to her chin and her arms tucked round them. In that moment she despised the man more than ever.

'Will you stay with me?'

Noreen nodded. 'I'll stay,' she promised. And she did. For many long hours she held Phoebe in her arms, and the two of them slept then woke and talked until they were exhausted. Sometime before daylight, when Phoebe was at last asleep, Noreen crept away and returned to the loneliness of her own empty room. She awoke with horror to discover that it was almost eight o'clock. As she came on to the landing, she could hear Phoebe moving about upstairs. Going to her husband's room, she tentatively inched open the door. There was no sign of him. Quickly she went downstairs to the dining-room. Still no sign of him. Nor was he in his study. 'What game are you playing now?' she muttered, keenly aware of his sadistic nature. Her next stop was the kitchen. 'No breakfast for me,' she told the maid who was already deep in preparations.

Daisy greeted her with surprise. 'Oh, there you are, ma'am,' she said churlishly. 'I was beginning to think everybody had died.' She gave a frown. 'Ain't the young 'uns going to work this morning?'

It was Noreen's turn to be surprised. 'Are you saying my daughter's still in bed?'

'I reckon so,' came the reply, then a giggle. 'When the cat's away the mice will play.'

'Have you seen Mr Dickens?'

'Oh, the master left a good hour ago.' Daisy was disgruntled because no one wanted breakfast. She'd already done the bacon to a crisp, and the eggs were sizzling on the stove. 'What am I expected to do with this food? I don't suppose Miss Phoebe will want any either?' she asked, sullenly slamming down the knife with which she'd been cutting the home-baked bread.

'I'm sure you'll find a good use for the food,' Noreen replied with a sly little smile. She was not unaware of the amount that Daisy consumed, nor was she in any doubt that certain pork legs and other juicy titbits found their way on to Daisy's own modest table. But it didn't matter to Noreen. As the master had so often reminded them, it was *he* who put the food in their bellies, and Daisy's belly could be just as hungry as anyone else's. 'You say Mr Dickens left the house a while ago?'

'That's right.' Daisy scooped the marmalade from the porcelain dish and plopped it back into the stone jar, afterwards wiping her little finger along the spoon and licking it clean. 'In a dreadful mood he were an' all,' she declared, looking at Noreen with a bemused expression. 'Fair snapped me head off when I asked him if he was ready for his breakfast.'

'Did he . . . seem all right other than his bad temper?' Noreen asked in a matter-of-fact voice. She knew how quick Daisy was when it came to a snippet of gossip.

'If you mean did he look well . . . it's no use asking me, because like I say, he hardly spoke two words. He rushed out of the door that smartly I wouldn't have known whether he was all right or about to fall dead at me feet.'

'He rushed out, you say?' It didn't sound as though he'd suffered any lasting effects from that knock on the head. More's the pity, thought Noreen savagely.

Daisy nodded, scratching her face thoughtfully. 'Aye. Came down the stairs just as I was taking me coat off in the kitchen. I came out straight away to ask whether he wanted a brew while breakfast was getting ready, and all he did was grunt some'at I couldn't make head nor tail of.' She flung out her arms in a gesture of frustration. 'Then he grabbed his hat and coat and went out the front door.' She peered quizzically at the other woman. 'Is everything all right, Ma'am?' she asked. Her nose told her there was something going on, and if there was anything she positively disliked, it was being kept in the dark.

Ignoring Daisy's little ploy, Noreen clarified the situation for her own ends. 'And you say my daughter refused her breakfast?'

'Didn't want nothing at all she said . . . no breakfast, and not even a brew o' tea. She were still in her dressing robe when she came down . . . intended looking in the study for her father, but I told her, "The master's gone, Miss." But she still looked in his study to satisfy herself. She even checked the hall stand to see if his hat and coat were gone, and o' course they *were*,' said Daisy indignantly. 'She told me she didn't want no breakfast, and then she went straight back to her bedroom and ain't been down since.'

'Thank you, Daisy. I'm sorry but it seems we've all lost our appetite this morning.' She forced a brighter smile. 'Maybe we'll make up for it tomorrow.'

Daisy was still grumbling when Noreen hurried from the kitchen and made her way back up to Phoebe's room. The girl was seated at the edge of her bed. There was a crumpled towel and a discarded nightgown flung over the back of the chair. Her eyes turned towards the door as it opened. She didn't say anything but her aunt knew instinctively what Phoebe was thinking.

'He's gone,' she explained, remaining at the door. Already she was regretting so much, including the way she had allowed her emotions to overcome her. She mustn't get too close to Phoebe. It went against everything she had promised herself. All the resolve of the previous night seemed to have vanished with the knowledge that he had gone from the house without seeking some sort of retribution. It bothered her.

'Why did he do it?' The question had drummed over and over in Phoebe's mind, and now she voiced it in a whisper, her eyes pleading. 'Why would he want to hurt me like that?'

Noreen's face was set like stone as she told Phoebe in a cool voice, 'I know it will be difficult for you . . . you have no other relatives, and no money of your own, but if the opportunity ever comes for you to leave this house, I beg you to take it.'

Astonished by the change in her aunt, Phoebe asked, 'Are you afraid of him . . . in danger?' Earlier, when she had opened her eyes after a fitful night, her aunt was gone. In all her life she had never felt so vulnerable. Scrambling from the bed, she had gone to the washroom where she scrubbed every inch of her aching body. Only his hands had touched her but she felt unclean . . . ravaged. Afterwards she returned to where she now sat, her heart heavy and her mind plagued by so many questions. And now her aunt had shut her out, just like before.

Noreen knew she had to be careful in the way she

answered Phoebe's pointed question because the girl's nature was such that she would never leave this house if she thought her aunt was living in fear. She smiled. 'Good heavens, child. Would I have done what I did if I was afraid of him?' she asked simply. 'I'm not in any danger,' she lied.

Phoebe wasn't entirely convinced. Margaret's words were still ringing in her head. 'Now *she'll* suffer for it, you can be sure of that.'

'Why did he do it?' she repeated. That question above all others haunted her. 'Something happened here, didn't it, between him and my mother?' She saw the colour drain from her aunt's face. 'Last night you asked me to forgive you. Why? What have you done that you should want to be forgiven?' As before, she sensed an undercurrent of something sinister. And it was to do with her own mother.

'My! You're like a dog with a bone. You never want to let go.' Noreen smiled then, displaying her kinder nature, but her heart was beating frantically. 'Don't read things into what I say,' she replied. 'It was just that I should have got to you sooner.' She didn't say she had lain in her bed, listening to Phoebe's cries until it was almost too late. 'Unfortunately I'm a deep sleeper.'

'That's all?'

'I've told you.' She half-turned to leave, but paused when Phoebe's brown eyes seemed to shadow over. 'Are you all right now?' she asked with genuine concern. The shocking events of the night were still visible in Phoebe's stricken brown eyes. That special glow had gone from her. Noreen prayed that it would only be temporary.

'What are your plans?' she asked. 'You surely can't go in to work?' She couldn't forgive herself for the confusion in those beautiful eyes, for the way they were now shadowed by the shocking experience. With her magnificent hair mutilated about her small white face, Phoebe seemed like the sorriest urchin. The marks on her bare arms were still red and angry. Soon they would darken into bruises.

'I don't know,' Phoebe said, closely watching the other woman's face. She had come to another decision which she had almost confided in her aunt. Now she wasn't sure. She still wasn't sure. One minute her aunt was a friend then she was almost a stranger. Phoebe suddenly realised that this woman's nature had been fashioned by another, evil one.

Noreen smiled. 'See how you feel,' she said, 'I'll come back in a little while.' There was a degree of tenderness in her now but she made no effort to come nearer. 'You might be better off at work . . . take your mind off things. But see how you feel.' She opened the door wider, preparing to leave.

'He won't get away with it,' Phoebe said grimly, her anger beginning to mount. She had decided to confide her intention. After all, she meant to go through with it even though her instincts now told her that her aunt would object.

'Oh?'

'I'm going to the constabulary.'

Noreen's face seemed to crumple. 'Good God, child! What are you saying?' She came into the room and closed the door.

'He should be made to pay for what he did.' Somewhere between sleeping and waking, Phoebe's terror had turned to dark anger. She wasn't afraid, and wanted him to know that.

'What will you tell them?' Noreen's voice was almost inaudible.

'That he assaulted me.' Phoebe's calm determined reply told the other woman that nothing she could do or say would deter her. 'I'll tell them how he tried to rape me.'

There was a moment when Phoebe thought her aunt was about to plead with her. But then the silence was broken and all she said was, 'You must do what you feel is right.' What she thought was, But it won't change anything. She knew because many years ago she had gone down that very same road.

When the door closed on her aunt, Phoebe sat on the edge of the bed, her shoulders hunched and her head bent forward in her hands. There was an ache in her. No, it was *more* than an ache; it was a deep hurt that she had never experienced before, not even when her mother died. Right from when she was small she had always been able to call on great reserves of strength, the same inner strength that had kept her going when she lost her father, her mother, and her home. Now it was as though she had used it all up and there remained only an empty void that threatened to swallow her whole.

'Look at you,' she said aloud, raising her head and staring into the mirror. 'Just look at you!' She was pale and tired, and there was a world of pain in her sad brown eyes. She looked different somehow. But then, she reminded herself, she *was* different, different in so many ways; not just outside but inside as well. Something had gone from her . . . a certain light, a particular brightness that gave her the ability to see only the good things. There was anger in her, it was true, and there was a sharp need for revenge that was only tempered by her affection for her aunt. At the back of her mind Phoebe still feared that Noreen would pay the price for having intervened.

'Why did he do it?' Phoebe asked herself, a deep frown cutting into the smoothness of her forehead. 'WHY DID HE DO IT?' And back came her answer. 'Because he wanted to hurt you, that's why.' But why did he want to hurt her? Again, Phoebe believed that it had something to do with her mother. She glanced at the photograph on the mantelpiece. Then she looked back at her own image. The same intangible quality had transferred itself from one to the other.

She looked again at the image in the tarnished mirror; at the rich auburn hair that was now ragged and unkempt. Strange how she mourned its loss. But it had been her joy, yes, and her pride . . . the abundance of waves, cascading down to her shoulders and beyond. 'Remember what your mam told you,' she murmured. 'Pride comes before a fall.' Maybe that was it. She had been too proud. *He* told her she was too proud. She didn't hate him. She didn't feel anything for him. All she wanted was that he should be made to pay for what he had done, and for what he might have done if her aunt hadn't stopped him. That more than anything had terrified her. But there was no terror now. Only cold reason.

In that moment Phoebe fell face down on to the pillow, her face hidden in her arms and her whole body shivering with the sobs that racked her. Only now, in her desperate loneliness did she realise the enormity of what had overtaken her since that day when her mother was laid to rest. She thought of the wonderful times she had shared with her, remembered the happiness of her youth, the laughter and the tears . . . all uniquely wonderful. Now everything was so empty. Her heart was empty. Her life was in chaos. And so she cried, and the crying healed. Afterwards she felt as though a clean breeze had rippled through every corner of her being. Her resolve was strengthened. She would go to the constabulary. It was the right thing to do.

Her aunt had said she'd be better off at work but Phoebe was suddenly afraid. Her mind was too alive with what had happened and the thought of actually going down the road, boarding the tram, and walking through the streets of Blackburn was too much altogether. Besides, she couldn't face Marcus. There would be too many questions . . . her hair, the marks on her arms. On top of that, her every limb felt bone weary. Her aunt would let Marcus know, say she had a chill or some such thing. Phoebe thought of his kindly face and knew that whatever happened, she had a loyal friend in him.

For the second time that day she made her way to the washroom where she diligently scrubbed every inch of her body. Tomorrow. Maybe she would go to work tomorrow.

It was two days before Phoebe caught the tram into Blackburn town centre. She had used the time between to gather her strength and mentally assess all that had happened. Twice more she had entreated her aunt to talk about the thing that had estranged Edward Dickens from his sister but each time Noreen had resisted. Her reluctance only fuelled Phoebe's suspicion that something awful must have taken place for her uncle to have disowned his only sister.

For two days Phoebe had not strayed from the house. For most of the time she had stayed in her room, avoiding her cousin and the ever curious Daisy, occasionally chatting to little Aggie who came to stand beneath her window. 'Is your cold better?' the child would ask. 'Daddy says he'll make you a strong brew that'll put the roses back in your cheeks.' Now and then Lou would wave to her from the other side of the road, and Greg would stand by the farm-gate watching, just watching, until Phoebe felt obliged to close the window and draw the curtains. He was another bad memory.

On this Wednesday morning she felt stronger of heart and able to face a brand new day, although the sense of shame that had risen in her was still there. 'Are you ready to face the world, Phoebe gal?' she asked, examining herself in the mirror for the umpteenth time. Did her face betray anything? Were there any marks that could easily be seen? Was she ready for any questions that Marcus might ask? And, most important of all, was she really prepared to talk about her ordeal with some strange man?

Collecting her bag from the bedside cabinet, she then took her grey cardigan from the hook on the door and flung it about her shoulders. Outside on the landing she paused a while, deep in thought. Suddenly the room was no longer her sanctuary. Like her, it had been violated.

The morning was overcast and the breeze spiteful. Pushing her arms into the cardigan, Phoebe quickened her steps. The tram was just about to leave. 'Hurry up, Miss,' the driver called through his window, and she ran the last few steps, swinging on to the inner platform just as the tram drew away. There were only four passengers on the lower deck – an old man with a tweed overcoat, two ladies chatting up at the front, and a tall thin personage with a narrow moustache and shining bald pate who seemed unable to keep his eyes off her. Resenting the intrusion, Phoebe quickly moved along the gangway to a forward-facing seat.

The constabulary was in the centre of Blackburn town a few short strides from where Phoebe alighted. The reception desk was manned by a short round man with a bright red face and dimpled hands that played on the counter top. 'What can I do to help?' he asked, taking a pen from behind his ear and preparing to write in the leaves of a rather bulky dog-eared ledger. His smile was encouraging and Phoebe was made to relax. 'How do I go about getting someone prosecuted?' she asked tentatively.

He stared at her a moment and thought her both incredibly lovely and unusually innocent. 'You've never been inside a constabulary before, have you?' he commented with a friendly smile. She shook her head. 'Let's start at the beginning then, eh?' he suggested. 'Now then, Miss . . . what's your name?' he asked, pen poised.

Phoebe gave her name. When she gave her address he looked up sharply, observing her anew. Phoebe met his stare with determination. 'I've answered your questions so far,' she pointed. 'Will you answer some of mine?'

Now that she was here, in this stark room, being quizzed by a uniformed officer, she felt less confident.

'That's what I'm here for, Miss,' he said kindly, but with a certain caution in his voice.

'If a young woman had been attacked by her uncle, what would she have to do to see that he's put away? What I'm saying is . . . would they take his word against hers?' Somehow she suspected that neither her aunt nor her cousin would substantiate her story.

'Ah!' He knew the way she was thinking and deliberately played along. 'If this . . . young woman . . . had been attacked and then made a formal complaint, then that complaint would be investigated. If it transpired that there was a case to be answered, the man would be brought before the courts. If he was proven to be guilty, he would be punished by the law . . . if he was proven to be innocent of the charge, then of course the case would be dismissed.' He regarded her more seriously now. The conversation was taking a turn that worried him. 'You say you live at Dickens House. Would that be the home of Edward Dickens . . . of Dickens' Gentlemen's Outfitters?'

'He's my uncle.' She took a deep breath before rolling up the sleeves of her cardigan to show him the bruises. She didn't explain them but the look on her face told him all he wanted to know and he was greatly alarmed.

'Wait a minute, Miss.' He made a gesture that told her she should cover up her arms, seeming greatly relieved when she did so. 'I think you should be aware that sometimes the court can come down heavily on someone who seeks to use the law for his or her own purposes. It's a very serious matter to make allegations against a prominent member of society. This "friend" of yours . . . this "young woman" who might have been assaulted . . . has she any witnesses to the event?'

'No. I don't expect so.'

'Is she hospitalised?'

'No.'

'I see.' He stared at her now. 'I think you should ask your "friend" to think very carefully before she brings a charge against anyone . . . especially if that person is a prominent member of society. Especially if that person is well respected hereabouts. And more especially if that person employs any number of people . . . paying good wages to those whose families might otherwise starve.' His own son was employed by Edward Dickens and work was increasingly hard to find these days. 'Domestic arguments should be settled within the confines of a family's own four walls. The law isn't appointed to act as referee,' he concluded firmly, replacing the pen behind his ear to indicate that the interview was at an end.

It was as Phoebe suspected. 'So you won't do anything?' she demanded.

'Can't!' came the reply.

'Won't, you mean!' she accused.

'Family fights don't come within our jurisdiction. If we wasted our time in settling family differences, there would be little time left for important issues.'

'Suppose I insisted on making a statement?'

'That's your choice, Miss,' he said, stiffening his back and regarding her with a hint of hostility. 'But you'd be well advised to go away and think about it first.'

'What you're really saying is, I ain't got no choice!' She waited for his answer but he merely pursed his lips and looked along his nose at her. 'I see,' she said. 'If it comes down to his word against mine, I won't have a leg to stand on, will I?'

'Like I said, Miss . . . it's really a domestic issue.' His whole attitude had changed the minute he realised she was looking to accuse none other than the proprietor of Dickens' Gentlemen's Outfitters. The very idea! Whatever next?

Phoebe didn't speak again. Instead she gave him a withering look and slammed the door on her way out. For one fleeting second he felt oddly belittled. 'Pretty little thing that,' exclaimed a colleague who had just arrived to take over the shift. He glanced at the desk ledger. 'Is there a problem?' he asked, seeing that no notes had been made there.

'No problem,' the desk sergeant returned. 'Just another family squabbling among theirselves.'

- The other man shrugged his shoulders. 'Some folk never learn, do they?' he declared with feeling.

'That's the way it goes.' The bald-headed one closed the ledger and placed his pen on top. 'Some things change and some things never will. Take young lasses these days . . all lipstick and bare legs. It's no wonder the parents get worried.' Thank God he didn't have no daughter or he might be tempted to tan her arse with the hard end of his boot.

Marcus had been watching for her. 'You had me worried,' he said. 'Your aunt told me you'd be back today, but she didn't say you might be later than usual.' His homely face was etched with concern. Before she could answer, he spied the cut of her hair. 'Oh, I see,' he said with a chuckle. 'You've been to the barbers, is that it? Sort of a "pick-me-up"?' He chuckled, regarding her with interest. In her blue polka-dot dress and long grey cardigan, she looked pretty as ever. Her hair, though, was frighteningly short, curled tightly over her small pink ears and dipping into the nape of her neck like a well-fitting collar. But she looked thin and peaky and he couldn't help but think that she'd come back to work too early. But he'd missed her. Dear God, how he'd missed her.

'I'm sorry for being late, Marcus,' Phoebe apologised, lying with a flush of shame. 'I missed the first tram.'

'Aw, that's all right,' he said brightly. 'Your hair looks nice, Phoebe . . . it suits you that way, I think.' Secretly, he hated the fact that she'd cut off all that beautiful hair but he wouldn't hurt her feelings by saying so. 'I don't really mind you being late, you know that.'

His smile was infectious and in that moment he seemed younger than his years. All weekend he'd been thinking about her, eaten with jealousy, seeing her in his mind's eye with the young man she had called Judd. For weeks he'd been on the verge of confessing how he felt, and now he believed that if he didn't speak up today, he would never find the courage. Since sneaking away from the barn-dance on Saturday, he hadn't known a minute's peace. These last few days had been the longest of his life. The thought of Phoebe lying ill in her bed had been a source of great anxiety to him; he'd wanted to go and see her, but thought it wouldn't be proper. He'd wanted to send her a huge bunch of flowers but was afraid such a personal gesture would cause gossip. Instead he sent his best wishes in a small plain card that said nothing of what he was feeling. Afterwards he spent his every minute agonising about how he might broach a certain subject to her on her return.

Yesterday, when her aunt took time from her shopping to tell him that Phoebe would be in this morning, he'd been beside himself with joy. This morning he had summoned his courage, waiting for her to come through the door. And when she didn't, his courage withered away. But now she was here and his heart wouldn't keep still. Soon, in a while, when she was settled, he would dare to ask her. For now though, the customers were beginning to find their way here. Mrs Arnold could be seen outside, gazing at the clogs in the window, and James Cartwright had promised to collect his boots any minute now. 'It's been busy from opening time,' he said, praying that Mrs Arnold wouldn't come in just yet, his heart sinking when she seemed to be making a move.

'Oh, Marcus, I'm really sorry to have left you without any help. I know how busy Mondays can be,' Phoebe said. Her body ached all over, and suddenly she felt incredibly weary.

'You're here now and that's all that matters,' he said softly. 'Anyway, it's me who owes *you* an apology.'

Phoebe had gone straight to the counter. Normally she would have gone immediately through to the back-room to hang up her cardigan but, determined that he shouldn't see the bruises on her arms, she rolled the sleeves right down to her wrist. 'What do you mean?' she asked, looking at him quizzically.

'Why . . . the barn-dance, o' course,' he explained,

hurt that she should have forgotten. Perhaps she hadn't even missed him at all? 'I expect you were wondering what happened to me?'

'You did say that it wasn't really your cup of tea,' Phoebe reminded him. 'I missed you, of course I did . . . looked everywhere for you. I was disappointed that you weren't there. But I do understand,' she assured him with a smile. 'Don't feel bad about it, Marcus. It's all right. Really.'

'I was there.' Unable to deceive her, he blurted the words out. Phoebe was shocked. At first she thought she'd misheard but the look on his face told her that he was about to make a confession.

Before the conversation could go on, the bell over the shop door rang out and Mrs Arnold bustled in. The first thing she noticed was Phoebe's hair. 'Good God above!' she exclaimed. 'Whatever have yer done, child?'

Marcus retired to the back-room and for the rest of the morning they were kept busy with their respective duties. It was the busiest Wednesday morning Phoebe could ever remember. Customers poured in with their repairs, and poured out again with their little yellow tickets: some folk went out carrying brown paper bags containing newly leathered boots or well-worn clogs with sparkling new irons beneath, and others just came in to browse and pass the time of day.

It was ten minutes past twelve when Marcus closed the shop door and turned the sign over to read 'GONE TO LUNCH'. Then he hurried upstairs, brewed the tea and came down with a look of embarrassment on his kindly face. 'You're right,' he said, resuming their previous conversation before Phoebe could question him. 'Barn-dances . . . *any* kind of dance . . . it's not for me. I've never been any good at that kind of thing.'

'But you said you went?' Phoebe took the mug of hot tea. Wrapping her two hands round it, she raised it to her mouth, slowly sipping and waiting for his explanation.

'Like I said, I didn't want to go in the first place, but then I thought as you'd been kind enough to ask me, I should at least make an appearance.' He paused, grinning sheepishly and wondering how he would tell her the reason for his going. And worse still . . . the reason for his coming away. But tell her he would for he couldn't face one more day keeping it to himself. 'I saw you,' he confessed.

'Well then, why on earth didn't you come up and keep me company?' she asked, puzzled.

'Because you were with him, and I didn't think I should intrude.' He saw the astonished look on her face and couldn't have known that for one terrible moment she suspected he might have seen her with Greg Peters . . . out there near the lake.

'Who?' she asked, deliberately keeping her voice calm. 'Who did you see me with?'

'A good-looking fella . . . taller than me, brownish hair, long, down to his collar. He were wearing dark trousers and a green shirt.'

Relief flooded through her. 'That was *Judd*!' she exclaimed. 'You know . . . Judd is Dora's brother, the friends I told you about.'

'Not a sweetheart then?' he said laughingly. His relief matched her own.

'No, not a sweetheart.' The idea seemed strange, but not as strange as she might have thought only a few months ago. 'Whatever made you think that?' she wanted to know.

'Well, he's a handsome young fellow. And you seemed happy in his company.' He wished he hadn't said that because now she seemed to be turning the observation over. The moment was nearly on him and he could hardly breathe. 'So you don't have a sweetheart then?'

Phoebe shook her head. The only image that came to mind was of her and Greg Peters. And that was something she would rather forget. 'No, I don't have a sweetheart.' She laughed then. 'Have you been saving all these questions up?'

'I've been thinking about one question in particular.'

'Oh, and what's that?' She was so intrigued by his nervousness that she put her cup of tea down and stared at him, asking directly, 'What is it, Marcus?' A thought presented itself. 'You're not about to finish me, are you? I know I was only here on trial but, well . . . I thought you were pleased with me.' If she lost her place here on top of everything else . . . Oh, it didn't bear thinking about.

She was stunned when he put his hand over hers, 'No, nothing like that, lass.' He smiled and the lines vanished from his face. 'I'm not saying this lightly because I've had plenty of time to think about it. Seeing you with that young man made me realise that I should speak my piece and face the consequences.' He swallowed hard, squaring his shoulders for the moment of truth. 'If you'll have me . . . I'd like for us to be wed.' When she reeled back and drew her hand from his, he feared he'd lost her for all time.

'Oh, I didn't mean to shock you,' he said softly, and there were actually tears in his eyes. 'And I don't expect you to give me an answer here and now. All I'm saying is . . . I've come to think a great deal of you, lass. When you were away, this little shop were that dark and empty. You're like a ray of sunshine to me, d'yer know that? Don't refuse me straight off, please,' he pleaded. 'I know you're not happy where you are, and I can give you a good life, I promise you that. I won't even ask you to share my bed until you think you're ready. I'm a good man, Phoebe, and I'd take good care of you.'

In all this time she hadn't taken her gaze off his face, her eyes reflecting her shock. 'Think about it, that's all I'm asking, lass,' he whispered earnestly. 'Will you do that for me? Think about it.'

And for the rest of that day, and for many days to come, Phoebe found herself thinking about little else.

Chapter Nine

The vehicle nosed its way through the winding lanes. Inside the pretty dark-haired young woman giggled and pushed the man's hand from her stocking-top. 'Watch the road, you naughty thing,' she chided, crossing her legs and so denying him the touch of her warm bare flesh. 'Whatever would people think if they could see us?' she asked in a whisper, the fetching pink blush of her cheeks belying the cunning of her nature. It had taken her a very long time to hook the prosperous Mr Edward Dickens and she wasn't about to let him taste of her so easily; at least not yet. She knew from experience that a man valued a woman most when she was hard to get.

'You little vixen,' he chuckled. His face was hot and red with desire and his hand trembled as he reluctantly drew it away. Later, he promised himself, later he would have his way with her, whether she wanted it or not. Although he sensed that she wanted it as much as he did, otherwise why had she given him the glad eye all these months, and why had she agreed to accompany him to the convention? Of course the two days they'd spent in Manchester had afforded them little time together. Too many meetings, too much business talk, boring men congregating until the early hours, had all prevented him

369

from making better acquaintance with his attractive clerk. The consequence was that his desire for her was unsatisfied and he was a man deeply frustrated. He turned his attention to another of his weaknesses. 'What do you think to the motor-car then?' he asked. 'Isn't she a beauty?' If he didn't get his thoughts off more carnal things, he might just go out of his mind.

'I know nothing at all about motor-cars,' she said proudly.

'Of course. Women don't, do they?' he acknowledged with a superior air that irritated her. Patting the dashboard he went on, 'She's a Morris Cowley . . . cost me all of one hundred and sixty-five pounds.' He smiled with delight when she gasped aloud. 'As you can see, I'm a man of expensive tastes,' he told her with a tight little grin.

'Oh, look!' She pointed out of the front window at a signpost. 'Appleby,' she read. 'Turn left. Isn't that the place we want?'

'So it is, my dear,' he confirmed, 'so it is.' He nudged the vehicle round the long curve of the road, his smile broadening as he relished the deviousness of his plan. The fellow he had come all this way to see, this John Soames, would be the one to put an end to this nonsense between his precious daughter and Hadley Peters. Dipping his finger and thumb into the top pocket of his waistcoat he took out a folded piece of paper which he then crumpled into the young woman's hand. 'We want Soames' Farm,' he told her. 'But first there's a lane . . . look at the address . . . what's the name of that lane?' He wasn't used to the back of beyond. He had always been a man of the town at heart. Indeed, there was a time when he had seriously toyed with the idea of moving even closer to the heart of Blackburn. But Dickens House had been in the family for so long now, and the older he got the more he seemed to cling to his roots. The house was his home but the world was his office. That was the way he saw it, and so far his philosophy had been a lucrative one.

The woman bent her head over the paper. After scrutinising it for a moment she read out, 'Green End Lane, that's it,' and raised her head and glanced at him. 'John Soames of Soames' Farm . . . Green End Lane.'

'Good!' He snatched the note back and thrust it into his pocket. 'Green End Lane . . . watch out for it. We don't want to hang about here longer than we have to.' He chuckled again. 'We can find better things to be doing, don't you agree, my dear?' He had an urge to stroke her knee but one glance revealed her legs were still tightly crossed and her knees securely covered with the tweed herringbone skirt. 'You're a devil,' he murmured gleefully.

'And so are you,' she replied with a coaxing smile. 'But, yes . . . there *are* better thing we could be doing.' Reaching out with slender fingers, she caressed his thigh. 'You still haven't told me what you want with this Mr Soames . . . is he a potential customer?' she asked, pouting her ruby red lips and leaning closer, knowing the effect she was having on him and loving herself for it.

He gave a long shivering sigh. Her touch was doing things to him that he could hardly bear; his loins were on fire and his member almost bursting from his trousers.

371

'You'd better stop,' he warned. 'Or I'll have to pull off the road and deal with you.' His voice was trembling and his eyes were watery bright as he turned to look at her. 'I think I *will* stop,' he moaned, but then he almost careered into the ditch and his attention was taken up in bringing the vehicle back onto the meandering lane.

'We'd better get your business over and done with,' she suggested, clinging to her seat as the vehicle swung from side to side, 'then we'll see, eh?' Wealthy and desirable as he was, Edward Dickens wasn't worth losing her life over. 'Keep your mind on the road,' she told him in a firmer voice.

'You're right of course, my dear,' he said breathlessly. 'I'll attend to this matter as you say . . . then we can enjoy ourselves to our heart's content. The inn where you've booked us a room . . . the Royal Oak, isn't it . . . I hope it's a pleasant and private place?' The sweat was dripping down his face and he had to undo his collar or it would have choked him. In all his life he had never wanted anything as much as he wanted her right now.

'I kept in mind everything you said when you asked me to find us a suitable hotel,' she told him in a surprisingly businesslike voice. 'According to the brochure, it fits the bill perfectly.' Touching his thigh with painted fingernails, she purred, 'Haven't I always satisfied you?'

'Oh, yes, you most certainly have, my dear,' he conceded. 'At least in the execution of your clerical duties.' Suddenly his hand jabbed out and clutched her fingers. 'But there are *other* ways to satisfy me as I'm sure you must know.' Raising her fingers to his mouth he pressed his lips against them. 'You're no fool,' he said, keeping her hand in his while watching the road ahead and easing his foot from the pedal. 'You know why I wanted you on this trip, don't you?' He glanced in the front mirror. She was smiling at him. Gratified, he returned her smile and then put both hands to the wheel. She knew all right.

It would be another two miles before they turned into Green End Lane, and in the fifteen minutes it took before they drew up in front of a dilapidated old farmhouse she provoked his annoyance by questioning him yet again as to his purpose in seeking out Mr Soames.

'If I thought you needed to know,' he told her flatly, 'I would have told you.' He cursed himself for having let her see the name on the paper. It was a dangerous and foolish slip which he hoped he might not come to regret.

The house was in a shocking state of disrepair; many slates were missing from the sagging roof, two attic windows were shattered, and the brickwork was eaten alive with rampant ivy that had even intruded into the house itself, through the many cracks and crevices. All along the apex of the roof, crows and other scavenging birds stood in a long dark line against the sky, their droppings layered on the grey slates below, bleached by the weather and forming a knobbly covering that resembled the icing on a cake. As the vehicle came closer and its engine slowed to a throaty roar, the birds rose in alarm, screeching madly as they flew high into the air, flapping their enormous wings to momentarily blot out the morning sunshine.

'Wait here, my dear,' he instructed her as he clambered from the vehicle and meticulously adjusted his trilby. 'You can depend I won't be a minute longer than is necessary.'

When she merely nodded her head and stared sullenly at the house, he sensed that she would have preferred to come with him. That would never do. What was about to take place between himself and John Soames was of such a nature that it must be kept strictly between the two of them. In fact, he knew it might have been much wiser if he had negotiated with this man from a distance. But that was not his way of doing things. Besides, if by any remote chance his carefully laid plans did go wrong, there wasn't a court in the land that would heed the words of an ex-jailbird against that of the eminent Edward Dickens. He had spent the best part of a lifetime building up a name and position for himself. Now he believed himself to be more established than the Town Hall itself. And it would take an earthquake to bring *that* down.

On determined footsteps he made his way to the house. The area between the dwelling and the place he had parked his car was strewn with all manner of debris; rusty old farm implements nestled in the knee-high weeds, and broken glass crunched underfoot. He shivered, pulling his jacket in and buttoning it tight. November had sailed in with a cutting breeze and the bright sunshine held little warmth. He dreamed about the woman in the car and a smile came to his face. Tonight he would be warm enough. 'Patience, my man,' he murmured, turning to bestow a delightful smile on her, 'and your reward will be tenfold.'

The first knock brought no response so he tried again, this time clenching his enormous fist and crashing it against the door as though it was a hammer. In a matter of minutes the door was flung open and there stood a man his equal in size. He was a rough-looking fellow with a droopy uncombed moustache and narrowed eyes bright with aggression; altogether he was a nasty sort, unkempt and unclean. 'Well?' he demanded, his eyes fixed on the visitor. He carried a primed shotgun which he pointed from the shoulder, his finger playing nervously at the trigger. 'State yer business or bugger off!' he snarled, laughing nastily. 'Unless yer fancy staying for good?' His implication was unmistakable as he hitched the gun up and levelled the barrel at Edward's temple.

With remarkable calm, he drew himself up to his full height. 'Put the bloody thing down, man,' he instructed in a forceful voice. 'You got my letter, didn't you? You knew I was making my way here today?' His whole manner was that of a man disgusted and disappointed when in truth his stomach was alive with sickening fear. This was his first experience of staring down the barrel of a shotgun and he was almost convinced that it might be the last thing he saw on this earth. The man was astonished then suspicious, glaring through his better eye and keeping the gun firm in his grasp.

'I'm Dickens, you bloody fool! Edward Dickens from Blackburn. I responded to your advert about the Peters family. Surely you haven't forgotten the letters we exchanged?' He began fumbling in the pockets of his jacket. His better instincts warned him to turn tail and run, but thoughts of his beloved daughter in Hadley Peters' bed kept him there. 'Damn and blast it, what the Hell's wrong with you?' he yelled. He was trembling with fear, and his anger was rising because of it. No man on this earth had ever made him tremble before.

Slowly, the gun was lowered as John Soames' twisted mind grasped who had come to his door. 'Edward Dickens?' he said, peering through bloodshot eyes. He smiled then, wiping a grubby hand on his trouser leg. 'Took yer sodding time though, didn't yer, eh?' he moaned. 'But you're here now. So come in, why don't you?' He raised his hand in greeting and frowned when it was sullenly refused. Stepping aside, he waited until his distinguished visitor was in the narrow darkened passage and then banged the door shut. 'Go on,' he urged, extending his arm to indicate the way ahead. 'We'll talk in there.'

Together they went along the awful-smelling passage and into a small square room leading from the last door on the right. 'Sit yerself down,' Soames said in a hostile gruff voice, pushing the other man in the back then realising his mistake when Edward turned to stare at him with the blackest hatred he had ever seen. 'Stand if you want to then,' he grumbled, eyeing Edward out of the corner of his eye. 'You don't fancy sitting on me chairs, but I don't expect you'll be so quick to refuse a drop o' the old stuff, will yer, eh?' he asked with a sly grin. Going to a sideboard he grabbed up a half empty bottle of whisky which he then brandished in front of Edward's nose. 'Been drowning me sorrows as yer can see,' he explained in a sorry voice.

When Edward made a gesture to indicate that he wanted none of the stuff, John Soames stared at him in disbelief and then started to cry. Tears ran down his face and his great shoulders shook. 'She left me, d'yer see?' He banged his fist on the dresser top, sending the dust-laden candlesticks into a tap dance. 'Me old woman's left me, I'm about to lose me home and me two sons are long gone.' He made a peculiar hiccuping noise that might have signified that he was choking until he went on in loud vengeful tones, 'I'm a bitter man. There's no man on this earth so filled with regret.' He thumped his chest with a clenched fist and stared at the other man with a fixed loathing; in that instance Edward Dickens could have been forgiven for thinking Soames was about to leap at his throat and strangle the life out of him.

'Have you got a daughter?' his question was so unexpected that, for a brief moment, Edward was rendered speechless. 'Answer me, damn yer eyes!' Soames insisted threateningly.

At once Edward was on his guard. 'My family is none of your concern,' he said. 'We're here to talk other business. But if you've changed your mind, then I'll be on my way.'

'No, you mustn't do that. There's business to be discussed, like you said. When all's said and done that's what matters.' He dropped his chin on to his chest and stared at the floor as though the burden of his thoughts was too heavy for him to hold up his head. He sighed from deep within. 'I had a daughter,' he began. 'Lucy, that was her name . . . Lucy Soames . . . the darlingest little thing you ever came across. She were me only daughter, y'sce? And when she needed her daddy most, he were in prison . . . put there because he couldn't keep his fingers off other folks' belongings.'

He raised his head and laughed, a horrible sound that rang through the house and put the fear of God into the man watching. But Edward Dickens had to watch, and had to suffer it because he needed to know everything. If his own plan was to succeed then he must be sure that he was dealing with a man enraged enough to do more than pilfer 'other folks' belongings'.

Soames' voice broke into a rending sob as he explained, 'She's been dead these past five years and more.' He sniffled and took a deep swig from the bottle. Afterwards he came across the room to stand before his visitor. 'D'yer know what it's like to lose a daughter?' he asked bitterly. 'Well, I'll tell yer.' He took another swig and laughed aloud. 'It's like having yer heart cut out,' he said. 'She was murdered, d'you see? That Peters fellow murdered her as sure as if he'd put a knife clean through her ribs.'

'If you've a story to tell, be quick about it, man,' Edward Dickens snapped. He wanted to be away from this place as quickly as possible not just because the smell that permeated the house made him feel nauseous, and not because the man himself was both filthy and aggressive – although these factors were reasons enough. This was an animal not a man and the house fitted him. The odd pieces of furniture were caked with dust and smattered with used pieces of crockery which themselves were littered with rancid food particles covered in tiny mountains of grey hairy mildew. Mice were ravenously gnawing at the putrid remains. Spiders had woven their nests round the decaying window frames, and the glass was so grimy that the daylight gathered on the outside, making weird shapes on the panes. These disturbing patterns were remarkably like the dirty faces of children peering in. There was a fetid smell everywhere. The man himself smelled worse than a drunk from the gutter. 'We've busi-

378

ness to conclude,' Edward reminded him. 'Although I'm not sure whether it wouldn't be a waste of time. You're drunk, man! Drunk out of your stupid mind!'

'Aye, mebbe so. But with good reason,' came the reply.

'What reason?'

'Reason enough.' The man began pacing the floor, his face was set grim and he had the look of a haunted man. Suddenly he came to a halt and looked directly into Edward's face. He took a long hard breath, and when he exhaled it seemed as though his whole body had shrunk. 'You'd like to know what happened,' he acknowledged, 'and to tell yer the truth, *I'd* like to know what really brought you out here.' He screwed up his eyes, regarding the other man with suspicion. 'What's in it for you, eh? What makes a man such as yourself want to help the likes of me.'

'You can be sure I haven't come all this way just to waste my valuable time,' Edward retorted angrily. 'I can help you find the man you're looking for. But there might be a price to pay.'

'Ah, now we're getting to it. What d'yer know?'

'First . . . why do you want him so badly?'

'Why do I want him? Well now, I'll tell yer, shall I?' There was a violent look about him as he stepped closer, his nose almost touching that of his visitor. When he saw that the other man was not ruffled, he stepped away and began to talk, softly at first, then growing excited. Slowly, tortuously, the story emerged. John Soames was a common thief, a hardened criminal who had recently been released from prison. During the eight years he was incarcerated, his sons had deserted, the farm had fallen to ruin, his daughter had grown besotted with a man by the name of Greg Peters. The same man had taken this virgin child and used her for his own ends. When she became pregnant, he turned his back on her. Soon after, Peters and his family left the area. 'Lucy was determined to find him. She would be gone for days on end . . . searching . . . looking everywhere. She loved him, d'yer see? She was barely a woman . . . heavy with his child. All she asked was that he should want the two of 'em . . . take care of 'em.' He paused, remembering, and hating all the more.

'And did she find him?'

'Oh, aye, she found him right enough. But she wouldn't let on where he was . . . she still loved him, wanted to protect him. Her mam said she'd been gone for weeks this time. When she came home she said she'd found him but he turned her away . . . told her to go to Hell, that he wanted nothing to do with either her or the brat. Said he didn't even know whether it was his or not.' His eyes blazed. 'Can yer imagine that, eh? I'm not much of a man, I'll not deny it, and I've done many things to be ashamed of, but as God's my judge I've never been guilty of anything so cruel. The day after she came back home, my Lucy went straight into labour. It was real hard. Her mam said she suffered bad. From that day on she was changed . . . saddened . . . grown old afore her time. Two weeks later she left her mam a note, saying as how she was taking the bairn to its daddy. In her letter she'd said as how when Peters saw that lovely little lass, his heart would melt and he'd take the pair of 'em with open arms.' There was a moment then when he couldn't go on.

He went to the grimy window and, closing his eyes, leaned his forehead against the glass as though it might cool his fevered thoughts.

'Go on, man.'

He laughed, lapsed into a strange silence and then continued, 'Poor little fool! He never wanted Lucy. Only what he could get from her. And he didn't want the girl-child neither. Turned 'em away he did . . . threatened her that if she ever came near his door again he'd have the authorities on her. The bastard!' He was quiet for a moment, thinking of what his wife had told him before she, too, walked out. 'Lucy's mam left me, y'know. Oh, I can't blame her, not after all that happened . . . none of us men were ever any good to her. We only ever brought her heartache. But *Lucy* . . . ah, she loved Lucy right enough. But there were nothing she could do. The top and tail of it is this . . . after Peters threatened her, turned her away again, Lucy fretted for days and weeks on end. Her mam were almost frantic. She said she saw it coming but there was nothing she could do. She tried talking to Lucy . . . threatening . . . cajoling. Saying as how Peters weren't worth the trouble. But, well, when a lass is in love, she can't see nothing else, ain't that the truth?'

The other man was made to think of his own daughter. 'I know,' he said simply, but there was a world of meaning in his voice.

'She killed herself.' Soames laughed again but the laughter soon turned to tears. 'My Lucy killed herself because that bastard used her then slung her away like so much rubbish.'

'And the girl-child?' Dickens had been both intrigued and delighted by the fellow's story, because hadn't it created enough loathing and revenge to suit his own purpose?

'Lucy left a note for her mam. She didn't want the child to be punished for her sins and so she intended leaving it on the doorstep for Peters to find. She said in the same letter: "I pray when he sees how like himself the child is, he won't have the heart to disown her." Her mam didn't know where to look or whether Lucy would do what she set out to. She were ill herself, y'know. A week later Lucy was found hanged in the woods. There were no sign of the girl-child.' His head was bowed now as he leaned heavily against the window frame. 'So help me, I've no idea what happened to the bairn. For all I know, Peters could well have done for her an' all.' He didn't look at the other man. He saw only one thing. And that was murder.'

'What about the authorities?'

'We told them nothing. Lucy's mam came to see me a lot at that time. I made her promise not to tell them about the child or the letter. I knew they wouldn't punish him. What did they know, eh? He made my lass pregnant then claimed the child weren't his. He hadn't committed no crime, had he? So what could the authorities do? No, I told Lucy's mam . . . hide the letter, tell the buggers nothing at all. She did as I asked and the authorities were glad enough to put it down as a straightforward suicide. Lucy's mam though . . . she couldn't stand no more heartache. It all preyed on her mind, d'yer see? Soon after that she stopped visiting me at the prison and then I never heard from her again. I don't begrudge her a new life because she's earned it. It were over between me and her, I knew that. All as mattered were what he'd done to Lucy . . . night and day, that were all I could think of. And so I bided me time . . . made meself a promise. When they let me loose, I went straight to the churchyard and made that same promise to my Lucy.'

'What did you promise, Soames?'

'The same thing as you yourself would promise . . . as *any* man would promise! There ain't nothing left in me life now. I've lost me sons and I've lost me wife. On the last day of this month the bailiffs will take the roof from over me head. I've got nothing to lose. I promised me daughter that Peters would pay for what he did to her. And, by God, he will!'

'You mean to murder him?'

'That's right, toff. I mean to murder him.'

'Good. Then it seems we might well be able to kill two birds with one stone.' Edward Dickens took off his hat and placed it on the chair. 'Perhaps I will have a measure of whisky after all,' he said, and his smile was devilish.

It was a little over an hour later when Edward Dickens emerged from the house. The young woman saw him approach and wondered at the benign smile on his face. He was walking with the air of a man who had just achieved something wonderful. She saw the rough-looking individual standing in the doorway of the dilapidated house, and was made to ponder. Why would an influential and wealthy man such as the respectable Mr Dickens associate with a fellow such as the one in the doorway there?

'Forgive me, my dear,' he said, flinging open the car

door. 'Business, you know . . . it all takes time.' He threw his hat on to the back seat in a cavalier fashion. 'But now it's done and we can concentrate on the more pleasurable aspects of our little trip.' He climbed into his seat, settled and fidgeted, and made a peculiar little wave to the man who watched. Turning to his companion he said with a cunning smile, 'There you see a fool of the highest order, my dear.' He then stroked her bare knee, sliding his fingers beneath her skirt to the top of her thigh; when she opened her legs, he could feel the dewy tenderness of her most private parts, and his excitement was more than he could bear. With the drink still on him, and his face leering with passion, he leaned over to press his lips on hers and, when she made no resistance, promised himself a night to remember.

As he had already told her, she was no fool. There was something strange going on here between Dickens and that scruffy fellow. And she wondered whether it might be worth her while to find out more. 'Be patient, you devil,' she murmured, snuggling up to him as he drove away. Her painted fingers caressed the bulge in his trousers. And all the while she wondered about that man back there. And the uncommon alliance. And how she might best benefit from it all.

'Cheerio then, Shirley. I'll see you later. Happen he'll be in a better mood by then.' Dora's smile was wide and happy but she was peeved at the way things were going. She stayed at the door for a brief time, watching the young woman cross the cobbles and then continue along the flagstones until she reached the bottom of the street where she turned the corner without a backward glance.

A moment later Dora had returned to the parlour where Judd was standing, legs astride, his back to the fire; he was still in his working overalls, sweat and grime was still etched into his skin. 'Well, our Judd,' she said angrily, 'I hope you're pleased with yourself?'

He didn't reply straightaway. Instead he looked into her face and there was a kind of sadness in his dark brown eyes. 'I've done nothing to be ashamed of,' he reminded her. 'All I said was that I'm not ready to take a wife.'

'And why not?' She sat down in the chair by the table and before he could answer put another question. 'Is it because you feel you'd be letting me down? Leaving me to care for our Dad?' Her mood softened then. 'I *want* to see you settled with a family of your own, our Judd,' she coaxed. 'There's any number of little houses going for rent. You could do a lot worse than Shirley. She's a good lass, you can't deny that.'

'No, I can't,' he readily agreed. 'But you've got it all wrong, our Sis. It has nothing to do with whether she's a good lass, and nothing to do with you having to cope with our Dad on your own . . . although there's no question that I would ever turn my back on my responsibilities.'

'What is it then? You're coming up twenty-seven now, and you've had enough girlfriends to keep a battalion of soldiers satisfied . . . and still there isn't one that's put the idea of marriage in your mind. It's time you took yourself a wife, our Judd.' She had been convinced that Shirley would be the one. Maybe she still would. At least he hadn't broken off the relationship altogether; not like he did with the others as soon as they started dreaming of wedding bells.

Dora wondered whether *she* was the root of Judd's

dilemma. She knew how he thought she ought to go out more often and maybe have a boyfriend. She could never convince her brother that she was content looking after her father. She could never contemplate being a wife; in fact, she had always been afraid of men in that particular way. Some women pined to wed and others were happy enough to stay single. Dora belonged to the latter category. If she had friends and money enough for her own needs, then that was all she wanted out of life. All her energies had been taken up with her parents, and though she would never openly admit it, when her old dad was gone she would enjoy being her own person again. A husband would only spoil all that. Besides, she had no wish to lie in a man's arms, and the thought of making babies terrified her.

Judd, though, he was another matter altogether. Red-blooded, charming and handsome, he had swept many a lass off her feet then disappointed them when he made it plain that he was not ready to put a ring on their finger. There were folks who were made for marriage, like Phoebe for instance. And Judd. There was no doubt in Dora's mind that he would make a wonderful husband when he finally chose the right lass. And it wouldn't surprise her if he didn't father a whole batch of young 'uns, because she'd seen him with the childer in the street. They loved him, that they did, just as she and their old dad loved him. He was a fine man and deserved a fine wife. Shirley was perfect for him and Dora could not get it out of her mind that Judd's happiness was marred by guilt. 'If I thought for one minute it were me that were holding you back, I'd sooner be six feet under the turf, our Judd,' she said sincerely.

'It isn't you, sweetheart,' he promised her. 'And it isn't Shirley. Like you say, she's a good lass and will make somebody a wonderful wife.' He laughed then. 'Who knows . . . she just might be the one to persuade me down the aisle one day.' He thought it highly unlikely, but there would come a day when he must settle down. He wanted a wife and a family of his own. Like any man, he had *always* wanted that. But it was Phoebe he needed to share his life with. And it was Phoebe's children he wanted to father. But she couldn't see him in the same way and now he believed she never would.

'Don't dismiss Shirley too quickly, will you, our Judd?' Dora asked now. 'She thinks the world of you.'

'Do you think I don't know that?'

'You'll not be too hasty in finishing with her then? You'll give it a while longer?'

He slowly shook his head, a loving smile on his handsome face as he said kindly, 'What a romantic you are, Dora Little.' He saw how anxious she was and conceded, 'All right. When she gets back from town, I'll go and see her . . . apologise for not taking a keen enough interest in the house in Railway Terrace. Though I'll not promise to rush round and see the landlord with a deposit, because I honestly don't see me and Shirley going that far together. And that's enough on the subject.'

He knew the house. He passed it every day on his way to and from work. It was a fine house, a house that could soon be a home, and he'd lost count of the times he'd stopped to gaze in at the windows, imagining himself and Phoebe sitting there by the fireside, lost in their love for each other, and mebbe a bairn or two tucked in their cots upstairs. It was a dream that sent him to sleep at night and woke him in the morning. A dream that drove him almost crazy when he was tempted to go to her and pour out what was in his heart. In all his life he'd never been afraid of saying what was on his mind, but he knew that one wrong word would only send her further away from him. He and Phoebe had grown up almost as brother and sister and he knew instinctively that she still saw him as that . . . a brother; her every letter confirmed it. More and more he'd come to realise how impossible his dream really was. And it was a well-known fact that dreams rarely come true. More often than not a body had to settle for second best.

'I'd better get cleaned up,' he said, going into the scullery and stripping the shirt from his back. He tried to thrust all thoughts of Phoebe from his mind. But it was getting harder and harder to do.

'And I'd best answer Phoebe's letter,' Dora called out. 'I reckon she and that Greg have had another fight.' She chuckled merrily. 'They do say as how true love never runs smooth.' She couldn't have known her words were like a stab to Judd's aching heart.

Part Two

1926

The Devil Sings

Chapter Ten

It was five minutes to six on a Friday evening. For six days now the weather had been atrocious; first the deluge of rain that saw out Christmas and the old year and now the snow. It had begun to fall on New Year's Day and four days later it was still pouring from the skies, big fluffy balls that fell on the ground to be hardened into ice by the bitter cold winds that swept down from the high ground.

Phoebe knelt by her window and gazed across the landscape. She loved the snow. It covered the ground with a shimmering cloak that glistened and sparkled like so many diamonds. All the dark corners were brightened and everything was equal; all that was ugly on the surface of the earth was now smooth and white, as beautiful as any wondrous landscape beneath. 'No one would ever know your secrets,' she murmured, staying a while longer and thinking deeper thoughts. She had a secret too. A frightening and terrible secret that haunted her every waking hour. *She was carrying Greg Peters' child!*

Just then a knock on the door cut through her thoughts, startling her. She swung round, eyes open wide, her heart quickened by the shame she must hide at all costs. 'Who's there?' she called out, her hand going instantly to the front of her dress, to the guilty secret there.

'It's only me.' It was her aunt's voice. Phoebe gave a huge sigh of relief. 'Phoebe . . . can I come in a moment? I want to talk to you.' There was a silence while the two women kept their own counsel; the one outside hoping her suspicions were unfounded and the one inside praying that her aunt had not guessed the truth.

It was a moment before Phoebe was composed enough to admit anyone into her little sanctuary. There was a strangeness in her heart, a feeling that she was being driven into a place where she was loath to go, a deepdown fear that what she had done would bring more than shame down on her head. What she felt was an odd, inexplicable sense of tragedy. All the same, she put on her brightest smile and opened the door. 'I was just about to make my way down,' she said.

Noreen came into the room and closed the door behind her. 'There's a few minutes yet,' she told Phoebe. 'Your uncle's closeted in his study . . . he and Margaret are discussing the forthcoming wedding.' She smiled then and Phoebe was yet again surprised by her aunt's prettiness. It was not a feature that showed itself too often for her smiles were rare.

'I still can't believe how Margaret managed to persuade her father,' Phoebe commented. 'Especially when he was so dead set against her being wed.'

Noreen gave a little sarcastic laugh. 'Margaret is nothing if not devious,' she admitted. 'All the same, if anyone had told me that Edward would change his mind about his precious daughter and Hadley Peters, I would have said they were talking out of the back of their head,' she said thoughtfully. 'And, yes, you're right, Phoebe. It *is* strange. Very strange.'

'What did you want to talk to me about?' She could count on one hand the number of times her aunt had been to her room. There was something different about this particular visit. She saw it in her aunt's eyes and in the way her small fingers were nervously winding round and round each other. She sensed that her aunt was more troubled than usual. And she was right to be.

'I've been meaning to talk to you for days now, Phoebe.' Noreen began pacing the floor, obviously very agitated. 'The trouble is, I don't quite know how to start.'

'Just say what's on your mind,' Phoebe suggested. Her aunt's nervousness had conveyed itself to her and now she was convinced that Noreen had guessed. 'Is it to do with me?' she asked, feigning both surprise and innocence. 'I can't think what I've done wrong. I've tried to stay out of their way . . . Margaret raises trouble with me every time her shadow crosses mine.' Since that awful night when her uncle had attacked her, Phoebe had been extra vigilant. But the minute she began to suspect that she was with child, other even more horrendous issues had overtaken her.

'No, Phoebe. It's nothing like that,' her aunt reassured her.

'What then?'

Noreen paused in her pacing to stare at Phoebe and there was an unusual affection in her countenance. Seeming embarrassed by Phoebe's quizzical and concerned gaze, she looked up to the ceiling, swallowing so hard that she made a little noise in her throat. She glanced at the bedside clock. In another minute they would be expected in the dining-room. All of this was very difficult for her. She had a liking for Phoebe and now was filled with a dreadful suspicion. Day and night she had thought about it, and now that she had plucked up the courage actually to come into her room and begin to tackle the issue, she mustn't falter. Downstairs, Edward and his daughter would soon be waiting. But for now Phoebe was also waiting . . . waiting for an explanation. It was now or never. But she would have to be very careful in the way she put it. The last thing she wanted to do was to raise any damaging thoughts in Phoebe's mind because already that young woman had voiced far too many questions about the relationship between her mother and Edward.

Taking a deep breath, she blurted out. 'The night your uncle came to your room . . . when he cut off your hair . . .' She couldn't ask it! Phoebe had suffered enough. Her courage began to waver.

Seeing the other woman's dilemma, Phoebe told her softly, 'You can talk about it. It's all right. I've dealt with it in my own way . . . it don't hurt me no more.' For many weeks she had shrunk from facing it all in her mind. But then she had come to realise that by being afraid she was letting him win. In her heart Phoebe knew that he was the weak one, the coward, the one who should be afraid. That belief gave her courage. And the courage gave her strength. 'It's all right,' she repeated in a calm voice. 'Please . . . you can say what you've come to say.'

'Did he . . . that night when he came into your room . . . did he touch you . . . intimately?' She was putting it badly but these past weeks she had a woman's intuition that Phoebe might be with child. And if he had done that to her! 'Dear God, if he's done that to you,' she cried in a hoarse voice. 'If he's forced himself on you in that way . . . *This time I will not stay silent.*'

Phoebe watched in amazement as her aunt's face crumpled and she gave a loud heart-rending sob. The tears spilled from her eyes and, too late, she turned away. Phoebe went to her then, putting her arm around the frail hunched shoulders. 'Is that what you've been thinking?' she asked in a whisper. When the other woman made a small nod but couldn't speak, Phoebe stood before her and, looking straight into her aunt's eyes, said kindly, 'You should have said something to me sooner . . . instead of worrying yourself like this. I thought you knew everything that had happened?' She smiled and shook her head. 'No. He didn't touch me in that way. Though I can't know what he might have done if it hadn't been for you.' The smile slid from Phoebe's face with her aunt's next words.

'Thank God for that, child. I'm sorry for having asked you these things but . . . well, you've looked so pale and unwell these past weeks . . . I got it into my foolish head that you might be pregnant. But I'm glad I was wrong.' Her face glowed with relief. 'We'd better hurry down or there'll be more trouble,' she warned. Without another word, she turned away and went out of the room, leaving Phoebe standing there, afraid and shocked. If her aunt had noticed a change in her, how many others had done the same? Suddenly she felt even more threatened. Even more alone.

She had no choice but to make her way downstairs. Many things were running through her mind as she came into the dining-room. One in particular kept raising itself. Something her aunt had cried out: 'Dear God, if he's forced himself on you in that way . . . *This time I will not stay silent.*'

Phoebe was so disturbed that she came to a halt on the stairs, her knuckles turning white as they gripped the banister. A picture began to emerge in her turbulent thoughts. Did it mean that Edward Dickens had forced himself on someone else? Had he made some woman heavy with child? Suddenly it all made sense and Phoebe was sickened to her stomach. Of course! Noreen herself. Suddenly it was easy to see what had been in the back of her aunt's mind just now. Suddenly Phoebe could understand the unnatural coldness between mother and daughter. The awful truth slowly dawned: Edward Dickens had forced himself on his own wife and made her with child. And who could blame that poor woman if she had no love in her heart for either her husband or for the cold calculating creature who had grown in his image? Many things began to make sense now, and Phoebe's heart went out to her aunt. But what could she do? Nothing. There was nothing at all she could do. Her aunt was a grown woman and would deal with things in her own way. Just as Phoebe herself must deal with the problems that loomed ever larger by the day. Up to now there was no telltale bump, but it was only a matter of time . . . maybe weeks rather than months. After that, the secret might be contained for a while because of her naturally slim figure and loose-fitting clothes. But then, soon enough, the whole world would know.

According to Phoebe's hazy calculations, the baby would find its way into the world some time in June or July. Being an only child herself, she knew little of such things. Not for the first time it crossed her mind to ask Marcus for a day off without telling her uncle. She could board a tram for Bury and pour out her heart to Dora. Time and again Phoebe had been on the verge of doing just this, but something held her back . . . shame perhaps? She could just about cope with Dora knowing how she had given herself freely to Greg Peters, but somehow she couldn't bear the thought of Judd knowing. All her life she had looked up to him in a way that she had never really looked up to anyone else. There was a kind of respect between the two of them, a closeness that she treasured. No, she couldn't tell Dora because that would be like telling Judd too. Or was it simply because she had never leaned on anyone else in the whole of her life and it was not an easy thing for her to do now.

Whatever the reason, Phoebe dismissed the idea. Somehow, she would have to find a solution. She remembered then what her mother used to say when trouble threatened: 'Trust in God.' That was what she had said. And that was what Phoebe would do.

When Phoebe came into the dining-room, three pairs of eyes turned to watch her. She felt as though they could see right inside her, and her heart turned over. 'I'm not late,' she said, taking her place at the table.

'Of course you're not, my dear,' her uncle said with a sudden smile. He sat down and everyone followed suit. 'All the same, it would please me if you could find your way to the table *before* the clock strikes the hour,' he said in a harsher voice. But he didn't want to be harsh, dear me no. Not when there was so very much to look forward to. Not when his plans had been honed to perfection. No, he didn't wish to appear surly. So he ate his meal noisily, occasionally bestowing a broad smile on one and all. And they in turn looked away with embarrassment.

All but Margaret, who returned his smile and was secretly thankful that at last he had come round to accepting the fact of her forthcoming marriage. She could never have allowed him to cut her out of his will . . . disown her. But then, she never really expected that he would or she might not have been so determined to have her own way. She hadn't been too surprised when his objections melted away. She had always been able to wind him round her little finger. Everything she'd ever wanted, she'd only had to ask and it was hers. Oh, there had been times when her father kicked and fussed, but in the end she always got her own way.

Hadley wasn't just another toy, another 'thing' she wanted, though. It had taken her a long time to make her father see just how important he was to her. If she was ever capable of loving a man other than her father, it was Hadley. It wasn't surprising that there had been some jealousy but that was only to be expected and, to tell the truth, she rather revelled in it. But, no. She wasn't surprised when her father gave way, just as he always had. And, yes, it was possible that there might come a time when she no longer wanted Hadley. But she wanted him *now*. She loved him *now*. And she meant to have him.

Noreen sat quiet throughout the meal and Phoebe had

little to say. Both women were lost in their own troubled thoughts. Mostly it was Margaret and her father who talked though once or twice Edward remembered to remind his daughter that, 'You are aware that you should not be talking during meals?' All the same when she fell silent it was he who started the conversation again and brought the smile back to her face. Occasionally he would glance at his newspaper and comment on this or that.

'I see the British troops are on the verge of pulling out of the Rhineland,' he said to everyone's lack of interest. And perhaps excited their curiosity just a little with: 'There's talk of a fellow called Baird having found a way to send moving images by radio.' At this point he lowered his newspaper and peeped over the top at each woman in turn. 'My word, we are sullen today,' he commented wickedly. Fixing his gaze on Phoebe he asked in a softer, more intimate voice, 'Cat got your tongue?'

He remembered little of the night when he had gone into her bedroom. Now his eyes appraised her short wavy hair, afire in a shaft of light that poured through the window. He knew that it was he who had ravaged her crowning glory and was delighted; he would have been even more delighted if the result had proved to be less attractive. He regretted not having shaved her head bald while he had the chance.

'And look at your plate,' he told her. 'That's good food you're wasting. If you didn't want a meal, you should have said so.' He folded the newspaper with meticulous precision, over and over, until it was no larger than a business envelope. Positioning it beside his plate, he regarded Phoebe curiously then turned to his wife and asked in a stern voice, 'Is she ailing or something?'

It was Phoebe who replied. 'No,' she said in a firm voice. 'I'm not ailing for anything.' She resented him immensely.

He visibly bristled. 'Have you still not learned to speak only when you're spoken to?' he demanded, his jaw bones clenching and unclenching. When she gave no reply, he told her sharply, 'Leave the table. You disgust me.'

Phoebe wasted no time in complying with his instructions. If her uncle thought that by sending her from the room he was punishing her, he couldn't be more wrong. Behind her she could hear her aunt explaining, 'The girl doesn't mean any harm, dear. She hasn't been all that well lately . . . perhaps she's coming down with a chill.'

'Then she had better keep her distance from the rest of us, don't you think?' he said sarcastically. 'Come to think, it might be a good idea if the pair of you were to take your meals in the shed.' Noreen was at once silent but Margaret's laughter could be heard all over the house. Until her father thumped his fist on the table, after which the meal was resumed in total silence.

It was eight-thirty when Hadley and Margaret presented themselves at the door of her father's study. He greeted them warmly and the three of them went inside with Margaret smiling sweetly at her mother who was making her way back from the kitchen. No sooner was the study door closed than Phoebe came down the stairs.

'I thought I might go across and see Aggie before she goes to bed,' she explained, coming to a halt at the foot of the stairs. 'Unless you'd like me to stay and keep you company?' There was something sad about her aunt.

Something that tugged at Phoebe's heart and made her want to be friends; although up to now, and in spite of the rare occasions when Noreen dared to reach out, Phoebe had never really managed to get close.

'You go on,' Noreen told her with a wan smile. 'Aggie will be pleased to see you, I'm sure. She's a delightful little girl. Friendly and open, just like her father.' She touched Phoebe on the arm and for one brief moment it seemed as though she was about to confide something in her. But all she said was, 'I shouldn't rush back. Your uncle won't even notice that you're gone.' She jerked her head in the direction of the study. 'They're all in there . . . discussing the wedding.' She shook her head, pursing her lips with a look of disbelief. 'I still can't believe it. He was so set against Hadley Peters . . . oh, a nice enough young man, I know. But I can't think what almighty thing must have happened to make Edward give them his blessing.'

'They love each other,' Phoebe said, her heart aching. Her own feelings were confused. There had been a point when she'd really believed she was in love with Hadley herself. Lately though, especially since her uncle had been persuaded to go along with the wedding plans, she wasn't sure quite how she felt anymore. When she'd first come to Dickens House she'd been adrift in a strange place. Hadley had been kind to her. Had made her feel welcome. She was confused and lonely and he seemed always to be there, strong and protective . . . just like Judd had always been. Only now Judd was a long way away, and courting into the bargain. At night, when the house was quiet, Phoebe often thought of him. But then, there were

401

other things to keep her mind occupied. Other more urgent matters that could prove to be her downfall.

'Margaret would have got wed, whatever her father said,' she told Noreen now. 'Happen he realised he could lose her for good if he wasn't careful.'

Noreen laughed, a low cynical laugh that surprised Phoebe. 'I don't think it would have come to that,' she said. 'Margaret knows she's the main beneficiary in her father's will . . . she wouldn't have thrown that away, believe me.' There was no bitterness in her voice. Only resignation. Aware that she had already said too much, she glanced nervously towards the study before turning away and hurrying in the direction of the dining-room.

Phoebe waited a moment, reflecting on what her aunt had said. Then she too went quickly along the hallway and out of the house, closing the door quietly behind her. She took a deep gulp of fresh air. Always, when she left the house, she felt as though a great weight had been lifted from her shoulders. Not today though. Today her aunt had voiced the suspicion that Phoebe was with child. For now she was content to be wrong but it was only a matter of time before other people too would make the same discovery. And Phoebe couldn't even begin to think about which way she could turn then.

'Come in, me beauty. Come away in.' Lou Peters was delighted to see her. The parlour was cosy as usual, and the cheery fire sent out a glow that warmed her. 'Now then,' he began as they sat down either side of the fireplace, 'why is it you've not been to see us these past few days? We were beginning to think we'd got the plague sure we were,' he laughed.

Aggie came rushing through the door then and he put the question to her. 'Isn't that right, me darlin'?' he called out as she threw herself into Phoebe's arms. 'Didn't the two of us wonder whether we'd caught the plague or what?' When there was no reply except the laughter of the other two, he threw up his arms in exasperation. 'What's a poor fellow to do?' he moaned, getting up from his chair. 'Put the kettle on, I expect, 'cause there ain't nobody listening to a word I say.'

Aggie sat on Phoebe's knee with one arm around her neck. 'Why haven't you been to see us?' she asked in that unnervingly direct way all children have. 'I wanted to come to your house but Daddy said I shouldn't be so cheeky.' She pulled a face. 'Anyway . . . your uncle might have opened the door, and I wouldn't have liked that. He stares like this.' She narrowed her eyes and peered into Phoebe's face. 'And he makes my stomach feel sick.'

Phoebe laughed out loud. Trust a child to describe Edward Dickens in such an apt way. She couldn't have put it better herself. 'When did he stare at you like that?' she asked, still chuckling. She wasn't aware that the child had been close enough for him to have stared at her in that particular way.

'On Friday when I lost my ball over the hedge and it rolled under his motor-car.' She set her mouth in a hard line. Then: 'He wouldn't let me get it. He just went right over it with his wheels. But it was all right,' she said, suddenly smiling, 'because he didn't pop it.'

'Well, I'm glad about that,' Phoebe said, secretly thinking what a hard-hearted old bugger her uncle was.

'Phoebe . . . *why* haven't you been to see us?' Her

brow crinkled and her mouth turned down. 'I've missed you.'

'I'm sorry, sweetheart. What with one thing and another, I haven't had a great deal of time to myself lately,' she lied. The real truth was she could have found a few minutes for Lou and Aggie but was desperately afraid that Greg would corner her. Whenever she glanced from her window he was there, looking up, smiling at her, seeming to watch her every move. On the last two occasions she'd been to the farmhouse, he'd almost managed to get her on her own. She didn't want that. She never wanted that. 'It's just that I've been staying on a bit later at the shop . . . helping Marcus to stocktake. I've been tired out with all the extra work.' It wasn't the work that had tired her out. It was her condition, she knew. What was more, she'd been off her food and wasn't sleeping too well. 'Do you want to read to me?' she asked with enthusiasm. She loved hearing the child read; it always raised a sense of great pride in her.

Aggie jumped down. 'Oh, yes!' she cried, eyes shining. 'Miss said I'm the best reader in the class now.'

'Well now, that's wonderful!' exclaimed Phoebe. She watched as the child skipped to the cupboard where she kept her little box of precious things. 'So I'm in for a treat then, aren't I?' she said lovingly.

The whole evening was a treat. Aggie wore herself out and was soon shipped off to bed; Lou talked himself almost hoarse, and Phoebe's spirits were lifted by his delightful sense of humour. Tonight, though, she found him to be less than his usual bouyant self, as though he had something very pressing on his mind. Now and then he would fall into a deep silence when he would stare into the fire, his head bowed and his hands clasped tight together, one palm working into the other as though he was desperately trying to grind something between them.

'Is everything all right, Lou?' Phoebe asked him, anxious to help with any problem he might have. She'd never seen him like this before, one minute making her laugh and the next seeming as though the world was weighing on his narrow shoulders.

'I'm fine, me beauty,' he told her with a ready grin that didn't quite dispel her suspicions. 'And what would be wrong with me, eh?' he demanded, straightening his back and looking at her with merry eyes.

'Well, if there *is* something,' Phoebe gently insisted, 'you know what they say? A trouble shared is a trouble halved.' Look at me, she thought, asking Lou to do what I can't myself. If she was threatened with murder, she still wouldn't be able to confide her own secret in anyone. At least not yet awhile.

'There's nothing at all for you to worry yourself about,' he promised her. 'If there is a problem . . . and I'm not saying there is, mind,' he quickly added, 'it'll be to do with family. And if it's to do with family, then it'll come right, sure as eggs is eggs.' He chuckled and was soon his old self. 'Families have a way o' causing theirselves a heap o' trouble and then it clears . . . like sunshine after a storm, it is.' The subject was dropped then and he talked excitedly of his son's forthcoming wedding. 'Though I'm not sure in me heart of hearts that he's chosen the right woman,' he confessed.

'But it's *his* choice,' Phoebe reminded him, thinking

405

this must be the reason for Lou's preoccupation and being relieved that it was nothing more serious.

'Yer right, sure ye are,' he conceded, his bright reply belying the truth. A terrible truth which he'd even kept from Hadley, and to good purpose, because if he knew about the advert which told how Lucy Soames' father meant to track them down, it would only deepen the awful bitterness between him and his brother. Lou didn't want that. Nor did he want Hadley taking the matter into his own hands. John Soames was dangerous. A relentless, bitter pursuer . . . and justifiably so, in Lou's opinion. But it was a known fact that the man was unbalanced. Besides which his long years in jail had probably inculcated a great hatred in him that would never be satisfied until blood was drawn. Lou had considered all of this. Day and night he'd gone over it all in his mind. He loved both his sons; a father had to, even when he was mortally ashamed of the weakness in one.

Only this morning he had come to a decision. The time had come to stop protecting a man who was so obviously without compassion or conscience. Because of Greg they had been forced to move home; because of Greg an innocent child had been robbed of her rightful parents; because of Greg a young woman had ended her own life; and now he had brought another man's vengeance down on them. This time, though, Lou had decided he would not run. For once in his miserable life, Greg would be made to face the consequences of his selfish actions. And God help them all!

It was late when Phoebe decided she'd better get home

before her uncle missed her although Hadley wasn't yet back and the three of them were probably still shut in the study. Edward Dickens liked to hear himself talking, and was no doubt laying down certain 'rules and regulations' with regard to the wedding of his dear daughter. According to Lou, Hadley had expressed his desire for 'a quiet affair'. Unfortunately, he was no real match for Margaret and her father. She was already planning on a much grander scale and no doubt her father intended giving her the grandest wedding Blackburn had ever seen. Certainly he gave every indication that this was what he planned. But then, there was no telling what was going on in that man's devious mind.

Lou walked Phoebe to the front door. 'Sure it's been grand seeing yer,' he said, reaching up to take his jacket from the peg. The night struck cool through the open door. 'Don't forget that me and the lass delight in your visits,' he gently chided. She kissed him fondly on the cheek and was intrigued when he asked, 'Is yer aunt keeping well?'

'Well enough,' she replied. 'Why don't you go over and see her tomorrow? She's in the house alone during the day . . . except for the time when Daisy's there.' In the lamplight she saw him cast his gaze down and thought he might be blushing. What a pity her aunt hadn't married someone like Lou. He was such a lovely, gentle man. 'I'm sure she'd like to see you.'

'Lord love and bless us! I can't go calling on another man's wife when he's not there,' he protested with mock horror, slipping into his jacket. 'Whatever would it look like?'

'It would look like a friendly neighbour calling on another, I would have thought.'

'Oh, aye? Well, all I can say is you don't know the trouble wicked tongues can cause,' he said thoughtfully. 'Your aunt is a good woman. I wouldn't want to do anything that might damage her reputation.'

'Yes, she is a good woman,' Phoebe readily agreed. 'But she's lonely too.'

'Now what makes yer say a thing like that?' He was surprised. 'How can a woman be lonely when she's got a family?'

'Being with people don't always mean you can't be lonely,' Phoebe told him softly. Even when she was sitting round that big old table, she felt isolated and unwanted; only her aunt sent her a small measure of warmth, but it was little compensation for the loss of her own mam and the love that had bound them for all time. Loneliness was a thing that grew inside, a cold unhappy feeling, a deep ache that was not relieved by the presence of other people. Since discovering she was with child, Phoebe had come to realise that more and more.

'Yer a strange little thing,' Lou observed affectionately. 'But you'd best be off now,' he warned, 'else I'll have your uncle after me, sure I will.' He looked out into the black night. 'I'll walk yer to the gate,' he said. But when there was a small cry from upstairs, he added cheekily, 'Wait a minute 'til I see what Madam wants.'

'No, it's all right,' Phoebe told him, going through the door and preparing to close it. 'It's only a step or two, and I'll be indoors before you've time to turn round.'

'Away yer go then, and don't forget what I said,' he

called out as he went up the stairs. 'We miss yer when you stay away.' He was gone then and Phoebe could hear him scolding the girl for having got out of her bed. Then: 'Did yer have a bad dream, sweetheart? Sure yer old daddy's here now and he'll chase it away, that he will.' She smiled as she gently closed the door. The love between Lou and that little girl was precious and wonderful . . . just as it had been between her and her mam.

Outside she paused and pulled her cardigan closer about her. It was a dark soulless night. A moment ago there had been a moon but now it was hiding behind uneasy shifting clouds. All around was pitch black. The eerie silence unnerved her as she set off towards the gate. On a night like this there were always creeping things, moving shadows and flitting shapes that followed every footstep. Phoebe felt them now as she hurried along the path. When she reached out to open the gate, she could almost smell danger. There was a sound behind her, a moment when her heart leaped in her throat, and then it was as if the darkness had solidified into a menacing shape that came at her out of nowhere, leaping at her throat, gripping her so that she couldn't move.

'Ssh . . . I won't hurt you,' he murmured, and his voice was like that of a lover. She couldn't see who it was that dragged her into the thicket, one arm round her waist and the other across her face. In his vice-like grip, and unable to turn her head, Phoebe found herself fighting for her very life. She kicked out, fury mingled with desperation, but then he lifted her from the ground and her legs were flailing in mid-air. She scratched and tore at his hands with her fingernails but he made no sound nor did he relax his hold. Instead he kept her tight, edging towards the spinney, taking her with him, and all the while murmuring, whispering endearments, caressing her name.

'Don't say you don't want me,' he warned lovingly, 'I know that you do.' He kissed her then, a soft and gentle brushing of the lips against her temple, and though she struggled like a mad thing, Phoebe felt her senses weakening.

In the spinney he laid her down with immense tenderness, keeping his hand across her mouth, seemingly unaware that he was slowly suffocating her. 'Phoebe,' he murmured, lying down beside her and pressing his lips to hers. 'You've been avoiding me. You shouldn't avoid me. I don't like it.' He laughed and relaxed his hold on her, his fingers clawing at her clothes, raising her skirt; his warm breath bathed her face, reviving her.

The cold night air invaded her body. She shivered and gasped it into her burning lungs. 'You!' she cried, lashing out at the grinning handsome face that was almost touching hers. She could feel the hardness against her, fumbling, wanting to enter. She would have screamed then but he sensed her intention. Cold thick fingers clamped themselves over her mouth.

'You didn't fight me before,' he said accusingly. 'Don't fight me now.' His voice softened. 'You must know how much I want you . . . since that first day when I saw you on the cart, I meant to have you.' He was smiling, incredibly handsome in the rising moonlight. He looked almost insane. 'I've been going crazy,' he moaned. 'You and me, we're the same kind of people . . . we don't want anything permanent. All I want is to have you again, just like before.'

He slid himself over her. The warmth of his bare flesh shocked her senses. Suddenly he was wrenched from her and the sky opened up like a dark vast ocean above her. There had been no warning, no sound, other than a fleeting whisper like the soft footsteps of night creatures scraping the earth.

As she fled from that place, Phoebe dared to glance back only once. The moon was high then, and what she saw was Greg Peters and his brother Hadley. Their fighting was fierce, their hatred all consuming. They lashed out, fists clenched like hammers, bone against bone. Equally matched, they fought with a hard and terrible strength.

Turning away she ran like the wind across the bank, into the road and towards the house, where she let herself in and slipped softly up the stairs. She was breathless and cursing herself for not realising he was certain to have been lingering somewhere outside the farmhouse, waiting for her, wanting her again. You should have known! she told herself angrily. You should have been more watchful. Quickly, she bolted the door against all who would invade her little sanctuary. Tense and restless, she paced the floor back and forth, thinking and planning. 'I've got to get away,' she muttered. 'Somehow I've got to get away from here.' There was urgency in her voice and now there was another man on her mind. Marcus, and she had not forgotten his offer of marriage.

Phoebe bathed and put on her nightdress. Sitting for a

while in front of the mirror, she brushed her short curled locks then leaned forward on her elbows, examining herself in the mirror. 'You're a fool, Phoebe Mulligan,' she told herself. 'And if he'd had his way with you, it would have bloody well served you right!'

She was angry with herself for having almost let it happen and was astonished at the thoughts that kept bursting upon her mind. 'Marcus,' she whispered, and felt even more shocked at the way her plans were shaping. Shaking her head, she actually smiled. 'You're running away with yourself, Phoebe, gal,' she said firmly. 'That's a dangerous thing to do.'

All the same, she couldn't entirely forget what Marcus had said to her. Nor could she forget what had happened here, in this very room, not so long ago. And now tonight, out there . . . Greg Peters, watching her, wanting her. Not wanting marriage, wanting only to use her in order to gratify his own lust. There was no peace for her now. Then there was the child . . . *his* child. The thought filled her with horror. 'He must never know it's his,' she murmured fearfully. Her mind came back to Marcus and it was a long time before she could calm herself enough to fall asleep.

Outside the night lengthened and grew steadily darker. The brothers fought until the night sky melted into dawn. They vented their longfelt hatred, inflicting pain, and the blood flowed fast between them. Too late now for forgiveness, too much had driven a distance between them. Now, because of one more wicked thing, because one was bad and the other was good, because of their father's suffering and their mother's before, because of the child and the girl, and because of Phoebe, there could be no reconciliation. Not yet. Maybe never. And so they fought and neither would admit defeat. When the morning sun was peeping over the horizon, when they were each broken and exhausted, they found their way home. And their father's heart was saddened all over again.

Chapter Eleven

Marcus had been singing all morning, going about his work as though he hadn't a care in the world when all the time he was steeped in thought. 'When did you say the wedding will be?' he asked, keeping his head bent and his tiny hammer tapping at the brass studs that skirted the pretty red clogs. 'My! What a performance it all is,' he added with a chuckle. Phoebe had explained how her uncle and cousin were forever closeted in his study, and how no one was allowed to forget what, in Margaret's words, was going to be 'a glamorous do'.

'I don't think the date's been set yet, although I reckon it won't be too long now,' Phoebe replied. 'But honestly, Marcus . . . anyone would think she was a film star the way she's going on!'

'Pampering herself, is she?'

Phoebe found herself laughing and it was a good feeling. Marcus did that to her. He always made her feel life wasn't too bad after all. 'You could say that,' she answered. 'In the past two weeks there's been a stream of dressmakers to the house, not to mention hairdressers and chefs from some of the best named establishments. And if she isn't talking about her dress, or planning the way she might wear her hair, she's prancing about with a book on her head, practising her "stately" walk down the aisle. But I'll tell you one thing for sure . . .'

'And what's that?'

'The prospect of being Hadley Peters' wife ain't made her a nicer person. Yesterday she even told her mam that she should stay away from the do. "You probably won't like all the fuss", that was what she said, but if you ask me, she's ashamed of the poor woman.' Phoebe had witnessed that very conversation and when she was bold enough to intervene: 'She gave me the same advice. "Stay away. I don't want either of you at the church," ' Phoebe told Marcus indignantly. 'And what was more, she meant it.'

He put down his hammer and quietly regarded her, saying in a fond voice, 'And does that bother you, Phoebe?'

'Not really. Though if I was to tell the truth, I suppose it would be grand to see how the toffs get wed.'

When she wasn't busy serving customers and she'd caught up with her own work, Phoebe often came to the doorway of the back-room from where she watched Marcus at his bench. She was there now, and as she watched him, fascinated by his extraordinary talents and never ceasing to be amazed at his total dedication to his craft, she was curious as to why he had never since mentioned the subject of his own proposal to her; although she couldn't really blame him, because she herself had given him no encouragement whatsoever. She supposed he was sorry he'd made the proposal in the first place and now wanted to forget it as quickly as possible.

'Oh, I haven't finished telling you yet,' she went on,

leaning against the door jamb, her brown eyes beginning to smile. 'I wasn't the only one to have heard Margaret's nasty instructions to her mother because unbeknown to any of us her dad overhead everything that was said. Afterwards he told Margaret in no uncertain terms that she was not to assume too much authority. He don't like that, you see. Anyway, with regard to the wedding he told her straight. He wants us *all* there. You could have knocked me down with a feather. And, oh, you should have seen her face. "Every member of this household will attend," he told her. "As will certain dignitaries, and any other guests that I choose to invite. This will be no ordinary wedding, my dear, I can promise you that." '

Phoebe mocked her uncle to perfection, making a stern face and stretching her chin in that peculiar manner of Edward Dickens' when he was exerting his authority. 'Sounds to me like he might even invite the *king*!' she said, bursting into a fit of laughter.

Marcus laughed too. The shop was always happy when Phoebe was here. And so was he. 'Do you think he'll invite a commoner like me?' he asked, bowing and scraping and making his whole countenance wonderfully humble.

'Why! I shall see to it at once,' Phoebe told him in a posh voice, smiling inside as she imagined herself confronting her uncle with her own list of guests, 'though he'll need to be in a better mood than he was at Christmas.' She thought about the Christmas period, and the way her uncle had frowned upon any celebrations, indignantly announcing, 'How am I expected to provide for a wedding *and* Christmas? I'm not made of money.'

When Phoebe bought a tree out of her own money, and struggled home with it from Blackburn town centre, he promptly forbade it in the house. There was no festive meal, and the only mention of Christmas itself was made in his unusually long and vigorous morning sermon, when he reminded one and all that 'greed and fornication are the means by which we pave our own way to Hell and damnation'.

Noreen and Margaret resigned themselves to a quiet Christmas, but Phoebe never could. Back home, Christmas had always been a time to remember the deeper issues and to pray for those less fortunate souls, but it was also a time for families, a time for love and joy, a special time. With this in mind, she took her tree across the road, where Lou stood it in a round earthenware pot in the corner of his parlour. Soon it was surrounded by pretty coloured presents and splendidly dressed in silver balls and trailing paper-chains lovingly made by Aggie and Phoebe in front of a cheery fire.

Even Margaret made mention of how lovely it looked, though Phoebe was afraid she might carry the tale back to her father; she never did though. In fact, when they all gathered round the table for Christmas Day tea, Margaret sat next to Hadley and appeared to enjoy herself as much as anyone, until she and Hadley very quickly retired to the front parlour; Greg was sullen but polite, and soon excused himself from the room. Lou, Phoebe and Aggie had the best time of all. They played hide and seek, opened their presents and laughed and chatted until Aggie fell asleep in the armchair. While Lou tucked her up in bed, Phoebe started the washing-up, and between the two of them they had the little kitchen spick and span in no time at all.

At ten o'clock, Phoebe went home laden with goodies for Noreen: big juicy slices from the best part of the plump turkey, dainty mince tarts made by Lou's own hands, and two little presents wrapped in pretty paper: a brooch from Phoebe and a scarf from Lou. Their kindness brought a fetching pink glow to Noreen's face. She had been asked to come to tea, but that was more than she dared to do. Still, she hadn't missed out altogether, and Phoebe for one was glad of that. Later, when Phoebe was in bed, she lay awake until the early hours, thinking of her mam, and missing it all.

'I'm glad you had a lovely Christmas, Marcus,' Phoebe said now, 'though I still think you should have been with us.'

'Nonsense! I've been to the same hotel in Blackpool every Christmas for the past four years. This year was no different,' he lied. In fact, Marcus had spent a miserable Christmas alone in his rooms above the shop. 'All the same, it was good of Lou to invite me, as I've said already.' He would have liked nothing better than to have spent Christmas with Phoebe, but he was afraid. He loved her too much. 'Still, Christmas is gone and today is Friday, the fourteenth of January. If we don't get on with our work, we'll have a queue at the door,' he reminded her.

This was the first time in almost two weeks that he'd seen even the semblance of a smile on Phoebe's lovely face. Before today she had been like someone weighed down, preoccupied and sombre of mood. It wasn't like her. He had so much wanted to help but dared not. Already he knew she had been shocked by his proposal of marriage, and though he still wanted that above all else, he didn't want to frighten her away for good. So he'd bided his time and now she was laughing again.

But something was still missing. The laughter didn't come from her heart. She was still deeply troubled. He saw it in her every move . . . in the way she slowly climbed the stairs when once upon a time she would have bounded up them like a child. When she served the customers, gone was the usual happy chat where she would lighten their day with a bright and wonderful smile. Often she would stand by the window, looking out at nothing in particular, and would be far away where he couldn't reach, where no one could reach. She looked so small sometimes . . . small and lonely and vulnerable, like a child.

But Phoebe was no child. Her loveliness had never been more pronounced. Her short auburn hair was rich and vital, reflecting the dark brown shine of her lovely eyes. In these past weeks she had assumed a kind of inner glow . . . more mature, a woman of inordinate quality and strength. She was still the warm, delightful Phoebe, and yet there was something . . . *something*. There were times when he felt her going away from him. And that, more than anything, filled him with dread. Not for the first time he thought carefully about his feelings towards her. How strange it was that these were sometimes oddly paternal rather than those of a man in love.

The rest of the day went with great speed, busier and busier as it wore on. The bell over the door hardly stopped ringing, and no sooner was one customer out of the shop than two more came in. There was little time for any further conversation between Marcus and Phoebe although they occasionally found time to smile at one another in between being rushed off their feet. All too quickly, though, the old clock on the wall had ticked away the hours and it was almost closing time.

'I don't think I've ever known it quite so busy,' Marcus said, stretching his back and groaning aloud. 'I shan't be sorry to pull the shutter down tonight, I can tell you.' He rose from his stool and rubbed the small of his back with his fists, all the while watching as Phoebe busied herself clearing the counter, filing away the receipt stubs and tidying the shelves; there was never enough time to stack the shoes on to the shelves as they were brought in so now she made sure that each and every pair of shoes or clogs was neatly parcelled in a brown bag and placed in order along the shelves . . . small repairs on the top rack, and those requiring full soles and heels on the bottom. She had just put the last parcel in place when the door bell rang out and in strode the flower-seller who kept a colourful stand at the top end of the boulevard.

'God love yer,' the woman gasped breathlessly, slapping a small yellow ticket stub on to the counter. 'I were sure you'd be shut up be now.' Sally Gromes was a dear little soul who would never see her fiftieth birthday again although she'd have swung for anybody who said so. Thin as a stick and so weathered that the wrinkles on her face resembled tram-lines, she had an unnerving way of screwing up her face and peeking at you through tiny rounded eyes.

She did this now to Phoebe, asking in a shrill little

voice, 'Is me clogs ready, lass? I know yer said Monday next but I can't be doing wi'out 'em no longer. Me feet ain't used ter these 'ere clumsy boots . . . and I ain't so rich as I can afford another pair o' good clogs.' She grinned at Marcus, showing a toothless mouth and merry eyes that danced when they smiled. 'Yer mek a bloody good pair o' clogs, Marcus Quinn,' she told him, 'I'll give yer that.'

'Thank you, Sally,' he replied. 'That's good of you to say so.' He came away from his stool and crossed into the main shop where he leaned against the counter. 'I've an idea I mended Sally's clogs only this morning,' he told Phoebe who was busy searching the shelves for the partner to Sally's yellow ticket.

'By! I hope they're ready, lass,' the old one moaned, rubbing her hands together and suddenly regarding Phoebe with renewed interest. On first coming into the shop, her sharp little eyes had noticed Phoebe's pale and tired features, and just now when she'd stretched up old Sally detected a slight telltale bump beneath the pretty grey dress.

The smile became a frown. Everyone knew the story of how Edward Dickens drove his own sister away with his dictatorial attitude, and how he had only reluctantly brought her child into his house. It was a known fact that he hadn't made life easy for the lass, and even her own cousin Margaret made no secret of the fact that Phoebe was merely tolerated. In contrast to her own blood kin, perhaps with the exception of that meek and timid creature who'd had the misfortune to be chosen by Edward Dickens as his wife, Phoebe Mulligan was a good-hearted, lovable creature without an ounce of malice in the whole of her being. Everybody liked her. No one that Sally knew had a bad word to say about the lass. But by God . . . if she'd gotten herself in the family way, there'd be Hell to pay and no mistake! Edward Dickens was not the kind of man to forgive such a terrible thing.

'Here we are!' Phoebe pulled out a brown paper parcel and checked the ticket again. 'Number 48,' she said with a warm smile, placing the parcel on the counter. 'That'll be ninepence if you please.' When the money was given over and the transaction complete, Phoebe asked with concern, 'How's the young 'un, Sally?' Some days ago, when she'd brought her clogs in to the shop, Sally had told them about her youngest who was going on twelve, and who'd been taken badly with a chill.

'Aw, yer a luv, what are yer?' she said gratefully. 'The lad's mending well, lass. Thank the good Lord I'm blessed wi' grand neighbours else I wouldn't 'a known what to do, 'cause I can't afford ter leave me flower stall and that's a fact.' She kicked off the ill-fitting boots and ripped open the brown paper bag, spilling the clogs on to the floor. Slipping her feet into them, she sighed with pleasure and rolled her eyes to heaven. 'By! Them's bloody comfortable,' she said with a chuckle. Stuffing the tatty boots into the torn paper bag, she went to the door. Phoebe went with her.

'Take care o' the lad,' Phoebe told her, opening the door and holding it ajar. She was surprised when the old woman leaned towards her. 'And you take care o' yerself an' all, lass,' she said in a whisper. 'It seems to me like there might be trouble brewing, eh?'

Something about Sally's expression made Phoebe's heart turn over. 'Whatever do you mean, Sally?' she asked in a strong voice.

'Aw, bless yer heart. Ain't I seen it all?' came the reply. 'Yer ain't the first lass to be tekken in by some fella's smooth tongue . . . an' yer won't be the last.' She glanced back at Marcus and then looked into Phoebe's brown eyes. In a low intimate voice she told her, 'If yer need to tek drastic action . . . well, there are certain folk who might be able to help.' She touched her nose and winked. 'If yer know what I mean.' She nudged Phoebe's arm. 'I'm allus at me stall if yer find the need ter talk,' she promised. 'An' I know when ter keep me mouth shut, yer needn't worry about that.' She tapped Phoebe on the arm in a friendly manner before going from the shop in a great hurry.

'What was all that about?' Marcus had seen the woman lean forward and whisper into Phoebe's ear. He had seen the look on the girl's face and suspected there was a secret of sorts between them. It troubled him.

It took a while for Phoebe to compose herself as she let the woman's words sink in. She deliberately took an extra minute or two in securing the door. 'It was nothing,' she said, and all the while her thoughts were flying ahead. SHE KNEW! Sally Gromes knew that she was with child. That was the second time someone had suspected. Oh, dear God! Dear God! She was more frightened than she could ever remember. What was she to do now?

She threw the bolt home, and her fingers were trembling; she laughed a little then, appearing surprised at his concern. Reluctantly she lied, reassuring Marcus that he was imagining things. Inside her heart was pounding and the tears were not far away. Soon the whole town would know, and she would be labelled a loose woman . . . a shameful thing, to be looked down on. There was no one at Dickens House who would stand by her, she knew that. Not even her aunt. But then, Phoebe would never ask that. What was to become of her? Where could she go? Who could she talk to? Perhaps she should take Sally up on her offer? No! She could never do that. There must be another way. But *what*? Awful thoughts came into her mind then . . . thoughts of throwing herself into the canal or falling beneath the wheels of a motor-car. Suddenly she was frantic. She hadn't realised that time was running out fast.

'There *is* something wrong, Phoebe. What is it? For God's sake, what is it?' Marcus had watched her every move. He had seen her fingers tremble as she bolted the door; he'd seen the way she delayed and fidgeted, keeping her back to him, evading his innocent question. And now she was slumped against the door, her face still turned from him and her whole body seeming to shudder. At once he was by her side. 'Can't you tell me?' he asked, tenderly touching her shoulder but not daring to encircle it. 'I'd hoped I was a friend.'

She turned to look at him then, her brown eyes brimming with tears. 'You *are* a friend,' she told him with the smallest smile. She had almost forgotten. Even so, she was afraid to confide in him.

'And what are friends for, if not to share your troubles with?' He hated to see her so unhappy. 'What is it, Phoebe?' he asked softly. 'What did Sally say to upset you so much?' He frowned. 'She can be a bugger at spreading tales,' he said with anger, glancing impatiently towards the door. 'Is it to do with your uncle? Has she been saying things about him?' In the back of his mind was something he'd heard, a lewd and distasteful rumour concerning Edward Dickens and that attractive clerk of his. 'You don't want to pay too much mind to Sally's wanderings,' he declared sternly, leading Phoebe across the shop floor and into the back-room where he made her sit down on the stool. 'Now then . . . you just think about what I said and I'll go upstairs and make us a nice brew of tea, how about that?' He hugged her then, wanting to protect her from the world.

Phoebe made no resistance. She sat in the back-room, not wanting to go home, not wanting to stay, not knowing exactly what she did want. Nervously she waited for his return, her frenzied mind churning over what had all too quickly become a desperate situation. She recalled what Marcus had said just now: 'What are friends for if not to share your troubles with?' And he was right. Suddenly it was as though a weight had been lifted from her shoulders. Raising her head she glanced towards the stairs, picturing him up there bustling about, putting out the cups, the milk and sugar, hurrying to return to her side. Urging the kettle to boil . . . all the mundane little things that people did, day in, day out, even in the heart of any crisis. Everyday things, comforting things that warmed her heart. It was good. *He* was good. The picture brought a smile to her lips. She knew then, that she *would* confide in him. Marcus was a fine and honest man. A man who understood loneliness. A man who, unlike so many others, might not be quick to condemn her. But what would he think? Oh, what would he think? That she was shameful? That she was no better than any streetwalker?

She heard him coming down the stairs and her courage wavered. Perhaps she should talk to Dora instead? But no. It would be unfair to burden Dora. She had her own troubles . . . cooped up in that tiny little house, at the beck and call of her ailing father. Besides, the thought of Judd knowing she was with child was more than Phoebe could bear. Lou then? No. Like as not he would want to strangle his son with his bare hands, when the fault was just as much hers. No. Not Lou . . . and not Hadley. Only Marcus. She could only confide in him. As he said, she needed to share her troubles with someone, and why not a good friend like him? Just to talk about it, to unburden her heart to someone, would help she knew.

'Here we are then.' Handing Phoebe one of the cups, Marcus then made himself comfortable on the workbench, his green eyes never leaving her downcast face. 'Did you think about what I said?' he asked softly.

'Yes, I thought about it.' Her hands were trembling so much that the tea almost spilled from the cup. She was thinking about her mother in that minute. It was strange how she seemed so close, almost like a physical presence in that humble little shop. And, for the very first time since they had been parted, Phoebe gave thanks that Jessica Mulligan was not here to witness this day.

'Do you want to talk it over?' He was afraid of pushing her too far. Afraid that she would run from the shop and he might never see her again.

Phoebe gave no answer. Instead she sipped at the strong sweet liquid, her mind in chaos . . . 'A friend' . . . 'Share your troubles' that's what he'd said. His voice echoed in her thoughts. She didn't look up then. She couldn't. Her own voice came to her, and it was like that of a stranger. 'I'm . . .' She swallowed hard, mustering courage to go on. He waited, sensing her trauma. 'I'm . . . with child,' she murmured, and such was the long silence that followed, she wondered if he had heard. Looking up, she saw how his face had drained of colour. He was shocked. And now she wished she hadn't told him. 'I'm sorry,' she muttered, rising from the stool and placing her cup on the bench beside him. She turned to go.

'No.' His head moved slowly from side to side. 'Don't go,' he pleaded. But she moved away and he was forced to follow her across the room. With his next question she was made to stop and stare at him with disbelief. 'I'm here if you want me, Phoebe,' he urged. 'I asked you before and I'm asking you again . . . LET'S GET WED.'

Now it was her turn to be shocked. 'You want me to *marry you*?' She laughed, a small painful sound. 'Didn't you hear what I said just now? I'M CARRYING ANOTHER MAN'S CHILD.'

'I heard. And yes . . . I still want to wed you.' He was in a strange state, excitement mingling with sadness, and for some reason unbeknown to him, it crossed his mind that Hadley Peters might be the father. 'There's just one thing I need to know,' he said in a serious voice.

'Don't ask me who the father is because I won't tell,' she said adamantly. 'I won't tell *anyone*.' Because then her shame would be even greater.

He smiled, and dared to touch her hand. 'No, I wasn't about to ask that,' he said truthfully. 'I was going to ask whether the fella would wed you . . . or whether you would wed him? But I think you've already answered my question by saying you'll never tell who he is.' There had been a time when he believed that he could never have a woman such as Phoebe. He'd believed his only chance of happiness had gone with Jessica. Now he wouldn't mind taking on another man's child, not if it meant he could have Phoebe too. 'Won't you consider what I've got to say?' he asked. 'Won't you let me look after you?'

Swinging away, Phoebe unbolted the door and inched it open. For a blind moment she didn't know what she was doing. She was in a whirl, confused and anxious. 'My bag,' she said. 'I mustn't forget my bag.' Going to the counter she reached beneath and withdrew a small cream-coloured hessian bag. 'I might have got all the way to the boulevard before I remembered it,' she said, smiling brilliantly at him as she returned to the door. Her fingers gripping the door-handle, she was astonished when his hands closed around her shoulders. 'I should never have told you,' she said lamely.

'I'm so glad that you did.' He shook her gently and made her laugh. 'Nothing is ever as bad as it seems.'

'What I've done is bad.'

Ignoring her comment, he asked again, 'Will you wed me?'

She shook her head. 'I can't do that,' she told him gently.

'Why can't you? Is it because I'm old enough to be your father?'

'No.'

'Or is it that I'm not well off?'

'You know that would never make a difference,' she chided him.

'What then?' Suddenly he realised. His eyes widened and the lines in his forehead deepened. 'You don't love me, is that it?' She lowered her gaze and he knew. 'Of course,' he said regretfully. There was a moment when she would have left him then, but he wasn't about to give up quite so easily. 'I don't expect you to love me, Phoebe,' he said, 'but I want to do what's best for you. It doesn't matter whether you love me or not. Sometimes a marriage works better when there's no love. It can be a painful thing.' And who knew that better than himself? 'Loyalty, friendship and affection can often be a wonderful substitute. We already have that, don't we, you and me?'

'Yes. We do have that,' she admitted.

'Then . . . will you at least stay awhile, Phoebe? See if the two of us can't thrash out a solution to your problem.' When he sensed her hesitation, he urged, 'You'd be doing me a great honour and a great favour. I'm lonely, Phoebe . . . like you, I'm terrible lonely. I wouldn't want anything from you that you don't want to give freely. You have my word on that.'

She blushed then. The thought of her and Marcus . . . it was too shocking. 'Don't think I'm not grateful,' she said warmly, 'because I am.' In fact, she was more grateful than he knew, and the more she thought about his offer, the more she realised it could be the answer to her prayers. Her every instinct said no. But then his argument bore a great deal of truth; she and Marcus had a strong bond between them. They were good for each other and, as he rightly pointed out, they were both 'terrible lonely'.

'Come back,' he urged her now. 'Let's talk, Phoebe. There's no need for you to be afraid . . . no need for this child to come into the world without a father. You and me . . . we can help each other. What d'you say?'

Phoebe didn't say anything then but when he quietly closed the door, she made no effort to stop him. A moment later the two of them made their way up to the tiny sitting-room above the shop; where they would sit and talk, and argue, and plan their lives as best they could.

At precisely ten-thirty on the following Sunday morning, Marcus Quinn set out on a short but very important journey; he looked exceedingly smart in his best checked coat and grey tweed cap which was newly acquired for the occasion. Some short time later he stepped out of the cab and looked up at Dickens House with a certain amount of trepidation. As he walked smartly to the front door he did not see Phoebe, standing at her window and following his every step with anxious eyes.

'Yes?' Daisy was all in a fluster. Already that day she'd overslept, been late for her work, spilled a whole jug full of milk on her quarry tiled floor, and accidentally broken the yolks of Edward Dickens' fried eggs – a dreadful misdemeanour when his greatest enjoyment before a lengthy sermon was popping the yellow yolk with his toast and afterwards mopping it up from the perimeter of his plate. 'Who are you? What do you want?' she asked impatiently, a deep frown distorting her face and her hair standing up on end. The look she gave him was so hostile that, for a minute, his nerve almost snapped.

'The name is Marcus Quinn,' he told her bravely, 'as you very well know since I've mended both yours and your husband's boots more times than I care to remember.'

At this her piggy eyes slowly widened as they appraised him from head to toe. 'Well I never!' she declared. 'So it is.' Chuckling, she opened the door wider. 'By! You look that different in your fancy togs, I couldn't for the life o' me see what was beneath.' She remembered then, and quickly became all smiles and gestures. 'You've come to see him, haven't you?' She jerked a fat misshapen thumb towards the inner sanctum. 'He's waiting . . . told me to show you right in soon as you arrived.' She regarded him more cautiously as he came into the hallway. 'By! You look the proper gentleman,' she said cynically. 'And quite right too . . . seeing as what you've come about.'

He was astounded. 'Are you saying you *know* what I've come about?' he demanded in a hushed voice. In his opinion matters such as this should be kept confidential until a proper announcement was made. He knew this woman of old and there was no greater gossip in the whole of Lancashire.

'Huh! You can't keep such things quiet for long, Mr Quinn,' she told him with some disgust. 'After all, you've nothing to hide, have you, eh?' She grinned, peeking at him with a crafty expression that was downright unnerving.

'If you'll just announce me now,' he suggested, not wanting to linger a minute longer beneath her suspicious gaze.

'Right away, of course I will,' she promised, immediately setting off down the hallway at an urgent pace.

He looked about at the grandness of the long wide hallway, at the polished banister and the sweeping stairway, at the quality dresser and the expensive ornaments on it. And he thought how very different Phoebe would find his own humble abode. He straightened his tie, cleared his throat, shifted from one foot to the other, and waited. In spite of everything he'd promised himself, he had been disturbed by the woman's insinuations . . . 'Nothing to hide, have you?' But yes, he did have something to hide. He and Phoebe had a secret that would stay just between the two of them for as long as was possible. Folk could raise their eyebrows and whisper among theirselves as to why a lovely lass such as Phoebe Mulligan would even consider marriage to someone like Marcus Quinn . . . a mere cobbler with nothing to offer her but his good name and a roof over her head. He wasn't a wealthy man and never would be. He was old enough to be her father, so why would she wed him? That was what folks were saying, he supposed. And in all truth he couldn't blame them. Because hadn't he asked himself the very same questions?

'He'll see you now.' Daisy was back in less than no time and urging him towards the master's study. 'You can thank your lucky stars,' she said as they went down the hallway. 'He were in a shocking mood first thing, but now he seems more mellowed.' She led him to believe that Edward Dickens had 'got out the wrong side of bed' when in fact his shocking mood was more to do with the hard fried egg she'd served him for breakfast. 'Good luck,' she said, gently tapping at the door and leaving him to wait there. She went quickly back to her kitchen and shut the door behind her. Later though, when the road was clear, she just might sneak back and put her ear to the door.

Marcus rubbed the toes of his shoes on the backs of his trousers, straightened his tie again, and waited. And waited. The silence seemed so solid that he could have cut it with a knife. Only the grandfather clock could be heard, slicing into the gloomy hallway, ticking the minutes away. He looked about. Daisy was gone and there was no one else in sight. He wondered whether he'd been altogether forgotten. He glanced about. For one fleeting moment he thought he saw a figure out of the corner of his eye, a woman . . . crossing from a room at the other end of the hall. Plucking up courage, he raised his fist to the door and knocked firmly. 'Mr Dickens,' he called out, 'Marcus Quinn to see you.'

No answer. The clock seemed to tick louder than ever. He waited, then: 'All right, Quinn!' He recognised the voice that summoned him with such authority and pushed open the door, all the while thinking of Phoebe. She gave him confidence.

Edward Dickens was seated at his desk. He didn't look up. Instead he pretended to be writing in a thick brown leather ledger. After quietly closing the door, Marcus went across the room to stand immediately before the desk. Still Dickens did not look up. Marcus remained patient. All manner of sensations assailed him . . . the familiar warm dry smell of leather; the pungent taste of polish liberally applied; a sense of luxury all around, and the feel of thick rich carpet beneath his best black boots.

His back began to ache from standing stiff. He coughed politely. Still the other man went on furiously writing, his head bent low, seemingly totally engrossed in the task at his finger-tips. Marcus coughed again. The finger stopped moving and for a moment the body went rigid. But still Dickens did not look up. He began writing again, slower this time. And then he spoke. 'You asked for an appointment,' he murmured, 'and I have been good enough to oblige. But I'm not pleased, you must know that. Sunday is my own time. You have invaded my own time.'

'I know. And I'm grateful that you agreed to see me.'

'And why couldn't this "business" be discussed yesterday at the store . . . when you brought me Miss Mulligan's wages?'

'Because what I have to ask is of a delicate and personal nature.'

'Hmm.' He put down his pen and looked up, his small grey eyes boring into the other man's face. 'Personal, you say?'

'Very personal, sir.'

Edward thrust back his chair, spread his large hands on the desk-top, then pushed himself into an upright position out of the seat. Silhouetted in the light from the window, he seemed immense. 'It had better be important,' he warned Marcus. Reaching into his waistcoat pocket he drew out a long silver chain, on the end of which was a bulky expensive watch. He flicked open the watch lid and peered at the face. 'I can give you five minutes,' he said.

'It's enough. Thank you.'

Edward Dickens would never admit that he might be

curious. His features remained impassive as he sat down again, stretching out an arm to indicate that Marcus should seat himself in the hard upright chair set before the desk. 'Say what you have to say, Quinn,' he instructed. 'And for your sake I only hope you haven't come here to waste my time.'

Marcus began, picking and choosing the right words, not wanting to shock and not wanting to alienate. Phoebe's uncle was both powerful and vindictive. He could put a man out of business with just one word in the right ear.

As Marcus went deeper into the reason for his being here, Edward Dickens listened intently. He made no comment but his expressions betrayed a whole gamut of emotions; at first he was shocked, then disbelieving. He smiled and made a face of wonder, and throughout the interview sat straight and stiff in his chair, his fists clenched in his lap.

At last Marcus had put his case and was now summing up. 'So you see, Mr Dickens, I have been bold enough to ask your niece for her hand in marriage, and she has been gracious enough to accept me. Oh, subject to your own approval of course!' he added swiftly. In actual fact it didn't matter whether this pompous man gave his blessing or not. Phoebe was of age, and Marcus had the necessary money earmarked from his own modest savings. But neither he nor Phoebe wanted to cause any trouble or go behind anyone's back. That particular route always seemed to lead to heartache one way or another. Besides, it was only right that he should come here and inform Phoebe's guardian of their intentions.

'You . . . and *my niece*?' The big man leaned in his

chair, regarding the other fellow through narrowed eyes. He laughed, a hard, lewd sound that almost betrayed his real thoughts. When he first put Phoebe to work at the cobbler's shop, he had hoped that this would happen. And now, after all this time, when he had almost given up, here was Marcus Quinn asking for Phoebe's hand in marriage. His hands were trembling. Oh, but it was music to his ears! Wasn't it true some people foolishly dug their own graves? Certainly, that was the case here. However, he had to tread carefully. He mustn't be seen to give his sister's girl away too easily. Nor must he let Quinn ever suspect that his affair with Jessica was known to him. When he thought of it now, his heart hardened and it was all he could do not to leap out of his chair and take the fellow by the throat. But *this* . . . Marcus Quinn and Phoebe, just as he'd planned! This was even better.

It crossed his mind to wonder why Phoebe would want a man so much older than her, but then he reminded himself that she had nothing. She came from an impoverished background, and the prospect of being the wife of a cobbler, a man who made a very good living by all accounts, must be very tempting. After all, she knew her stay here would be short-lived, and like the crafty creature she was, had set her sights on a better prize. Well, they didn't know it but these two had let themselves in for a great deal of shame and heartache. Let them enjoy each other. And afterwards . . . they would be outcasts of the very worst kind. He wanted to laugh out loud, but now, as he addressed Marcus, he forced himself to talk in a serious voice and with a formal manner suited to that of a guardian.

Upstairs Noreen Edwards lay meditating on her bed.

This past week she had deliberately kept out of Phoebe's way, and so she had no idea why Marcus Quinn had come calling. It preyed on her mind. The idea of her husband shut away in the study with Jessica's former lover made her nervous. 'What are you up to, you old tyrant?' she muttered. Whatever it was, she suspected it would bring a heap of trouble in its wake.

Phoebe couldn't keep still. She went to the window, then she sat on her bed, then she went to the washroom, then she came back and brushed her hair. And now she was on the landing, leaning over the banister, her anxious brown eyes searching the hall below. He's not out yet, she told herself. Even now she wasn't sure whether she was doing the right thing. But, thanks to Marcus, she was less afraid of the future. He said they should wed quickly, and leave folks to their suspicions. 'It wouldn't be the first time a couple got wed in a hurry,' he told her. 'Once there's a ring on your finger, lass, they'll leave well enough alone, I can promise you that.' She wanted so much to believe him, but somehow she couldn't rid herself of the feeling that she had taken a wrong turning somewhere. A deep-down, uneasy feeling that in the end she would be made to pay the full price for having sinned.

Chapter Twelve

On a Saturday afternoon in February 1926 Phoebe and Marcus were pronounced man and wife. It was not a grand affair. Conducted in a bleak register office on the outskirts of Blackburn town, it was a brief and soulless ceremony, concluded in less time than it took to walk through the door from the outer courtyard, then across the room to stand before the long table, which was covered with a white cloth and bedecked with huge, extravagant artificial flowers. The registrar was a tall stick of a man who spoke down his nose and kept his eyes glued to the book before him. His wife stood beside him, a permanent grin on her face and her hands nervously rubbing one over the other as though mentally counting the money that Marcus Quinn had paid over.

The room was austere and chilly. Dressed in the lovely cream gown that her mother had made, and carrying a beautiful posy of flowers, Phoebe looked exquisite; her hair was brushed into a mass of deep shining waves that curled about her ears and teased against her forehead. Her dark brown eyes, though serious throughout, held a depth of gratitude to the man beside her. The blue shawl with silver threads was new, a gift from him and one which suited her colouring to perfection. Her dainty blue shoes were also from him; with their tiny heels and delicate crossover ankle straps, they showed off her shapely ankles as no other shoes could do. It had taken Marcus ten days to make them, after carefully choosing the softest leather and dying them the exact shade of blue to match the shawl. He kept his secret well, working when Phoebe was out of sight, keeping his back bent to the task until the small hours and hiding them until the morning of the wedding when he had them delivered to the Rose and Crown by special messenger. There wasn't another pair like them in the whole of Lancashire, and he had been clever enough to guess her exact size. Phoebe loved the shoes, and now she wore them with pride.

Around her neck she wore the tiny silver heart given to her by Dora, and though it was her own wish that only the smallest number of people should attend the ceremony, Phoebe was deeply sorry that her friends from Bury were not here.

'All right, are you?' Marcus whispered in her ear, his hand holding hers and a warm reassuring smile on his homely face.

Phoebe gave a small nod, returning his smile and thinking how very smart he looked. In her heart she wished it could all have been very different. For the first time since coming to Blackburn, though, she felt safe. Marcus had done that for her. 'I'm fine,' she whispered. And he was satisfied.

From the back of the room, Lou and Aggie watched with pride. Hadley was there too. He had told Margaret in no uncertain terms what he thought of her feud with Phoebe; though, judging by what Margaret told him, he was increasingly convinced that the bad feeling which existed between these two young women was as much Phoebe's fault as her cousin's. But then, he thought, it was only natural that there should be a certain amount of jealousy between them.

When the ceremony was over, the paid witness made his formal signature, the registrar and his wife wished the happy couple well, and outside in the grey-paved court-yard Marcus proudly posed beside his new bride, shifting and grinning until the photographer was satisfied that he had at least one good picture. Later, the picture was to show how sad was the look on Phoebe's face, and how she clung to Marcus, as though he might suddenly run away and leave her to a terrible fate.

The back room at the Rose and Crown looked delightful. There were colourful streamers overhead, a table weighed heavy with food, and a pianola playing in the background. 'We allus like to do well for our newlyweds,' boasted Gloria the landlord's missus. 'Known for it we are.' The food was wholesome, the drinks flowed freely, and Marcus had put a tidy sum over the counter to ensure that there was enough for all. Greg went without though, and soon left in a sullen and morose mood.

'Are you happy, Phoebe?' Hadley asked. He had given his good wishes to her husband, and now he felt the need to assure himself that Phoebe was in good hands. 'Will he treat you right, do you think?' he asked, offering her a pork pie from his plate. His question was accompanied by a light-hearted grin but underneath there was serious concern.

Waving her hand to show that she wasn't in the mood

for food, Phoebe answered warmly, 'I suppose you could say I was happy. And, yes, he will treat me right.' She knew that much if she knew nothing else.

'He's a fortunate man.' His eyes appraised her face, that uplifted shining face with the quiet eyes that held so many secrets. 'I'm sorry Margaret saw fit to stay away,' he apologised. 'I don't pretend to understand the mind of a woman but I hope you two can become friends in time.' When he saw that she wasn't about to discuss the subject, he told her, 'How is it that your friends from Bury didn't come?'

'Because I didn't ask them.' Phoebe knew she could be honest with this man, and knew he was genuinely concerned about her; although she still felt she could only confide in him to a point. After all, he would shortly be Edward Dickens' son-in-law. 'I didn't tell them I was getting wed,' she confessed.

'But whyever not?'

'It's complicated.' How could she explain how shame had prevented her from telling them? Even now the thought of what Judd in particular might have to say made her spirits dip.

He shrugged his shoulders. He didn't understand the mind of a woman. 'I expect you have your reasons,' he told her.

'I have,' she agreed. And then she was whisked away by one excited little girl who had a great deal to say about everything, from the pretty pink dress which Lou had bought for the occasion to Phoebe's sparkling wedding band. 'When I grow up I'm gonna have a ring with little hearts all over it,' Aggie said. 'And I want a beautiful black carriage and four big black horses with feathers between their ears.'

Lou had come up behind, winking at Phoebe so she wouldn't betray his presence. 'Sure it sounds more like a funeral than a wedding,' he exclaimed, grabbing Aggie by the waist and swinging her high into the air. 'It's time you were home and getting ready for your bed, young lady. You've had enough excitement for one day!' he cried, tickling and teasing her, making her squeal and struggle, while everybody laughed at their antics. After a time he put her down and told Phoebe in a low breathless voice, 'It does me old heart good to see you happy.' He'd known right from the start that Phoebe would find small contentment in Edward Dickens' house. She was too lively, too young and down to earth. There was a world of difference between the life she'd left and the life her uncle might want to break her into.

'Thank you for that,' she replied affectionately. 'I won't forget what a good friend you've been.'

'And me,' a small voice piped up. 'You won't forget *I've* been a good friend too?'

Stooping to kiss the uplifted face, Phoebe asked in a stern voice, 'Now how could I forget you?' And what she got for her trouble was a skinny pair of arms round her neck and a kiss that left sticky jam all over her face.

The evening went all too quickly. At eight o'clock everyone had gone and the room was unbearably quiet. Ten minutes later, Phoebe and Marcus were making their own way home. In the cab he held her hand and she tried not to look at him. 'We'll be home in no time,' he promised, and he couldn't have known how the thought of it turned her heart. Home. Phoebe's emotions were mingled. It wasn't her place of work anymore. Suddenly it was home, and that was a strange, frightening thing.

Back in the cosy rooms above the shop, they looked at each other and smiled and he said how good it was of the Peters family to come, although he secretly wished Hadley had stayed away. And Phoebe said how she thought the landlord had put on a good spread. And Marcus agreed wholeheartedly. Then, a long uneasy silence fell between them when each was plagued with their own thoughts, shy and afraid to voice them. Until Phoebe offered to make a brew, and Marcus was shocked. 'What! I'll not have you spoiling that lovely dress your mother made you,' he declared. She laughed then, and he felt at ease.'If you want to change in the bedroom, I'll not get in the way,' he promised.

'And where will *you* change?' she asked, trying not to appear nervous. When he replied that he wasn't in a hurry to change, she visibly relaxed. He watched her go into the bedroom and watched her come out, dressed now in a pretty khaki-coloured jumper and a straight black skirt. He was glad that he'd had the sense to hide Jessica's photograph where Phoebe would never find it.

'Come and sit beside me,' he invited, patting the settee cushion. 'I reckon you and me need to talk.'

Phoebe did as she was bid, because she too thought they needed to talk. Not that they hadn't gone over most things during these past days, but there were still things playing on her mind. Things which only he could reassure her about. 'It was a lovely reception,' she said earnestly. 'Thank you.' She smiled into his eyes and he thought he had never seen anyone so lovely. Jessica had been lovely too but in a different way. He could see her in Phoebe – in the way she inclined her head when she was thinking, in that full rich mouth – and sometimes, like now, he felt that Jessica was close.

'I'll look after you, Phoebe,' he felt the need to reassure her. 'You do know that, don't you?'

'Yes, I know.' Suddenly, she was afraid. Somehow it all seemed so very wrong, her being here, being Marcus Quinn's wife. And yet, inexplicably, it was so very right.

'You're not sorry you married me, are you?' He felt too old, too inexperienced. 'I know I'll never be good enough for you, but I do so want to make you happy, Phoebe . . . make up for those precious things you've lost,' he said now. He wanted to hold her hand, but suddenly he felt foolish. There was something wrong. He felt awkward. 'Why didn't you ask Dora and Judd?' he asked. 'You never did tell me the reason.' He recalled the night of the barn-dance, when he'd seen her with Judd. They'd looked so right together. 'It would have been nice for your friends to come,' he told her gently. 'You know I would have paid for them to stay at the Rose and Crown with you.' He couldn't understand. Unless she was ashamed of him, he thought. But he didn't say that. He wouldn't do that to her.

Phoebe felt his discomfort and was instantly mortified. 'Don't ever ask me if I'm sorry to have wed you,' she told him. 'I'll *never* be sorry about that.' Suddenly she knew she never would be. 'You're everything to me,' she said fervently. And in that moment he was. 'As for Dora and Judd, I know you would have looked after them, but

I thought it best to tell them *after* the event. You know I didn't want a big fuss.' That was only partly true because in the back of her mind Phoebe suspected that either Dora or Judd would try and talk her out of marrying a man so much older than herself, and in such haste too. The last thing Phoebe wanted was for Dora to guess that she was with child. There would be time enough for that to become known, and no doubt Dora would have plenty of questions to ask. But Phoebe didn't want that yet. No, not yet.

'Whatever you say,' he conceded. 'But for the life of me, I can't understand why you didn't want to leave from your uncle's house. I didn't like you being on your own the night before our wedding.' It was a hurtful thing, and he had his own suspicions, which Phoebe had strongly denied. 'You're sure your uncle didn't throw you out . . . you wouldn't lie to me about that, would you?' he asked with immense concern. He had asked that same question many times over the past few days, and Phoebe's answer had always been the same.

It was the same now. 'No, he didn't throw me out. Like I said, there was a bad atmosphere there . . . there's *always* been a bad atmosphere in my uncle's house. I was glad to get out,' she said truthfully. But she didn't reveal everything to Marcus. She didn't tell how her aunt and uncle had quarrelled because of her, and she didn't tell how Margaret had grown increasingly spiteful towards her since learning that she too was going to be wed; it was as though she was afraid that Phoebe might steal some of her glory. Then that spoilt young woman was further antagonised when Hadley came over especially to wish

Phoebe all the best. Lou and Aggie had been over the moon. 'Marcus Quinn is a grand fella,' Lou told her, and Aggie instructed Phoebe in a grown-up voice: 'You have to come and visit every once in a while!' Phoebe had given her word that she wouldn't forget to call on them occasionally, and they all seemed satisfied with that. As for Greg Peters, he lingered around, smiling in that devilishly handsome way he had, as though he knew that she was marrying Marcus because she was with child . . . *his* child.

That thought had given her many a sleepless night. But then, she assured herself that he couldn't know. Only she and Marcus knew that she was with child. And only *she* knew the identity of the child's father. All the same, Greg began to unnerve her. Everywhere she turned he was there. On top of that, Margaret was growing more bitter and hostile by the day, her aunt seemed to be deliberately avoiding her, and her uncle had made it perfectly clear that he had given Marcus word and now wanted no more to do with the matter.

Phoebe sensed that he was always on the verge of saying something to her . . . something else, something that he couldn't quite bring himself to say. It bothered her. In that cold unfriendly house, she had become more and more uncomfortable.

'No, Marcus,' she said again. 'My uncle didn't throw me out. I just thought it best to make a clean break and move into the Rose and Crown for those last two nights.' She had been bitterly disappointed that her aunt had not been at the service today; she had invited her, and that was all she could do. But then, Phoebe wasn't surprised, not when her uncle had already warned her: 'Of course, you and Mr Quinn must make your own arrangements, my dear. It's best if we don't promise to be there, you understand. Your aunt and I already have one wedding to cater for, and that's quite enough.'

Margaret's wedding had been set for Easter Saturday, some two months away, and already there was great excitement. Every customer who came into the shop was full of it. It seemed they all intended watching the bride emerge from her house in all her splendour, and those who couldn't make it that far out of town would be waiting outside St Peter's Church to see the procession arrive. In her mind's eye Phoebe could see the sightseers lining the entire length of Preston New Road and all the streets leading right into the heart of Blackburn town. Folks loved a wedding. They loved it even more if it was a grand affair.

'Marcus.' Phoebe sat straight and stiff beside him, not knowing how to broach the subject. When he looked at her with eager eyes, she felt the blush spread from her neck right up to her ears. Turning away, she wondered how she might talk with him about what was on her mind, what had been on her mind all day and for days before that.

'Yes, Phoebe, what is it?' Marcus sensed her dilemma. He suspected it was the same as his own.

'I . . . do you mean to . . .' The words stuck in her throat as she glanced towards the bedroom.

He knew then, and his heart went out to her. 'Don't you remember what we said, my lovely?' he asked, taking her hand in his and smiling at her with loving eyes. 'I won't ask anything of you that you're not prepared to give. If and when I come to your bed, it'll be when *you* ask me . . . and not before.' He saw that she was visibly relieved and his emotions were a mixture of regret and relief. 'There,' he said, gently patting her hand, 'is that what you were so afraid to say?'

'Oh, Marcus.' The lump in her throat melted and there was a burning sensation behind her eyes. The tears welled up and suddenly she was crying. It was as though the whole of her life was passing before her and she realised she need never be afraid. 'I'm sorry, she said brokenly; she couldn't say any more as the tears flowed down her face and misery overwhelmed her. She felt herself being drawn into his embrace, and there she stayed, safe in his arms, comforted by his love yet fearing she could never return it in the way a wife should. 'I'll try,' she promised. 'I will try.'

'No, no, sweetheart. I don't want you to promise anything,' he protested, holding her close and resting his head on hers. 'It's enough that you're here with me, and that the child will have a name.'

Phoebe made no reply. Instead she saw herself as selfish and ungrateful. Marcus was a man of unique goodness and would never take advantage of any woman, she was sure. A man like that deserved the best from a woman. She was his wife now. A wife did not turn her husband away, and neither would she. Wiping her eyes, she looked up at him. Her eyes were still shining from the tears, but there was a certain look in them now, a look of love and gratitude. And he was shocked to the core by what that tender look might be implying.

'I still can't fathom out what made your father change his

mind about me,' Hadley said. After the reception at the Rose and Crown, Margaret and Hadley had gone to the Palace in Blackburn town where they had danced until the doors closed at midnight.

Now they were back at Dickens House, tired yet full of plans for their future. They had talked and talked, kissed and cuddled, and wanted desperately to make love. But they would have to be patient. It was almost one a.m. and the man of the house might return at any minute. That fact didn't deter Margaret too much but Hadley was made of stronger stuff.

'Not here,' he told her. And she knew he was right. Her father was like a volcano ready to erupt. The slightest thing could well make him change his mind about Hadley, never mind finding the two of them rolling about near naked in his own front room.

'He knows it was either you or him,' she replied now. 'It took time and cunning but I got him round to our way of thinking in the end,' she boasted. 'Though I'm not sure whether I want to marry you now,' she taunted. 'Not after what you did today!'

At first when Hadley came knocking on the door earlier that evening, she kept him waiting on the doorstep, sulking because he had gone to the reception at the Rose and Crown in spite of the fact that she had refused to accompany him. But when he rounded on her in a calm and dignified manner, accusing her of being childish and insensitive, she quickly changed her tack. Margaret was nobody's fool. She knew how determined Hadley could be when he believed himself to be in the right and there was no point in letting Phoebe Mulligan put up barriers between them. When they were married, though, Margaret intended being just a little more forceful about having her own way. For now, she would have to keep her temper under control.

'There isn't a girl in the whole of Lancashire who wouldn't envy me now,' she said. She looked at him with a gluttonous expression on her pretty face. He was so handsome, a man to show off to her town friends. He was standing in front of the fireplace, tall and straight, one arm stretched up to the mantelpiece and the other held out to her. She went to him then, cuddling sensuously into the crook of his arm and smiling up at him with baby blue eyes. 'Kiss me,' she said teasingly, raising her face and pressing herself against him. Aroused, he put both his arms round her and bent his head to hers. Neither of them heard the door open.

Enraged, Edward Dickens slammed the door shut, deliberately startling them. 'It's late,' he said gruffly, staying by the door, legs astride and his grim features set like stone. He addressed Hadley direct. 'I'd be obliged if you'd leave now.' He might have been more careful not to betray his real feelings in front of these two but his own evening had not gone to plan and he was vexed because of it. He'd spent the last few hours at his favourite hideaway, where he and his lady-friend often tasted of each other's delights. Tonight though she'd been keener to talk than to fornicate, seeming more interested in their last encounter . . . and in particular his visit to John Soames. Not for the first time he'd cursed himself for having been so reckless as to take her there with him. Suspicious of her motives, and angry that she rejected his advances to bed her, he sent her on her way, and now, after indulging his other expensive weakness and losing a great deal of money because of it, he was drunk and looking for trouble.

Margaret was the first to speak. 'It's *not* late!' she snapped, coming forward to confront him. 'And Hadley's not going so you might as well leave us be and get yourself off to bed.' She regarded him with disgust. 'You're drunk,' she told him, her face expressing her loathing.

Sensing a row brewing on his account, Hadley quickly stepped between the two. 'Your father's right. I ought to be getting home,' he said, taking Margaret by the hand. 'I'll see you tomorrow.'

'We'll go somewhere special,' she said wickedly. 'Find a quiet place. Just the two of us . . . together.' Her intention was to goad her father but Hadley merely replied, 'We'll see'. He had long thought Margaret's relationship with her father a strange and dangerous one. There was love between them, but there was also hate.

'You're a sensible young man.' Dickens glowed with his own self-importance as he brushed Margaret aside and saw Hadley to the door. When it was closed, his false smile slid away. In its place came a look of cunning. He would have to be more careful in future, but it was hard trying to suppress his rising excitement at what was in store.

When he returned to the sitting-room, Margaret was waiting for him. 'You bastard!' she cried, lunging at him but stopping short when he grabbed her wrists and riddled her with those hard grey eyes. 'You had no right to do that,' she whimpered, snatching away. 'You had no right to throw him out. Go away! I don't want to talk to you.' She went to the fireplace, keeping her back to him, hoping he would see that he wasn't loved and leave.

But he had no intention of leaving. That night he'd gone to meet his lady-friend with his loins on fire and his passion roused to a fever pitch; it was still roused, and his loins were still on fire. 'Oh, my dear,' he murmured softly, coming forward and placing his hand on her shoulder. 'But I didn't throw him out. How can you say such a thing?'

Shrugging his hands from her, she spun round. 'Yes, you did!' she said savagely. 'And I thought we'd come to an understanding, you and I. It's either you or Hadley. As far as I'm concerned, nothing's changed.'

'Well, I *know* that, my dear,' he protested, 'and I'm happy to go along with your plans, of course I am.' He laughed, leaning his head against her shoulder and cringing inside when she pulled away. 'I wouldn't want to do anything that might upset my little girl,' he assured her in a more serious manner. Suddenly he was afraid she might suspect that he had a deeper motive with regard to the wedding.

'I'm not your little girl any more,' she said cruelly, thrusting him away. 'I won't be your little girl ever again! Do you understand what I'm saying?' She emphasised her words with a knowing little smile that was the worst cruelty to him. There had always been something between them, a certain bond that tied them together in a terrible way. It was broken now and he visibly shivered at her words. 'I can see you *do* understand,' she said, laughing in his face, her wicked heart hardened against him.

He reeled away from her, his mouth wide open and his shocked eyes like two small glittering stones. 'Oh, my dear,' he moaned. 'My dear girl. I had hoped there would be no need to hurt you but now I see that there is no other way.'

She looked at him in surprise. 'What do you mean?' she asked softly, then in a stronger voice, 'What do you mean? . . . Hurt me? . . . No other way?' She came to stand before him, challenging him to answer. 'WHAT DO YOU MEAN?' she demanded. 'Are you threatening to spoil everything for me? Well, you won't. I intend to have Hadley Peters, and there's nothing you can do about it!'

'My, my!' He had seen his daughter in the worst of tempers and had witnessed her cruelty against others, including her own mother and the impoverished Phoebe Mulligan. But he had never seen her so vehement against himself. It frightened him. He must not lose her. Even though he was risking everything in what he planned, he must not lose his precious daughter. 'What a suspicious mind you do have,' he gently chastised. 'To think I want to spoil everything when I'm going out of my way to see that you have the finest wedding money can buy.' He reached out to touch her but drew away when she continued to glare at him. 'I don't want to do anything that would make you sad, my dear,' he promised. 'I love you more than anything else in this whole dreadful world. You must know that.' For one heart-rending minute he recalled saying exactly the same to another lovely young thing. He didn't want to 'spoil' things for her either, but his sister had turned on him then . . . just as his daughter was turning on him now. He began to cry aloud, repeating the very words he had spoken once before. 'I don't want to hurt you. I just want to love you. Only say that things can go on as before?' he pleaded.

'You're drunk. I won't talk to you when you're drunk.' Her father had always been the stronger of the two, but now she was in charge and liked the sense of power it brought. Tomorrow might be different but tonight he was at her mercy. 'I intend to marry Hadley,' she told him viciously. 'And what's more, although Hadley doesn't know it yet, I have my eye on a splendid house with land some miles away. I want us to start our new life in a new area. The further the better. Thanks to your generosity over the years, I've managed to put by quite a considerable sum of money. Besides which, Hadley is a shrewd and clever man who will see to it that I never want for anything. So you see, I really don't need you anymore, do I? To tell you the truth, once I have a husband to cater to my every wish, I wouldn't care if I never saw you again. You might as well accept that. And you should realise that from this moment on, things can never be the same as before.' As she stormed from the room, she could not know how her words only fuelled the terrible tragedy he was brewing.

It was two a.m. His wife and daughter were asleep but for Edward there was no rest. His mind was too alive. There was a need in him, that same driving need that always lurked beneath the surface – a need to hurt and maim and even to kill. He paced his study, every now and then stopping to fill his glass. Nothing satisfied him.

He threw the glass across the room, smashing it into the fireplace. 'BASTARDS!' he roared. 'You all forget too quickly what I've done for you.' He went to the desk, opened the drawer, and grabbing the contents he scattered them across the carpet. Swiping the paraphernalia from the top of his desk, he screamed out, frustrated, filled with a terrible rage that burned like a flame in every corner of his being. 'Things can never be the same again,' that's what she'd said. But they would, 'THEY WILL!' he shouted to the ceiling. 'THEY WILL BE THE SAME.' He would make sure of it.

Upstairs, the two women heard him ranting and raving. They lay in their beds listening until he became quiet. They knew that tomorrow he would remember nothing of his rage. Margaret turned over and went to sleep. Noreen, however, could not. A gentle soul, she was always terrified by the sounds of anger, his voice yelling and shouting. She was terrified now. Fear made her sit in the bed, hunched up against the pillows, waiting, unsure as to whether he might try her door. She made herself watch the handle, riveted with fear. Sick to her stomach. It made her thirsty. Her throat was dry, her tongue stuck to the roof of her mouth. If he came to the door what in God's name could she do? What had his sister been able to do? What could any of them do? But he didn't come to the door, and little by little, she began to relax. The house grew quiet again.

She was sleepy now, and her thoughts began to wander. She wondered about Phoebe. She had so much wanted to see the girl wed but he forbade it and it was more than she dared do to defy him. Was Phoebe happier now? Did

the wedding go off all right? No doubt she looked lovely.
But had she done the right thing? Had she made the right
decision? What would Jessica think of it all? And *why*
had Phoebe married Marcus? Although he would make
a fine husband, the girl could have done better. She could
have wed someone more her own age. She could have
waited. But, no. She could *not* have waited. More than
ever, Noreen was sure that Phoebe was with child. She
missed her but she was glad that at least one of them had
escaped from this house. From him.

She was sleepy. And thirsty. So very thirsty. Reluctantly she got out of bed and listened at the door. It was
quiet. He must be asleep. 'Drunk to the world, I shouldn't
wonder,' she muttered. Putting on her dressing robe she
opened the door and listened again. Not a sound. The
house was slumbering. Slowly, she went down the stairs
on bare feet. Her throat was closing up. She was still
afraid. She was still thirsty. Not daring to take a candle
or a lamp, she felt her way down the steps, holding on
to the banister as she went. Thankfully, she had been
down these stairs so many times she could do it with her
eyes blindfolded.

Pausing outside his study, she listened. The crude snoring sound told her that the monster slept. The tiniest
smile curved her mouth as she went softly into the
kitchen. Once inside she felt her way to the table in the
centre of the room. Her hands touched against the oil
lamp and the matches situated alongside, just as Daisy
always left them. Carefully, she took off the glass dome,
struck a match and put the issuing flame to the oil-soaked
wick. At once it sucked the flame in and soon the room

was bathed in a soft yellow glow.

Hardly daring to breathe, she went to the sink. In her usual conscientious manner, Daisy had returned all the crockery to the cupboard. On tiptoe, Noreen went across the room, gently opening the cupboard door and taking out a small chunky glass. Quickly now, she made her way to the pantry. What she wanted was an invigorating measure of sarsaparilla. Opening the door to the pantry, she went inside. There it was, the large stone jug that was always brimming with Daisy's home-made sarsaparilla. With both hands she took it down from the shelf carefully, not daring to make the slightest sound. The cork was rammed tight home. She gripped it firmly with her fingers and tugged hard, panicked a little, afraid that she had been here too long. Her feet were cold, her whole body was trembling. Hurry up, she told herself. Hurry up. Suddenly the cork popped out, making a small sucking sound. She smiled, greatly relieved, her throat was parched as never before. She raised the jug and began pouring the dark brown liquid into the glass.

In his room, the monster stirred. Something had disturbed him. He opened one eye. Noticing the light coming in through the chink beneath the door, he opened the other. For a long moment he remained perfectly motionless, his two eyes narrowed to slits, staring at the light while his fuddled brain tried desperately to make sense of it. He sat upright in the chair, stretching his arms above his head and moaning. He sniffed, wiped the end of his nose with finger and thumb, and slowly pushed the chair back. Someone was in the hall. 'Margaret,' he murmured affectionately. It was Margaret come to make up. They had rowed before. But she always came to make up afterwards. And here she was, at his door, wanting to come in. His smile spread across his large features like the sun coming up. He rose from the chair, patted his hair, smoothed his crumpled waistcoat, and went on soft unsteady footsteps across the room; his shoes remained under the desk where he'd thrown them, and his jacket hung haphazardly across the back of his chair. In his shirt sleeves he seemed an amiable homely figure. At the door he paused a moment, composing himself. He heard it then, a soft plopping sound. Curious now, he silently turned the key and inched open the door. There was no one there. No one waiting to come in . . . no Margaret anxious to make up. He scowled, deeply disappointed, inconsolable. But then he realised that there was someone in the kitchen; that was where the light had come from, filtering in beneath his door. He reached behind the study door, his fingers curling round the handle of a whip which hung there. Once he had it safely in his grasp, he went forward at a cautious pace, pushing the kitchen door open and peeking in. There was no one to be seen, but there *was* someone here . . . the pantry door was open. He crept up, carefully now, because the drink was still on him and his senses were ragged.

Noreen had returned the jug to its place on the higher shelf. She was so engrossed in her task that she didn't hear either the kitchen door open or the relentless footsteps approaching. When the pantry door was flung open she slewed round to see the figure of a man silhouetted in the lamplight. Before she could scream he darted forward and flicked the cat o' nine tails round her throat. His face bore down on her. 'What the hell are you creeping about for at this hour of the morning?' he demanded, shaking her so hard that she fell against the glass and sent it shattering to the floor. 'Were you spying on me? Answer me, damn you!' he screamed, almost breaking her back as he twisted her upwards towards him.

She tried to speak but her voice came out in a croak. She shook her head, her eyes pleading with him, but still he wouldn't release her. The drink blurred his vision, but he felt as though he had the strength of an ox. 'I thought it was her,' he said in a whisper. Drink always made him emotional. It made him want to cry. 'Why couldn't you have been her?' he asked in a small childish voice. She shook her head again and he stared at her face, at the pretty, frightened eyes, at the way her robe was twisted from her shoulders exposing the rise of her breasts. And he grew confused, 'Jessica?' He stared at her, blinking and staring again. 'JESSICA?' He shivered, his bloodshot eyes gazing at her face then at the leather throng that was biting ever deeper into her neck. 'Oh . . . oh, Jessica, I don't want to hurt you,' he sobbed. 'Don't make me hurt you.' There was terror in him then. He stiffened, his horrified gaze never leaving her face. 'You won't forgive me, will you, Jessica? You'll never leave me be, will you?' he pleaded. Suddenly he relaxed his hold on her and slumped forward as though mortally wounded.

Noreen watched him in astonishment, her two hands caressing the red raw marks on her throat. In that moment she believed he was losing his mind. She knew things concerning him and Jessica. She knew he had suffered regrets and nightmares about the things he had done,

460

about the way he had abused his sister in the name of righteousness. She had long suspected that he had made Jessica with child, but she was never sure. She knew how Phoebe's arrival here had caused him deeper anguish than he would ever admit. Yet, for all his guilt, he never blamed himself. Always he blamed Jessica, that lovely gentle creature whose only 'sin' had been to fall in love. In spite of everything, he never forgot and he never forgave. With a tingling shock, Noreen wondered if he meant to punish Jessica? To kill her? Suddenly she was in fear for her own life. 'I'm not Jessica,' she whispered. She prayed that once he realised she was not his sister, he would leave her to go peaceably.

He seemed not to have heard. He continued to stare at her, his eyes bulbous now, tears spurting out to course down his face and trickle into his open mouth. 'Jessica, I'm sorry.' The sound of his voice was strange. Small wet drops spattered across her face as the tears sprayed from his lips. 'I have to punish you, don't you see? It wasn't my fault. *None* of it was my fault. You tempted me . . . made me bad, because you were bad. You have to tell the truth now. It was *Marcus*, wasn't it? The father of your child . . . it was Marcus. SAY IT!' He was sobbing out loud now. 'You shouldn't have come back,' he cried, his voice was like thunder as he raised the whip high and brought it crashing down on her. The first vicious stroke took the robe from her back. The second took her skin. Her awful screams did not deter him. He wasn't striking her, he was striking *himself*! There was madness in his heart. A frenzy that saw no reason. Again and again, until the walls were sprayed with her blood, and she lay

461

at his feet, a whimpering, broken thing. Only then did he turn away. Wearily, he closed the pantry door and turned the key. Then he went away, exhausted but greatly exhilarated. As he went slowly across the kitchen, the whip trailed behind him, making spidery crimson patterns on the quarry tiles. At the door, he glanced back and sighed. Then he raised his head proudly and smiled to himself, before departing the room and climbing the stairs to his bed.

Some time before the dawn, he woke from a nightmare, heavy with sleep, and sweating profusely. Already his mind was filled with thoughts of Margaret, of a certain wedding, and a certain wicked scheme. The time was drawing near, and there were things to do; a particular journey to make.

Daisy sang as she came into the kitchen, but suddenly she reminded herself that it was Sunday and that meant being forced to listen while the master spouted forth in his own private little 'church' upstairs. 'Prayers and singing today, Daisy gal,' she moaned. 'And him telling you how to live a good Christian life.' She snorted and tossed her head in defiance. 'Edward Dickens, you're a bloody hypocrite,' she muttered, taking off her coat and hanging it on the back of the door.

She flung open the curtains and enjoyed the rush of sunlight that sped in through the window. 'A better day than yesterday,' she said, smiling to herself and beginning to sing again. ' "On a hill far away, there's an old rugged cross . . . a . . ." ' She looked at the floor. 'What's that then, eh?' she asked, bending closer. 'Well now, just look at that!' she declared angrily. 'How many times have I said that once I've shut this kitchen up and gone home, folks would have to clear their own mess up behind 'em? And they can't blame Phoebe Mulligan . . . oh, it's Phoebe Quinn now,' she said with a chuckle. 'Well, they can't blame her, 'cause she ain't here no more, is she?'

Realising she would have to clear up the spillage, she collected a bucket from beneath the sink, a long mop from outside the door, and a splash of washing powder from the box on the window-sill. The stain was a stubborn one, but not as stubborn as Daisy, and soon the floor was shining clean again. 'There!' she said, regarding it closely, hands on hips and a look of determination on her face. 'I shall have something to say about this and no mistake,' she grumbled.

It was seven-thirty. The table was laid for breakfast and the kettle was boiling on the gas ring. And still there was no sound from any quarter of the house. 'Lazy buggers,' she moaned. 'They don't know what it's like to get up of a Sunday and face a full day's work. Moneyed folk! Huh!' She didn't resent folks having money. She just wished it was shared more evenly, that's all. 'They're rich and I'm poor, and that's the way of it,' she muttered. 'What's more, I'd best get the breakfast underway else he'll be down the stairs to catch me unawares then I'll not even have a *job* to call me own.'

At first the pantry door wouldn't budge, as though it was jammed from inside. She put the key in and out two or three times but couldn't push it open. 'Well, I'm blessed!' she declared. 'As if I ain't got enough troubles.' Turning the key once more, she took a deep breath and, leaning the whole of her considerable weight against the door, thrust herself forward. The door groaned, inching open bit by bit. Suddenly she cried out as it flew open, throwing her into the gloomy interior. Her foot trampled on something soft. She looked down and for one shocking minute couldn't believe her own eyes. Her hands flew to her face, covering her mouth as though to stem the scream that welled up inside. But the horror of what lay in that room was too much. Hysterical now, she fled from that place, tripping and stumbling up the stairs to Miss Margaret's room terrified that the devil who had done such a thing would find her and do the same to her.

They managed to get her up to her room. Daisy was all for pronouncing her mistress dead, but Margaret insisted, 'She'll be all right, I tell you.' She looked down at the pathetic figure in the bed and wondered how he could have done such a thing. All these years he had used the slightest excuse with which to punish this woman who was her mother. All these years he had ruled her with a rod of iron and never once had she retaliated with like ruthlessness. Noreen Edwards was too soft, too frightened a creature ever to defend herself, and her daughter despised her because of it. She despised her now. 'You fool!' she muttered beneath her breath. 'What did you do to antagonise him this time?' And even as she was asking the question, the answer came to her. *He had punished the mother because the daughter had displeased him!*

'Is she dead?' Daisy had done as she was told and now she was returning from the kitchen with a bowl of hot water and her pinny pockets stuffed with various artefacts.

'Don't talk nonsense!' Margaret snapped. 'She's no

more dead than you or me.' There had been a moment downstairs when she herself had thought her mother to be dead. Daisy's screams had put the fear of God in her, and the awful scene that greeted her downstairs would stay with her for longer than she could ever imagine . . . the blood-spattered walls, that slight figure lying on the floor, crooked and torn, mercilessly beaten within an inch of her life. Yes Margaret had thought, this time . . . this time, he had gone too far. Now, though, she saw the flicker of life in her mother, and was thankful. At least he wouldn't be tried for murder.

'I've brought some carbolic and a packet of salt,' Daisy said, setting to work on the open wounds. 'It's an old sailor's remedy that,' she said. 'When they were lashed at sea, their wounds soon healed with a dose of salt rubbed in.' She gently washed the torn skin, dabbing at it with hands that were still violently trembling. 'Dear God!' she moaned, and straightened from her task to turn to the other woman. 'Dear God above . . . this poor woman,' she said in a whisper. Her next question was uttered without forethought, and she instantly regretted it, 'Did *he* do it?'

'Whatever do you mean?' Margaret was shocked. 'It was plain what happened here, you fool,' she retorted. 'My mother was surprised by a burglar. Mr Dickens was celebrating, as he does on a Saturday night as you well know. Afterwards he was in a deep sleep . . . that's why he didn't hear whoever it was. As for me, I heard nothing until you woke me with your screeching.' She glared in a way that reminded Daisy of her master.

'If you say so, Miss.'

'I most certainly *do* say so.' She was anxious to make certain that this woman knew to keep her mouth shut. If this got out, her father might still be called to answer to the authorities. Besides, her wedding was coming up all too soon, and she had no intention of letting anything spoil it. 'Come to think of it,' she said cunningly, 'I do believe your husband has knowledge of this house, hasn't he? Correct me if I'm wrong, but didn't he visit last summer? A man could quite easily perceive the layout of such a house as this . . . and, of course, you yourself are aware that it contains items of considerable value?'

Daisy was alarmed. 'What are you saying, Miss?' she asked, staring at the other woman with stricken eyes. There was no doubt in her mind that this one was every bit as wicked as her father.

'All I'm saying is that someone . . . a burglar . . . disturbed my mother downstairs. My father and I slept through the entire incident.' She smiled then. 'Wouldn't you say that was what happened, Daisy?' she warned.

Daisy thought a moment. She thought about how her husband had been in trouble with the law a long time ago; she thought about how the authorities always had a long memory when it suited them. She thought about how it was really none of her business if the toffs wanted to beat each other to death. And most of all, she thought about how unbearable life would be if she didn't have a wage to take home on a Friday night. 'It's a sin and a shame that such things go on, isn't it, Miss,' she slyly conceded. What was it to her anyway?

'It is, Daisy,' Margaret replied sweetly. 'Indeed it is. And you're a very sensible woman. No doubt you would find it distasteful even to discuss such things, isn't that right?' She waited for Daisy to nod her head. 'Of course. And I'm quite certain the matter will not be carried beyond these four walls,' she said meaningfully.

'I've never been one for telling tales.' Not when they could lose me my livelihood, Daisy thought bitterly.

'That's very wise,' Margaret told her. 'And unless you want her to die, I suggest you get on with seeing to her.' She pointed to her mother. Already Noreen was stirring, softly moaning, her face rucked with pain.

'But she'll need more than me, Miss,' Daisy protested, her little eyes popping open. 'She'll need somebody to watch her carefully. I mean, *anything* could happen. These are bad wounds . . . real bad, Miss. If they should fester and go wrong . . .' She threw her arms up in despair. 'There's no telling what it might lead to. No, I'm sorry, Miss, but your mother needs proper medical treatment.'

'There'll be no doctor at this door,' came the sharp reply. 'No medical treatment except yours. You can leave all your other duties to be at her beck and call. She's a strong woman . . . stubborn I think you might call her . . . but, like you say, her wounds are not at all pleasant and there may very well be a risk of infection. So you had better do what you can, hadn't you, Daisy?'

Daisy sighed at the immense responsibility that had been placed on her. 'Very well, Miss. I'll do my best. But I hope I'll not be held responsible should anything go wrong?'

'Nothing will go wrong,' Margaret told her. And with that she might have left the room. But then she recalled how she and Hadley were taking the tram into Blackpool today; according to him, a walk along the front would be refreshing. Margaret would much rather have been doing other, more interesting things, such as viewing houses, but there was still time enough for her to persuade him on that issue, even though he was under the illusion that she would be living at the farm with him and his family. Hmh! The very idea that she would reside under the same roof as Lou and Greg Peters was ludicrous. But Hadley was a loyal son and he would not forsake his responsibilities lightly. Still, he would come round to her way of thinking. One way or another he would see things her way. 'I'm going back to my bed,' she said in a surly manner. 'Be sure to wake me in an hour's time.'

Margaret had one more stop before she retired to her bed. She believed she might have been a little harsh on her father. Whatever he was guilty of, she couldn't help but adore him and her only wish now was to heal the rift between them. However, she soon discovered that the reconciliation would have to wait. Softly, she opened her father's bedroom door and looked inside. The bed appeared not to have been slept in. She went inside. A glance in his wardrobe told her that his valise was missing, together with certain items of clothing. It was obvious that he was greatly upset by his daughter's harsh words, otherwise he would have exercised a little more control over the beating he'd given his unfortunate wife. And now, quite wisely to Margaret's thinking, he had decided to take a short holiday until this whole thing had blown over; possibly even taking with him a decidedly attractive and obliging clerk. 'You're a wicked man, Father,' she chuckled. 'A wicked, wicked man.'

She was still chuckling when she returned to her own room and clambered back into bed. Snuggling down beneath the silken sheets, she sighed and smiled, and closed her eyes to picture herself in that wonderful gown which would make her the envy of every budding bride.

Daisy spent the next hour attending to her mistress. She carefully bathed the wounds, dressed the jagged skin and dabbed it with salt every now and then. She made a special herbal broth that was known for its medicinal benefits and persuaded the patient to take a small amount of food. Gradually, the colour came back to Noreen's cheeks and she was able to move without too much pain. 'There y'are then,' Daisy declared proudly as she returned the pretty china cup to the tray. 'You're looking better already, if you don't mind me saying.'

Noreen glanced at the domed brass clock on her dresser. She had heard her daughter's instructions to Daisy. 'Wake me in an hour' she'd said. She shifted her gaze to Daisy and pointing at the clock murmured, 'You'd better go.' Her voice was hardly audible and Daisy didn't hear what was said. Instead, she looked in the direction where Noreen was pointing.

'Good Lord!' She saw the time and was straight away in a panic. 'I'll go now!' she cried, crossing the room at an awkward run. 'By! It's a good job *somebody* remembered.' Without looking back she promised breathlessly. 'You lay still now, and I'll be back afore you know it.' She couldn't help thinking it was almost as though the mistress *wanted* her daughter out of the way. 'My! They're a rum lot an' no mistake,' she muttered as she went at a furious pace along the landing.

Noreen lay in her bed, stiff and sore and anxious for

Daisy to hurry back. She had heard her daughter's footsteps go past her door and was glad. With Margaret out of the way, it would be easier for her to do what was needed. She only hoped that her husband would not wake before the deed was done. She imagined him lying in his bed and loathed him. No doubt he'd gone from the kitchen into the study where he'd likely steeped himself in booze until he could just about drag himself upstairs to his room. No matter. When he was like that, he often slept right through until the evening. She recalled what he'd said to her, and knew she would not rest until she'd spoken to Marcus. If Edward even suspected what she was about to do, he wouldn't stop at flaying the skin from her back next time. He wouldn't stop until he'd flogged the last breath from her body. But she had to speak out. And she prayed it was not too late.

'Well now, d'you think you can manage a lightly boiled egg, Ma'am?' Daisy bustled into the room and came to stand by the bed. 'You need to have something more substantial than broth, if you want to be up and about,' she declared. 'And it seems like I've got all the time in the world to tend you. I've seen Miss Margaret off, and according to her instructions she'll not be returning until late.' She frowned then. 'It also happens that the master won't be wanting any meals prepared either, on account of he's gone out as well . . . "For a few days", or so Miss Margaret says.'

Relieved that she would have no interference either from her husband or her daughter, Noreen gave up a small prayer of thanks that, apart from Daisy, she was alone in the house and would be for the rest of the day at least. All the same, there was no time to waste. Not if what Edward had told her was true. She opened her mouth to speak, but her throat was closed tight. The words came out incomprehensible.

'What's that?' Daisy leaned forward. 'What are you trying to say, Ma'am?' All she could hear was a hoarse whisper and it was unnerving the way Mrs Dickens was staring straight at her like that, as though she was about to have some kind of fit. 'I can't make out what it is you want?' she said worriedly. Leaning nearer, 'Are you wanting your daughter back again, is that it?' If it was, then no one would have been more surprised than Daisy herself, because she knew there was no love between them two.

Noreen was in a considerable amount of pain. Every inch of her body hurt, and she found it difficult even to speak. When Daisy thought she might be wanting her to fetch Margaret back, she panicked, tugging at the other woman's pinny and drawing her towards the pillow. 'Mar . . . cus,' she whispered, and the effort exhausted her.

Daisy wondered whether she'd heard right. 'Are you saying you want me to fetch *Marcus Quinn*?' she asked, the tip of her nose brushing Noreen's temple. When the other woman closed her eyes in frustration, Daisy took that to mean yes. Shocked, she moved back a pace. 'Well, I never!' she said. 'Marcus Quinn, eh? You want me to fetch Marcus Quinn . . . here? To your bedroom?' Whatever next!

Noreen had more to say than she could speak so she indicated that Daisy should fetch the note-pad and pen from her dresser. When Daisy delivered them to her, Noreen scratched down these words: 'Take the tram to Blackburn and tell Mr Quinn I must see him at once. On no account are you to let Phoebe hear you tell him this.' She handed the note to Daisy and waited for the woman's response.

Daisy was never a scholar and so it took her a moment to decipher the scribbled words. Holding the paper at arm's length, she screwed up her eyes and read the words out loud, like a child who was learning might do. When she looked up, it was with astonishment. 'I can't do that!' she cried. 'It's Sunday . . . how can I go to the shop on a Sunday when it's closed? Besides, even if I was to knock on the door, like as not Phoebe herself would answer it and then what would I do?' She was getting herself into quite a state. 'I can't very well say, "I'm sorry, Mrs Quinn, but I don't want to see you. It's your *husband* I'm calling on." ' She looked aghast. 'Now, that *would* look a fine kettle o' fish, wouldn't it, Ma'am?' On top of which, if her old man ever found out, he'd give her a hiding to remember and no mistake!

Noreen could see the poor woman was working herself up into a frightening state. She shook her head, placating Daisy with a reassuring smile. 'Thank God for that, Ma'am,' Daisy muttered with a sigh of relief. Now, when Noreen indicated that she wanted to write something else, she gave her the pad and pen and waited patiently to see what new idea her mistress had in mind. When the pad was handed back again, she read the message out loud as before. 'Tomorrow morning, before you come into work, I want you to take a pair of my boots to Marcus Quinn.

Tell him I'd like them soled and heeled. You'll be carrying a very important letter, Daisy. The letter will be addressed to Marcus AND ON NO ACCOUNT MUST PHOEBE SEE IT. Hand it to Marcus and say nothing of this to anyone. Do you understand?' On the last word, Daisy looked at her mistress with inquisitive eyes. She saw how Noreen was waiting for her assurance, and reluctantly she gave it. 'I don't like doing things underhand,' she moaned. 'But if it's that important to you, Ma'am, then I'll deliver your letter.' Noreen fell back against the pillow as though a great weight had been raised from her. 'But if I'm to deliver it before I come to work, that means I'm to take this letter home with me?' Noreen nodded. 'Gawd luv us, I hope my old fella don't go nosing in me pockets,' she groaned. At this Noreen looked alarmed. 'Oh, bless your heart, Ma'am,' Daisy told her at once, 'a woman knows where to hide such things, don't you know?' She chuckled lewdly. 'It wouldn't be the first time I've managed to keep things where he can't get his hands on 'em!' Daisy was in no doubt as to what might happen if she didn't know how to contain her curiosity on what was inside the sealed envelope. Yet, she was no fool. Edward Dickens could be a bad enemy. And she was not about to jeopardise either her position, or her good health. Not just so she could peek inside a letter she wasn't!

All the same, when her work was done and she got home to her own little parlour on Viaduct Street, Daisy was riddled with curiosity. After a meal of hot pot and apple duff, her husband snoozed in the rocking chair, while she cunningly hid the letter beneath the carpet edge.

She tried to put it out of her mind then, but it was awful
hard. Like a cat on hot bricks, she paced up and down,
sitting in her own smaller rocking chair and rocking back
and forth, her eyes constantly going to the ragged carpet
beneath the window where the letter was safely secreted.
In all of her life, she had never been more curious. And
it was to her credit that, not once, until the following
morning when she was about to walk out the door, did
she recover that long white envelope from its hiding place.
Then, before she could be tempted further, she rammed
it into the pocket of her pinnie, put her coat on over the
top, and went smartly out of the house.

Chapter Thirteen

It was six o'clock on a Monday morning. Already the outer window of the little cobbler's shop was strung with rows of colourful footwear, and beneath these, the wooden table that Marcus brought back and forth each day was laid with a selection of second-hand articles, such as children's clogs, leather shopping bags with brand new handles, handbags with shining new clasps, and gentlemen's boots; all of which Marcus was forced to sell when, after a certain long period, they appeared to have been abandoned by their owners. 'Beats me how folk can afford to do it,' he told Phoebe. But when she pointed out that certain folk might have died, or maybe couldn't even afford to collect their belongings, his conscience was touched. Not only did he agree to wait a while longer, until it was impossible to find another square inch of space inside his store-room, but he went to the trouble and expense of placing a small advert in the local paper. It drew no response at all. Consequently, on this bright sunny morning he had cleared his back shelves and the wooden table was laid end to end with bargains. 'I wouldn't be surprised if the folk who come along to buy these things are the same absent-minded lot who left them here in the first place,' he told Phoebe with a grin.

'I can't believe that,' Phoebe said, laughing, although she knew that stranger things had happened. For instance, here she was, less than a year since she'd left her home in Bury, married to a man she didn't love and carrying another man's child. If anyone had told her it would happen, she would never have believed *that* either. Suddenly she needed to stay out in the morning sunshine. 'I'll make the table a little more attractive,' she told Marcus as he went back inside. 'See if we can't tempt passers-by to part with their brass.'

'There you are, I knew you'd make a formidable businesswoman,' he called out. She heard him laugh and then he was gone from her sight.

Phoebe set about the display. It was good to be out in the fresh air, to feel the sun on her face. She couldn't feel the sun in her heart though. She wondered if she ever would again. She'd been a married woman for almost two days now, and still she couldn't come to terms with the fact that she was Mrs Marcus Quinn. Her thoughts deepened and she found herself thinking of Judd. She wondered what he was doing right now. But of course, he'd be at work, earning a wage to keep his sister and dad. She smiled then, her heart a little warmer. She missed him. She missed Dora. She thought about what they might say when they knew she was a married woman. Last night she had actually sat down to write the letter that would tell them, but twice her courage gave out and she abandoned the idea. It was Marcus who persuaded her to finish the letter and so she did, promising Dora that they would be able to 'catch up with the news that's overtaken us' when she and Judd came to her cousin

Margaret's 'posh wedding'. To that end, Phoebe enclosed the two invitations which her uncle had so generously given her. His thoughtful act had been so out of character that Phoebe had been taken aback, although she did recall him saying that he wanted the affair to be a well attended one. To be honest, she would rather not have gone but that would be an insult to her aunt and Phoebe could never knowingly hurt that inoffensive little woman.

The street was wide awake now. Folk pushing along, late for their work, and others dashing to catch an early tram. 'Nice day,' said the postman as he went about his business. 'I ain't going to school!' yelled a particularly loud little boy, kicking his mother's ankles. 'And yer can't make me.' Her answer was a resounding slap round his ear and the threat that, 'You're bloody well going, whether yer like it or not.' The two of them went down the street, he struggling and biting, and she every now and then giving him a lift with the toe of her boot. Phoebe watched them go. 'Little sods, ain't they, dear?' chimed in a woman of enormous size as she pushed Phoebe to one side in order to see the goods on the table. 'Good God!' she said, grabbing a pair of well-worn buckled shoes. 'Them's *mine*!' She glared at Phoebe. 'Them's mine I tell you. Damn and bugger it! I wondered where they'd gone. Where is he?' She marched towards the shop door, holding the shoes aloft as though she'd just fished them out of the sea. 'I want a word with him,' she threatened, charging in and routing Marcus from his work. Phoebe couldn't help but chuckle when she heard the irate woman ranting and raving, and poor Marcus couldn't get a word in edgewise.

Some way down Lord Street, Daisy stood back for a moment, half hidden in the pawn shop doorway. She had seen Phoebe outside the shop and was in a quandary as to what to do next. Recalling Mrs Dickens' strict instructions she kept the letter folded in her fist, and her fist tightly thrust into her pocket. If it was up to her, she'd give the blessed thing to Phoebe and ask *her* to pass it on to Marcus Quinn. But the mistress had been adamant so she had better do exactly as she'd been told. Taking a deep breath, she set her best foot forward, hoping that Phoebe would be good enough to stay outside while she herself went into the shop and quickly did what she'd been sent to do. 'Morning, Miss Phoebe,' she said brightly, coming nearer. 'Oh, I forgot. It's Mrs Quinn now, isn't it?' she corrected herself.

Phoebe was surprised to see her. Swinging round at the sound of a familiar voice, her smile betrayed her delight. 'Daisy!' she cried. 'Whatever are you doing here?' Not once the whole time she'd been at Dickens House had Phoebe known the little woman to take a day off; not even when Edward Dickens made her life miserable. A dreadful thought occurred to her. 'Oh, Daisy! He's no given you your cards, has he?' Lord knows he'd threatened it often enough.

'No, he has not,' Daisy replied, a look of horror on he face. The very thought sent shivers down her spine an reminded her of the errand she was sent to do. 'No. It' just that, well . . . Mrs Dickens has sent me here with pair of boots she wants mending.' Afraid that Phoeb might grow too curious, she said, 'I can see you're bus so I'll not disturb you another minute. Besides, I want t catch the eight-fifteen tram.' She hadn't seen the other woman go in but her voice sailed out to the pavement. 'By! Somebody's got out the wrong side of the bed this morning,' Daisy chuckled, pointing her hand towards the shop door. 'In there, is he . . . Mr Quinn?'

'As far as I know,' Phoebe replied with a smile. 'Look, I've almost finished here. Let me see to you, eh?'

Daisy was flustered. 'Not a bit of it!' she declared, hurrying towards the shop. 'You're doing a grand job there and I wouldn't dream of taking you from it. No, I'll not be a minute afore I'm in and out and gone altogether.' With that she rushed inside the shop, leaving Phoebe with no choice but to finish the task she'd started.

Having said her piece and paid her dues, the other woman marched out again. 'I never thought you'd sink so low as to sell other folks' belongings,' she told the beleaguered Marcus. 'What's more, it'll be a long time afore you'll see me set foot inside these premises, I can tell you.' As she furiously slammed the door behind her, he prayed she meant what she said. Turning to Daisy, he asked, 'You haven't come to bawl at me as well, have you, Daisy?' When she gave no answer but glanced nervously towards the door before looking at him in a strange manner, he was momentarily lost for words. What was the matter with everybody this morning?

'I'm here on Mrs Dickens' instructions,' she explained in a furtive whisper, glancing again at the door to satisfy herself they were not about to be disturbed. 'On no account is Phoebe to set eyes on this letter . . . that's what I'm to tell you,' she explained, dredging it from her pocket and placing it on the counter. Out of the corner of her eye she saw that Phoebe was about to enter the shop. 'Quick!' she told him impatiently, shoving the letter along the counter towards him. 'Mrs Dickens was most emphatic . . . Phoebe mustn't see it.' She actually sighed aloud when he grabbed the letter up and thrust it into his overall pocket. 'And you can rest assured that nobody else has clapped eyes on it neither,' she said, letting him know that she was unaware of its contents. 'Here,' she went on, plucking the boots from her wicker basket and plonking them on to the counter. 'I ain't got time to stop, but you'll see what wants doing, I expect,' she told him. And with that she went swiftly out of the door, grumbling to herself and wondering why it was that in this life, some folks did the telling, and others did the bidding.

'Cheerio, Daisy,' Phoebe called as the little woman went past her in a great rush. 'Give my regards to my aunt, won't you?' Noreen was the only one at Dickens House for whom she had any warm feelings. 'She's all right, ain't she? Only I was expecting her to come and see me wed but she never turned up.' Phoebe still hadn't got over her disappointment though she suspected her uncle was at the root of it all.

'Aye, she's all right,' lied Daisy as she pressed on down the road. 'I expect she'll come and see you in her own good time.'

'Don't call us, we'll call you . . . that's what she's saying,' Marcus said kindly. 'You know as well as I do why your aunt wasn't there to see you wed. Edward laid the law down, I shouldn't wonder.' *Just like he laid the law down with your poor lovely mam all those years since,* he thought bitterly. *But it was a long time ago since he* and Jessica were madly in love. Now the good Lord had smiled on him and brought him Phoebe. Just when he thought he was destined to be lonely forever, he'd been given a second chance. What more could any man want?

'Marcus?' Phoebe stood behind the counter, her face a study in deep thought.

'Mmm?' He too had lapsed into deep thought; his hand touching the letter in his overall pocket as he wondered what message it conveyed and why Phoebe should not set eyes on it. 'Is there something on your mind, lovely?' he asked, gathering his wits and smiling warmly at her. She seemed aglow this morning. The soft cream of her dress brought out the brown of her eyes.

'Oh, I was just thinking,' she replied, 'why do you think my uncle gave his blessing for us to be wed?' She had been astonished when Marcus reported that Edward had greeted the news with some delight. It puzzled her then, and it puzzled her still. 'I mean . . . I really expected him to go mad.' She chuckled, 'I really expected him to throw you out.'

'Did you now?' he said with some amusement. The same thing that puzzled Phoebe also puzzled him. 'I expect he was glad to be rid of what he saw as a burden,' he suggested. 'After all, you said yourself he didn't want you there in the first place.'

'Yes but, well . . .' She shook her head in disbelief. 'I still can't believe he didn't have something to say. I really expected him to punish me in some way.'

Marcus came to her then, wrapping his fingers over hers and saying firmly. 'Now why should he "punish" you, eh? You've done nothing to be punished for.' Again

481

his thoughts flew back to Jessica. To this day he wondered what influence had been brought to bear on her. But then he remembered that it was Jessica herself who had made the choice, and who was he to question it? The door opened and in came two young ladies. Conversation was over.

Leaving Phoebe to attend to the customers, Marcus retired to the back-room and discreetly opened the letter which Daisy had brought. As he read on, his heart turned somersaults and his whole world spun upside down.

Dear Marcus,

I don't know rightly even how to begin what I'm about to tell you for I know it will come as a great shock. Years ago, you believed that no one knew of your affair with Phoebe's mother. You were wrong. Edward knew. And I knew, because I overheard certain heated conversations between him and Jessica. Looking back, I see how wrong I was not to speak to you, but to my shame I did nothing.

There is no point in dredging up the past but unfortunately the past has a strange way of rearing its head, just as it has done now. Something happened recently that makes me now want to speak out. You did not know but when Jessica broke off her relationship with you, she was with child. That child was Phoebe. And I have reason to believe that *you may well be Phoebe's father*.

I know what a shock this must be, but only you can know whether there are any grounds for my suspicion. If there is even the remotest chance that you *are* Phoebe's father, then my heart goes out to you, and I pray this letter has not come too late.

I leave the matter in your hands. Please do not come to the house. Do not try to contact me on this issue, because there is nothing further I can add to what I have said here.

I beg you to destroy this letter at once.

Noreen Dickens

Marcus stared at the letter, every word emblazoned in his mind. He felt numb, unable to take in the real implications of what Noreen had told him. Slowly folding the letter as though it was something very precious, he slipped it back into his overall pocket. Memories came flooding back. Memories of a young woman much the same age as Phoebe . . . and, oh, how his heart ached. He never knew that she was with child. Jessica never confided in him. And, yes, the child could well have been his. In his heart, he knew it must be. He and Jessica had loved each other. That was why he could never understand why she left him in the way she did. But then, of course, there was always the influence of her brother. Edward Dickens was a formidable man and Jessica a gentle unassuming soul. Marcus knew above all else that Jessica would not have lain with any man other than himself. He would stake his life on that. He gasped aloud when the full impact of his thinking dawned on him.

'Dear God above!' he moaned softly. 'Me and Jessica . . . Phoebe!' Closing his eyes tight, he tried to shut out the awful realisation. The truth stabbed at him . . . He was Phoebe's father! Now, when he opened his eyes they were misted with tears. Blinking them back, he looked towards the doorway, to the room where even now Phoebe was going about her work as though nothing had happened. As though everything was the same. But it was not the same. It would never again be the same. And the thought of what he had done was harrowing. *He had wed his own daughter!* His mind was in chaos. All he could think was that he had to get away . . . make up some story that would get him away where he could think about what to do. He knew Phoebe would have to know but the thought of telling her horrified him. No, he must get away . . . give himself time to think, to work out what must be done, and in a way that would spare Phoebe any more pain.

He couldn't work. All he could think about was the letter and the devastating news it had brought. 'What's wrong, Marcus? Are you ill?' Phoebe had seen how agitated and drawn he looked, and was greatly concerned.

'No, I'm not ill,' he assured her. But he *was* ill. He was ill with worry, and would not rest until he'd found a solution to this shocking dilemma. 'All the same, if you can manage all right I think I'll go for a walk,' he suggested. 'Get some fresh air.'

'Go on then,' Phoebe told him, going to the door where she took his jacket off the hook. 'I'll be fine. Don't hurry back on my account.' He looked so grey and worn, Phoebe thought a walk in the fresh air would do him good.

Marcus went along Lord Street and out towards the business area of town. His intention was to consult a solicitor. Surely to God a solicitor must know what could be done. All manner of questions were rushing through his mind. Would it be possible to have the marriage annulled? How could this awful thing be resolved without shaming Phoebe? What of the child? And, least of all, would he be sent to prison? As he went up the steps to the grand panelled door which was laden with brass plaques bearing the names of solicitors, Marcus prayed there was someone there who could find a solution to the awful nightmare that had engulfed both him and the innocent Phoebe.

'Our Dad's in a difficult mood this morning,' Dora yawned as she came into the parlour where Judd was pulling on his boots. 'We've none of us had five minutes' sleep altogether,' she told him. 'And look at you, you're still half asleep. I reckon you'd best give work a miss today, our Judd,' she said, coming to sit beside him on the settee.

Judd was bent down, tying his laces, but now he looked up, smiling at her through sleepy dark eyes. 'Oh, aye? And what about you then?' he asked.

'What d'you mean?'

Finishing his task before replying, he sat up and put his arm round her chubby shoulders. 'I mean . . . what about you? If I'm to take the day off, will you do the same?' he said kindly.

Dora was startled. 'I can't do that!' she retorted, her eyes popping like marbles. The very idea!

'And neither can I. Besides, what would we do when Friday came and I was a day's pay short in my packet, eh?' he wanted to know. 'I don't reckon the landlord would take kindly to having his rent cut back because I took a day off work, do you?' Having made his point, he gave her a cuddle and got up to put on his jacket. 'You look worn out. Try and get a rest if you can,' he said. Jerking his head towards the ceiling, he asked, 'Is he sleeping now?' He'd never known his dad to be so agitated through the night, and it worried him.

'Yes, he is,' Dora told him with a sigh. 'All the same, do you reckon I should get the doctor to him, our Judd?'

'It might not be a bad idea.' He moved his head from side to side reliving the trauma of the last few hours. 'He weren't in any pain though,' he recalled. 'Or so he said. But, yes, it might be as well if the doctor took a look at him.' He glanced towards the china jug on the dresser top. There was precious little money left in there, he knew. 'There's money in the front parlour,' he said. 'You know where it is. Take what you need.'

'But that's your nest-egg, our Judd,' she cried, scrambling from the settee. 'I'm not touching that. I've a few shilling left in the jug yet.'

'Dora, if he needs a doctor, you're to take the money from the front parlour,' he stressed. 'I'll not hear any arguments. Is that understood?'

'All right. But happen I'm wrong, and he'll be fine when he's had a good rest.'

Judd went to the scullery then where he collected his snap-can. Another minute and he was ready to leave. 'I'll go up and have a peep at him before I go,' he said, bending to kiss her on the top of her head. 'Remember what I said . . . try and get some rest.'

'I will,' she promised. And she would, because she felt fit for nothing as she was now.

Upstairs, Judd softly opened the door and peered inside. The old fellow was sleeping soundly. 'See you tonight, Dad,' he murmured. Then he crept down the narrow stairs, waved his hand at Dora who was standing in the parlour doorway, and went out of the house. At five o'clock on a Wednesday morning there were few folk about apart from others like himself who made the daily journey to their place of work. In another half-hour the cobbles would echo to the sound of clogs as other workers responded to the call of the mill siren. He hoped the piercing sound wouldn't disturb his father. It didn't as a rule, but the old fellow had been strangely restless these past few nights.

As he trudged along the streets, past the old familiar places where he'd played as a child, Judd was immersed in thoughts of Phoebe. 'Where are you now?' he asked with a heavy heart. 'Tucked up in bed and lost in your dreams, I shouldn't wonder.' He smiled a sad smile, and his pain was a strange kind of ecstasy. 'Wherever you are, I don't expect you're giving me a thought, are you, eh?' he murmured pensively.

Usually, when Phoebe pressed hard on his mind, he managed to thrust her away. This morning, though, he couldn't do it. Not when the smoky sky was marbled with flashes of gold and the silence bore into his deepest thoughts. Not when he could so clearly see her lovely face in his mind's eye. And not while her laughing brown eyes heightened the ache in him, 'Oh, Phoebe! Phoebe!' he groaned. 'Why are we always so afraid to say what's in our hearts?' Suddenly, he slowed his steps. He had stopped being a brother to Phoebe these many months. What would he have to lose by telling her how he felt?

Surely, there had been enough time now? His heart soared in leaps and bounds. What *did* he have to lose? Even if she turned him down, he couldn't feel any worse than he did right now. Oh, but was it wise? He still had Phoebe's love and respect in another way, and he didn't want to lose her altogether. All the same, the thought persisted. Maybe it was time for him to say what was in his heart. And with that idea growing steadily in his mind, he went on his way with a lighter step and a feeling deep down that all was not yet lost.

It was late afternoon. Dora had been up and down the stairs all day, with little time for anything else but to attend her father; he'd wanted a never ending stream of tea since Judd had gone off to his work that morning. 'I'm fair tuckered out,' she muttered, falling into the deep armchair beside her father's bed. 'If you don't soon settle, our Dad, I reckon I'll have to fetch the doctor to you after all,' she went on, believing the sickly old fellow to have drifted back to sleep.

'You'll do no such thing!' He shifted in the bed and stared up at her. 'I don't want no doctor when I've got you, Dora luv.' When he tried to smile his face folded into itself as though it was made of crêpe paper. 'Come here and talk to your old dad,' he whispered.

Dora laughed aloud. 'Why! You old codger,' she teased, 'I thought you were fast and hard asleep.' Coming to his bed, she sat down on its edge. Taking his hand in hers, she tenderly stroked it. 'You *should* be sleeping, our Dad,' she chided.

'Away with you. I'll be sleeping the long sleep soon enough, I dare say.'

'Don't talk like that,' she told him, her heart breaking. 'I won't have you saying things like that.' For too long now she had cared for her father and loved him more than ever.

'It has to be said, our Dora. And if I was tell the truth, I won't be sorry to stand afore the good Lord.' He stroked her face with gnarled fingers. 'You've been a good lass,' he told her lovingly. 'No man could have wished for better. You've looked after me, and I've never yet heard you grumble.'

She chuckled, admitting sheepishly, 'Hmm! Well, all I can say is . . . you couldn't have heard me at three o'clock this morning, after you woke me for the umpteenth time.'

'I'm sorry, lass. I haven't been much use to you and Judd have I?' When she made to protest, he shook his head. 'I know you both love me, though, and I thank God for that.' He closed his eyes and soon was in a deep sound slumber, his mouth loosely open and his hands twitching at the eiderdown with such frenzy that she wondered what he was fighting in his dreams. 'You're sleeping though,' she murmured thankfully. 'At last you're sleeping.' With that, she settled down in the deep armchair and closed her eyes to slumber. Soon the house was silent, save for the old man's gentle snoring.

Some time later, it was the silence that woke her. When she gazed on his blanched still face, the shock was momentarily paralysing. Her father was gone to a better place. She saw a peace in his old features that she had not seen for many a long year. She gathered him in her arms and her tears washed over his face. And it was only then that she realised the full extent of Phoebe's loss when her mam had been taken.

When Judd came home some half-hour later, it was a kindly neighbour who greeted him at the door. 'The lass is upstairs,' she said, and her voice was a warning to him. 'It's your father . . .' Her words were lost on him as he raced along the passage and up the stairs. At his father's bedroom door he stopped, his wide open arms clutching at the door frame on either side. Dora was kneeling beside the bed, holding her father's hand and murmuring words meant only for him. When Judd came to the door, she turned her tear-filled eyes on him. 'He's gone, Judd,' she said in a broken voice. 'Our Dad's gone and he's never coming back.' Then she broke into a fit of sobbing. He went to her and cradled her in his strong arms. As he looked at the face of his father, Judd felt a great sense of emptiness, as though he had lost more than a father, he had lost a whole way of life. He comforted his sister in her grief but there was no one to comfort him. And yet, in that moment, Phoebe came into his heart to give him strength.

The good neighbour looked round the parlour, at the uncleared breakfast dishes on the table and the ashes still in the fire-grate. 'I expect the poor lass has had more to worry about than dirty dishes,' she said to herself. She had already found the post that was still lying on the front door-mat. 'Better put these somewhere safe afore I get to work,' she muttered, glancing down at the two envelopes in her hand; one was a bill of sorts, and the other a small white envelope addressed in fine handwriting. It was postmarked Blackburn. 'Hmm! They do say as how the Mulligan girl was sent away to Blackburn,' she said absent-mindedly, then went to the sideboard and placed the two letters in the top drawer there. 'Poor little sod,' she muttered. 'Whatever became of her, I wonder?' There was a knock at the door then and she quickly closed the drawer. 'I expect that's the authorities,' she said, going out of the parlour and down the passage. 'Them buggers don't waste no time and that's a fact.' When she saw the tall sombre-faced gentleman with the long black coat and top hat, she thanked her lucky stars that it wasn't *her* he'd come to measure.

'Is there something troubling you, Marcus?' Phoebe had little appetite herself this Friday morning, but it worried her to see how Marcus had hardly touched his breakfast again and she'd particularly gone to Dewsbury's butcher's for that black pudding he so loved. 'Is it me?' she wanted to know. 'Have I done something to upset you?' She scraped his leftovers on to her plate and piled the plates one on top of the other. 'You would tell me if I was in the wrong, wouldn't you?' she asked anxiously, leaning across the table. For days now he had seemed so preoccupied. And, in spite of his reassurances, Phoebe sensed that he was deeply troubled. She tried not to think about the more intimate aspects of their marriage. She felt too ashamed.

'You're not at fault in any way,' he told her fondly, but when he looked at her, she could see the pain in his eyes. 'Its just that I'm having problems with one of my suppliers, that's all,' he lied. 'I've had these difficulties before and they've always worked out fine. But, that's the price you pay for running your own little business. I'll work it out, don't you worry.' He smiled, reaching out as though he might lay his hand over hers, but then he swiftly drew back. Phoebe opened her mouth to speak, and he cursed himself for allowing her to see that he was troubled. 'Not another word now, please,' he insisted. 'We've a shop to open and the customers won't wait while we discuss the ins and outs of running a cobbler's.' His manner was affectionate as always.

Pushing her chair back, Phoebe said nothing. Instead, she went about her work, clearing the table and piling the crockery on the drainer. She wasn't angry but she was hurt. A trouble shared was a trouble halved, was what she believed. She glanced at him now. Normally, at ten minutes past six, he'd be down in his workroom, bent over his bench, and happy in his labour. But here he was, still seated at the breakfast table, his mind obviously on other things. 'And you're sure there's nothing I can do?'

'I've told you, I'll deal with it.' Rising from his chair he said in a gentler voice, 'I've arranged to see the supplier concerned at four o'clock this afternoon. As it's Friday and custom tails off at about that time, we might as well shut shop. If you want, that is?'

'No, I'd rather stay open, Marcus.' Phoebe loved the little shop, and anyway when she was busy it stopped her from thinking too much. Thinking brought its own heartache.

'Fair enough.' He stretched his back and made himself smile at her. 'I'd best get to my work then . . . get started on that pile of repairs that came in yesterday.' He turned about and was quickly gone.

Phoebe stood at the pot sink, her arms up to the elbows

in suds, feeling unusually low. 'Whatever it is that ails you, Marcus?' she murmured, 'I've a feeling it's my fault.' In spite of his contradictions, she was convinced that his 'problem' was more than just a little hiccup with a supplier. She chided herself then, wondering why she should have the gall to question his word. 'Anyway, Phoebe Mulligan, what do *you* know about business, eh?' she asked herself. She even chuckled. But somehow, his mood had conveyed itself to her, and she couldn't shake off a deep-down feeling that something awful was in the making.

At ten minutes past four, soon after Marcus had left for his business appointment, Daisy came into the shop, bearing a letter. 'Mrs Dickens told me to fetch this afore the master claps eyes on it,' she told Phoebe. 'He's away at the minute but could be back any time.' Daisy was peeved at having to run errands. 'You'd best see to it that your friends know your new address,' she warned, ''cause *I'm* not running backards and forrads like no postman, and that's a fact.'

'I'm sorry, Daisy.' Phoebe was puzzled when she saw that the letter was postmarked Bury, Lancs. 'I did write and tell Daisy my new address, over a week ago.'

'Well then, you'd better tell her again, because it seems like she's forgot,' Daisy retorted. She didn't have to show respect to Phoebe, not now she was Mrs Quinn and out of the Dickens House. 'I've got better things to do than run about after you,' she said. 'Anyway, I suppose I've to be grateful, seeing as how Mrs Dickens told me to go straight home afterwards.' That brought a smile to her sour face.

Phoebe waited until Daisy was well on her way before she opened the letter.

Dear Phoebe,

I'm writing with some very sad news. Our Dad passed away this afternoon. I suppose it was expected but as you must know that never makes it any easier. Dora is inconsolable. She was always the closest to him, and it's hit her the hardest.

I hope you don't mind me asking this but do you think your uncle would mind you coming to the funeral? I know Dora would want you here at such a time. You're her friend, and God knows she made precious few when all her time was taken up with our Dad, Lord rest his soul.

It would be a tonic for us both, to see you again. The funeral is on Monday at nine a.m.

God bless,
from
Judd

It was a moment before Phoebe recovered. She sat on the chair by the counter, her eyes going over and over the letter. 'Poor Dora,' she kept saying. 'Poor Dora.' Because she knew what the old fellow had meant to her friend. Judd too, of course. Although he didn't wash and feed the old man, he adored him just the same and her heart went out to them both. Judd was right. Even though it was 'expected', it didn't ease the heartache when you had to say goodbye to a loved one. Strange though, Phoebe thought, how the letter had only confirmed her instincts that something awful was waiting to happen.

Going to the door, she clicked the sneck and turned the sign over to display the 'Closed' side. Marcus had said she could shut the shop and the idea had seemed unthinkable to her. Now, though, it would seem unthinkable to keep it open at a time like this.

Upstairs in the tiny sitting-room, Phoebe looked at the letter again. There was no question in her mind but that she must go to them. She wanted only to comfort her friends in their hour of sorrow, just as they had comforted her. She looked at the envelope, examining the address and wondering what made Judd send it to Dickens House when she'd clearly given Dora this address. And why was the letter addressed to Phoebe Mulligan when her name was now Phoebe *Quinn*? On top of that, Judd had asked whether her uncle would allow her to come to the funeral. It was as though her own letter had never arrived. 'But then again, it ain't surprising you forgot my new address and the fact that I'm now a married woman,' she murmured softly. No doubt Dora and Judd were too swept along by what was happening in their own little home, to concern themselves about what was happening in anybody else's.

'I'm sorry, Mr Quinn, but she has to be told.' The solicitor was a small shrewish man with rimless spectacles and a goatee beard. 'You should not even be under the same roof. I thought I made that clear the last time you came to see me?' He sighed. 'There's no point in you paying me good money for advice if you're not going to heed it,' he reprimanded sharply.

Marcus shifted uncomfortably in his seat. 'I don't know what to do,' he said softly, rubbing the palms of his hands together. 'How can I tell her?'

'I can't advise you on that, Mr Quinn. All I can say is that you *must* tell her. You must not stay under the same roof.' He glared at the little man. 'You do understand there's a very real possibility that you could go to prison?'

'Yes, I understand.'

'Then you'll do as I say? Or I cannot handle this case.'

'I don't want her blamed in any way. She knew nothing of my relationship with her mother.'

'I can't promise what the outcome will be, but I'll do my best, Mr Quinn, you can rely on that. Only, you have to listen to what I'm telling you.'

Marcus nodded. 'Don't worry.'

'Good.' The solicitor clapped his hands together and told his client, 'This is a very delicate business and needs to be handled most carefully.' He inclined his head towards the door. 'My secretary will arrange the next suitable appointment. Good day, Mr Quinn.' He bent his head to his desk, and didn't raise it again until he heard the door close. Then he stroked his beard, saying sadly, 'Before this is done Mr Quinn, I'm afraid you may *both* go to prison!' He opened the file in front of him and began to peruse it with renewed interest. 'Jessica Dickens, eh? Hmm . . . sister to Edward, would you believe!' He knew the fellow well though had no liking for him. Few people did.

Phoebe was waiting for Marcus' return. When she heard him coming up the stairs, she went to greet him. At once he saw the unhappy look on her face and his heart nearly stopped. He was surprised to see that she had closed the shop after all; when Phoebe said something she usually kept to it, and she had said she had no intention of shutting. Now here she was, with tears in her eyes and anxiety written all over her. His first thought was that somehow she had discovered where he'd been and the reason for his errand. He didn't speak first. He dared not. Instead he stood on the top step, looking up at her and just once glancing apprehensively at the letter in her hand.

'It's from Judd,' Phoebe explained, handing him the letter. 'His father's died and Dora's taking it very badly.'

'Oh, Phoebe, I'm so sorry to hear that.' But he *wasn't* all that sorry because he was weak with relief that his fears were unfounded after all. Phoebe still didn't know the shocking truth, thank God! He came into the sitting-room and stood beside her, his eyes devouring the letter. When he came to Judd's request, his relief was tenfold. 'But of course you must go!' he told her. 'It's obvious that your friend needs you right now.'

'Oh, Marcus!' Phoebe knew he would feel that way. He was such a good man. 'Are you sure? What about the shop? How will you manage without me?'

'I managed before, didn't I?' he asked, wagging his head at her. 'If I need assistance, there are plenty of folks who'll put in a few hours behind the counter for a shilling or two.'

'You really don't mind then?' Phoebe was remembering his mood that morning and for days before that. 'I mean . . . I'm sure Dora and Judd would understand.' She hated the thought of letting them down but in the back of her mind she knew Marcus would never allow that. 'The funeral's on Monday morning. So I should be back by Tuesday at the latest.'

Marcus was adamant. 'You must stay for as long as they need you.' He was sorry for Phoebe's friends in their grief, but was thankful that here was an opportunity to get her out of the way. 'You don't have anything black, do you?'

'No. But I can make do with my dark blue skirt and my jacket,' Phoebe offered. She had kept them smart, but in all truth it was not altogether a suitable outfit for a funeral. The jacket had white trimming on the pocket tabs and the skirt was shorter than she would have liked.

'I'll not hear of it,' Marcus declared. Striding across to the sideboard, he opened the left hand drawer and took out a round tin box. 'We're not so short of money that you have to make do,' he told her firmly, counting out one guinea. 'Take yourself off to the stores and buy what you need.'

'But I don't need *that* much,' Phoebe was horrified at the thought of spending Marcus' hard-earned money.

'Get what you need,' he told her. 'If you go now, you'll catch the stores open. Then an early night and you can be away on the first tram in the morning. I know the funeral isn't until Monday but I'm thinking Dora will need you before then.'

Phoebe had been in her uncle's store only once before and that was when she went with Marcus to deliver a batch of black patent leather shoes. It was a grand place, a place for gentlemen of means. There were two main showrooms; upstairs was reserved for overcoats, shirts and soft clothing, while downstairs was for shoes, umbrellas and other such apparel.

As Phoebe went by the front of the store now, she was interested to see that the window display was in the process of being changed about; there were naked dummies with their backs to her, and various items strewn across the floor. She paused, slightly regretting the fact that she had not been given the opportunity to work in such a splendid establishment. At that moment the young woman who had been altering the display came back into the window. It was Margaret. At first she seemed taken aback at the sight of Phoebe looking in. But then she inclined her head in reluctant greeting, a sly look on her face and a feeling of satisfaction glowing inside her. This was her domain, hers and her father's. There was no place here for the likes of Phoebe.

Deliberately turning her back, Margaret set about her work. Phoebe continued along Ainsworth Street. It was a pity she and her cousin had got off to such a bad start. It was a pity too that her cousin had turned out to be the kind of selfish, nasty person she was. There was more of her father in her than her mother, that was certain

'That looks really lovely on you.' The assistant fussed and fretted, patting the padded shoulders on the dress and standing back to admire the smart and sophisticated garment. She had seen Phoebe in a state of undress and was made curious; it struck her that this young lady could well be with child. 'You've chosen well, if you don't mind me saying,' she offered with one of those glued-on smiles that came with the job. 'Being designed on Empire lines, it is very concealing.' Her sharp eyes fell to Phoebe's midriff.

'There is a long line jacket to go with it,' she added hopefully. 'It's the sort of outfit that you can wear again and again, for any occasion.'

'I do like it,' Phoebe said, choosing not to satisfy the woman's obvious curiosity as to whether her customer was with child or not. In any case, she realised it wouldn't be too long now before her condition was obvious to one and all. The thought niggled at her, but as Marcus had told her time and again, 'We'll cross that bridge when we come to it.' She looked in the long narrow mirror, turning this way then that and thinking how she had never in her life had such a beautiful dress on her back; with the exception of the one her mother made, of course. The dress was black from top to bottom but there was nothing mournful about it; in fact, it was unusually beautiful and, as the assistant had quite rightly pointed out, could be worn for any occasion. The shoulders were gently padded, it had a 'V' neck without a collar, and the material was sheer and exquisite to the touch. The sleeves were long and fastened at the wrist with tiny black pearl buttons, and the whole thing fitted neatly beneath the breast before falling in generous folds to a calf-length hem. Phoebe also thought it to be cleverly concealing. 'It's exactly what I want,' she told the delighted assistant.

'Then you must try the jacket.' She hurried away to lose herself in a long deep cupboard with a glass front. 'Here we are,' she cried, emerging with a long line jacket clutched in her hands. When Phoebe tried it on, she cooed and sighed and made a great fuss but her customer would not be rushed. All the same, it took only a few minutes for Phoebe to realise that the jacket might have been made for her. With deep turnback revers and huge bone buttons, it was a perfect partner for the dress, yet it could be worn with any other outfit and so was not a waste of Marcus' hard-earned money.

Next came the hat. Phoebe tried only three before she chose the right one – a grey cloche hat with a pretty black silk rose sewn into the brim. 'My dear, you look absolutely wonderful!' exclaimed the assistant. This time her smile was genuine for she had never seen such beauty as she saw now; Phoebe's rich auburn hair peeped out in tiny wispy curls from beneath the hat, forming a delightful frame for her lovely face; her brown eyes sparkled, and there was a glow about her that took the woman's breath away. In the pretty blue shoes that Marcus had made for her, and with her slim shapely ankles, Phoebe made a most attractive figure. 'I'm beginning to think I should have bought the outfit for myself,' the assistant laughed, although she knew that even if she were to wear the crown jewels and a robe of gold, she would still seem dowdy and clumsy in comparison.

The entire outfit cost fourteen shillings. Phoebe would much rather have made do with what she already had in her wardrobe, but having seen herself began to think Marcus was right. This was the very first time she had been to a clothes shop and bought herself a brand new outfit. Standing there, seeing herself in the mirror, wearing something that had not been worn before or chosen for her by somebody else, had been a new and exhilarating experience. It was only a pity that it had transpired because she was about to attend a funeral.

'Give my condolences to your friends, Phoebe.' When the conductor rang the bell, Marcus stepped off the tram platform. 'Take care of yourself,' he called as it pulled away. 'And remember . . . I want you to stay as long as it takes. I'll be fine. There's no need for you to worry.' He watched the tram as it rattled along the meandering lines. He saw Phoebe wave just before it turned the corner, and then he was left alone. 'You must never come back,' he whispered, his shoulders bowed as he went across the boulevard and up Lord Street. He knew that never again would he and Phoebe live beneath the same roof. He remembered what the solicitor had warned, 'You realise you could go to prison?', and he was prepared for anything as long as Phoebe was not held to blame.

Chapter Fourteen

Thoughts of his late father pressed heavy on him but when he answered the knock at the door and saw Phoebe standing there, Judd's heart soared with joy. Choked with emotion he grabbed her in his arms. 'Oh, Phoebe! We so much hoped you would be able to come,' he said, holding her too close for much too long. Suddenly realising he might be embarrassing her, he reluctantly released her. 'I'm sorry,' he murmured. 'It's just that I'm so glad you're here.' Collecting her small portmanteau from the doorstep, he told her in a subdued voice, 'She's taking it badly.' Then his face broke into a warm smile. 'Bless you for being here,' he said, and Phoebe was deeply moved to see tears in his handsome dark eyes.

'You knew I wouldn't stay away,' she said simply. For one brief minute there was a longing in her, a deep inexplicable longing that he should take her in his arms again and hold her close, like a man in love might do.

Shocked by her own thoughts, she turned away. What in God's name was the matter with her? 'Where's Dora?' she asked, not even daring to look at him but glancing down the passage towards the parlour.

'She's upstairs.' He touched her on the hand. 'Please, Phoebe, go on up. I'll fetch your case, then I'll see about getting you a bite to eat.'

She found Dora in her father's room, gazing out of the window across the chimney-tops with tears streaming down her face. When Phoebe entered the room she made no move, thinking it was Judd for he had been in and out so many times in his efforts to persuade her to come downstairs.

On soft footsteps, Phoebe crossed the room. Even when she was at her friend's side, when she was able to reach out and touch her, Dora remained deep in thoughts of her father. Phoebe touched her tenderly on the shoulder. 'Dora,' she said softly. 'Won't you let me help?'

Dora swung round, bloodshot eyes staring in disbelief, 'Phoebe! she cried, and the tears poured unashamedly. 'Oh, Phoebe, he's gone,' she sobbed. 'Our Dad's gone.' She fell into Phoebe's arms. 'I miss him,' she sobbed. And Phoebe held her tight, soothing her with tender words and remembering how it was. She knew what Dora was feeling. Because weren't there times even now, when she felt that same crippling grief herself?

Judd went to the room that had been Dora's. It was a cosy place with frilly curtains and peg-rugs, and potted plants adorning the mantelpiece. It smelled of lavender and it was bright and sunny. Judd placed the portmanteau on the bed. 'You'll be comfortable enough here, Phoebe,' he muttered with satisfaction. To have her here, under the same roof, was something he'd thought could never happen. It was just a pity that she had to come under such sorry circumstances. A few minutes later he went across the tiny landing to the room opposite where he knew Phoebe and Dora to be. He raised his hand to open the door but then stopped himself when he heard them talking. It was the first time Dora had opened her heart and he thought it best to leave them be. Dora had a lot to tell and Phoebe was a good listener. On softer footsteps he continued downstairs.

It was some twenty minutes later when the two women emerged. Dora was still wet-eyed but there was a marked difference in her countenance. Judd had never doubted that Phoebe could bring his sister solace. 'There's paste butties and a chunk of pork pie each,' he told them. 'How's that?' He pointed proudly at the table. There was a huge pile of sandwiches in the centre, together with a round pork pie, a full steaming teapot, milk jug and sugar bowl. 'I knew you'd be hungry,' he told Phoebe, pulling out two chairs one after the other. 'Sit yourselves down,' he told them masterfully. '*I'm* doing the waiting-on today.'

Phoebe and Dora looked at each other in amusement. They'd each noticed that there were no plates, knives or forks, no cups, not even a knife to cut the pie with. 'That's very commendable, our Judd,' Dora remarked, 'but haven't you forgotten some'at?'

Curious, he examined his handiwork. It only took a minute to see why the two women were amused. Slapping his hand to his forehead, he laughed. 'Well, it's obvious I'm better at laying roads than I am at laying tables,' he admitted. With that he chuckled and soon the three of them were laughing. It was the first time since their dad had died that he'd seen Dora so relaxed; it was like the sun had poured into the house with Phoebe and he loved her all the more.

That evening, when Judd took the old mongrel out for

his walk, Dora and Phoebe sat beside the fireplace in the back parlour and talked of so many things: they reminisced about their childhood and discussed the future. But, to Phoebe's surprise, at no time did Dora mention what Phoebe had put in her letter. After a while, she asked nervously, 'Did you not get my letter, Dora?'

'When? Which letter do you mean?' Dora was puzzled because she was about to ask Phoebe why she hadn't written in such a while.

'You should have had it a week ago.' It occurred to Phoebe that the letter must have gone astray. 'It was a rather particular letter,' she said.

'Oh?' Dora was intrigued. 'What was "particular" about it then?'

Phoebe's heart fell inside her. She would have to go through it all from the beginning, and that included confessing about Greg Peters. She couldn't bring herself to say it. 'This may not be the time for you to think about it, Dora, but there were two invitations in that letter. My uncle's invited you to his daughter's wedding.' She wondered how she might break the other news: the news that she and Marcus were wed; the news that she was carrying another man's child.

'Well I never!' Dora had not expected to be invited to such a posh do. 'What brought that about?' she wanted to know.

'I think he just wants to show the whole world how splendidly he sends his precious little girl off,' Phoebe said. 'But, to tell you the truth, I'm surprised he's even allowing her to get wed in the first place.'

'Possessive, is he?'

'You could say that.'

'I expect it'll be a grand do though, won't it?'

'Oh, it'll be that all right. No expense spared from what I can make out.'

'When is it?'

'Easter Saturday.'

'I'd like to see how the well-off get wed, but I don't know, Phoebe, what with our Dad an' all.'

Phoebe understood. 'We'll not talk about it now, eh? There's time enough.'

'What else?'

'What do you mean?'

'The letter. You said it were a "particular" letter. Was it just the wedding invitations you meant?' She saw how Phoebe lowered her gaze and sensed that there was something else. 'What news have you, Phoebe?' she insisted. 'There's nowt wrong, is there?'

Unable to sit still beneath Dora's inquisitive gaze, Phoebe got out of the chair and went to the sideboard where she stood with her back against it and her fingers curled over the top. Leaning her weight on her hands, she looked at the carpet then stared at the ceiling. Then she was looking directly into Dora's bright little eyes. 'I'm wed,' she told her quickly before she lost her courage altogether.

'You're what!' Dora sprang from the chair, her eyes going to Phoebe's wedding finger, and sure enough there was the band of gold, sparkling in the lamplight. 'Who?' she asked excitedly. 'Who have you gone and wed behind my back?' She was thrilled, but at the same time anxious. 'Oh, Phoebe, what have you done? And why didn't you let me know afore now?' she demanded, not giving Phoebe time to answer any of her questions. 'Who is it then? Who have you gone and wed?' Hadley Peters came into her mind but then she realised it couldn't be him. But who then? And *why* had Phoebe done it so underhand? It wasn't like her at all.

'I'm wed to Marcus.' Now, when she said it out loud and Dora was looking at her with her mouth open in disbelief, Phoebe was made to question the sense of the enormous step she'd taken. Marcus was a fine man. But she had to ask herself whether she had done the right thing after all.

'MARCUS QUINN?' Dora was visibly shocked. 'You're wed to the cobbler?' She shook her head and took Phoebe's hand in hers. 'What in God's name made you do such a thing? The fella's old enough to be your dad.' She knew how Phoebe respected her employer and was aware that he'd been good to her, but . . . 'Why?' she wanted to know. 'Why did you do it? Was it to get away from your uncle, is that it?' It suddenly occurred to her there was the remotest possibility that Phoebe might have a deeper motive. 'Do you love him?'

Phoebe's dark eyes were bright with tears. Dora's questions echoed the ones in her own heart and it was hard not to see the mistake she had made. In answer to Dora's last question she couldn't bring herself to speak and so she prayed, her lips tight together and the tears threatening. Here, with Dora, with this woman who was like a sister to her, she didn't have to hide anything and it was as if a dam had opened up inside her. Taking Dora's hand, she placed it ever so gently on the mound of her stomach.

where, these past few days, she had felt the child begin to move. She didn't say anything but watched Dora's face which mirrored her revelation; first there was puzzlement, then slowly but surely the truth dawned and her eyes grew wide with astonishment. Her mouth fell open and she just stared at Phoebe with disbelief. Phoebe realised she was about to ask another question and anticipated it. 'No it isn't his,' she said shamefully. 'Marcus isn't the father.'

It was too much for Dora. The news that Phoebe was wed had been enough of a shock, and then to discover it was Marcus Quinn she was wed to, and now this! 'I'll have to sit down,' she said, wagging her head from side to side. She returned to her chair. Phoebe followed her. 'I'm sorry, Dora,' she said softly. 'I should have waited to tell you. This isn't the time. Not now.'

'If you *hadn't* told me, I'd 'a wanted to know the reason why, my girl!' Dora retorted. 'I can see now why you chose not to tell me about you getting wed . . .'cause you know I'd have had some'at to say about it all.' She regarded Phoebe with sharp accusing eyes. 'You should have told me, all the same.'

'I know,' Phoebe could see that now.'But, I thought I could work it out better on my own.'

'Who is it then?' Dora asked in a kinder voice, her own sadness diminished by Phoebe's awful news. At least she had Judd, a shoulder to cry on whenever the need came to her. 'It's me that ought to be sorry, lass,' she apologised. 'I shouldn't be judging you, Phoebe. I can only imagine what you must have gone through to take the decision you did. Do you want to tell me who the father is?' A dreadful thought came into her mind. 'Oh, Phoebe, it's not . . .' She couldn't even bring herself to say it.

'Hadley Peters?' Phoebe knew what was on her friend's mind. 'No, it isn't him?'

'But you had a liking for him. You told me so yourself.'

Phoebe smiled sadly. 'I was lonely,' she explained. 'He was kind, and I had a foolish notion, that's all. There was never any real substance to it.'

'I'm glad to hear that.' Dora breathed a sigh of relief. 'That cousin of yours sounds like the kind who'd turn the world upside down if she thought you were after her man.' She asked again, 'Do you want to tell me then?'

And so Phoebe told her. She told her about how Greg Peters had cornered her when she was most vulnerable, and how she had given herself to him willingly, and how she had come to regret it ever since. She told Dora how she had lived in fear of her uncle finding out, and of the way in which Marcus had come to her rescue. And all the time Dora listened, and saw that Phoebe had gone from one trap to another. 'But you're not content, are you?' she asked lovingly.

Phoebe couldn't lie. Marcus had been good to her but she couldn't lie anymore, not to Dora and not herself. 'No,' she admitted. 'I'm not content. But then, I don't deserve to be.'

'Do you sleep with him?'

Phoebe was surprised by Dora's abrupt question until she told herself that only a good and close friend could ask such a thing. 'We've never slept together, me and Marcus,' she answered truthfully. 'When he suggested that we should get wed, he said he wouldn't ask anything of me that I wasn't prepared to give, and he's kept his word.' For that much at least Phoebe was thankful. 'He sleeps on a put-me-up in the sitting-room, and I have the bedroom.' She wanted Dora to know. 'He's been very good to me, Dora. If it hadn't been for Marcus, I dread to think what might have become of me.' There was just one more thing. 'Don't mention any of this to Judd, will you?'

Dora was astounded. 'But he'd want to know. Judd would want to help, you know that.'

'Please, Dora. When he needs to know, I'll tell him.' The thought of Judd knowing how she'd shamed herself was an even deeper shame to Phoebe.

'And if he sees your wedding ring?'

'*You* didn't.'

'No, I didn't,' Dora conceded. 'And they do say a man is less observant than a woman, so he might not.' She saw that Phoebe seemed deeply agitated. 'Aw, don't worry, I promise you I'll not say a word, if that's the way you want it. But he loves you as much as I do, Phoebe. Don't forget that, will you?' She had her own suspicions about Judd and the way he felt about Phoebe, and this news had shocked her more than she could say.

They sat a while longer, two dear friends happy together, each with their own regrets but secure in their affection for each other. At nine-thirty, Dora said goodnight. 'I'm out on me feet,' she told Phoebe. 'You'll not mind if I make me way to me bed, will you?' Phoebe promised she wouldn't be far behind and so Dora left her there, sitting by the fireside, warm and cosy, lulled by the warmth from the glowing embers in the grate and dreaming of how it used to be, here in this narrow street with its back-to-backs, every flagstone a milestone through her childhood, everywhere another memory. Alone in that little parlour, with the feelings of nostalgia too much to bear, Phoebe softly cried. It had all gone wrong. Somehow, it had all gone hopelessly wrong.

'Hey, what's all this then?' Judd had come into the room and so engrossed in her thoughts was she that Phoebe hadn't heard him. Now, when he spoke, she looked up in surprise, surreptitiously dabbing at her eyes and hoping he didn't see her crying. 'Judd! I didn't hear you come in,' she said, forcing a bright smile.

He came across the room and sat in the chair opposite her. Remaining silent for a moment he studied her face; in the flickering firelight he thought she was the loveliest creature he had ever seen. 'You were crying,' he said. Her dark eyes still glittered with tears, and he wanted so much to hold her, to keep her safe and love her for all time.

'Just thinking,' she admitted.

'About the old days?' He smiled at her then, and suddenly he was so different from the boy she had grown up with. His smile touched her heart in a way she could never have dreamed and her regrets were all the deeper.

'About everything,' she answered. 'When we were kids life was so much simpler.' The tears trickled from her eyes and she let them fall; somehow they eased her aching heart. 'I miss it all so much,' she said brokenly.

'What do you miss most, Phoebe?' he asked tenderly.

'Oh, everything.' She laughed. 'The makeshift rafts or the cut and the way we always used to think we were intrepid explorers making our way through the swamps

Winter-time when we used to gather the snow off the window-sills and pelt old Jackson's fruit-barrow. Getting sent to bed early because we'd torn our best Sunday clothes. My mam.' She threw her arms out and laughed at the memories. 'Oh, everything, Judd. I miss it all.'

'Do you miss me?' His voice crept softly into her heart.

She looked at him then, at his brown eyes and the soft loving gaze that mingled with hers, at that handsome face which smiled in a way that made her tremble, and she was torn asunder. 'Of course I miss you,' she said, a little too quickly, her heart fluttering at his nearness. It's the fire-glow, she thought, and the lamplight. It's the loneliness in me that makes me imagine things.

'I should never have let you go away,' he murmured lovingly, reaching out to touch her hair. 'Because I've missed you every minute of every day.' Her dark eyes were wide and confused, and he loved her all the more. Choosing that moment to take her in his arms, he gently raised her from the chair, pressing her close to him. 'I was a fool,' he whispered. 'I love you, Phoebe. More than I could ever love anyone else.' He gazed into her upturned face and her beauty shocked him. Pressing her close, he bent his head and entwined his fingers in her hair. Drawing her to him, he kissed her long and passionately. When she shivered in his arms and pulled away, he buried his face in her hair. 'Marry me,' he murmured. 'Let me take care of you, my love.'

In that moment, Phoebe knew what was in her heart. She hadn't seen it before because they had been too close, her and Judd. She was blinded by the nearness of him. But now she knew the truth and it broke her heart. She loved him! She had *always* loved him. If only she'd realised it earlier. There were no words to tell him. No way she could explain without hurting him. 'It's impossible,' she whispered. It wasn't what she wanted to say. It was what she *must* say. Looking up into those intense brown eyes that clouded at her harsh words, she would have given anything to turn the clock back. But it was too late, all too late. His hurt was her hurt, and there was nothing she could do to ease it. 'I'm sorry, Judd,' she said softly.

'You don't love me?'

She gave the only answer she could.'I *can't* love you.'

'Forgive me then,' he said, and in a moment he was gone. And all of Phoebe's joy went with him.

'It was a fine service, Dora, and you've given your father a grand send-off.' The woman had been a good neighbour these many years, and she was the last to leave the little parlour. 'It's easier somehow when they're laid beneath the ground. You know it's final and you have to come to terms with it.' As she departed, she reminded Dora, 'You know where I live if you need anything.'

'Thank you, Mrs Bethnall. I'll remember that.' Dora was glad to see the last mourner leave. Sinking into the armchair, she told Phoebe, 'Well, we've done us duty by him.' A small sob escaped her but she choked back the tears and drew in a long deep sigh. 'I'm glad you're here,' she said. ''cause I don't know what I'd 'a done without you.'

'I'm glad I was here too,' Phoebe replied. Her mind was still on Judd. Throughout the service he had kept his eyes forward, his head up and his shoulders straight; only once did she see them shake, and that was when they lowered his father into the ground. He looked at her then, a longing, loving look that spoke volumes, and the agony in his face cut through her heart. Afterwards, he did his duty by Dora and welcomed the visitors into his father's house. But when he saw that his sister was coping well enough, he left. Phoebe had gone to the window to watch him stride away down the street, a lonely figure. If only she could have gone after him, she thought sadly. If only there was a way that things could be right between them. But there wasn't. Too late she had realised the love between them. She had a husband now, and a child on the way. There was no turning back. 'You rest now,' she told Dora, 'I'll get started on this lot.' She left the parlour rolling her sleeves up. There was much work to be done, and the more the better, because it might help to keep her mind off the mess she'd made of her life.

Dora didn't argue. She rested her head back against the chair, and closed her eyes. In a minute she would help. But in a minute she was gently sleeping and Phoebe went quietly about her work until the place was spick and span; every piece of crockery and every item of cutlery washed and put away. It had been her intention to stay a few days, but now, if Dora was all right, she wanted to get back to Blackburn. There was uneasiness there it was true, but there was heartache here. Besides, her presence would only make for an impossible situation between her and Judd.

She made herself a cup of tea and sat in the chair opposite Dora and thought about Judd; and she thought about Marcus, and she thought about the child, and her head began to spin. Yes, she must leave here, she decided. First thing in the morning if possible.

Later, when she was rested and gently wakened with a cup of tea, Dora smiled at Phoebe's concern for Judd. She told Phoebe that he always went walking when things crowded in on him. 'He'll stride the fells, and sit awhile until his troubles are more bearable.' she said. 'I'm not worried about him. I know our Judd too well. He's strong and has his own way of dealing with our Dad's death.'

How could she know that besides suffering the loss of his dad, his heart was weighed down with another loss; a loss that bespoke more the future than the past; a loss that weighed heavy on him? Phoebe had been his hope and his love for so very long. And now the hope was gone. But not the love, he thought bitterly. His love for Phoebe was a hard physical pain inside him. It would always be there. There could never be anyone else for him.

He walked the streets until the night closed in all around. He knew that Dora would be all right. She had done her grieving, and Phoebe was there to give her the love she could never give to him. He tried to harden his heart against her. But the more he tried, the more her lovely image flowed in and softened it again. He turned the corner into Albert Street. Outside number fourteen he paused and looked at the house. There was a light on. Through the parlour window he could see Shirley; she was seated at the table, her head bent over a newspaper. Only days ago he had told her things wouldn't work out between them. He knew she would be more than pleased to see him. He began his way up the path and stopped. He turned away. Tomorrow, he would see her. Tomorrow, his mind might be clearer.

It was midnight when Judd came home. Dora was fast and hard asleep in the room which had been her father's. Phoebe lay awake in the opposite room. Time and again she had gone to the window and stared into the night, searching for that familiar figure, praying he would soon be home. Somehow, she felt responsible for him being out so late, alone in his grief, alone in his love. But then so was she, she mused, so was she.

She had only just gone back to her bed when the sound of footsteps took her back to the window. Her heart leaped when she saw that it was Judd. He came to the front door and suddenly he glanced up. Startled, she jerked her head back. He hadn't seen her. She watched him enter the house and for a moment was tempted to go down and tell him why it was that she could not return his love, although in her heart she had already done so. The temptation quickly passed. The thought of seeing his face when he realised how easily she had given herself away was more than she could bear. Going back to her bed, she lay there awhile, listening to his movements in the parlour below. She heard him come up the stairs, and it took every ounce of her strength for her not to run out and throw herself into his arms. But the shame was still on her, more so now she knew how he loved her. Like her mam used to say, she had made her bed and now she must lie on it.

And so that was exactly what she did. But sleep eluded her. She turned and fretted all night long. Soon after dawn she heard someone moving about downstairs. Thinking it must be Dora, she threw her robe about her shivering body and went down. Pushing open the parlour door, she looked inside. There was a fire already cheerfully blazing in the grate and the lamp on the mantelpiece sent out a warm welcoming light. There was no sign of Dora. Hearing someone in the scullery, Phoebe made her way there. Judd was bent over the sink, stripped to the waist, his flesh glistening as he vigorously worked the soap into a lather, over his thick muscled arms and across the dark hairs on his chest.

'I'm sorry. I thought it was Dora,' Phoebe said, staying by the door. 'I was worried that she couldn't sleep.'

'Phoebe!' He hadn't heard her come into the parlour and didn't realise she was watching him. They looked at each other for what seemed an age and then he spoke again, but this time he was over the shock and his voice was impersonal. 'I always light a fire before Dora comes down. These old houses can be chilly of a morning,' he said. Putting his arms into the water, he rinsed them off. 'There's a brew made if you want one,' he offered, wiping himself dry.

Phoebe was out of her depth. Seeing him like that, knowing that he was being deliberately cold to her, was too hurtful.'I didn't mean to disturb you,' she said. 'I'll go back upstairs for a while.' She lowered her gaze and prepared to leave.

She was almost at the parlour door when his hand touched hers. 'Phoebe.' He said her name softly. When she turned, he put his hands on her shoulders; he could feel the warmth of her skin and his senses reeled. 'Are you sure . . . about us? There really is no chance that you could love me?' His gaze was soft yet intense. 'Have I lost you altogether?' he asked, a world of emotion in his voice.

Phoebe was close to telling him the truth but couldn't bring herself to do it. Besides, it would only cause him more pain, she knew. Steeling herself against his touch, not daring to look at the adoring light in his dark eyes, she told him gently, 'I'm going home today, Judd.'

'I see.' The intonation in her voice left him in no doubt that he was given his answer and it was the same as before. His hands dropped to his sides and he smiled at her, but it was a cold smile. 'A safe journey then, and thank you so much for coming, Phoebe. You helped Dora through a bad time, and I'll always be grateful.' Just that, and then he returned to the scullery where he busied himself in getting ready for his work. But when he heard the door close behind her, he clenched his fists together, his eyes closed in anguish as he realised she was going out of his life for ever.

On Tuesday afternoon at four-thirty Phoebe alighted from the tram at Blackburn Boulevard. Some ten minutes later she was astonished to see that the shop door was shut and the 'Closed' sign showing. Quickly she turned her key in the lock and went inside. 'Marcus,' she called out once or twice as she went hurriedly up the stairs. But he wasn't there, and, judging by the state of the larder which still held all the food she'd bought especially for him while she was away, he hadn't been there for two days.

Puzzled and concerned, she looked around the room.

It was then that she saw the letter propped against the clock on the mantelpiece. It was addressed to her.

Dearest Phoebe,

I'm going away for a few days. It's nothing at all for you to worry about. It has to do with business, and I'm simply pursuing a few possibilities.

Ruby, at number eight, has offered to come in and help, if you need her. You'll find that I've caught up with all the repairs, and they're ready for collection. You may not want to open the shop at all, but I'll leave you to decide. There's money on the mantelpiece, which should keep you going 'til I get back. If you need more, go along and see the bank manager. He knows I'll be away, and everything has been arranged.

I'm not sure how long I'll be gone, but I'll keep in touch, don't worry.

Marcus

It was a strange thing for him to do, and Phoebe didn't know what to think. She knew he'd been having difficulty with suppliers, or so he'd said, but with regard to any other business interests he might have, she knew nothing at all. Glancing at the mantelpiece again, she noticed the wallet lying there. 'You should have confided in me, Marcus Quinn!' she chided aloud. 'But you needn't worry about me going to no bank manager,' she promised. 'And you needn't concern yourself about your interests at this end because it'll be business as usual until you get back!'

Ten minutes later she was knocking on the door of

number eight. A lady of large and scruffy appearance flung open the door. 'Mrs Quinn, ain't it?' she asked. And before Phoebe could answer, she snapped, 'If you've come for our Ruby, you can forget it. I know your old man said there might be a job open for her at the cobbler's, but she can't afford to wait for folks tekking their time and knocking on this 'ere door just when it suits their own ends. I've put her to work at the ironmongers' and she'll not be leaving there in a great hurry, I can tell you. What's more, Arnie Clapham pays a better wage than yon cobbler so I'll thank you to look elsewhere for yer cheap labour.' With that she shut the door and left Phoebe in a quandary. Yet, as she walked back to the shop, another possibility presented itself to her, and her heart brightened at the thought.

Friday came, and Marcus was still not home although a letter arrived to tell Phoebe that he was well and things were going according to plan. He gave no explanation but she was reassured by the letter. Something else had put her in a bright and cheerful mood this Friday morning because in twenty minutes she would meet Dora off the tram.

'There!' With her polishing cloth in one hand and a tin of beeswax in the other, Phoebe surveyed her handiwork. She had gone through the living quarters with a fine tooth comb because she so much wanted to make a good impression on Dora. The curtains were tied back to let the sunlight in and everything was sparkling bright; there was even a vase of flowers standing in the hearth. Next she checked herself in the wardrobe mirror; she looked fine and dandy with her hair brushed into a manageable mass of curls and waves, and the blue blouse with the darker loose-fitting ankle-length skirt suited her a treat. She patted the rise of her stomach. 'You won't be able to put off going to the doctor much longer, my girl,' she told herself. She tried not to think about that. At the best of times she had a wariness of men in authority, and so intended putting the visit off for as long as was possible.

A few minutes later Phoebe was making her way down Lord Street towards the Boulevard. In spite of being anxious about Marcus, she wouldn't let herself dwell on the idea that he was in some kind of trouble. Marcus knew what he was doing, she assured herself. He was an accomplished man of business, and though he might not be in the same league as her uncle, he had developed and maintained a thriving little business. It had been going well long before she came and there was no reason now why there should be any problems. In fact, since reading his letter, Phoebe had convinced herself that he was look-ing to expand his business in some way and didn't want to say anything until it was all cut and dried. But she daren't think about it too much because instead of being overjoyed at the thought of her and Marcus working together to achieve even greater success, her heart just wasn't in it. Today she intended to dwell on more pleasant things. Dora was on her way to stay for a while, the sun was shining, and even though it would never be possible for her and Judd to have a life together, she had been warmed to the heart by his admission of love for her.

As she approached the tram-stop, there was a definite spring in her step. Almost at once the Bury tram pulled in and there was Dora, already waiting on the platform and eager to disembark. The tram jerked to a grinding halt and Dora tumbled off the platform into Phoebe's waiting arms. 'Oh, I'm that glad to see you,' she said, her fat little arms clinging to Phoebe. Collecting her huge tapestry bag from the pavement where she'd dropped it, she ordered, 'Lead on then, gal. Let's see this little shop o' yourn.'

Phoebe went to take the bag from her, but Dora clutched it tight. 'What!' she cried. 'I'll not have you carry my bag, not in your condition, I won't.' Two pompous ladies in front turned round to stare. At once she realised she might have said the wrong thing and that maybe these two were known to Phoebe. 'I mean . . . you don't want to go putting too much strain on them varicose veins now do you, eh?' she remonstrated to Phoebe's great amusement. 'You know very well what the doctor said.' Smiling at the ladies, she told them, 'Runs in the family it does . . . veins as wide as tramlines. The doctor's told her, any strain and they'll be big as balloons in no time at all.'

The larger of the two ladies declared in a sympathetic voice, 'You don't have to tell me, my dear. I'm a martyr to varicose veins. A *martyr*, I tell you.' She sighed and tutted then shook her head in despair and went on her way. Behind her, both Dora and Phoebe were engulfed in merriment.

'You should be ashamed,' Phoebe laughed, linking her arm with Dora's and taking her across the tram-lines. Oh, it was wonderful having her friend here, and it was good to know that she wasn't alone in her troubles. It had taken a great deal of courage for her to confide in Dora but now she was thankful she had. She knew Dora would keep her promise not to betray her shame to Judd; he would know soon enough, she thought sadly.

'How far is this 'ere cobbler's shop?' Dora asked breathlessly as they rushed out of the path of an oncoming tram.

'Not too far,' Phoebe answered. 'There's Lord Street there.' She pointed to the narrow street just ahead.

'Have you heard from Marcus?'

'No. But I expect I shall soon.'

'Won't he mind me staying?'

'He won't mind one bit,' Phoebe said, hugging her arm tighter round Dora's. 'In fact, it's a wonder he didn't suggest it himself.'

The happy chatter continued all the way along Lord Street, and even when Phoebe was unlocking the shop door she was delighted to hear Dora exchanging pleasant-ries with one or two of the friendlier neighbours. 'Hey, this is a grand little street,' she said as they entered the shop.

'Reminds me of home,' Phoebe said. Lord Street was very similar to the street she and Dora were brought up in. The tiny houses and the crooked little shops nestling against each other, the snotty-nosed, raggy-arsed kids who played on the cobbles, were all part of her dearest memories.

Dora went through the shop and into the back work-room; she rummaged about in the store outside and thought it was magical. 'I've never seen the inside of a cobbler's afore,' she said, her eyes shining. Phoebe took her all over the living quarters, and she couldn't believe how roomy it was. 'Well, I never! From the outside it looks like a doll's house,' she laughed.

Dora and Phoebe laughed a lot that day, and in the days to follow. At night, though, when the curtains were drawn and the world shut out, they opened their hearts to each other. The only things Phoebe kept back were the things Judd had said to her and her own love for him. There was nothing to be served by revealing them.

Dora was a godsend. Phoebe opened the shop and the customers poured in. And even though she warned them that their shoes wouldn't be repaired for some time, on account of Marcus being called away on suppliers' business, they still left their footwear, saying there was no one else they'd trust to mend them except Marcus Quinn. Dora helped behind the counter and enjoyed every minute. 'By! I reckon I might take it up when I get back home,' she said enthusiastically. 'After all, I'll be well experienced, won't I?' And Phoebe had to agree.

The following Monday there was another letter from Marcus. It told Phoebe that all was going well and that she wasn't to worry. He couldn't say when he'd be home, but hoped it wouldn't be too long now.

Some sixty miles away, in a guest house situated in the outskirts of Liverpool, Marcus had also received a letter. It was from his solicitor. The news was not good, but there were certain other avenues the solicitor wished to pursue before he called Marcus to his office. The main stipulation was as before, but this time couched in stronger terms: 'Under no circumstances should you and Miss Mulligan reside under the same roof'. A lonely man, aching for his shop, longing for his work, and missing Phoebe's warm companionship, Marcus put on his coat and left the house. Just as he had done every night since ostracising himself from all that he loved, he went to the docks and for a while watched the great ships there. He saw the men who sailed them coming and going, and envied them their work. Without his own work to busy his hands and ease his heart, he was a man with nothing. But he would give it all up if he could only save Phoebe from scandal and disgrace.

Chapter Fifteen

John Soames stepped off the train and glanced at the clock high up in the rafters of Blackburn railway station. Under his arm he carried a dark oddly shaped carpet bag, which he kept close to his body as he weaved his way through the Easter Saturday travellers. He was a man with a mission, a man who had waited many years for this day, a bitter man who had lost all reason, confusing right from wrong, mistaking revenge for justice. His grim face betrayed the urgency in him. But he would have to be patient a while yet. The situation was not entirely under his control. He had instructions to wait in a certain isolated place not too far from the centre of Blackburn town. He was on his way there now.

'You're a clever bastard, Dickens!' Soames muttered under his breath, a dark wicked smile enveloping his features. Edward Dickens was a man after his own heart. All of his instructions had been delivered personally. Not once had he written anything down, because the written word could be damning, even for a man of Edward Dickens' influence, whereas the word of a crook was easily dismissed out of court. Not that John Soames cared one way or the other for he intended that when this day was over, his own life would be at an end.

Just as Phoebe had predicted, it seemed as though the entire population of Blackburn had come out to see the bride in her pomp and finery. Edward Dickens and his family were as near to royalty as this town was ever likely to see close up. They clustered outside his fine house, and they lined the route from Preston New Road into Blackburn, and they watched the shining black carriage as it took the bride through the highways and byways to St Peter's Church.

There the bride came carefully out of the carriage, revelling in all the attention and looking like a Hollywood starlet in her beautiful silken gown, the bejewelled veil flowing from a sparkling coronet and the long magnificent train of satin and sequins fanning out behind her. Her yellow hair was pinned up high, splendidly dressed with glittering mother-of-pearl combs and tiny red roses that matched the many blooms in her exquisite bouquet. She smiled, and she waved, and she adored it when they gasped in astonishment, wide-eyed with wonder at such extravagance.

'I've never in all my life seen anything like it!' Dora was aglow. 'I don't have much liking for that young madam. But, oh, isn't it wonderful?' she told Phoebe. 'I wouldn't have missed it for the world.'

'She does look beautiful,' Phoebe admitted. 'Happen she'll change for the better when she's wed to Hadley, eh?' she remarked, her brown eyes shining with delight, and only the slightest regret murmuring in her heart. Every girl dreamed of such a wedding, but it was only the very privileged few whose dreams came true. 'I suppose we'd better go into the church,' she suggested, 'or the bride will be there before us.' She and Dora had waited by the gate for Margaret to arrive. The bridesmaids were already in place at the altar; a pretty dark-haired girl from Edward Dickens' store who had for some reason found favour with her employer's daughter and little Aggie whose dream of being a bridesmaid had also come true. The two dresses were in a delicate shade of blue, falling to just below the calf, with a flounce at the hem, and over their pretty curls they each wore a plain white head-band wound with flowers to match the bride's bouquet. Their slippers were blue satin and their beautiful posies were shaped from tiny blue and white flowers.

'My! But they couldn't have wished for a better day,' Dora whispered as she and Phoebe made their way out of the brilliant sunshine and into the cold interior of the church. The flowers were breathtaking: on every aisle, every window-ledge, the candle-holders and either side of the altar steps, winding their way up the columns and hanging from the sides of the pews – every available space and corner was alive with the scent and blossom. Perfume filled the church and the sun poured in through the arched windows. On such a day as this, when dreams came true, and holy vows exchanged, when love was blessed and life held such promise, everything was so right. But danger was never far away.

The church was packed to capacity. Noreen Dickens wore a pretty suit of pastel green, and her husband looked the part in his dark long-tailed coat and top hat. Throughout the service he stood like a proud man, tall and erect, his chin jutting out and a glisten of tears in his eyes. Noreen remained taut and unmoved, devoid of emotion and wishing the service at an end so she could hurry back to hide herself away in the privacy of her little shed. Attending the ceremony under sufferance, she had been rejected, belittled and unloved for too long by this magniloquent man and his cossetted child. Now, there was no brightness in her life, no joy, no hope that things might improve, and nothing to look forward to when she began each new day. Like a discarded shell she was empty and hollow. The church was teeming with people but they meant nothing to her and she meant nothing to them with the exception of two kind souls.

Lou Peters was filled with pride as Aggie stood before the altar, her face shining like the moon on a starry night and a look in her eyes that he would remember for the rest of his life. But his attention was divided, for he had seen how Noreen Dickens might have been alone for all the consideration her husband gave her. He thought her a handsome woman, much like the wife he had loved and lost. He was touched by the sadness in her countenance, and somehow it tainted the day for him.

Phoebe also had seen how small and insignificant her aunt seemed beside the man whose ring she wore. And she too wondered how such a gentle quiet woman could have come into the hands of such a man. Later, she would make it her business to draw her aunt out. She might even persuade her to come and have a bite to eat with her and Dora. Yes, that would be really nice, she thought, and the thought cheered her no end.

Outside the photographer waited patiently, occasionally checking the time with the church clock against his pocket watch; he had another wedding in just over an hour and it was a good twenty minutes' journey away. As the hands of the clock shifted round and there was still no sign of the bride and groom, he grew more and more impatient. No more than two strides away from where he stood, the other man waited also. But this man didn't mind waiting because he had already bided his time for more than five years. A few more minutes was next to nothing now. Hiding the dark oddly shaped bag behind a tree, he sauntered over to the photographer. 'Lovely day,' he said, thrusting his hands in his pockets and giving a friendly smile.

The photographer was in a sour mood. 'That so?' he said, without turning his head.

'The couple getting wed . . . is the man's name Peters?' he asked. After all this time, he didn't want to make any mistakes. Edward Dickens had already given Soames his instructions and this was the right church he knew. According to Dickens, this was where Greg Peters would be taking himself a bride today. It stuck in his craw like a stone. Taking himself a bride. He thought of Lucy and hatred burned inside him like a fever.

'Peters?' The other man tilted his head to stare at Soames with curiosity. There were so many brides, so many grooms, he had to apply his mind. 'Peters?' he muttered. 'Yes, that's his name . . . Peters. But you've missed the major part of the ceremony. They're due out any minute now, I shouldn't wonder.'

Soames made no reply but nodded and withdrew into the shrubbery behind. The man watched him. 'Strange fellow,' he said under his breath. But then a wedding always drew the misfits out of the woodwork.

The organ played the procession out of the church and into the sunlight. Everyone was smiling and relieved. The official part was over, and now came the laughter and the partying; there was to be a grand reception at Blackburn's poshest hotel, with champagne flowing until the early hours, and music to dance the night away.

From his hiding-place, John Soames watched as the photographer assembled the smiling group and went through the laborious task of lining up his cumbersome camera. Grinning at the irony, he collected the oddly shaped bag from the foot of the tree. Opening it he dipped his hand inside and began taking out its contents with loving care, his eyes raking the wedding group. Edward Dickens was already known to him, and not for the first time he wondered why a man should want to bring such tragedy to his own daughter's wedding day. But then, he wasn't concerned with Dickens *or* his daughter. He was only concerned with the man who stood beside her. Greg Peters was the reason he was here today. The *only* reason. The rest of them could go to Hell and back as far as he was concerned.

He waited until the photographer had the group in his sight, and he too was ready. There was a fullness in him, a kind of exhilaration. 'At last,' he whispered. 'For Lucy.' A solitary tear trickled from the corner of his eye and blurred his vision. There was the briefest moment when he questioned what he was about to do. He lowered his head and closed his eyes against the bright sunlight, his mind in turmoil. But then he thought of Lucy and his heart was hard with revenge. Quickly now, he raised the shotgun to his shoulder and set his eye to the sights.

Wait though, he cautioned himself. Pick your moment, Soames.

Phoebe was one of the last out of the church. She had lingered a while at the altar, on her knees offering up a small prayer. She gave thanks for what the good Lord had given her yet at the same time expressed her sorrow that he had not thought to bring her and Judd together before circumstances had parted them for ever.

Unaware that the photographer was about to take his pictures, she pressed through the foyer towards the church steps. She could see Dora standing some way off, frantically waving her hand, indicating that Phoebe should wait a minute before coming out. She stepped back, and in that split second her eyes were drawn by the glint of the sun on the shotgun barrel.

Realising he'd been seen, Soames panicked and squeezed the trigger. The shot rang out, rending the air with such violence that all the birds were sent screeching into the air, but the ensuing silence was just as shocking: an eerie unearthly silence when the world stood still. A woman screamed, there were shouts of horror, and people fleeing in all directions. At first Phoebe wasn't sure as to what had happened. She saw how Hadley reeled back, his arms flung wide, his whole body lifted from the ground as though he was a rag doll; Margaret fell against the wall, big round eyes staring, her beautiful gown splattered with crimson patches, hands over her ears and her mouth open, screaming but not screaming; she was obviously in deep shock, trembling uncontrollably, her face drained grey.

Phoebe's horrified voice broke the awful silence.

'HADLEY!' Instinctively she rushed forward. Another shot split the air, spinning her round. As she stumbled, her eyes rolled up and she saw them running towards her. Dora's stricken face was the last thing she saw before her body was engulfed in a sea of black fire.

As they converged on him, Soames frantically reloaded the shotgun. His mission was done. Greg Peters was dead. He waited until they were almost on him, and then he opened his mouth, laughed in their faces, and pressed his finger against the hard metal. One lurching, crazy heartbeat, and it was all over.

Part Three

1926

Going Home

Chapter Sixteen

Phoebe knew they were there. Through the haze that fogged her brain, she saw them leaning over her, heard their voices, kind and loving, soothing her senses. But she was tired, so very tired. The darkness was always on her, drawing her down, taking her away. In her dreams she saw her mother, the way they had been, laughing together, sharing and content. 'Come away, child,' Jessica murmured, and Phoebe held out her hand, going towards that smiling face without fear or regret. In her heart she felt as though at long last she was going home.

'What chance does she have, doctor?' Judd was devastated. It was *his* life too that lay in the balance, for without Phoebe he had nothing. No future, no hope, nothing. 'I want the truth, mind,' he said brokenly. 'Don't fob me off with clever words.' He swallowed hard, afraid to ask yet afraid not to. 'Will she live?' His heart stood still while he waited for the doctor's reply, and when it was given he shrank inside.

'She's very ill, I'm afraid. God only knows how she wasn't killed outright. The shot tore through her temple although that itself will heal. But it's the trauma, the shock to her system . . . the loss of the child. She just isn't responding.' He shook his head sadly. 'You asked for the truth, and there it is. We've done all we can. It will take a miracle for her to pull through.'

'Then we'll *pray* for a miracle,' Judd told him. 'If there's a God up there, He won't let her die, I'm sure.'

The doctor nodded. 'Faith is a great help in times like these,' he conceded. 'But, like I said, she's gravely ill.' With that he touched Judd on the shoulder and went about his business. As he strode down the corridor, he mused on Judd's words. 'If there's a God up there, He won't let her die.' How many times had he heard those very same words? And how many times had the patient died anyway? But still, he mustn't dwell on such thoughts, because if he was to be swayed from his detached clinical stance he would never last the day.

Judd returned to Phoebe's bedside. He had been there day and night since the horror that had taken Hadley Peters to an early grave. He had watched over his love, tending to her, whispering words of encouragement and pouring out his love, praying that somehow it would penetrate the grey fog that kept them apart. There were times, like now, when he felt as though she was slipping away from him and his heart was broken all over again.

Outside, Marcus and Dora sat on a bench; they too had spent many long hours with Phoebe. They had all prayed and cried. Dora was crying now. 'She mustn't die,' she sobbed. When Marcus put his arm around her, she leaned on him. 'It isn't fair,' she said. 'She's so young, and she's already suffered too much.'

'We have to put our trust in God,' he said softly. 'Phoebe's strong, you know that.'

'But what if she doesn't *want* to live?' Dora had thought

long and hard about this. 'If she's lost her will to live, then nothing in the world will save her, isn't that right? Isn't that what the doctor said?'

'No. They weren't his exact words.'

'But it's what he meant right enough.' Dora looked up at him, 'She's been through so much, Marcus. She's lost everything, and now she's lost the baby too.'

'All the same, Dora, we mustn't lose hope.'

She heard the break in his voice and lifted her head. 'I'm sorry,' she said, taking out her handkerchief and wiping away the tears. He had a great weight on his mind, she knew. Marcus had told her and Judd all about his own fears and the dreadful situation that had come about between himself and Phoebe. It was clear that he was riddled with guilt. Now, she was at death's door, and for some inexplicable reason he blamed himself.

'It's ironic, isn't it, Dora?' he said with a wry little smile. 'Me and Jessica all those years ago . . . the possibility that Phoebe might be my own daughter; the fear that we might both be sent to prison. And now, all it needs is for Phoebe and me to make a declaration to the court, stating under oath that neither of us were aware that we were committing any crime. If the court believes us, there's a good chance that we could annul the marriage without prejudice. Oh, Dora . . . she's got to live. She's just got to.' He couldn't speak now but his thoughts raced ahead. If only he had run away with Jessica long ago. If only Edward Dickens had not set himself between them. If only he had been at the church with Phoebe, he might have held on to her . . . if only . . . if only. His thoughts were in turmoil. All that mattered was Phoebe.

He went across the corridor and peeped in through the door of that tiny ward. Phoebe's face was stark white against the pillow, her eyes closed and her two hands lying on top of the covers. She was still, so beautiful. Judd was in the chair, head bent into his fists and his whole body shaking. When he raised his face, he looked like a man haunted. Without a word, he reached out and tenderly took Phoebe's small slim fingers into his large capable hands, cupping them in his palms, occasionally caressing them with his mouth, but all the time his eyes were on her face. 'Don't leave me, sweetheart,' he begged in a trembling voice, and the tears spilled down his pale handsome face. 'I love you so much. Do you hear me, Phoebe . . . I love you.' He stroked her forehead and pushed back the tumbling auburn locks. 'Everything will be fine,' he promised. 'I didn't understand but I do now. And I want to take care of you for the rest of our lives. Can you hear me, Phoebe? I love you so much, sweetheart.' His voice broke then and he bowed his head.

Marcus closed the door softly. There was so much love in that little room. So much wanting. 'Listen to him, Lord,' he murmured, raising his face. That was all he could ask. It was all any of them could ask.

Chapter Seventeen

'Get out!' Lou was the smaller of the two men but his anger was mountainous. 'Because of you, I've lost the best son a man could ever have,' he said, crying unashamedly. 'I had to wait until Hadley was laid to rest but now I'm telling you. GET OUT!' Throwing open the front door, he went on in a low threatening voice. 'As long as I live, I don't ever want to set eyes on you again.'

Greg smiled, but made no answer. Instead, he looked with contempt at the bag his father had packed for him and thrown along the passage. He made no effort to pick it up. Without a word, he turned his back on his father and on his own daughter who had cried herself to sleep every night since Hadley was killed. He was glad to be leaving. There was nothing to keep him here. There never had been.

Outside in the moonlight he looked back towards the farmhouse. 'It's no loss,' he murmured cruelly. Turning his attention to the house across the way, he saw that the light was on in the lower bedroom. His smile deepened and he went across the road to wait. Wherever he was going, he didn't intend to be alone. Of course, there could well be a time in the not too distant future when he just might have to discard the old and then on with the new.

For now, though, a little feminine company wouldn't harm.

His thoughts were interrupted by raised voices and an angry exchange. He had a mind to leave then but the road ahead looked lonely and at heart he was the worst coward. So he leaned against the tree trunk, huddled further into his coat, lit a cigarette and waited.

Edward Dickens straddled the doorway of his daughter's bedroom. He had been drinking heavily and was unsteady on his feet. 'You're not going, damn you!' he roared. 'You'll leave this house only over my dead body.'

'If that's the way you want it.' Margaret stood before him, holding a portmanteau in each hand; even at this moment when she was unsure which way her path might lead, she couldn't bear to leave her beautiful clothes. There was pure hatred in her eyes as she regarded him now. 'You killed him,' she hissed. 'I don't know how you were involved, but I know that you were responsible for Hadley's death. You thought that by getting him out of the way, things could go on as before. But they can't. They won't ever again.' Her laughter was awful to hear and it unnerved him. 'You old fool!' she went on. 'Did you think I really loved you?'

'What do you mean, my dear?' He couldn't understand, he didn't want to. He deliberately lowered his voice. 'How can you say such a wicked thing, after all we've been to each other?' He grinned at the shocking memories. 'You're upset, that's all . . . shaken by what's happened. But it was for the best. I did it for you. You'll forget him, I promise. He wasn't good enough. There isn't a man alive that's good enough for my little darling. I'll help you forget him, you'll see.' A look of sheer terror

542

came into his face. 'But, please . . . you mustn't say you don't love me. That would break your daddy's heart, don't you see? Of *course* you love me.' He went to touch her, but she reeled away.

'I loathe you,' she said in a shivering voice. 'With every ounce of breath in me, I loathe and detest you. Hadley was my escape.' She watched with pleasure as he was visibly shaken by her terrible words, and before he could recover, pushed her way past him. He followed, crying and moaning, pleading for her to come back. When the door slammed shut behind her, he fell to the floor, sobbing like a baby.

Outside she could hear him calling but her heart was like hardened steel. 'Where are we headed?' she asked her companion.

'Wherever takes your fancy,' he said, collecting one of the portmanteaux and linking his arm with hers as they went down the street. 'Where would your ladyship like to go?'

And she answered, 'Anywhere. Just as long as we never come back here.'

'Oh, I think I can promise you that,' he replied. At least *he* would not be coming back. When the day came that he no longer found pleasure in her company and she was left all alone, there was no telling what *she* might want to do. But, 'Let's enjoy our freedom while we can,' he suggested with a light-hearted kiss. She kissed him back. 'Why not?' she said, and their laughter echoed as they went down Preston New Road, away from Blackburn, away from all that had been familiar and comfortable and safe.

* * *

Noreen had fled the house when Margaret came home to tell her father that she was leaving. The row had been fierce and frightening. Her every instinct told her that it was not over yet and so she remained in the shed, in the dark, crouched in the corner. The door was locked and she dared not move a single muscle in case he heard her there. In these past few minutes he'd been out twice, calling her name, kicking at the door and threatening all manner of retribution if she didn't: 'Show your face, woman!' But she knew she must not do that or he would flay her within an inch of her life. Every part of her body ached and groaned and still she didn't move. Bent and stiff, hurting inside and out, she curled tighter into the corner, waiting for daylight, praying for help. She couldn't know that help was already in the offing, nor could she know that it would be Edward himself who would be her salvation.

In his desperate haste to find his daughter, he left the front door wide open. He shivered. The night was chilly, and he was dressed only in his trousers and a thin shirt with the sleeves rolled up. He followed her footsteps down the road, calling her name at every turn, but the night was silent all around. He came back, taking the path towards the lake. 'Margaret,' he cried, but there was no answer. He climbed the bank, stumbling and falling, his steps sluggish with drink and his mind grief-stricken with the loss of his love. On the top of the rise, the moon threw shadows all around. Imagining he saw her, he cried out again, pushing forward towards what he thought to be her, slipping and sliding on the mossy bank. The shadows dodged him, played with him and confused him. He held ut his arms, grabbing at the whispering shapes. Only air. Only empty space.

No one heard his terrible screams. Only the night knew. And the sleek black waters that closed over his head. One day those same waters would give him up. But not yet. Not for many a moon.

Chapter Eighteen

The day had hardly begun when Phoebe opened her eyes.
At first she was blinded by the dawn that rose outside her
window. Slowly her vision cleared and she looked around
the room: small and square with white-washed walls and
pretty floral curtains. She turned her head and saw him
there; his arms folded into a pillow on the bed and his
head resting against them. His sleeping face was turned
towards her, that strong handsome face that she knew so
well. Her heart swelled with love when she realised that
it was Judd. And yet she wondered why he was here. The
last time she had been with him, they'd parted sadly. For
one confused moment she was unsure what had happened. Then she remembered . . . the wedding, Hadley
going down, the large spreading patches of crimson on
Margaret's gown. She groaned then. The pain was
intense. Hadley was dead, she knew. She recalled how
she had run forward, then the searing pain and darkness
closing in. But she wasn't dead. Astonishment rippled
through her. Closing her eyes, she lay back against the
pillow once more. Somehow she had to shut out those
awful images.

She turned her eyes to Judd; his fair hair was tousled
like a child's. 'Judd,' she whispered softly, reaching out

to entwine her fingers in that thick unkempt hair. How long had he been here? How long had she been lying in this hospital bed? The smell was unmistakable . . disinfectant, and that clean sharp tang that stuck in you throat. 'Judd,' she murmured again. She felt drained incredibly weak, strange deep down inside. Suddenly i struck her. The child! There was no life inside her. The tears came then, warm and stinging against the pallor of her skin. Judd wakened and took her in his arms. Hi tears were tears of joy. 'Oh, Phoebe,' he cried, cradling her to him. 'Thank God!' And he held her as though he would never let her go.

On 2 June 1926 Marcus and Phoebe attended court Standing side by side before the bench, they addressed themselves to the grim-faced officers in authority. Declar ations made by them both were read out and studie and meticulously perused before the officers retired t chambers in order to discuss them further. 'Try not t worry,' Marcus whispered. 'We've told the truth as it is and we have nothing to be ashamed of.' All the same he kept his fingers crossed behind his back. Everythin depended on what transpired here today. His life Phoebe's happiness, it was all at stake, and he dared no think about the outcome.

Phoebe felt Judd's eyes on her. When she turned roun it was to see his smiling face; she felt his encouragemen and her heart was quieter. When Marcus had first tol her about his relationship with her mother, she had bee both shocked and horrified. But then she came to realis how her mother could have loved him. Throughout it a

548

he had been dignified and totally honest, and she had come to feel that it would be an honour to discover that she was after all the daughter of Marcus Quinn, the cobbler.

Judd had been a tower of strength, and the knowledge that they could love without fear was like a gift from heaven itself. Standing here in a court-room, she might have felt alone and afraid, but she had made many friends and they were all here, with the exception of little Aggie who had only recently returned to school after suffering nightmares about that fatal day when she was bridesmaid at her brother's wedding. But children were resilient and Aggie had the love of a devoted 'father' to bring her through. Wisely, he had not told her that Greg was her real father. 'There's no need for the child to know,' he told Phoebe. 'And I pray there never will be.' She agreed, although Lou's graphic account of how the tragedy had developed . . . of Greg, and Lucy, and John Soames' part in it all, was a startling revelation to her.

Judd sat in the front row, looking at her and silently giving her strength. Dora sat beside him, and Lou beside her. Noreen came next, and it gladdened Phoebe's heart to see how her aunt and Lou were discreetly holding hands. Noreen Dickens was a woman transformed; her daughter's departure then her husband's drowning had set her free. Life had taken on a new meaning. Her eyes sparkled and there was a brightness about her that shone out. It was obvious to Phoebe that Lou was in love and that her aunt had come to reciprocate.

The officers returned. The one in the middle regarded her then Marcus and with immense deliberation took up the paper before him and began reading.

'We have read the declarations signed by you both, and it is our considered and unanimous opinion that what transpired here is an honest and unfortunate error. Therefore we declare the marriage between you Marcus Quinn, and you Phoebe Mulligan, to be null and void.'

While the decision was being read out, Phoebe was stiff with fear. The thought of going to prison was always in the back of her mind as was her concern for Marcus. Now she visibly relaxed, her senses reeling. She could hear Marcus laughing and crying all at the same time, and suddenly she was in Judd's arms. 'Do you know what this means?' he cried jubilantly. 'It means we can be wed! Oh, Phoebe! WE CAN BE WED.' She felt herself being swung round and everyone was clapping. She wanted to laugh and cry and sing and shout; she wanted the whole world to know how she and Judd were free to love each other. The officers hurried away else they might have been obliged to detain everyone for breach of the peace. It was rare to see such happiness in this court-room and it did their old hearts good.

Phoebe's wedding was neither grand nor extravagant. It was a simple but beautiful service, conducted by the same vicar who had spoken over her mother and her father before; the same vicar who had baptised her as a tiny infant. He looked at her with pride as he asked softly, 'Do you, Phoebe Mulligan, take this man to be your lawful wedded husband?' He saw how she turned to her man and was greatly moved by the love that flowed between them. In a voice that was strong and true, she answered. Another moment, then the words she had so long waited to hear: 'I pronounce you man and wife.' Judd took her hand, they kissed, and every dream she had ever dreamed blossomed to fullness in her heart.

As she walked down the aisle towards the sunshine, Phoebe was a proud and contented woman. It didn't matter that there were still those who thought she could never be a 'lady', for there were more important things in life. She was as the good Lord made her, without fancy trimmings or fine clothes. Judd was her man, and she was his woman, and that was all that mattered to her.

In his coat pocket Judd had the key to the house which he had passed many a morning on his way to work when he would gaze longingly through the window, picturing himself and Phoebe there and imagining their children upstairs fast asleep. The house was theirs now and life was good. 'You look lovely,' he whispered, squeezing her hand and thinking that no man was ever more fortunate. He had never seen Phoebe look more exquisite; her rich auburn hair was longer now, an abundance of waves and wild wispy ringlets that teased her face and heightened the beauty of her warm brown eyes.

No splendid gown for her, no bejewelled train or satin shoes. Instead Phoebe had chosen to wear the cream dress her mother had made her. On her dainty feet were the prettiest white shoes which Marcus had given her that very morning; her coronet was woven with flowers gathered by Lou and Noreen, and her veil was a special present from Aggie. As she emerged into the daylight, the sun glinted on the silver chain around her neck: Dora's gift of friendship. Precious things, from darling people.

'Let's go home, sweetheart,' Judd whispered as they climbed into the carriage.

'Go home,' she murmured. How wonderful those words sounded. Home to the little house that was not too far away from friends yet far enough away for her and Judd to be alone together. She glanced up at the sky and for one brief moment it seemed as though her mother's darling face smiled down on her. 'Did you hear that, Mam?' she asked beneath her breath. 'At long last, I'm going home.' Judd was beside her, her friends were all around, and she would never be alone again. What else could any woman want?

With a full heart, Phoebe gazed up at her husband and realised that all the riches a woman could have were hers in that moment. And she would cherish them for ever.

Headline hope you have enjoyed reading JESSICA'S GIRL and invite you to sample the beginning of Josephine Cox's compelling new novel, NOBODY'S DARLING, out now in Headline hardback . . .

Chapter One

'Don't go putting on airs and graces, my girl. Fame and riches ain't fer the likes of us, and you'd do well to remember that.' Lizzie Miller shook her head and sighed noisily, 'God help us, but I can't help wondering what's gonna become of yer,' she muttered impatiently.

Seated in the old horse-hair armchair, with the contented bairn sucking at her flat drooping breast, Lizzie had been secretly watching her eldest daughter for these past ten minutes or so. Not for the first time she wondered how someone as plain and unbecoming as herself could ever have given birth to such a perfect and lovely child as Ruby. The girl didn't take after *her*, and she was unlike any of the other childer. All the same, Lizzie thanked the good Lord for sending her such a precious little parcel. But, oh wasn't it shocking how quickly the young 'uns grew up? she asked herself now.

Going on fifteen years old, Ruby was already showing the signs of womanhood. On a Friday night when all the childer were washed in the old tin tub, Lizzie had been astonished at the changes in her daughter's body; the small budding nipples and the fine dark hairs just poking through above her private parts, the way she seemed suddenly to be losing the awkwardness of a child, and gaining that special grace with which some young women were blessed. With her small shapely figure, the abundant spill of rich brown hair and those magnificent speckly dark-blue eyes, it was plain to see that Ruby Miller was set to be a beauty. And, for some reason she couldn't rightly fathom, Lizzie was fearful for the girl. It was true what they said about there always being at least one child who would cause a mother the greatest worry, because of all her brood – and there were six of them – it was *Ruby* who gave her the worst sleepless nights.

Surprised and embarrassed, Ruby swung round, 'Oh, Mam!' she cried, blushing bright pink as though she'd been caught in the act of thieving, 'You've been peeking at me again.' Lately it seemed that her mam was always 'peeking' at her.

'It ain't surprising that I'm fascinated with yer comical antics, is it, eh?' Lizzie asked with a chuckle, thinking how Ruby looked the grandest little lady in the cast off clothes which she herself had worn as a young woman; the long flouncing skirt with its deep frilly hem, the cream-coloured shawl with pretty lace workings all round the edge, and a big-brimmed hat decorated with long black feathers above large silk flowers. In that moment, Lizzie realised with a little shock that she hadn't always been 'ugly' and 'clumsy'. When Ruby's dad came courting her some eighteen years ago, she had been thin enough for him to encircle her waist with one arm. She was twenty-one then, foolish and full of dreams. Now she was going on forty, with six young 'uns round her arse, and a waist as far round as the gasworks at the end of Albert Street. Life hadn't been easy since then, what with three childer taken young by the whooping cough, and always a struggle to make ends meet. Yet, for all that, the thought of her husband, Ted, brought a warm glow to Lizzie's tired old heart, 'Yer a pretty little thing, our Ruby,' she said now, 'an' yer deserve pretty things.'

Ruby looked thoughtful as she chewed her bottom lip and thought on her mam's words. Presently she said softly, 'Dad says *you* looked lovely when you were young.'

'Aye well, yer dad's a silly ol' bugger,' Lizzie laughed. 'Anyway, he were in love, an' it's a known fact that fellas are daft as brushes when they're in love.'

'But you *did* look lovely, didn't you, Mam?' Ruby insisted. She couldn't imagine her dad being 'daft as a brush'. And anyway, sometimes, when her mam smiled at the babby, Ruby thought how pretty she really was; and when she raised her face for a kiss from Ruby's dad, Lizzie's soft hazel-coloured eyes sparkled like jewels. Anybody could see that Lizzie had been a good-looking woman, and Ruby wouldn't have it any other way. 'I expect you think I'm fancying myself, don't you?' Ruby asked, a sense of shame washing through her; if her mam had taught her anything, it was that she must never get carried away with grand ideas. Ruby found that very hard, because she had so many 'grand' ideas, and the greatest of all was that one day, she might somehow be able to give her mam and dad a better life. Day and night, she never lost sight of that dream, although she was careful not to say it out loud to anyone, not even to Johhny Ackroyd.

'Aw, bless yer heart, it don't matter if yer fancy yerself

in yer mam's old togs,' Lizzie told her, carefully shifting the babby from one shrivelled titty to the other. 'So long as yer don't forget yer station in life, it don't hurt to pretend just a little bit. Only don't forget what yer mam's allus told yer.' She shook her grey head and stared hard at the girl. 'It don't do no good to spend yer life dreamin' for what yer can never have, lass. Wishing for the stars can only end in heartbreak. The plain truth is that when yer born poor, yer meant to end yer days the same way, an' that's a fact.'

'Who says so?' Try as she might, Ruby had never seen the reason in that.

'*I* say so, my girl!' In the early days, Lizzie had dreamed her own dreams, and she had always been bitterly disappointed when they came to nothing. She had never revealed her own secret longings, and she never would. But she didn't want no child of hers to suffer the feelings of being 'second-hand', in the same way she did. In time, Lizzie had come to accept her lot, and now she wanted her young 'uns to do the same. 'Wanting what you can't have is a sure way to hating what the good Lord has already seen fit to give you,' she retorted sharply. She didn't like putting Ruby down in that way, but she believed it was for the best. There was something about the girl that was too strong, too deep-down yearning. And such ambitions were dangerous.

'But, I *like* to dream, Mam,' Ruby said wistfully. She dropped the hat onto a stand-chair, then, slipping out of the garments, she sat opposite her mam by the empty firegrate. 'I don't think the Good Lord would mind me wishing, 'cause I don't want Him to give me anything for nothing. I'll work hard, Mam, I promise, and I won't be bad. All I want is for you and our dad to have lots of nice things, like you deserve.' She smiled the deepest smile, 'Oh, our Mam, wouldn't it be lovely if the childer could have grand presents of a Christmas, and if our Lottie could have a pretty white shawl like the grocer's babby?' She lowered her gaze until it rested on her mam's face, and the magnificent blue-black eyes were darkly serious. 'I don't think it can be wrong, wanting special things for people you love. And I don't thing it's wrong wanting to live in a house where the rats don't come in from the brook and run round the young 'uns' legs when they're playing in the yard.'

'Well, it *is* wrong!' Lizzie yelled. 'And I don't want to hear you talking like that, d'yer understand? Get rid o' them fancy bloody ideas, my girl . . . else I'll have to ask yer dad to knock 'em out of yer.' Ruby put Lizzie in mind of herself when she was younger, and it frightened her. 'D'yer hear what I'm saying?' she insisted. 'Yer ain't rich yet famous, and yer never will be.'

It took a moment for the girl to answer. In her young heart she was convinced that she was right, but she wouldn't upset her darling mam, not for all the world, she wouldn't. 'I'm sorry, Mam,' she said reluctantly, her wounded gaze falling away to the threadbare mat. There was bitterness in her then, and it tasted nasty. She was angry and hurt. Part of her wanted to promise that she would never again think above her station, but she couldn't bring herself to say it. Her dreams were too precious, and the thought that one day she might make them come true was too fierce inside her. Sometimes in the middle of the night, when it was dark and she lay in her chilly bedroom listening to the fidgets and snores of the other childer, it was only her dreams that kept hope alive. She couldn't give them up. They were too much a part of her.

Getting up from the chair, Ruby came to kneel at her mam's feet, and there was such love in her eyes that it made the woman ashamed. 'I'm sorry, our Mam. I didn't mean to make you mad at me,' she said, stretching out her hand to stroke the infant's sleeping face. There was so much more she could have said, but not now, because the words wouldn't come easy. She could have said how she hated to see her dad come home from the quarry worn and weary; she could have explained how sad it made her when little Lottie was laid to bed in an old orange-box instead of a proper cot. She might have reminded her mam about the ragged clothes that the childer went to school in and how the other kids from better families made fun of them. And what of her mam? When was the last time she had something new to wear? When did she last go out and enjoy herself? Why was there never enough money to buy that dear woman a new frock or a pair of boots? Ruby had thought and thought about all of these things and it only made her all the more determined. She wanted to speak of it, but she knew it would only hurt her mam all the more, and so she said nothing except, 'I do love you, Mam.' She saw Lizzie's gaze soften, and her young heart was full.

One glance at Ruby's downcast face had warned Lizzie that she might have been too harsh. No mother should have a favourite, but if she was to tell the truth and shame the devil, Lizzie would have to admit to herself that her first-born was closer to her than the five that came after; although Hell and high water could never drag that admission from her. Lowering the sleeping child to her ample lap, she fastened her blouse and smiled at the girl. 'Aw, lass,' she said in a gentler voice, 'I'm sorry an' all, 'cause I should never 'ave shouted at yer like that. Yer know I wouldn't ask yer dad to do any such thing as knock yer about . . . not that he ever would,' she added with a wry little chuckle. The chuckle died away and she was serious again. 'But, I want yer to listen hard to what I'm saying, sweetheart. Dreamin' and wishing can make yer bitter if yer let it get out of hand. Oh, I expect it don't do no harm to pretend now and then. But, yer have to know which is pretending, and which is real.' She hoped she was making herself understood.

'I know what you mean, Mam,' Ruby assured her. 'And I *do* know the difference.'

Lizzie was visibly relieved. 'That's all right then,' she said, 'just so long as yer know.' She struggled forward in the chair and waited for Ruby to stand up before placing the child in her outstretched arms. 'Mek her comfortable, lass,' she instructed. 'Then yer can help yer mam get summat on the table afore yer dad comes home from his work.'

Lizzie watched with pride when Ruby pressed the infant close to her as she went towards the makeshift cot in the corner. Here she laid the child down and fussed about it for a while, tucking its legs beneath the patched eiderdown and stroking its face with tender fingers. There was no doubt that Ruby was very special . . . 'An old head on young shoulders' was how her dad described her and he wasn't far wrong. Lizzie deeply regretted the harsh scene that had just taken place between her and the lass, and she was eager to make amends. 'Set the table, sweetheart,' she instructed, 'then see if yer can round the others up for their teas. Afterwards, yer can fancy yersel' all yer like.' She strutted across the floor, mimicking the manner of a fine lady, 'Oh, la de da!' she said in a grand voice, clasping the girl to her when they both collapsed with laughter. 'Only don't break that there mirror with all yer rouge and finery,' she warned, ' 'cause it were a present from yer old Irish granmer. I don't want the ol' bugger turning in her grave when that mirror cracks from top to bottom at the sight of you in yer old mam's long begones. We don't want the divil to come down on us with a sack full o' bad luck, do we, eh?' she teased.

'No. It's all right, thanks, Mam,' came the reply. Ruby looked into her mam's hazel eyes, putting the fear of God in her when she said firmly, 'Your clothes are lovely, Mam, but they're not *mine*. And you needn't worry about Granmer's mirror, because I'll put it back in the cupboard where it'll be safe. The next time I look in it, I'll be wearing my own finery.' Realising she had said more than intended, she promised, 'I'll put the clothes back upstairs when Lottie settles.'

'Aye, you do that, lass,' Lizzie told her softly. When Ted came home, happen she would persuade him to have a quiet word with his daughter.

'Isn't she lovely, our Mam?' Ruby was fascinated with the infant. When her mam had gone into labour with this latest addition to the Miller family, Ruby had been the only one there and so she had seen the whole wonderful birth from beginning to end. It was an experience she would not easily forget.

'Yer *all* lovely,' Lizzie retorted, and you most of all, she thought, gazing at the dark brown tumbling hair and the sparkling blue-black eyes that looked on the tiny infant with such wonder. In that moment Lizzie knew instinctively that never again would Ruby dress up in her mam's old clothes. Never again would she allow others to see her 'pretending'. It was a sad thing to Lizzie, but suddenly she knew that her little girl was gone forever. It was another stage in Ruby's development, another step to being a woman.

'Take the things back upstairs then, and put them in the box where yer found 'em,' Lizzie said. She watched the girl a moment longer; loving her all the more when the child began crying and Ruby's soft lilting voice sang her back to sleep. It made a very special picture for Lizzie, one that she would cherish 'til the end of her days.

Still singing, Ruby gathered the clothes together and went up the stairs two at a time. In a minute she was running back down, and in another minute she could be heard at the front door, calling out to the childer, 'Come on you lot. Mam says you've to get washed for your teas.'

Lizzie smiled to herself and shook her head, 'Kids!' she moaned. 'Nowt but trouble.' Taking a small oval tin from her pocket, she opened the lid and with her finger and thumb, she pinched out a generous helping of the brown stuff, afterwards pushing it up into her nostrils and coughing from the shock. Taking snuff was a weakness of Lizzie's, and she rarely did it in public; although the

563

tell-tale brown signs beneath her nose were an obvious giveaway. 'By! That's some strong stuff,' she spluttered, quickly putting away the tin before the childer should come rushing in through the door.

Glancing at the mantelpiece clock, she was astonished to see that already it was nearly five o'clock. In less than an hour her husband would be home, wanting his tea after a hard day's work. She hurried into the scullery where she filled the big old black kettle to the brim with water. As usual when she placed it on the gas ring, Lizzie stood well back. The rusty ring had an unnerving habit of spitting and popping the minute a lighted match was put to it. All the same, this was the time of day she loved best; when Ted was on his way home, and soon all the family would sit round the table, cosy in each other's company. Lizzie smiled at the thought. The sight of her man seated at the head of the table always gave her a rush of pleasure. It was strange how she and Ted could still be so much in love, after all these years of ups and downs, and so many childer between. A feeling of warmth and contentment spread over her as she went about her work.

But suddenly a strange emotion rippled through her, and somehow she couldn't seem to settle inside herself. It was a peculiar feeling, an instinct that something awful was waiting to happen; and yet there was no rhyme or reason as to why she should think it, unless it was because of those few hasty words with Ruby just now. 'Aw, stop worrying about the lass,' she muttered. 'Yer daft ol' bugger, Lizzie Miller! She'll sort herself out, you see if she don't.' She then launched herself into the business of peeling the onions, and in spite of the burning tears streaming down her face, she was soon in a happier mood.

If you would like to find out whether Ruby's dreams do come true, the hardback of NOBODY'S DARLING is available from all major bookshops and is priced £15.99.